HEART OF THE MATTER

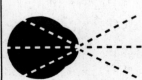

This Large Print Book carries the
Seal of Approval of N.A.V.H.

HEART OF THE MATTER

EMILY GRIFFIN

LARGE PRINT PRESS
A part of Gale, Cengage Learning

GALE
CENGAGE Learning

Detroit • New York • San Francisco • New Haven, Conn • Waterville, Maine • London

GALE
CENGAGE Learning·

LIBRARY OF CONGRESS CATALOGING-IN-PUBLICATION DATA

Giffin, Emily.
  Heart of the matter / by Emily Giffin.
    p. cm. — (Thorndike Press large print basic)
  ISBN-13: 978-1-4104-2640-6
  ISBN-10: 1-4104-2640-8
  1. Stay-at-home mothers—Fiction. 2. Single mothers—Fiction.
3. Pediatric surgeons—Fiction. 4. Life change events—Fiction.
5. Triangles (Interpersonal relations)—Fiction. 6. Psychological
fiction. 7. Large type books. I. Title.
PS3607.I28H43 2010b
813'.6—dc22   2010001520

ISBN 13: 978-1-59413-451-7 (pbk. : alk. paper)
ISBN 10: 1-59413-451-0 (pbk. : alk. paper)

Published in 2011 by arrangement with St. Martin's Press, LLC.

For Sarah, my sister and lifelong friend

ACKNOWLEDGMENTS

Deepest gratitude to Mary Ann Elgin, Sarah Giffin, Nancy LeCroy Mohler, and Lisa Elgin for their unwavering generosity from page one. I couldn't do it without you and could never thank you enough.

I owe so much to my editor, Jennifer Enderlin, and my publicist, Stephen Lee, along with everyone at St. Martin's Press, especially Sally Richardson, Matthew Shear, John Murphy, Matt Baldacci, Jeanne-Marie Hudson, Nancy Trypuc, Mike Storrings, Sara Goodman, and the whole Broadway and Fifth Avenue sales forces. Because of you, I feel lucky every day.

I am indebted to my superb agent, Theresa Park, and her team: Emily Sweet, Abigail Koons, and Amanda Cardinale. You are the consummate professionals, yet you make the journey fun, too.

Thanks also to Carrie Minton, Martha Arias, Stacie Hanna, Mara Lubell, Mollie

Smith, and Grace McQuade for their support; to Allyson Wenig Jacoutot, Jennifer New, Julie Portera, Laryn Gardner, and Brian Spainhour for their input; and to Dr. Christopher A. Park and Joshua Osswald for their insight on matters of medicine and tennis, respectively.

I am grateful to my readers for their warmth and enthusiasm, and my friends for their good humor and love.

Finally, a huge, heartfelt thank-you to Buddy Blaha and my entire family, for more reasons than I could ever name.

And to Edward, George, and Harriet — you can come up to my office and interrupt my writing anytime.

1
TESSA

Whenever I hear of someone else's tragedy, I do not dwell on the accident or diagnosis, or even the initial shock waves or aftermath of grief. Instead, I find myself reconstructing those final ordinary moments. Moments that make up our lives. Moments that were blissfully taken for granted — and that likely would have been forgotten altogether but for what followed. The *before* snapshots.

I can so clearly envision the thirty-four-year-old woman in the shower one Saturday evening, reaching for her favorite apricot body scrub, contemplating what to wear to the party, hopeful that the cute guy from the coffee shop will make an appearance, when she suddenly happens upon the unmistakable lump in her left breast.

Or the devoted young father, driving his daughter to buy her first-day-of-school Mary Janes, cranking up "Here Comes the Sun" on the radio, informing her for the umpteenth time that the Beatles are "without a doubt the greatest band of all time," as the teenaged boy, bleary-eyed from too many late-night Budweisers, runs the red light.

Or the brash high school receiver, full of promise and pride, out on the sweltering practice field the day before the big football game, winking at his girlfriend at her usual post by the chain-link fence, just before leaping into the air to make the catch nobody else could have made — and then twisting, falling headfirst on that sickening, fluke angle.

I think about the thin, fragile line separating all of us from misfortune, almost as a way of putting a few coins in my own gratitude meter, of safeguarding against an *after* happening to me. To *us*. Ruby and Frank, Nick and me. Our foursome — the source of both my greatest joys and most consuming worries.

And so, when my husband's pager goes off while we are at dinner, I do not allow myself to feel resentment or even disappointment. I tell myself that this is only one meal, one night, even though it is our anniversary and the first proper date Nick and I have had in nearly a month, maybe two. I have nothing to be upset about, not compared to what someone else is enduring at this very instant. This will not be the hour I will have to rewind forever. I am still among the lucky ones.

"Shit. I'm sorry, Tess," Nick says, silencing his pager with his thumb, then running his hand through his dark hair. "I'll be right back."

I nod my understanding and watch my husband stride with sexy, confident purpose toward the front of the restaurant where he will make the necessary call. I can tell, just by the sight of his straight back and broad shoulders navigating deftly around the tables, that he is steeling himself for the bad news, preparing to fix someone, save someone. It is when he is at his best. It is why I fell in love with him in the first place, seven years and two children ago.

Nick disappears around the corner as I draw a deep breath and take in my surroundings, noticing details of the room for the first time. The celadon abstract painting above the fireplace. The soft flicker of candlelight. The enthusiastic laughter at the table next to ours as a silver-haired man holds court with what appears to be his wife and four grown children. The richness of the cabernet I am drinking alone.

Minutes later, Nick returns with a grimace

and says he's sorry for the second, but certainly not the last, time.

"It's okay," I say, glancing around for our waiter.

"I found him," Nick says. "He's bringing our dinner to go."

I reach across the table for his hand and gently squeeze it. He squeezes mine back, and as we wait for our fillets to arrive in Styrofoam, I consider asking what happened as I almost always do. Instead, I simply say a quick prayer for the people I don't know, and then one for my own children, tucked safely into their beds.

I picture Ruby, softly snoring, all twisted in her sheets, wild even in her sleep. Ruby, our precocious, fearless firstborn, four going on fourteen, with her bewitching smile, dark curls that she makes even tighter in her self-portraits, too young to know that as a girl she is supposed to want the hair she does *not* have, and those pale aquamarine eyes, a genetic feat for her brown-eyed parents. She has ruled our home and hearts since virtually the day she was born — in a way that both exhausts me and fills me with awe. She is exactly like her father — stubborn, passionate, breathtakingly beautiful. A daddy's girl to the core.

And then there's Frank, our satisfying

baby boy with a cuteness and sweetness that exceeds the mere garden-variety-baby cute and sweet, so much so that strangers in the grocery store stop and remark. He is nearly two, but still loves to cuddle, nestling his smooth round cheek against my neck, fiercely devoted to his mama. *He's not my favorite,* I swear to Nick in private when he smiles and accuses me of this parental transgression. I do not have a favorite, unless perhaps it is Nick himself. It is a different kind of love, of course. The love for my children is without condition or end, and I would most certainly save them over Nick, if, say, all three were bitten by rattlesnakes on a camping trip and I only had two anti-venin shots in my backpack. And yet, there is nobody I'd rather talk to, be near, look at, than my husband, an unprecedented feeling that overcame me the moment we met.

Our dinner and check arrive moments later, and Nick and I stand and walk out of the restaurant into the star-filled, purple night. It is early October, but feels more like winter than fall — cold even by Boston standards — and I shiver beneath my long cashmere coat as Nick hands the valet our ticket and we get into our car. We leave the city and drive back to Wellesley with little conversation, listening to one of Nick's many jazz CDs.

Thirty minutes later, we are pulling up our tree-lined driveway. "How late do you think you'll be?"

"Hard to say," Nick says, putting the car into park and leaning across the front seat to kiss my cheek. I turn my face toward him and our lips softly meet.

"Happy anniversary," he whispers.

"Happy anniversary," I say.

He pulls away, and our eyes lock as he says, "To be continued?"

"Always," I say, forcing a smile and slipping out of the car.

Before I can close the door, Nick turns up the volume of his music, dramatically punctuating the end of one evening, the start of another. As I let myself in the house, Vince Guaraldi's "Lullaby of the Leaves" echoes in my head where it remains long after I've paid the babysitter, checked on the kids, changed out of my backless black dress, and eaten cold steak at the kitchen counter.

Much later, having turned down Nick's side of the bed and crawled into my own, I am alone in the dark, thinking of the call in the restaurant. I close my eyes, wondering whether we are ever truly blindsided by misfortune. Or, somehow, somewhere, in the form of empathy or worry or a premonition deep within ourselves, do we feel it coming?

I fall asleep, not knowing the answer. Not knowing that this will be the night I will return to, after all.

2
VALERIE

Valerie knew she should've said no — or more accurately *stuck* to no, the answer she gave Charlie the first dozen times he begged her to go to the party. He had tried every angle, including the "I don't have a daddy or a dog" guilt trip, and when that got him nowhere, he enlisted the support of his uncle Jason, who was longer on charm than anyone Valerie knew.

"Oh, come on, Val," he said. "Let the kid have a little fun."

Valerie shushed her twin brother, pointing toward the family room where Charlie was building an elaborate Lego dungeon. Jason repeated himself verbatim, this time in an exaggerated whisper as Valerie shook her head, declaring that six years old was too young for a sleepover, especially one outdoors in a tent. It was a familiar exchange as Jason habitually accused his sister of being overprotective and too strict with her

16

only child.

"Right," he said, smirking at her. "I've heard that bear attacks are on the rise in Boston."

"Very funny," Valerie said, going on to explain that she didn't know the boy's family well enough, and what she *had* gleaned of them, she didn't much like.

"Lemme guess — they're loaded?" Jason asked teasingly, pulling up his jeans, which had a way of sliding down his spindly frame, exposing the waistband of his boxers. "And you don't want him mixing with *that kind?*"

Valerie shrugged and surrendered to her smile, wondering how he had guessed. Was she that predictable? And how, she wondered for the millionth time, could she and her *twin* brother be so different when they had grown up together in the same brown-shingled house in their Irish-Catholic neighborhood in Southbridge, Massachusetts? They were best friends, sharing the same bedroom until they were twelve when Jason moved to the drafty attic to give his sister more space. With dark hair, almond-shaped blue eyes, and fair skin, they even *looked* alike, often being confused for identical twins as babies. Yet according to their mother, Jason had come out of the womb smiling, while Valerie emerged scowling and worried — which was how things remained throughout their childhood, Valerie the shy loner, riding on the coattails of her popular, outgoing, older-by-four-minutes brother.

And now, thirty years later, Jason was as happy as ever, an easygoing optimist, flitting from one hobby and job to the next, utterly comfortable in his own skin, especially since coming out of the closet just after their father died during their senior year in high school. A classic underachiever, he now worked in a coffee shop on Beacon Hill, making friends with everyone who walked through the door, making friends wherever he *went,* just as he always had.

Meanwhile, Valerie still felt defensive and out of place much of the time, despite all of her accomplishments. She had worked so hard to escape Southbridge, graduating at the top of their high school class, attending Amherst College on a full scholarship, then going to work as a paralegal at a top Boston law firm while she studied for the LSAT and saved money for law school. She told herself that she was as good as anyone, and smarter than most, yet she never truly felt a sense of belonging after leaving her hometown. Meanwhile, the more she achieved, the more she felt disconnected from her old friends, especially her best friend, Laurel, who had grown up three houses down from Val and Jason. This feeling, subtle and hard to pinpoint at first, culminated in a complete falling-out one summer during a barbecue at Laurel's house.

After a few drinks, Valerie had made an offhanded remark about Southbridge being suffocating, Laurel's fiancé even more so. She was only trying to help, even suggesting that Laurel move into her small Cambridge apartment, but she regretted it as soon as the words were out, doing her best to suck back the comments and apologizing profusely in the days that followed. But Laurel, who had always been quick-tempered, summarily wrote Valerie off, spreading rumors of her snobbishness among their old circle of friends — girls who, like Laurel, lived with their high-school boyfriends-turned-husbands in the same neighborhoods they'd grown up in, frequented the same bars on the weekends, and worked the same dreary nine-to-five jobs their parents held.

Valerie did her best to counter these accusations, and managed to fix things on a surface level, but short of moving back to Southbridge, there was really nothing she could do to return to the way things once were.

It was during this lonely time that Valerie

started acting out in ways she couldn't explain, doing all the things she'd vowed never to do — specifically, falling in love with the wrong guy, getting pregnant right before he left her, and jeopardizing her plans for law school. Years later, she sometimes wondered if she had subconsciously tried to sabotage her own efforts to fully escape Southbridge and create a different kind of life for herself — or perhaps she just didn't feel worthy of the Harvard Law School acceptance letter she hung on her refrigerator along with her ultrasound photographs.

In any case, she felt caught between two worlds, too proud to crawl back to Laurel and her old friends and too embarrassed by her pregnancy to maintain her college friendships or forge new ones at Harvard. Instead, she felt more alone than ever, struggling to make it through law school while caring for a newborn. Jason understood how tough things were for her during those early months and years of motherhood. He could plainly see how overwhelmed she was by constant exhaustion and work and worry, and had endless respect for how hard his sister worked to support herself and her son. Yet he couldn't understand why she insisted on walling herself off, sacrificing any semblance of a social life except for a few casual friendships. Her excuse was lack of time, as well as her devotion and singular focus on Charlie, but Jason didn't buy this, constantly calling his sister out, insisting that she used Charlie as a shield, a way to avoid taking risks, a way to avoid more rejection.

She thought about her brother's theory now, as she turned back toward the stove, pouring a dozen perfectly symmetrical silver-dollar pancakes. She wasn't an accomplished cook, but had mastered all breakfast dishes thanks to her very first job, waitressing at a diner, and her infatuation with one of the short-order cooks. That was a long time ago, but to Jason's point, she still felt more like that girl refilling coffee than the woman and successful attorney she had become.

"You are such a reverse snob," Jason said, ripping off three paper towels to use as napkins and then setting the table.

"I am *not,*" Valerie retorted, turning the term around in her brain, sheepishly admitting to herself how often she drove past the stately homes on Cliff Road and assumed that the people inside were superficial at best, and at worst, unflinching liars. It was as if she subconsciously equated wealth with a certain weakness of character and shifted the burden of proof on these strangers to show her otherwise. It wasn't fair, she knew, but there were a lot of things in life that weren't fair.

In any event, Daniel and Romy Croft had done nothing to prove her wrong the night she met them at the open house at school. Like most families at Longmere Country Day, the private elementary school in Wellesley that Charlie was attending, the Crofts were intelligent, attractive, and affable. Yet as they skimmed her name tag and made adroit small talk, Valerie had the distinct feeling that they were looking past her, right through her, scanning the room for someone else — someone *better.*

Even when Romy spoke of Charlie, something rang false and patronizing in her tone. "Grayson just *adores* Charlie," she said, purposefully tucking a strand of white-blond hair behind her ear, then pausing, hand in the air, seemingly to showcase the mammoth diamond on her ring finger. In a town full of big rocks, Valerie had never seen one quite this impressive.

"Charlie really likes Grayson, too," Valerie said, crossing her arms across her flamingo-pink blouse and wishing she had worn her charcoal suit instead. No matter how hard she tried, how much money she spent on her wardrobe, she always seemed to choose the wrong thing from her closet.

At that moment, the two little boys ran across the classroom hand in hand, Charlie leading the way to the hamster cage. To even a casual observer, they were best buddies, unabashed founders of a mutual admiration society of two. So why, then, did Valerie assume that Romy was being insincere? Why couldn't Valerie give herself — and her own son — more credit? She asked herself these questions as Daniel Croft rejoined his wife with a plastic cup of punch and rested his free hand on her back. It was a subtle gesture she had come to recognize in her relentless study of married couples, one that filled her with equal parts envy and regret.

"Honey, this is Valerie Anderson . . . Charlie's mother," Romy prompted, giving Valerie the impression that they had discussed her prior to this evening — and the fact that there was no father listed in the school directory alongside Charlie's name.

"Oh, sure, right." Daniel nodded, shaking her hand with boardroom vigor as he made fleeting, apathetic eye contact. "Hello."

Valerie returned the greeting, and a few seconds of empty chitchat ensued before Romy clasped her hands and said, "So, Valerie, did you get the invitation to Grayson's party? I sent it a couple weeks ago?"

Valerie felt her face grow crimson as she replied, "Yes, yes. Thank you very much." She could have kicked herself for not RSVPing, feeling certain that not responding in a timely manner to an invite, even to a child's party, was among Romy's chief pet peeves.

"So?" Romy pressed. "Can Charlie come?"

Valerie hesitated, feeling herself caving to this impeccably groomed, endlessly self-assured woman, as if she were back in high school and Kristy Mettelman had just offered her a drag of her cigarette and a ride in her cherry-red Mustang.

"I'm not sure. I'll have . . . to check the calendar . . . It's next Friday, right?" she stammered, as if she had hundreds of social engagements to keep track of.

"That's right," Romy said, her eyes widening, smile broadening, as she waved to another couple just arriving with their daughter. "Look, honey, April and Rob are here," she murmured to her husband. Then she touched Valerie's arm, flashed her one last perfunctory smile, and said, "It was *so* nice to meet you. We hope to see Charlie next Friday."

Two days later, holding the tent-shaped

invitation, Valerie dialed the Crofts' number. She felt a surge of inexplicable nervousness — social anxiety, her doctor called it — as she waited for someone to answer, followed by palpable relief when she heard the automated recording prompting her to leave a message. Then, despite all of her big talk to the contrary, her voice rose several octaves as she said, "Charlie would be *delighted* to attend Grayson's party."

Delighted.

This is the word she replays when she gets the call, only three hours after dropping Charlie off with his dinosaur sleeping bag and rocket-ship pajamas. Not *accident* or *burn* or *ambulance* or *ER* or any of the other words that she distinctly hears Romy Croft say but can't begin to process as she throws on sweats, grabs her purse, and speeds toward Massachusetts General Hospital. She cannot even bring herself to say them aloud when she calls her brother from the car, having the irrational sense that doing so will make everything more real.

Instead, she simply says, "Come now. Hurry."

"Come where?" Jason asks, music blaring in the background.

When she does not answer, the music

stops and he says again, more urgently, "Valerie? Come where?"

"Mass General . . . It's Charlie," she manages to reply, pressing the gas pedal harder, now going nearly thirty miles over the speed limit.

Her grip on the steering wheel is sweaty and white-knuckled, but inside, she feels an eerie calm, even as she runs a red light, then another. It is almost as if she is watching herself, or watching someone else altogether. This is what people do, she thinks. They call loved ones; they speed to the hospital; they run red lights.

Charlie would be delighted to attend, she hears again, as she arrives at the hospital and follows signs to the ER. She wonders how she could have been so oblivious, sitting there on the couch in her sweats with a bag of microwave popcorn and a Denzel Washington action flick. How could she not have known what was happening at the palatial home on Albion? Why had she not followed her gut about this party? She curses aloud, one lone, hoarse *fuck,* her heart filled with guilt and regret, as she peers up at the looming brick and glass building before her.

The night becomes hazy after that — a collection of disjointed moments rather than a smooth chronology. She will remember leaving her car at the curb despite the NO PARKING sign and then finding Jason, ashen faced, inside the glass double doors. She will remember the triage nurse, calmly, efficiently typing Charlie's name before another nurse leads them down a series of long, bleach-scented corridors to the PICU burn unit. She will remember bumping into Daniel Croft on their way, and pausing as Jason asks him what happened. She will remember Daniel's vague, guilt-filled reply — *They were making s'mores. I didn't see it* — and her image of him typing on his BlackBerry or admiring his landscaping, his back to the fire and her only child.

She will remember the first horrifying glimpse of Charlie's small, motionless body as he is sedated and intubated. She will remember his blue lips, his cut pajamas, and the stark white bandages obscuring his right hand and the left side of his face. She will remember the beeping monitors, the hum of the ventilator, and the bustling, stone-faced nurses. She will remember her raw appeal to the God she has all but forgotten as she holds her son's good hand and waits.

But most of all, she will remember the man who comes to examine Charlie in what feels like the middle of the night, after her worst fear has receded. How he gently uncovers Charlie's face, exposing the burned skin beneath the bandages. How he leads her back to the hallway where he turns to her, parts his lips, and begins to speak.

"My name is Dr. Nick Russo," he says, his voice deep and slow. "And I am one of the leading pediatric plastic surgeons in the world."

She looks into his dark eyes and exhales, her insides unclenching, as she tells herself that they would not send a *plastic* surgeon if her son's life were still in danger. He is going to be okay. He is not going to die. She knows this as she looks in his doctor's eyes. Then, for the first time, she considers how Charlie's life has changed. How this night will scar him in more ways than one. Feeling a fierce determination to protect him no matter what the outcome, she hears herself ask Dr. Russo if he can fix Charlie's hand and face; if he can make her son beautiful again.

"I will do everything I can for your son," he says, "but I want you to remember something. Will you please do that for me?"

She nods, thinking he will tell her not to expect miracles. As if she ever dared to do so, even once in her whole life.

Instead, Dr. Russo holds her gaze and says

the words she will never forget.

"Your son *is* beautiful," he tells her. "He is beautiful *now.*"

She nods again, both believing and trusting him. And only then, for the first time in a very long time, do her tears come.

3
TESSA

Sometime in the middle of the night, I awaken to the solid warmth of Nick beside me. With my eyes still closed, I reach out and run my hand over his shoulder, then down his shirtless back. His skin smells of soap from his usual post-work shower, and I feel a wave of attraction that is quickly expelled by an even greater dose of fatigue. Par for the course since Ruby was born — and certainly since she was joined by Frank. I still love having sex with my husband, as much as ever once we're under way. It just so happens that I now prefer sleep to most everything else — chocolate, red wine, HBO, and sex.

"Hi there," he whispers, his voice muffled against his pillow.

"I didn't hear you come in . . . What time is it?" I ask, hoping that it's closer to midnight than to the kids' automatic seven o'clock wake-up, more unforgiving than any alarm clock and without a snooze option.

"Two-thirty."

"Time to see a dentist," I murmur.

It is one of his endearing exchanges with Ruby: *What time is it, Daddy?* To which Nick grimaces, points to his mouth, and replies: *Tooth hurty. Time to see a dentist.* A real crowd-pleaser.

"Uh-huh," Nick says distractedly, clearly in no mood for conversation. But as I open my eyes and watch him turn and stare intently at the ceiling, my curiosity gets the better of me. So I ask, as casually as I can given the nature of the inquiry, whether it was a birth defect — which comprises a significant portion of Nick's work.

He sighs and says no.

I hesitate and tentatively guess again. "A car accident?"

"No, Tess," he says, so patiently that it gives away his impatience. "It was a burn. An accident."

He adds this last bit as a disclaimer. In other words, it was *not* child abuse — sadly, far from a given; Nick once told me that about ten percent of all pediatric burns are the result of child abuse.

I bite my lower lip, my mind racing with the usual possibilities — a boiling pot from the stove, a scalding bathtub, a house fire, a

31

chemical burn — and I'm unable to resist the inevitable follow-up. The question of *how*. It is the question Nick resists the most, his typical reply going something along the lines of: *What difference does it make? It was an accident. Accidents are just that. They happen.*

Tonight he clears his throat and resignedly gives me the facts. A six-year-old boy was roasting marshmallows. He somehow fell into the fire and burned his hand and cheek. The left side of his face.

Nick's speech is rapid and detached, as if he's simply relaying the weather forecast. But I know that this is only an act — a well-practiced cover-up. I know that he will likely be awake much of the night, unable to fall asleep from the adrenaline of the night's events. And even tomorrow morning — or more likely, afternoon — he will roll downstairs with a remote expression, pretending to be engaged with his own family, while he dwells on a little boy's hand and cheek.

Medicine makes a jealous mistress, I think, an expression I first heard during Nick's first year of residency, from a bitter doctor's wife who, I later learned, left her husband for her personal trainer. I vowed then that I would guard against ever feeling this way. That I would always see the nobility in my husband's work — even if that meant a certain measure of loneliness.

"How bad is it?" I ask Nick.

"It could be worse," he says. "But it's not great."

I close my eyes, searching for the silver lining, knowing that this is my unspoken role in our relationship. Nick might be the eternal optimist at the hospital, brimming with confidence, even bravado. But here at home, in our bed, he relies on me to bring the hope — even when he's silent and self-contained.

"Are his eyes okay?" I finally muster, remembering that Nick once confided in me the enormous complexity of repairing what everyone believes to be the window to the soul.

"Yeah," he says, as he rolls onto his side, toward me. "His eyes are perfect. Big and blue . . . like Ruby's."

His voice trails off as I think that this is a dead giveaway — when Nick compares a patient to Ruby or Frank, I know he has begun to obsess.

"And he has a pretty decent doctor, too," I finally say.

I can hear the smallest of smiles in Nick's voice as he rests his hand on my hip and replies, "Yeah. He does have that going for him, doesn't he?"

The following morning, just after Nick has returned to the hospital, I am making breakfast while I endure the standard meal-time whine-a-palooza, compliments of my firstborn. To put it mildly, Ruby is not a morning person, another trait inherited from her father. In fifteen minutes, she has already complained that Frank is "looking" at her, that her banana is too mushy, and that she prefers Daddy's French toast from the griddle to my toaster variety.

So when the phone rings, I happily retrieve it, feeling relieved for civilized adult companionship (the other day, I was excited when a pollster called) and even more so when I see Cate's name light up my caller ID. Cate Hoffman and I met nearly sixteen years ago at an off-campus party the first week of our freshman year at Cornell, when we were formally introduced to the collegiate world of beer pong, quarters, and "I never." Several drinks into the night, after being asked too many times if we were sisters and acknowledging a certain full-lipped, strong-nosed, blond-highlighted resemblance, we made a pact to look out for each other — a promise I made good on later, saving her from a leering frat boy, then walking her back to her dorm and holding her hair out of her face as she puked in a bed of ivy. The experience bonded us and we remained the best of friends for the next four years and beyond graduation. Since our mid-twenties, our lives have diverged — or, more accurately, mine has changed and hers has stayed very much the same. She still lives in the city (in the same apartment we once shared), is still serial dating, is still working in broadcasting. The only real difference is that she is now in *front* of the camera, hosting a cable network talk show called *Cate's Corner,* and, as of very late, has achieved a modicum of fame in the New York area.

"Look, Ruby! It's Auntie Cate!" I say with exaggerated cheer, hoping that my enthusiasm will rub off on my daughter, who is now in mourning because I will not add chocolate syrup to her milk. I answer the phone and ask Cate what she's doing up so early.

"I'm headed to the gym . . . on a new fitness regime," Cate says. "I really need to drop a few."

"Oh, you do *not,*" I say, rolling my eyes. Cate has one of the best figures I've ever seen, even among the childless and airbrushed. Sadly, people no longer confuse us for sisters.

"Okay, maybe not in real life. But you *know* the camera adds at *least* ten pounds," she says, and then changes the subject with her usual abruptness. "So. What'd you get? What'd you get?"

"What did I get?" I ask, as Ruby moans that she wants her French toast "whole," which is a radical departure from her usual demand that her toast be unveiled to her in "tiny square pieces, all the same exact size, no crust." I cover the phone with one hand and say, "Honey, I think someone may have forgotten the magic word?"

Ruby gives me a blank stare, indicating that she does not believe in magic. To this point, she is the only preschooler I know who has already questioned the veracity of Santa Claus, or at the very least, his travel logistics.

But magic or not, I hold my ground until she amends her request. "I want it *whole.* Please."

I nod as Cate eagerly continues, "For your anniversary? What did Nick give you?"

Nick's gifting is one of Cate's favorite topics, perhaps because she never graduates beyond the "thanks for last night" floral arrangements. As such, she says she likes to live vicariously through me. In her words, I have the perfect life — words she delivers in what vacillates between a wistful and an accusatory tone, depending on her latest dating low.

It doesn't matter how many times I tell her that the grass is always greener and that I'm envious of her whirlwind social schedule, her hot dates (including a recent dinner with a Yankee outfielder), and her utter, blissful freedom — the kind of freedom you take for granted until you become a parent. And it doesn't matter how often I confide my standard complaints of stay-at-home motherhood — namely, the frustration of ending a day no further ahead than where you started, and the fact that I sometimes spend more time with Elmo, Dora, and Barney than with the man I married. None of this registers with her. She still would trade lives with me in a heartbeat.

As I start to reply to Cate, Ruby unleashes a bloodcurdling scream: "*Nooooo!* Mommy! I saaa-iiid *whole!*"

I freeze with the knife in midair, realizing that I've just made the fatal mistake of four horizontal cuts. *Shit,* I think as Ruby demands that I glue the bread back together, even making a melodramatic run for the cabinet where our art supplies are housed. She retrieves a bottle of Elmer's, defiantly shoving it my way as I consider calling her bluff and drizzling the glue over her toast — "in a cursive *R* like Daddy does."

Instead, I say with all the calmness I can muster, "Now, Ruby. You know we can't glue food."

She stares at me as if I'm speaking Swahili, prompting me to translate for her: "You'll have to make do with *pieces*."

Hearing this bit of tough love, she proceeds to grieve the toast that might have been. It occurs to me that a pretty easy fix would be to eat the French toast myself and make a fresh piece for Ruby, but there is something so thoroughly maddening about her expression that I find myself silently reciting the advice of my pediatrician, several how-to books, and my stay-at-home-mother friends: *do not surrender to her demands.* A philosophy that runs in marked contrast to the parenting adage I normally subscribe to: *choose your battles* — which I confess is secret code for *hold your ground only if it's convenient; otherwise, appease the subject in order to make your life easier.* Besides, I think, as I prepare for an ugly gridlock, I am trying to avoid carbs, starting this morning.

So, my cellulite settling the matter, I purposefully set Ruby's plate on the table before her and announce, "It's this or nothing."

"Nothing then!" Ruby says.

I bite my lip and shrug, as if to say, *Bring on the hunger strike,* then exit to the family room where Frank is quietly eating dry Apple Jacks — one at a time — the only thing he'll touch for breakfast. Running my hand through his soft hair, I sigh into the phone and say, "Sorry. Where were we?"

"Your anniversary," she says expectantly, hungry for me to describe the perfect romantic evening, the fairy tale she clings to, aspires to.

On most days I might hate to disappoint her. But as I listen to my daughter's escalating sobs, and watch her attempt to roll her toast into a Play Doh–like ball in order to prove that I *am* wrong, and that food can *indeed* be reassembled, I delight in telling Cate that Nick got paged in the middle of dinner.

"He didn't switch his call?" she says, crestfallen.

"Nope. He forgot."

"Wow. That sucks," she says. "I'm so sorry."

"Yeah."

"So you didn't exchange gifts? Not even when he got home?"

"No," I say. "We agreed not to do presents this year . . . Things are kind of tight these days."

"Yeah, *right,*" Cate says, refusing to believe something else I tell her about my life — that plastic surgeons aren't loaded, at least the ones who work at academic hospitals helping children rather than in private practice enhancing breasts.

"It's true," I say. "We gave up one income, remember?"

"What time did he get home?" she asks.

"Late. Too late for s-e-x . . ." I say, thinking that it would be just my luck for my gifted daughter to memorize the three letters and spout them off to, say, Nick's mother, Connie, who recently hinted that she thinks the kids watch too much television.

"So what about you?" I ask, remembering that she had a date last night. "Any action?"

"Nope. The drought continues," she says.

I laugh. "What? The five-day drought?"

"Try five weeks," she says. "And sex wasn't even an issue . . . I got stood up."

"Shut up," I say, wondering what man would stand her up. Beyond her perfect figure, she is also funny, smart, and a huge sports fan, rattling off baseball trivia the way most women can recite Hollywood gossip. In other words — she is most guys' dream. Granted, she can be high-maintenance and shockingly insecure, but they never glean that at the outset. In other words, she's break-up-able, but not stand-up-able.

Ruby preaches from the next room that it's not nice to say *shut up* as Cate continues, "Yeah. Before last night, I always had that going for me. Never been stood up and never dated a married man. I almost thought the former was my reward for the latter. So much for karma."

"Maybe he *was* married."

"No. He definitely wasn't married. I did my research."

"Wait. Was this the accountant from eHarmony or the pilot from your last trip?"

"Neither. It was the botanist from Starbucks."

I whistle as I peek around the corner and catch Ruby taking a surreptitious bite of French toast. She hates to lose almost as much as her father, who can't even make himself lose to her at *Candy Land.*

"Wow," I say. "You got stood up by a botanist. That's impressive."

"Tell me about it," she says. "And he didn't so much as text an explanation or apology. A simple, 'Really sorry, Cate, but I think I'd rather curl up with a good fern tonight.' "

"Well. Maybe he just . . . *forgot?*" I offer.

"Maybe he decided I'm too old," she says.

I open my mouth to refute this latest cynical tidbit, but can think of nothing particularly comforting to say other than my usual standby that her guy is out there somewhere — and she will meet him soon.

"I don't know about that, Tessa. I think you might have gotten the last good one."

She pauses in such a way that I know what's coming next. Sure enough, she adds a wry, "Correction: the last *two* good ones. You bitch."

"Any idea when you're going to stop bringing him up?" I ask, both of us referring to my ex-fiancé. "Just a ballpark estimate?"

"Hmm. How about never?" she says. "Or . . . let's just say when I get married. But wait — that's the same thing as never, isn't it?"

I laugh, and tell her I have to run as my memory is jarred back to Ryan, my college sweetheart, and our engagement. And by engagement, I don't mean that Ryan had just proposed. Rather, we were mere weeks away from our wedding day, knee-deep in honeymoon itineraries, final dress fittings, and first-dance lessons. Invitations had been mailed, our registry completed, our wedding bands engraved. To everyone in my life, I was a typical, glowing bride-to-be — my arms toned, skin tanned, hair shiny. *Literally* glowing. Everyone but my therapist, Cheryl, that is, who, every Tuesday at seven o'clock, helped me examine that blurry line between normal wedding anxiety and commitment issues stemming from my parents' recent, bitter divorce.

Looking back, the answer was obvious, the mere inquiry suggesting a problem, but there were so many factors clouding the issue, confusing my heart. For starters, Ryan was all I really knew. We had been dating since our sophomore year at Cornell and had only ever slept with each other. I couldn't imagine kissing anyone else, let alone loving someone new. We had the same circle of friends with whom we shared precious college memories I didn't want to taint with a breakup. We also shared a passion for literature, both of us English majors turned high-school teachers, although I was about to start grad school at Columbia with the dream of becoming a professor. In fact, just a few months before, I had talked him into moving to the city with me, convincing him to leave his job and his beloved hometown of Buffalo for something more exciting. And although it was exciting, it was also scary. I had grown up in nearby Westchester, making frequent trips to Manhattan with my brother and parents, but living *in* the city was a different matter, and Ryan felt like my rock and safety net in the uncertain, scary real world. Reliable, honest, kind, funny Ryan with his big, boisterous family and parents who had been married for thirty years and counting — a good sign, my mother said.

Check, check, check, check, check.

Finally, there were Ryan's own sweet assurances that we were perfect for each other. That I was just overthinking things, being my usual neurotic self. He truly believed in us — which on most days was enough for me to believe in us, too.

"You're the kind of girl who will never be completely ready," he told me after one session with Cheryl, the details of which I always divulged to him with only the most minor edits. We were sitting at an Italian restaurant in the Village, waiting for the gnocchi special, and he reached his long, lanky arm across the table and patted my hand. "It is one of the things I love most about you."

I remember considering this as I surveyed

44

his pragmatic expression, and deciding, with a certain degree of sadness and loss, that he was probably right. That maybe I wasn't hardwired for the sort of all-consuming, unconditional passion that I had read of in books, seen in movies, even heard some friends, including Cate, describe. Maybe I would have to make do with the cornerstones of our relationship — comfort and compatibility and compassion. Maybe it was good enough, what we had, and I might look for the rest of my life and never find better.

"I *am* completely ready," I said, finally convincing myself that it was the truth. I still wasn't sure whether I was settling, but in my mind at least the *issue* was settled. I was going to marry Ryan. Final decision, last word.

Until three days later, that is, when I first laid eyes on Nick.

I was on the subway, during my crowded morning commute to school, when he walked onto the train two stops after mine, holding a tall thermos of coffee and wearing blue-gray scrubs. His dark, wavy hair was longer than it is now, and I remember thinking he looked more like an actor than a doctor — and that maybe he *was* an actor playing a doctor, on his way to a TV set. I remember looking into his eyes — the warmest brown eyes I had ever seen — and feeling overcome by a crazy, gut feeling that can only be described as love at first sight. I remember thinking that I was saved by a moment, by a person I didn't know and probably would never know.

"Hello," he said, smiling, as he reached out and held the same pole I was gripping.

"Hi," I said, catching my breath as our hands touched, and we rattled our way uptown, making small talk about topics we've both, remarkably, forgotten.

At one point, after we had delved into a few personal matters, including my Ph.D. program and his residency, he nodded down at my diamond ring and said, "So when's the big day?"

I told him twenty-nine days, and I must have looked grim when I said it, because he gave me a knowing look and asked if I was okay. It was as if he could see straight through me, into my heart, and as I looked back at him, I couldn't stop myself from welling up. I couldn't believe I was crying with a complete stranger when I hadn't even broken down on Cheryl's tweed couch.

"I know," he said gently.

I asked *how* he knew.

"I've been there," he said. "Of course, I

wasn't on my way to the altar. But still . . ."

I laughed through an unattractive sob.

"Maybe it will be okay," he said, looking away, as if to give me privacy.

"Maybe," I said, finding a Kleenex in my purse and gathering myself.

A moment later, we were stepping off the train at 116th Street (which I would only later learn wasn't Nick's true destination), the crowd dispersing around us. I remember how hot it was, the smell of roasted peanuts, the sound of a soprano folksinger crooning from the street above. Time seemed to stand still as I watched him remove a pen from the pocket of his scrubs and write his name and number on a card I still have in my wallet today.

"Here," he said, pressing it into my palm.

I glanced down at his name, thinking that he looked like a Nicholas Russo. Deliciously solid. Sexy. Too good to be true.

I tried it out, saying, "Thank you, Nicholas Russo."

"Nick," he said. "And you are . . . ?"

"Tessa," I said, feeling weak with attraction.

"So. Tessa. Give me a call if you ever want to talk," he said. "You know . . . Sometimes it helps to talk to someone who's not . . . vested."

I looked into his eyes and could see the truth. He was as vested as I was.

The next day I told Ryan I couldn't marry him. It was the worst day of my life to that point. I had had my heart broken once before him — granted, on a much more adolescent level — but this was so much worse. This was heartbreak *plus* remorse and guilt and even shame over the scandal of calling off a wedding.

"Why?" he asked through tears I still can't bear to think about too closely. I had seen Ryan cry before, but never because of me.

As hard as it was, I felt that I owed him the truth, brutal though it was.

"I love you, Ryan. But I'm not *in* love with you. And I can't marry someone I'm not *in* love with," I said, knowing that it sounded like a canned breakup line. Like the sort of unsubstantial, shallow excuse middle-aged men give before divorcing their wives.

"How do you know?" Ryan asked. "What does that even *mean?*"

I could only shake my head and think of that moment on the train, with the stranger named Nick in the blue-gray scrubs, and say again and again that I was sorry.

Cate was the only one who got the full story. The only one who knows the truth, even today. That I met Nick *before* I broke up with Ryan. That if it weren't for Nick, I would've married Ryan. That I'd probably *still* be married to Ryan, living in a different city with different children and a different life altogether. A watered-down, anemic version of my life now. All the same downsides of motherhood, none of the upsides of true love.

Of course, there was speculation about infidelity among some of our more partisan friends when Nick and I started to seriously date only a few months later. Even Ryan (who at the time still knew me better than anyone, Nick included) expressed doubts about the timing of things, how quickly I had moved on.

"I want to believe you are a good person," he wrote in a letter I still have somewhere. "I want to believe that you were honest with me and would never cheat. But I have a hard time not wondering when you and your new boyfriend actually met."

I wrote him back, despite the fact that he told me not to, declaring my innocence, apologizing once again for the pain I caused him. I told him that he would always have a special place in my heart, and that I hoped, in time, he would forgive me and find someone who loved him the way he deserved to be loved. The implication was clear — I had found what I wanted for him. I was *in* love with Nick.

It is a feeling that has never wavered. Life isn't always fun, and is almost never easy, I think, as I return to the kitchen in my troubleshooting mode, ready for my second cup of coffee, but I am in love with my husband and he is in love with me. It is the constant in my life, and will continue to be so, as our children grow, my career changes, friends come and go. I am sure of this.

But I still find myself reaching out and knocking twice on our wooden cutting board. Because you can never be too sure when it comes to the things that matter most.

4
VALERIE

The following morning, Charlie is moved across the street, from the ER at Mass General to Shriners, which Valerie has been told repeatedly is one of the leading pediatric burn centers in the country. She knows they are in for a long, uphill struggle when they get there, but she also feels relief that Charlie's condition is no longer a life-or-death emergency, a feeling that is bolstered by the sight of Dr. Russo waiting for them in their new room.

It has not even been a full day since their first conversation, but she already trusts him as much as she's ever trusted anyone. As he steps toward her, clipboard in hand, Valerie notices how striking his features are, admiring the curve of his bottom lip, his elegant nose, his liquid brown eyes.

"Hello," he says, forming each syllable carefully, his manner and posture formal. Yet there is something familiar, even comforting, about him, too, and Valerie fleetingly considers whether their paths have crossed before, somewhere, in a much different context.

"Hi," she replies, feeling a twinge of embarrassment for crumbling the night before. She wishes she had been stronger, but tells herself he has seen it all, many times, and will likely see more tears from her before they are finished.

"How are you?" he asks with genuine concern. "Did you get any sleep?"

"A little," she says, even though she spent most of the night standing beside Charlie's bed. She wonders why she's lying — and further, how any mother in the world could possibly sleep at a time like this.

"Good. Good," he says, sustaining eye contact with her for several seconds before dropping his gaze to Charlie, who is awake but still heavily sedated. She watches him examine Charlie's cheek and ear, with the efficient aid of a nurse, the two exchanging instruments, ointment, gauze, and quiet commentary. Then he turns to Charlie's hand, using tweezers to peel back a dressing from the charred, swollen skin. Valerie's instinct is to look away but she does not let herself. Instead, she fights a wave of nausea, memorizing the sight of his mottled skin, red and pink in places, black in others. She tries to compare it to her visual from a few hours before, when his bandages were last changed, and studies Dr. Russo's face for a reaction.

"How does it look?" she asks nervously, unable to read his expression.

Dr. Russo speaks quickly but kindly. "We're definitely at a critical juncture here . . . His hand is a bit more swollen from all the fluids he's taking in . . . I'm a little worried about the blood flow, but it's too soon to tell whether he'll need an escharotomy."

Before she can ask the question, he begins explaining the foreboding medical term in simple detail. "An escharotomy is a surgical procedure used on full-thickness, third-degree burns when there is edema — or swelling — that limits circulation."

Valerie struggles to process this as Dr. Russo continues more slowly. "The burns have made the skin very rigid and hard, and as Charlie becomes rehydrated, the burned tissue swells and becomes even tighter. This causes pressure, and if the pressure continues to build, the circulation can become compromised. If that happens, we'll have to go in there and make a series of incisions to release the pressure."

"Is there a downside to the procedure?" she asks, knowing instinctively that there is always a downside to everything.

Dr. Russo nods. "Well, you always want to avoid surgery if you can," he says, an air of careful patience to his words. "There would be a small risk of bleeding and infection, but we can typically control those things . . . All in all, I'm not too worried."

Valerie's mind rests on the word *too,* analyzing the nuances and gradations of his worry, the precise meaning of his statement. Seeming to sense this, Dr. Russo smiles slightly, squeezes Charlie's left foot through two layers of blankets, and says, "I'm very pleased with his progress and hopeful that we're moving in a great direction . . . He's a fighter; I can tell."

Valerie swallows and nods, wishing her son didn't have to be a fighter. Wishing she didn't have to be a fighter for him. She was tired of fighting even *before* this happened.

"And his face?" she asks.

"I know it's difficult . . . But we have to wait and see there, too . . . It will take a few days to determine whether those burns are second or third degree . . . When we declare those injuries, we can devise a game plan from there."

Valerie bites her lower lip and nods.

Several seconds of silence pass as she notices that his dark beard has come in since the night before, forming a shadow across his jaw and chin. She wonders whether he's been home yet, and whether he has children of his own.

He finally speaks, saying, "For now, we'll just keep the skin clean and dressed and keep a close eye on him."

"Okay," she says, nodding again.

"*We* will keep a close eye on him," Dr. Russo says, reaching out to touch her elbow. "*You* try to get some sleep tonight."

Valerie musters a smile. "I'll try," she says, lying again.

Later that night, Valerie is wide awake on her rocking chair, thinking of Charlie's father and the night they met at a dive bar in Cambridge, mere days after her big fight with Laurel. She had come in alone, knowing that it was a bad idea even before she saw him sitting in the corner, also alone, chain-smoking and looking so mysterious and beautiful and thrillingly angst-ridden. She decided that she needed a mindless hookup, and if given the chance, she would leave with him. Which is exactly what she ended up doing, four glasses of wine and three hours later.

His name was Lionel, but everybody

called him "Lion," which should have been a red flag. For starters, he looked like a lion, with his striking gold-toned skin and green eyes, his thick mane of curly hair, and huge, callused hands. Then there was his temperament — remote and languid with flashes of anger. And like a lion, he was perfectly content to let the lioness in his life do all the work — be it his laundry, the cooking, or taking care of his bills. Valerie chalked it up to his preoccupation with his work, but Jason insisted his laziness stemmed from a sense of entitlement typical of beautiful women. She could see her brother's point, even in the throes of infatuation when most women are blinded by their attraction, but she simply didn't care, and in fact, found his flaws compelling, romantic, befitting a sculptor and painter.

"He's an artist," she told Jason repeatedly, as if it were a blanket excuse for all his shortcomings. She knew how she sounded, knowing that Lion was something of a cliché — a temperamental, self-centered artist — and she an even bigger cliché for falling in love with him. She had visited Lion's studio and seen his work, but had not yet seen him in action. Still, she could perfectly envision him splattering red paint on giant canvases with a flick of his wrist. The two of them together, reenacting the Demi Moore–Patrick Swayze pottery scene in *Ghost,* "Unchained Melody" playing in the background.

"Whatever," Jason said, rolling his eyes. "Just be careful."

Valerie promised that she would. But there was something about Lion that made her throw all caution to the wind — and condoms to the wind, for that matter, as they had sex everywhere, all over his studio, her apartment, the cottage at the Vineyard where he dog-sat (which turned out to be his ex-girlfriend's house and dog — the source of their first significant argument), even in the back of a taxi. It was the best sex Valerie had ever had — the kind of physical connection that made her feel invincible, as if anything was possible. Unfortunately, the euphoria was short-lived, replaced by jealousy and paranoia as Valerie discovered perfume on his sheets, blond hair in his shower, lipstick on a wineglass that he hadn't even bothered to put in the dishwasher. She interrogated him in fits of rage, but ultimately believed his stories about his visiting cousin, his professor from the art institute, the girl he met at the gallery who he swore up and down was a lesbian.

All the while, Jason did his best to convince Valerie that Lion wasn't worth the angst. He was just another troubled, not very talented artist, a dime a dozen. Valerie pretended to agree, *wanted* to agree, but could never really make herself believe those things were true. For one, Lion wasn't *that* troubled — he didn't have a drug or alcohol problem, had never been in any trouble with the law. And for another very unfortunate thing, he *was* talented — "brilliant, clear-eyed, and provocative," according to the critic in the *Boston Phoenix* that reviewed his first exhibit at a Newbury Street gallery, incidentally a gallery owned by a saucy, jaunty young socialite named Ponder, the very girl Lion would next conquer.

"*Ponder?* How pretentious can you get?" Jason said after Valerie spotted Lion kissing her on the street outside his apartment and rushed home, devastated, to give her brother the news.

"Lion and Ponder," Jason continued. "They deserve each other, with names like those."

"I know," Valerie said, taking some solace in her brother's scorn.

"Ponder *this*," Jason said, flipping off the pair with both middle fingers.

Valerie smiled, but couldn't bear to tell Jason the real bitch of the breakup. She had taken a pregnancy test the day before, and was pregnant with Lion's baby. She wasn't sure why she was hiding it from her brother, whether from shame, grief, or the hope that it wasn't true — that she had the first false positive pregnancy test in the history of pregnancy tests. Days later, after the blood test at the doctor's office confirmed the fetus growing inside her, she wept in her room and prayed for a miscarriage — or the strength to go to the clinic on Commonwealth Avenue that several of her friends had visited in college. But deep down, she knew she couldn't do it. Maybe it was her Catholic upbringing, but more likely it was that she really wanted the baby. *Lion's* baby. She vehemently denied that it had anything to do with wanting him back, but she still called him, repeatedly, imagining a change of heart, a transformation of character.

He never answered the phone, forcing her to leave vague, needy messages he would never return, even when she informed him that she had something "really important" to tell him.

"He doesn't deserve to know," Jason said, declaring Lion the first person he ever hated.

"But doesn't this baby deserve to have a father?" Valerie asked.

"If the choice is binary — Lion or nothing — the kid is better off with nothing."

Valerie could see Jason's point, recognizing that there is more heartbreak in continuous disappointment than a void, but she also felt that it was wrong to keep it from him in the same way ending her pregnancy felt wrong. So one lonesome evening late in her third trimester, she decided to call him one last time, give him one final try. But when she dialed his number, a stranger with a Middle Eastern accent informed her that Lion had moved to California with no forwarding information. She wasn't sure whether to believe this person, or whether he was a co-conspirator, but either way she officially gave up, just as she had given up with Laurel and her friends back home. There was nothing more she could do, she decided — and she took surprising comfort in that feeling of futility, reminding herself of this during every difficult moment that followed: when she went into labor, when she brought Charlie home from the hospital, when he kept her up late at night with colic, when he had ear infections and high fevers and bad falls. She reminded herself of this when Charlie was finally old enough to ask about his father, a heartbreaking moment that Valerie had dreaded every day of her son's life. She had told him the modified truth, one that she had scripted for years — that his daddy was a talented artist, that he had to go away before Charlie was born, and that she wasn't sure where he was now. She had brought out the only painting she had of Lion's, a small abstract covered with circles, all in hues of green, and ceremoniously hung it over Charlie's bed. Then she showed him the only photo she had of his father, a blurry snapshot she kept in an old hatbox in her closet. She asked Charlie if he wanted it, offering to frame it for him, but he shook his head, returning it to the hatbox.

"He never met you," Valerie said, fighting back tears. "If he did, he would love you as much as I do."

"Is he ever coming back?" Charlie asked, his eyes round and sad, but dry.

Valerie shook her head and said, "No, honey. He's not coming back."

Charlie had accepted this, nodding bravely, as Valerie told herself again that there was nothing more she could do — other than be a good mother, the very best mother she could be.

But now, years later, staring up at the hospital ceiling, she finds herself doubting this, doubting herself. She finds herself wishing she had tried harder to track Lion down. Wishing that her son had a father. Wishing they weren't so alone.

5
TESSA

On Sunday afternoon, Nick, Ruby, Frank, and I are shopping for Halloween costumes at Target — our idea of quality family time — when I realize that I've officially become my mother. It's certainly not the first time I have sheepishly caught myself in a "Barbism" as my brother calls such moments. For example, I know I sound like her whenever I warn Ruby that she's "skating on thin ice" or that "only boring people get bored." And I see myself in her when I buy something I truly don't want — whether a dress or a six-pack of ramen noodles — simply because it is on sale. And when I judge someone for forgetting to write a thank-you note, or driving a car with a vanity license plate, or, God forbid, chewing gum too enthusiastically in public.

But as I stand in the costume aisle at Target, and tell Ruby no, she cannot get the *High School Musical* Sharpay outfit, with its jeweled, midriff-revealing halter and tight gold lamé capris, I know I have traversed deep into Barb terrain. Not so much because of our shared feminist sensibility, but because I promised my daughter that she could select her own costume this year. That she could be "anything she wants" — which is exactly what my mother told me when I was a girl and then a young woman. When what she *really* meant, time and time again, and apparently what *I* meant in this instance, was, "Be anything you want, as long as I approve of your choice."

I cringe, remembering all the conversations I had with my mother last year after I told her I was quitting my tenure-track position at Wellesley College. I knew she'd have something (a *lot*) to say about it as I was used to her giving me her unsolicited two cents. In fact, my brother and I often laugh about her visits and how many times she begins her sentences with "If I might make a suggestion" — which is simply a gentle launching pad for her to then go on and tell us how we are doing things all wrong. *If I might make a suggestion: perhaps you should lay Ruby's clothes out the night before — it would really avoid a lot of morning arguments.* Or, *If I might make a suggestion: you should probably allocate one command spot for all the incoming mail and paper. I've found that it really cuts down on clutter.* Or my personal favorite, *If I might make a suggestion: you need to try to relax and create a soothing environment when you nurse the baby. I think Frankie senses your stress.*

Yes, Mom, he most certainly *does* sense my stress. And so does everyone in the house — and the world at large. Which is why I am quitting my job.

This, of course, was not an explanation that satisfied her. Instead, she was full of more "suggestions." Such as, *Don't do it. You'll be sorry. Your marriage will suffer.* She went on to cite Betty Friedan, who called staying at home "the problem that has no name" and Alix Kates Shulman, who suggested that rather than quitting their jobs, women should simply refuse to do 70 percent of the housework.

"I just don't see how you can give up all your dreams," she said in her ardent way that conjured her bra-burning, flower-child days. "Everything you worked so hard for. So that you can sit around in your sweats, folding clothes and cooking pot pies."

"It's not about that," I replied, wondering if she could somehow see me through the phone lines, standing at the stove, making bacon and black truffle macaroni-and-cheese from a recipe I had just clipped from a magazine. "It's about spending time with Ruby and Frank."

"I know, honey," she said, "I know that's what you believe. But in the end, you will have sacrificed your soul."

"Oh, puh-*lease*, Mom," I said, rolling my eyes, "don't be so dramatic."

But she went on, just as fervently, "And before you know it, those kids will be in school all day. And you'll be sitting around, waiting for them to come home, peppering them with questions about *their* day, living *your* life through them — and you will look back and regret this decision."

"How do you know how *I'll* feel?" I said indignantly, just as I did in high school whenever she tried to, in her words, raise my consciousness. Like the time I tried out for cheerleading and she scoffed, in front of all my cheerleading friends no less, insisting that I should be "on a real team" and not "jump around for a bunch of boys."

"Because I know you . . . I know this won't be enough for you. Or Nick. Just remember — Nick fell in love with the young woman who followed her dreams. Her heart. You *love* your work."

"I love my family more, Mom."

"They aren't mutually exclusive."

"Sometimes it feels that way," I said, thinking of the time I came home to find our nanny squealing with delight over Ruby's first steps. And the countless other things I missed — both big benchmarks and quieter moments.

"What does Nick say?" she asked. I could tell it was a trap, a test with no right answer.

"He supports my decision," I said.

"Well, that doesn't surprise me," she said, with just enough of a caustic note to make me wonder for the hundredth time what she has against my husband — or perhaps all men other than my brother.

"What's that supposed to mean?" I challenged her, knowing that she was viewing this the way she viewed everything — through the lens of her own divorce and her hatred of my philandering father.

"Well, let me just say that, in part, I think it's a very noble thing for Nick to support you in this," she began, switching to her calm, patronizing tone, only slightly less annoying than her strident one. "He wants you to be happy — and thinks this will make you happy. He's also prioritizing time over the extra income — which can be a wise thing . . ."

I dipped a wooden spoon into my bubbling cheese sauce, and tasted it. *Perfect,* I thought, as she continued her rant. "But Nick's dreams aren't being put on hold. And as the years pass, this could create a wall between you. He will have this stimulating, challenging, rewarding, *vibrant* life, completely separate from you, Ruby, and Frank. Meanwhile, all the drudgery, all the domestic details, will be yours —"

"I'll still have a life, Mom. I'll still have interests and friends — and more time to cultivate both . . . And I can always go back and teach one or two classes as an adjunct professor if I miss it that much."

"That's not the same. It would be a *job,* not a *profession*. A pastime, not a passion . . . and over time, Nick might lose some respect for you. And worse, you might lose respect for yourself," she said, as I inhaled and prepared myself for what I felt certain was coming next.

Sure enough, she finished with a note of heavy, bitter innuendo. "And *that* —" she said, "that is when your marriage becomes susceptible."

"Susceptible to what?" I asked, playing dumb to make a point.

"To a midlife crisis," she said. "To the siren call of shiny red sports cars and big-breasted women with even bigger dreams."

"I don't like red cars or big breasts," I

said, laughing at my mother's colorful way of expressing herself.

"I was talking about Nick," she said.

"I know you were," I said, resisting the urge to point out the inconsistencies of her argument — the fact that Dad's dalliances began after she started her own business as an interior designer. In fact, her work redecorating a Murray Hill brownstone had just appeared in *Elle Decor* the very week she uncovered my father's final affair, busting him with an *unemployed* woman with no particular dreams other than to perfect the art of leisure. Her name was Diane, and my father was still with her today. David and Diane (and their dogs Dottie and Dalilah). *D*s monogrammed on everything in their home, a portrait of second-marriage bliss, the two of them smugly pursuing hedonism together, wallowing in the fruits of her trust fund and his retirement from the white-shoe law firm where he worked for over thirty years.

But I stopped myself from telling her that work was not a foolproof insurance policy, both because I didn't want to hurt her feelings and because I didn't want to imply that I had anything other than the utmost respect for her. She may not have handled her divorce with textbook poise (such as the day she discovered Diane and took a bat to my father's Mercedes convertible), but she did the best she could. And despite every setback in her life, she always managed to emerge victorious, strong, even, against all odds, genuinely happy. From raising my brother and me, to her brief but intense bout with breast cancer (which she miraculously hid from us in elementary school, insisting she shaved her head due to the intense New York heat wave), to the career she built from nowhere, Barbie was one tough, *beautiful* cookie, and I was always proud to have her as my mother, even at her most overbearing.

So instead, I simply held my ground and said, "Mom. Listen. I know your heart's in the right place. But this is the right choice for *us*. For *our* family."

"Okay. Okay," she relented. "I hope I'm wrong, Tessa. I truly hope I'm wrong."

I think of this conversation now, and my vow to try to support Ruby's choices even when I don't agree with them. But as I survey the Sharpay photo, taking in the red lipstick, high heels, and provocative pose, I lose my resolve and attempt to carve out a "no hoochie-wear" exception and change my daughter's mind. Just this once.

"Ruby, I think it's a little too mature for

you," I say casually, trying not to entrench her position.

But Ruby only shakes her head resolutely. "No it's not."

Grasping at straws, I try again. "You'll freeze trick-or-treating in that."

"I'm warm-blooded," she says, clearly misunderstanding her father's biology tutorial this morning.

Meanwhile, I watch another mother-daughter pair, dressed in matching purple velour sweats, happily agree on a wholesome Dorothy costume. The mother smiles smugly, then, as if to show me how it's done, says in a suggestive voice clearly intended for Ruby, "Look at this *darling* Snow White costume. This would be perfect for a little girl with dark hair."

I play along, to show her that her flimsy tricks would never work in my house. "Yes! Why, Ruby, you have dark hair. Wouldn't you like to be Snow White? You could carry a shiny red apple!"

"No. I don't want to be Snow White. And I don't like apples," Ruby retorts, her expression stony.

The other mother gives me a playful shrug and an artificial smile as if to say, *I tried. But my mother-of-the-year prowess can only go so far!*

71

I flash a fake smile of my own, refraining from telling her what I'm really thinking: that it's an unwise karmic move to go around feeling superior to other mothers. Because before she knows it, her little angel could become a tattooed teenager hiding joints in her designer handbag and doling out blow jobs in the backseat of her BMW.

Seconds later, as the two continue along their yellow brick road, Nick rounds the corner carrying Frank in one arm and an Elmo costume in the other, proving once again that, at least in our house, boys are easier. Ruby's eyes light up when she sees her father, and she wastes no time in busting me in the highest volume possible.

"Mommy said I could be *anything* I want for Halloween and now she says I can't be Sharpay!" she shouts.

Nick raises his brows. "Mommy wouldn't go back on a promise like that, would she?" he asks.

"Oh, yes she would," Ruby says, pushing out her lower lip. "She just did."

Nick glances my way as I reluctantly nod. "See for yourself," I mumble, pointing at the glammed-up photo, and feeling a rush of secret satisfaction as I read his mind. On the one hand, I know his basic instinct is to indulge his daughter, make her happy at

72

virtually any cost. On the other, he's as overprotective as they come, with a strong preference that his little girl not roam the neighborhood resembling a child prostitute.

Feeling hopeful, I watch Nick kneel beside Ruby and give it his best shot. "I think this looks a little . . . *old* for you, Ruby," he says. "Maybe next year?"

Ruby shakes her head. "It's not too old, Daddy. It's my size!" she says, pointing to the 4T in the upper corner of the packaging.

At this first sign of resistance, Nick stands and surrenders, shooting me a helpless look.

"Well, then," he says to Ruby. "It looks like this is between you and Mommy."

I think of my mother again — both trying to imagine what she would say to Ruby, and perhaps more important, what she would say about Nick's laissez-faire fathering. *The domestic details will be yours,* I hear ringing in my ears. Then I heave the burdened sigh of mothers everywhere and say, "A promise is a promise. Sharpay it is."

"Yay!" Ruby says, scampering toward the checkout line.

"Yay!" Frank echoes, as he and Nick follow her.

"But no lipstick," I say, now talking to myself, just as my mother does. "And you're

73

wearing a turtleneck, young lady. Like it or not."

Later that night, after the kids are finally in bed, I glance at our calendar and discover that tomorrow is Ruby's day to be "special helper" at her preschool. This is fantastic news for Ruby who, according to the "special helper" handout, will get to feed the class goldfish, choose the book to be read at story time, and be first in line to the playground. Unfortunately, it also means that it is *my* day to provide a healthy yet delicious snack for sixteen children, one that does not contain peanut products or tree nuts, because of a lethal allergy in the class — which pretty much rules out anything that we might have on hand.

"Dammit," I mumble, wondering how I missed the neon-orange highlighter that I used to underline "special helper" only two weeks ago.

"You want the Napa or the Rhone?" Nick says, holding a bottle in each hand.

I point at the Rhone and make another disgruntled sound at the calendar as Nick slides the Napa back onto the wine rack and rifles through the drawer to find an opener. "What's up?" he says.

"Ruby's the 'special helper' tomorrow . . .

74

In school."

"So?"

"So we have to bring the snack," I say, using *we* even though this assignment falls squarely in my domain — and did even when I was working. Unfortunately, I no longer have the excuse of my job — which I always felt lowered expectations slightly.

"So what's the problem?" he asks, utterly clueless.

"The cupboards are bare," I say.

"Oh, c'mon," Nick says nonchalantly. "I'm sure we have *something* here."

"We don't, actually," I say, thinking of the piecemeal lunch and dinner I threw together today, using leftovers from last week.

He uncorks the bottle, pours two glasses, and then strolls toward the pantry. "Aha!" he says, pulling out an unopened bag of Oreos — one of my many guilty pleasures.

"Oreos?" I say, smiling.

"Yeah. Oreos. You know — cookies and milk. Old-school."

I shake my head as I consider the exhilarating freedom of being a man, the daddy. Of thinking that Oreos could *possibly,* in any school or stratosphere, be brought as a snack, let alone the *class* snack.

"Wrong on so many levels," I say, amused. "Aren't you a doctor? Isn't this sort of like the preacher's daughter having sex? A cobbler's kid going barefoot in the city?"

"Did you really just say *cobbler?*" Nick says, laughing. And then, "C'mon. Kids love Oreos. Besides, your analogy is suspect — I'm not a *dentist.* I'm a plastic surgeon."

"Okay. Oreos are unacceptable."

"Why?"

"For one, I'm sure they contain peanut products," I say, scanning the ingredients. "For another, they're loaded with sugar. For another, they're not homemade. And they don't look like they *could* be homemade . . . Do you have any idea what the other mothers would say behind my back if I handed out Oreos?"

Nick hands me my glass as I continue my playful rant. "I'd be totally shunned for the rest of the year. For years to come. I mean, I might as well go in there, light up a cigarette, and toss out the F-bomb. 'Fuckin-*A*, these Oreos hit the spot' . . . The reply-all button would be in full abuse mode in a mass gossipfest."

Nick cracks a small smile and says, "Are these mothers really that judgmental?"

"Some," I say. "More than you could imagine."

"Do you care?" he asks.

I shrug, thinking this is the crux of the issue. I don't want to care about this sort of trivia. I don't want to care about what other people think, but I *do*. Especially lately.

As if on cue, the phone rings and I see that it's my friend April calling. April is my second-closest friend, after Cate — and definitely my closest everyday Mommy-friend, even though she makes me feel inadequate much of the time. She doesn't do it on purpose — but she is just so damn perfect. Her house is tidy, her children well behaved *and* well dressed, her photo albums and scrapbooks current and filled with gorgeous black-and-white photography (her own, of course). She does everything the right way, especially when it comes to her children — from nutrition to finding the best private school (and requesting the best teacher at that school). She's read and researched it all and earnestly shares any and all information with me and anyone who will listen, particularly when there is an underlying note of doom. A water bottle contains excessive levels of lead? A suspicious man driving a white van in the neighborhood? A new study linking vaccines to autism? She will be the first to give you the scoop. Unfortunately for me, her daughter, Olivia, is a year older than Ruby and now attending kindergarten at another school

(Longmere Country Day — which is, of course, the best in town); otherwise, she would have reminded me of my snack duties.

"It's April," I tell Nick. "Let's ask her about the Oreos."

He rolls his eyes as I pick up the phone and say hello.

April immediately launches in with an apology for calling so late — which is how she begins almost every conversation. Usually it's the "I know this is a really bad time" disclaimer — which is interesting because I've never seen or heard any evidence that she endures particularly chaotic bedtimes or bath times or mealtimes, the grueling rituals that unravel lesser mothers. At the very least, she's trained her children not to whine or interrupt when she's on the phone. In fact, Olivia is the only child I've ever heard use the word *pardon.*

"You know we don't have a calling curfew," I say (knowing that she has a firm eight o'clock cutoff and that it is now 7:55). Then, before I let her ramble, I say, "Quick question for you. Ruby's snack day is tomorrow. Only thing we have in the pantry is Oreos. Do you think that'll work?"

I put the phone on speaker, but there is only silence on the other end.

78

"April?" I say, grinning. "Are you there?"

To which she replies, "Oreos, Tess? Are you *for real?*"

"No . . . But Nick is," I say.

She gasps as if I've just confided that Nick delivered a left hook to my eye during an argument and then says worriedly, "Tessa? Am I on speaker?"

"Yeah," I say, knowing she'll kill me for this later.

"Is . . . Nick right . . . *there?*" she whispers.

"Yeah. He's here," I say, grinning wider.

"Why, hello there, April," he says, rolling his eyes again. Nick likes April well enough, but doesn't understand why we're so close and accuses her of being neurotic and overly intense — both irrefutable. But I've explained to him that when you live on the same suburban street, and have children the same ages (her son, Henry, is six months older than Frank), that's all it really takes to bond. Although, in truth, I think our friendship runs deeper than circumstance or convenience. For one, she is the sort of friend who would do absolutely *anything* for you — and she doesn't just make the empty offer; she actually initiates and always follows through. She brings the soup when you're sick. She loans you the dress when you have nothing suitable to wear and forgot to go shopping. She babysits your kids when you're in a pinch. For another, she is a planner who consistently puts together fun things for us to do, either with the kids, the couples, or just the two of us. And finally, she is quick to pour a glass of wine — or two or three — and becomes hilariously frank and irreverent when she drinks. It is a surprising quirk in an otherwise utterly disciplined persona and one that always makes for a good time.

But now she is all business — the helpful, earnest perfectionist I love, sometimes in spite of herself.

"It was a good thought," she says in a patronizing tone I don't even think she knows she's adopted. "But I'm sure we can come up with something better."

I picture her pacing in her kitchen, her lean, tennis-toned arms and legs working overtime as always. "Oh! I got it . . . I just made the most yummy carrot muffins. They'd be perfect."

Nick winces — he hates food adjectives like *yummy* and *tasty* and, his least favorite combination of them all, *moist and chewy.*

"Hmm. Yeah. Not so sure I have time to *make* muffins," I say.

"They're *soo* easy, Tessa. A cinch."

To April, everything is easy. Last year, she

actually had the audacity to call beef Wellington "a cinch" when I told her I had to come up with something for Christmas dinner. Incidentally, I ended up ordering the entire meal and then getting busted when my mother-in-law asked me how I made the gravy, and my mind went perfectly blank as to how to make *any* gravy, let alone the kind residing on my table.

"Yeah. I think I'll have to go store-bought on this one," I say, taking the phone off speaker to spare Nick from hearing more.

"Hmm. Well, there's always fruit skewers," she says, explaining that I need only pick up little plastic stirrers at the party store and then spear the grapes, strawberries, pineapples, melon. "Then just pick up a few bags of organic popcorn . . . that Pirate's Booty stuff is pretty tasty . . . although popcorn *is* listed as a leading choking hazard in a recent consumer report, along with grapes, hot dogs, raisins, gum, and candy . . . So maybe not such a good idea . . . Choking always scares me. That and drowning. And *God* . . . not to be a *total* downer, but that's . . . sort of why I'm calling . . ."

"To warn me against choking hazards?" I say, knowing that it's not out of the realm of possibility.

"No . . . Didn't Nick tell you?" she asks, her voice returning to a whisper.

"You're off speaker," I say. "Tell me what?"

"About the accident?"

"What accident?"

At the word *accident,* Nick shoots me a look — somehow, we both know what is coming.

"The little boy in Grayson Croft's class . . . Charlie Anderson?"

"Yeah?" I say.

"He was burned at Romy's house — in a campfire accident."

I am speechless as my mind ticks through the few degrees of separation which are so typical in Wellesley: Romy Croft is one of April's closest friends on her tennis team. Romy's son and April's daughter are in the same kindergarten class at Longmere Country Day, apparently along with Nick's patient.

Sure enough, April says, "Isn't Nick his doctor? That's the word going around . . ."

"Yes," I say, marveling that the rumor mill can churn so efficiently over the weekend.

"What?" Nick asks, now staring at me.

I put my hand over the phone and say, "Your patient Friday night. He was at Romy Croft's house when it happened . . ."

"Who?" he asks, proving once again how bad he is with names and any sort of social networking. He is so bad, in fact, that sometimes it seems as if he is doing it on purpose, almost as a point of pride. Especially when it involves a high-profile type, like Romy, who throws lavish, renowned dinner parties, is involved in just about every charity in town, and is on the board of Longmere — which I hope Ruby will attend next year.

I shake my head and hold up one index finger, indicating that he'll have to wait a second. Meanwhile, April is telling me that Romy is *beside* herself with worry.

"How did it happen?" I ask.

"I don't know . . . I swear she must be going through post-traumatic stress syndrome where she sort of blanked out the details."

"She doesn't remember anything?"

"Not really . . . No specifics, although she was right there, along with Daniel, carefully supervising . . . But at some point, Daniel ran in to get more Hershey bars or graham crackers or marshmallows . . . and Romy was alone with the boys . . . and I guess a few of them started to roughhouse . . . and somehow Charlie must have tripped and fallen . . . She can't remember anything after that, other than yelling at Daniel to call 911 . . . God, it's just *so* awful."

"Horrible," I murmur, picturing the gruesome, terrifying scene.

"I mean, I've *never* seen Romy so upset. She's usually cool as a cucumber about everything . . . But now . . . She's mostly worried about Charlie, of course, but Grayson, too. She said he cried himself to sleep — and then woke up with nightmares. She's going to make an appointment with a child psychiatrist to deal with everything."

"Yeah," I say. "I can imagine."

"And of course this is totally off the record, but Romy and Daniel are freaking out about a potential lawsuit . . ."

"Do you really think they'll *sue?*" I say, thinking of the drama that would unfold if one parent in a class sued another. And I thought it was bad when a little boy in Ruby's class bit another child last week.

"She," April says. "There *is* no father. She's a single mother . . . And nobody really knows her too well . . . Of course, I sent out an e-mail to the other mothers and teachers, letting everyone know what happened . . . But so far, nobody has spoken to her . . . at least as far as I know . . . So it's really anybody's guess what she'll do."

"Right," I say, feeling myself tense for a reason I can't quite place. "I'm sure she's not even thinking along those lines right now."

"Of course not," April says, realizing that her focus, too, might be insensitive. As such, she quickly adds, "So how's he doing? Charlie?"

"Um . . . I'm not really sure," I say. "Nick and I haven't really discussed the specifics . . . I didn't realize there was . . . a connection."

"Oh. Well . . . can you ask him?"

"Uh . . . yeah . . . hold on a sec," I say. Then I look at Nick who vehemently shakes his head, clearly sensing the direction of the conversation. This is no surprise; when it comes to ethics, Nick is by the book.

Sure enough, he whispers, "C'mon, Tess. You know I can't discuss my patients like that . . ."

"Should I tell her that?"

"I don't know . . . Just tell her something general — you know, that I haven't declared the burns yet. That it's too soon to tell."

"Declared?" I say, recognizing the terminology but forgetting the exact meaning.

"Whether they're second or third degree. Whether he'll need surgery," he says, his voice becoming impatient.

I nod and then walk into the family room, just out of Nick's earshot, and say, "Hey,

I'm back."

"What did he say?"

"Well, from what I understand," I say, clearing my throat, "the boy's face and hand are burned pretty bad . . . but that's off the record. You know, patient confidentiality and all."

April sounds the slightest bit defensive as she tells me she totally understands. "I just hope he's okay. I feel so bad for *everyone* involved . . ."

"Yeah. It's really awful. Things can happen so quickly," I say, wondering why I feel conflicted in this conversation. I tell myself that there are no sides to be taken.

"I think Romy's going over to the hospital tomorrow," she says. "To bring a care package and try to speak to the boy's mother . . . And I'm going to organize a dinner drop-off or something. Pass along a sign-up sheet over at the school. People will want to help. It's such an amazing community — a really tight-knit place."

"Have you met her? Charlie's mother?" I ask, identifying with her rather than Romy, although I'm not sure why.

"No. Although I remember her from the open house the other night." April then launches into a physical description, saying, "She's very petite . . . and pretty in a plain

86

sort of way. Dark, straight hair — that slippery wash-and-go kind. She looks young, too . . . so young that you wonder if it wasn't a teenaged-pregnancy sort of thing . . . Although I could be totally wrong about that. She could be a widow for all I know."

"Right," I say, feeling sure that April will get to the bottom of things soon.

She continues, as if reading my mind. "I don't want to get overly involved, but I *am* involved . . . You know, as Romy's friend and a mother at the school . . . And, in a way, as a friend of yours and Nick's. Jeez, I can't believe what a small world it is . . ."

"Yeah," I say, returning to the kitchen for a much-needed sip of wine.

"So anyway," April says, her tone lightening suddenly, dramatically. "Do you need help with those skewers? Just went shopping and our fruit bowl is bountiful — I could run some over?"

"Thanks," I say. "But too much effort. I think I'll just pick something up in the morning."

"You sure?" she asks.

"I'm sure," I say.

"Okay," April says. "But no Oreos."

"No Oreos," I repeat, wondering how I could have been so stressed, even for a moment, about something as trivial as a pre-school snack.

6
Valerie

The view outside Charlie's third-floor room at Shriners is a pleasant one, overlooking a courtyard planted with pink and white hydrangeas, but Valerie prefers to keep the blinds drawn, the thin northern exposure allowing virtually no light to work its way through the plastic slats. As a result, she quickly loses track of day and night, in a way that is a bittersweet reminder of Charlie's infancy, when all she wanted to do was be near him and take care of his every need. But now, she can only watch helplessly as he endures dressing changes while bags of fluids drip nutrients, electrolytes, and painkillers into his veins. The hours pass by slowly, punctuated only by Dr. Russo's twice-daily rounds and the endless cycle of nurses, social workers, and hospital staff, most of whom come for Charlie, a few to check on her, some simply to empty the wastebaskets, bring meals, or mop the floors.

Valerie refuses to sleep on the stainless-steel cot that one of the many nameless, faceless nurses wheeled in for her, its pilled white sheets and thin blue blanket stretched and neatly tucked into the sides. Instead, she stays put on the wooden rocker near Charlie's bed, where she watches his narrow chest rising and falling, the flutter of his eyelids, the smile that sometimes appears in his sleep. Every once in a while, despite her best efforts to stay alert, she dozes for a few minutes, sometimes longer, always awaking with a start, reliving the call from Romy, realizing once again that her nightmare is real. Charlie is still too drugged to fully understand what has happened, and Valerie both dreads and prays for the moment she will explain everything to him.

On the fourth or fifth day, Valerie's mother, Rosemary, returns from Sarasota where she had been visiting her cousin. It is another moment Valerie has been dreading, feeling irrationally guilty for cutting her mother's visit short when she almost never gets out of Southbridge, and guiltier still for adding another tragic chapter to her already tragic life. Widowed twice over, Rosemary lost both husbands — Valerie's father and the salesman who followed — to heart attacks.

Valerie's father had been shoveling the driveway after a particularly large snowfall (stubbornly refusing to pay the teenaged boy next door for something he could do himself) when he collapsed. And although it was never confirmed, Valerie was pretty sure her mother's second husband died while the two were having sex. During the funeral, Jason had leaned over to Valerie and opined about the number of Hail Marys it would require to pay for the sin of nonprocreative, lethal carnal relations.

It is one of the many things Valerie loves most about her brother — his ability to make her laugh in the unlikeliest of circumstances. Even now, he attempts casual one-liners, often at the expense of the more zealous or chatty nurses, and Valerie forces a smile as a way of thanking her brother for his effort, for always being there for her. She thinks of her earliest memory, the two of them in a red wagon, flying down the steep, grassy hill near their house, laughing so hard that they both wet their pants, the wagon filling with the warm liquid that they blamed on their next-door neighbor's dachshund.

Years later, he would be the one to hold her hand at Charlie's first ultrasound; and drive her to the hospital when her water broke; and take on night duty when she couldn't stand it another second; and even support her through law school and studying for the bar exam, insisting again and again that she could do it, that he believed in her. He was her twin brother, best friend, and since the falling-out with Laurel, only real confidant.

So it is no surprise that he handles things now, too, bringing Valerie toiletries and clothing, phoning Charlie's school and her boss at the law firm, explaining that she will need an indefinite leave of absence, and, just this morning, picking up their mother at Logan Airport. Valerie can hear him debriefing Rosemary, gently suggesting the right and wrong things to say. Not that it will do much good, for despite the best intentions, their mother has an uncanny knack for saying the exact wrong thing, especially to her daughter.

So it is no surprise that when Rosemary and Jason return from the airport and find Valerie in the cafeteria, staring into the distance with a fountain soda, an untouched burger, and full plate of crinkly fries before her, her mother's first words are critical rather than comforting.

"I can't believe a hospital serves such junk food," she says to no one in particular. It is an understandable position after losing two husbands to heart disease, but Valerie is not in the mood to hear it now, especially when she has no intention of eating anything anyway. She pushes the red plastic tray away and stands to greet her mother.

"Hi, Mom. Thanks for coming," she says, already feeling exhausted by the conversation they have not yet had.

"Val, honey," Rosemary says. "There is no need to *thank* me for coming to see my *only* grandson."

It is the way she always refers to Charlie — which Jason once joked is the saving grace of Valerie's single motherhood. "Charlie might be a bastard," he said, "but he'll get to pass on the family name."

Valerie laughed, thinking that she would not have tolerated that word from anyone else in the world. But Jason had a free pass, good for life. She could count on one hand the number of times he had angered her. Lately, the opposite seemed to be true of her mother. She initiates a reluctant hug with her now, one that Rosemary awkwardly reciprocates. The two women, with their willowy builds, are mirror images of one another, both self-contained and stiff.

Jason rolls his eyes, having recently posed the question of how two people who love each other could have such a hard time showing it. Valerie feels a wave of envy toward her brother, remembering the first time he brought a boyfriend (a handsome stockbroker named Levi) home to meet the family, and how taken aback she felt watching the two casually touch, hold hands, even, at one point, hug. Valerie's surprise had nothing to do with her brother being gay, which she had known for years, maybe even before Jason knew it himself, but rather his ability to show such easy, natural affection.

She remembers Rosemary glancing away at such moments, seemingly in denial about the nature of their "friendship." She had stoically accepted Jason's news when he broke it to her (more stoically than she had received the news of Valerie's pregnancy) but had not acknowledged it since, other than to offhandedly mention to Valerie that he *sure didn't seem gay,* as if hoping there had been some sort of mix-up. Valerie had to admit this was true, that Jason did not hew to the usual stereotypes. He talked and walked like a straight man. He lived for the Red Sox and Patriots. He had little fashion sense, dressing almost exclusively in jeans and flannel shirts.

"But he *is* gay, Ma," Valerie said, recognizing that part of love is acceptance — and that she wouldn't change a thing about her brother, just as she wouldn't change a thing about her son.

In any event, Valerie has feared her mother's reaction to Charlie's injury, anticipating either breezy denial, a stockpile of guilt, or endless *if only*s.

She picks up her tray now, dumping the contents into a nearby wastebasket and leading her mother and brother to the cafeteria exit. By the time they've arrived at the elevator, Rosemary has asked her first loaded question. "I'm still a little hazy here . . . How in the world did this happen?"

Jason gives his mother an incredulous look, as Valerie sighs and says, "I don't know, Ma. I wasn't there — and I obviously haven't talked to Charlie about it yet."

"What about the other little boys at the party? Or the parents? What did they tell you?" Rosemary asks, her angular face moving back and forth like an old-fashioned windup toy.

Valerie thinks of Romy, who has left her multiple voice mails and has been by the hospital twice, dropping off handmade cards from Grayson. Despite her desire to know every detail about that night, she cannot bring herself to see Romy, or even call her back. She is not ready to hear her excuses or apologies, and she is certain that she will never forgive. Valerie and her mother have this in common, too, Rosemary holding grudges more firmly than anyone she's ever known.

"Well, let's go see him," Rosemary says, exhaling ominously.

Valerie nods, as they ride the elevator up two floors and then walk in silence to the end of the hall. As they approach Charlie's room, Valerie hears her mother mumble, "I really wish you had called me straight-away."

"I know, Ma . . . I'm sorry . . . I just wanted to get through those first hours . . . Besides, there was nothing to be done long-distance."

"Prayer," Rosemary says, lifting one eye-brow. "I could have prayed for him . . . What if, God forbid . . ." Her voice trails off, a wounded expression on her heavily lined face.

"I'm sorry, Ma," Valerie says again, keeping silent tally of her apologies.

"Well, you're here now," Jason says, flashing Rosemary his most captivating smile. It is no family secret that Jason is her favorite child, his homosexuality notwithstanding.

"And you," Rosemary says, giving Jason a once-over that he would later joke to Valerie looked like a search for signs of AIDS. "You're way too thin, honey."

Jason drapes one arm over Rosemary's shoulder, further charming her. "Oh, come on, Ma," he says. "Look at this face. You know I look *good*."

Valerie considers his statement and feels herself tense. Not so much because Jason is talking about his handsome, unscarred face, but because of the glance he shoots her afterward. It is a look of worry, of sympathy, of realizing that he, too, just said the wrong thing. Valerie knows this look of pity well and feels an ache in her heart that her son will now come to know it, too.

The following morning, while Charlie is still dozing, Dr. Russo comes to examine his hand. Valerie can tell right away that something is wrong despite his impassive expression and slow, deliberate movements.

"What's wrong?" she says. "Tell me."

He shakes his head and says, "It's not looking good. His hand. There's too much swelling . . ."

"Does he need surgery?" Valerie asks, steeling herself for bad news.

Dr. Russo nods and says, "Yeah. I think

we need to go in there and release the pressure."

Valerie feels her throat constrict at the thought of what "going in there" entails until he says, "Don't worry. It'll be fine. We just need to release the pressure and do a graft on his hand."

"A graft?" she says.

"A skin graft, yes."

"From where?"

"His leg — the thigh area. Just a little strip of skin is all we'll need . . . Then we'll put it in a meshing machine and expand it — and secure it to his hand using a few surgical staples."

She can feel herself wince as he continues, telling her the whole graft will be nourished by a process called plasmatic imbibition — which means that the graft literally drinks plasma, then grows new blood vessels into the transplanted skin.

"You make it sound easy," she says.

"It *is* pretty easy," he says, nodding. "I've done thousands."

"So there's no risk?" she asks, wondering if there's a judgment call involved, whether she should seek a second opinion.

"Not really. The main concern is fluid accumulation under the graft," he continues. "To prevent this from happening, we'll mesh the graft with tiny rows of short, interrupted cuts." He makes a small cutting motion in the air and continues. "Then, each row will be offset by half a cut-length, like bricks in a wall. In addition to allowing for drainage, this allows the graft to both stretch and cover a larger area . . . and more closely approximate the contours of the hand."

She nods, feeling queasy but reassured by the precise science of it all. "I'll also be using VAC therapy — Vacuum Assisted Closure — which does pretty much what it sounds like it does. I'll place a section of foam over the wound, then lay a perforated tube onto the foam, securing it with bandages. A vacuum unit then creates negative pressure, sealing the edges of the wound to the foam, and drawing out excess blood and fluids. This process helps to maintain cleanliness in the graft site, minimizes the risk of infection, and promotes the development of new skin while removing fluid and keeping the graft in place."

"Okay," she says, taking it all in.

"Sound good?" he asks.

"Yes," she says, thinking she does not want a second opinion, that she trusts him completely. "And then what?"

"We'll keep his hand immobilized in a

splint for four or five days, then continue therapy and work on function."

"So . . . you think he'll be able to use it again?"

"His hand? Absolutely. I'm very optimistic. You should be, too."

She looks at Dr. Russo, wondering if he can tell that optimism has never been her go-to emotion.

"Okay," she says, resolving to change that.

"Are you ready?" he asks.

"You're going to do the surgery *now?*" she asks nervously.

"If you're ready," he says.

"Yes," she tells him. "I'm ready."

7
TESSA

The accident seems to be all anyone can talk about — at least among the stay-at-home mothers in town, the ranks of whom I'm slowly infiltrating. The subject arises at Frank's playgroup, Ruby's ballet class, on the tennis courts, even in the grocery store. Sometimes the women know of Nick's connection to the boy, openly giving their condolences to pass along. Sometimes they have no clue, relaying the story as if it were the first time I'd heard it, exaggerating the injuries in ways I'd discuss with Nick later. And sometimes, in the most annoying instances, they know, but pretend not to, transparently hoping that I will divulge some inside information.

In almost all cases, they speak in hushed voices with grave expressions, as if, on some level, relishing the drama. "Emotional rubbernecking," Nick calls it, disdainful of anything smacking of gossip. "Don't these women have anything better to do with their time?" he asks when I report happenings on the grapevine, a sentiment I tend to agree with, even when I am a guilty participant in the chatter, speculation, and analysis.

Even more striking to me, though, is the distinct sense that most of the women seem to identify more with Romy than the little boy's mother, saying things like, "She shouldn't be so hard on herself. It could happen to anyone." At which point, I nod and murmur my agreement, both because I don't want to make waves and because, in theory, I believe it's true — it *could* happen to anyone.

But the more I hear talk of how poor Romy hasn't slept or eaten for days, and what happened in her backyard wasn't really her fault, the more I begin to think that it *is* her fault — and that she and Daniel *are* to blame. I mean, for chrissake, who lets a bunch of six-year-old boys play with fire? And if you *are* responsible for such an egregious lapse of judgment and plain common sense, well, I'm sorry, you probably *should* feel guilty.

Of course I downplay these feelings to April, who has become understandably obsessed with Romy's emotional (and potential legal and financial) plight, sharing all the details with me in the way that close friends always share details about other close friends. I do my best to be sympathetic, but one afternoon, when I meet April for lunch at a little bistro in Westwood, I can feel myself losing patience when she starts in with an indignant tone. "Valerie Anderson still refuses to speak to Romy," she says, seconds after our lunch arrives.

I look down at my salad as I smother it with blue cheese dressing which, I realize, defeats the point of ordering the salad — and certainly of ordering dressing on the side.

April continues, her tone becoming more impassioned. "Romy's been by the hospital with artwork from Grayson. She's also sent Valerie several e-mails and left her a couple of messages."

"And?"

"And nothing back. Absolute stone-cold silence."

"Hmm," I say, poking a crouton with my fork.

She takes a dainty bite of her own salad, tossed with fat-free balsamic, then chases it with a liberal gulp of chardonnay. Liquid lunches are April's favorites — the salad an afterthought. "Don't you think that's rude?" she finishes.

"Rude?" I repeat, gazing back at her.

"Yes," April says emphatically. *"Rude."*

Choosing my words carefully, I say, "I don't know. I suppose so . . . But . . . at the same time . . ."

April absentmindedly reaches up to shift her long ponytail from one shoulder to the other. Her looks, I have always thought, do not match her true personality. Her curly auburn hair, combined with her smattering of freckles, perky nose, and athletic build, conjure a laid-back, outdoorsy type — a former field-hockey player turned go-with-the-flow soccer mom. When, in fact, she is as uptight and *indoorsy* as they come — her idea of camping is a four-(rather than five-)star hotel; and to her, ski trips are about fur coats and fondue.

"But at the same time, what?" she asks, pressing me to put into words what I'd rather leave to implication.

"But her son's in the hospital," I say bluntly.

"I know that," April says, giving me a blank stare.

"Well, then?" I make a gesture that would be captioned, *Well, then, what is your point?*

"Okay," April says. "I'm not saying Valerie should be all buddy-buddy with Romy or anything . . . but would it kill her to return

104

a simple phone call?"

"I suppose that would be the right thing to do — at least the *nice* thing to do," I say reluctantly. "But I don't think she's really thinking much about Romy. And I don't think we really know what this woman is going through."

April rolls her eyes. "We've all had sick children," she says. "We've all been to the ER. We all know what it's like to be scared."

"C'mon," I say, appalled. "Her kid's been in the hospital for *days*. He has third-degree burns on his face. His right hand — the hand he uses to write and throw a ball — is totally messed up. He's had one surgery already and there will be more to come. And he will probably *still* have some functional impairment. And scars. For the rest of his life."

I almost stop there, but can't help adding a footnote. "You know what that's like? You know that kind of worry? Really?"

April finally looks sheepish. "He's going to have scars for the rest of his life?" she asks.

"Of course," I say.

"I didn't know . . ." she says.

"C'mon. He's a burn victim. What did you think?"

"I didn't think they were that bad. The

105

burns. You didn't tell me."

"More or less I did," I say, thinking of the numerous times I've given April vague updates.

"But I've heard Nick say he can do skin grafts that are . . . unnoticeable. That burn surgery has become totally sophisticated."

"Not *that* sophisticated . . . I mean, yes, they've made a ton of progress over the years — and yeah, I'm sure you've heard him talking his big surgeon game about how seamless his grafts are . . . But still. As good as Nick is, he's not *that* good. That little boy's skin was still badly burned in places. As in burned *off.* Gone."

I bite my tongue from contrasting this to Olivia's fall off her front porch last year, when she chipped a baby tooth, reducing April to tears for weeks, as she lamented all the many photographs that would be ruined before her adult tooth came in and Googled "gray, discolored dead teeth" ad nauseam. A cosmetic blip as far as injuries go.

"I didn't know," she says again.

"Well," I say softly, carefully, "now you do. And you might want to pass the word along to Romy and tell her that maybe . . . maybe this woman just needs some time to herself . . . And Jesus, she's a single mother on top of it. Can you imagine dealing with this kind of crisis without Rob?"

"No," she says. "I can't."

She purses her lips and looks away, out the window next to our table to a very pregnant woman strolling along the sidewalk. I follow her gaze, feeling the same twinge of envy that I always feel when I see a woman about to have a baby.

When I turn back to her, I say, "I just don't think we should judge this woman unless we've walked in her shoes. And we certainly shouldn't be vilifying her . . ."

"Okay, okay," April says. "I hear you."

I force a smile. "No hard feelings?"

"Of course not," April says, dabbing her lips with the white cloth napkin.

I take a long sip of coffee, eyeing my friend, and wondering whether I believe her.

8
VALERIE

As the days pass, Charlie slowly begins to understand why he is in the hospital. He knows that he was in an accident at his friend Grayson's house and that his face and hand were burned by the fire. He knows that he's had surgery on his hand and that he will soon have one on his face. He knows that his skin needs time to heal, and then lots of therapy, but that in time he will return to his own bed and school and friends. He has been told these things by many — nurses, psychiatrists, occupational and physical therapists, a surgeon he calls Dr. Nick, his uncle and grandmother, and most of all, his mother, who is constantly at his side, day and night. He has seen his face in the mirror, and studied his naked hand with worry, fear, or mere curiosity, depending on his mood. He has felt the pain of his injuries ebb and flow along with his doses of morphine and other painkillers, and has cried in frustration during therapy.

Still, Valerie has the troubled sense that her son does not fully grasp what has happened to him — either the gravity of his injury or the implications for the months, maybe years to come. He has not interacted with anyone outside of the hospital bubble and has yet to encounter any stares or questions. Valerie worries about all of this, and spends much mental energy preparing for what lies ahead, for the lucid moment of truth when Charlie asks the inevitable question she has asked herself again and again: *Why?*

The moment comes early Thursday morning, nearly two weeks after the accident. Valerie is standing at the window, watching the first snow flurries of the season, anticipating Charlie's excitement when he awakens. She can't remember ever seeing snow — even a few flakes — in the month of October. Then again, it might be the sort of thing one overlooks when bustling about in the world, hurrying to get to one thing or another. She lets out a long sigh as she contemplates taking a shower or at least having a cup of coffee. Instead, she shuffles back to her rocking chair, her slippers making a whispering noise on the hard, cold floor. Then she sits very still and stares at images flashing on the small, muted television bolted to the wall above Charlie's bed. Al Roker is spreading cheer out on Rockefeller Plaza, chitchatting with all the ebullient tourists who are holding their handmade signs up for the cameras. HAPPY SWEET SIXTEEN, JENNIFER . . . HELLO, LIONVILLE ELEMENTARY . . . CONGRATULATIONS, GOLDEN GOPHERS.

Valerie wonders when she will feel such simple, sign-waving joy again when she hears Charlie softly call her. She quickly glances away from the TV to find him smiling at her. She smiles back at him as she stands and walks the few steps over to his bed. She lowers the side rail on his bed, sits on the edge of his mattress, and strokes his hair. "Good morning, sweetie."

He licks his lips, the way he does when he's excited or about to tell her something good. "I had a dream about whales," he says, kicking off his covers and tucking his knees up toward his chin. His voice is sleepy and a little hoarse, but he no longer sounds drugged. "I was swimming with them."

"Tell me more," Valerie says, wishing her own dreams had been as peaceful.

Charlie licks his lips again, and Valerie notices that the bottom one is chapped. She leans over to retrieve a tube of Chap Stick in the drawer next to his bed as he says, "There were two of them . . . They were *huge.* The water looked freezing cold like the pictures in my whale book. You know the one?"

Valerie nods, reaching over to apply the pale pink stick to his lips. He briefly puckers for her and then continues, "But in my dream, the water was *really* warm. Like a bathtub. And I even got to ride one of them . . . I was sitting right up on his back."

"That sounds wonderful, sweetie," Valerie says, basking in the feeling of normalcy even as they sit in the hospital together.

But one beat later, Charlie's expression becomes faintly troubled. "I'm thirsty," he says.

Valerie feels relieved that his complaint involves thirst rather than pain, and quickly grabs a juice box from the refrigerator in the corner of the room. Gripping the waxy container, she angles the straw toward his lips.

"I can do it," Charlie says with a frown, as Valerie remembers Dr. Russo's advice the day before, to try to let him do things for himself, even when it's difficult.

She releases her hold, watching his expression become gloomy as he awkwardly grips the box with his left hand. His right hand remains still, in a medicated splint, elevated on a pillow.

Valerie feels herself hovering, but is unable to stop herself. "Can I get you anything else?" she says, an anxious knot growing in her chest. "Are you hungry?"

"No," Charlie says. "But my hand itches so *bad.*"

"We'll change the dressing in a minute," she says. "And put on your lotion. That will help."

Charlie says, "Why does it itch so much?"

Valerie carefully explains what he's been told several times already — that the glands that produce oil to lubricate his skin were damaged.

He glances down at his hand, frowning again. "It looks terrible, Mommy."

"I know, honey," she says. "But it is getting better all the time. The skin just needs a while to heal."

She considers telling Charlie about his next skin graft — his first for his face — which is scheduled for Monday morning, when he asks a question that breaks her heart. "Was it my fault, Mommy?" he whispers.

Valerie's mind races as she tries to recall specific articles about the psychology of burn victims, as well as warnings from

Charlie's psychiatrists — *There will be fear, confusion, even guilt.* She pushes all of the words and advice aside, realizing that she doesn't need anything other than her own maternal instincts.

"Oh, honey. Of *course* it wasn't your fault. It wasn't anyone's fault," she says, thinking about Romy and Daniel and how much she actually blames them for what happened, a feeling she hopes she will never reveal to Charlie. "It was just an accident."

"But why?" he asks, his big eyes wide and unblinking. "Why did I have to have an accident?"

"I don't know," she says, studying every curve and angle of his perfect, heart-shaped face. His broad forehead, round cheeks, and little, pointed chin. Sadness wells up inside her, but she does not flinch or falter. "Sometimes bad things just happen — even to the best people."

Realizing that this concept does not satisfy him any more than it does her, she clears her throat and says, "But you know what?"

She knows she is speaking with the voice of false cheer, the one she uses to, say, make a promise of ice cream in exchange for good behavior. She wishes she had something to offer him now, something — *anything* — to make up for his suffering.

"What?" Charlie asks, looking hopeful.

"We will get through this together," she says. "We're a great, unstoppable team — and don't forget it."

As she swallows back tears, Charlie takes another sip of juice, gives her a brave smile, and says, "I won't forget it, Mommy."

The next day, after a painful round of occupational therapy for his hand, Charlie is on the verge of frustrated tears when he hears Dr. Russo's trademark hard double knock on the door. Valerie watches her son's face clear and feels her own spirits lift, too; it is a close call as to who looks forward to his visits more.

"Come in!" Charlie calls out, smiling as his doctor strolls into the room. Valerie is surprised to see him dressed not in his usual scrubs and tennis shoes but in dark denim, a light blue shirt open at the collar, and a navy sport coat. He looks casual but elegant, down to his black loafers and silver cuff links.

Valerie suddenly remembers that it is Friday night — and assumes he has dinner plans with his wife. Valerie has long since observed the gold band on his left hand, and has slowly gathered details about his life from his many talks with Charlie. She knows that he has two young children, a daughter and a son. She knows the little girl has a stubborn streak — the naughty-Ruby tales are among Charlie's favorites.

"How're you feeling today, buddy?" Dr. Russo asks as he musses Charlie's curly blond hair, in dire need of a cut. Valerie remembers thinking he needed a trim the day of Grayson's party.

"I'm great. Look, Dr. Nick, I got an iPod from my uncle Jason," Charlie announces, holding up the tiny silver device he received the week before. It is the sort of expensive gift Valerie never would have allowed before the accident. She knows that many things will become measured and categorized like this: *before the accident, after the accident.*

Charlie hands his iPod to Dr. Russo, who flips it over in his hand. "Very cool," he says admiringly. "It's much smaller than mine."

"And it holds a *thousand* songs," Charlie says, watching proudly as his doctor scrolls through his playlist.

"Beethoven. Tchaikovsky. Mozart," he says and then whistles. "Who-*ah*. Buddy, you've got some sophisticated taste in music."

"My uncle Jason downloaded all my favorites," Charlie says, his words, voice, and expression transforming into those of a

115

much older child. "They're relaxing."

"You know what? . . . I feel the same way. I love listening to classical music — especially when I'm worried about something," Dr. Russo says, still scrolling along. At some point, he pauses, glancing over at Valerie for the first time since entering the room, and mouths hello. She smiles back at him, hoping he knows how much she appreciates the way he addresses her son first, before her. And more important, how much she appreciates his effort to connect with Charlie in ways that have nothing to do with his injuries, always making him feel important, an effect that lingers long after he's departed.

"I just listened to the *Jupiter* Symphony on the way over here," Dr. Russo says. "You know it?"

Charlie shakes his head no.

"Mozart," Dr. Russo says.

"Is he your favorite composer?"

"Oh, boy. That's a tough one. Mozart's awesome. But I also dig Brahms, Beethoven, Bach. The three *B*s," Dr. Russo says, taking a seat on the edge of Charlie's bed, his back now to Valerie. She watches the two huddled together and feels a pang of sharp sadness, wishing Charlie had a father. She has long since accepted her situation, but at moments like this one, she still finds it astonishing that Charlie's father knows absolutely nothing about his son. Not his love of classical music or *Star Wars* or blue whales or Legos. Not the funny way he has of running with one arm straight at his side or the happy, crinkly lines that form around his eyes when he smiles — the only child she's ever seen with crow's-feet. Not the fact that he is in a hospital now, discussing composers with his plastic surgeon.

"Do you like 'Jesu, Joy of Man's Desiring'?" Charlie asks breathlessly as Valerie fights back unexpected tears.

"Of course," Dr. Russo says, then belts out a few loud, staccato notes, as Charlie joins in with the English lyrics, singing in his high, sweet voice, " 'Drawn by Thee, our souls, aspiring! Soar to uncreated light!' "

Dr. Russo turns to give Valerie another smile and then says, "Who taught you all this about music, buddy? Your mom?"

"Yeah. And my uncle Jason," Charlie says.

Valerie thinks that she can take no credit for this one — it is all Jason — although she remembers playing classical music when she was pregnant, holding the CD player up to her belly.

Dr. Russo nods, handing the iPod back to Charlie, who reaches across his body to accept it with his good hand, then rests it on his thigh and scrolls with his left thumb.

"Try your right hand, buddy," Dr. Russo says softly. Charlie frowns, but obeys, the web of purple skin between thumb and forefinger stretching taut as he clicks through the songs.

"Here ya go," Charlie finally says, pushing the play button and turning the volume dial up. Keeping one of the earbuds, he hands Dr. Russo the other and they listen together. "I like this one."

"Ahh. Yes. I love this one," Dr. Russo says.

"It's great, isn't it?" Charlie asks intently.

Several soft seconds pass. "Yes," Dr. Russo says. "It's beautiful . . . And those horns — they sure sound happy, don't they?"

"Yes," Charlie says, beaming. "Very, *very* happy."

A beat later, Rosemary arrives unexpectedly, along with a bag of dollar-store gadgets for Charlie and a plastic container of her famous chicken tetrazzini. Valerie knows how hard her mother is trying, how much she wants to be there for them both. Yet she finds herself wishing she had not come, at least not at this moment, and marvels at how her mother manages to suck the peaceful feeling out of the room by her mere presence.

"Oh! Why, hello," Rosemary says, staring at Dr. Russo. They have not yet met, but she has heard much about him, mostly from Charlie.

Dr. Russo abruptly turns and stands with a polite, expectant smile, as Valerie makes an introduction that feels both awkward and somehow revealing. Since their arrival at the hospital, Valerie and Charlie have made a few friends, but she has remained a vigilant gatekeeper of all personal information. Only occasionally has a detail slipped out, sometimes unwittingly, sometimes by necessity. Dr. Russo knows, for example, that there was only one parent signing consent forms — and anyone can easily observe that there are no male visitors other than Jason.

"Very nice to meet you, Mrs. Anderson," Dr. Russo says, as he extends his hand toward Rosemary.

"It's wonderful to meet you, too," she says, shaking his hand with a flustered look of awe, the same expression she wears after church when talking to the priests, especially the young, handsome ones. "I just can't thank you enough, Dr. Russo, for everything you've done for my grandson."

It is an appropriate thing to say, and yet Valerie still feels annoyed, even embarrassed by the slight tremor in her mother's voice. More important, she is conscious of Charlie, listening intently, and resents her mother's melodramatic reminder of why they all are here. Dr. Russo seems to be aware of this dynamic, too, because he quickly murmurs, "You're welcome." Then he turns back to Charlie and says, "Well, buddy, I'll let you visit with your grandma . . ."

Charlie's face scrunches into a frown. "Aww, Dr. Nick, can't you stay a little longer? Please?"

Valerie watches Dr. Russo hesitate, and then rushes in to save him. "Charlie, honey, Dr. Russo needs to go now. He has a lot of other patients to see."

"Actually, buddy, I need to talk to your mom for a few minutes. If that's okay with her?" Dr. Russo says, shifting his gaze to Valerie. "Do you have a minute?"

She nods, thinking of how much her life has slowed since they came here. Always before, she was rushing everywhere; now she finds herself with nothing but time.

Dr. Russo squeezes Charlie's foot and says, "I'll see you tomorrow. Okay, buddy?"

"Okay," Charlie says reluctantly.

Valerie can tell Rosemary's feelings are hurt by her second-fiddle status and she overcompensates with forced exuberance.

"Look! I brought a seek-and-find book!" she shrills. "Wouldn't that be fun?"

Valerie has always maintained that searching for words in a grid of letters is among life's most boring games, and she can tell from her son's lackluster reaction that he agrees. His grandmother might as well have just asked him to count the dimples on a golf ball. "I guess so," he says, shrugging.

Dr. Russo gives Rosemary a nod good-bye before exiting the room. Valerie follows him, remembering the night they met, and their first conversation out in a sterile hall just like this one. She thinks of how far she and Charlie have come, how much her fear and horror have subsided, replaced by a large measure of stoic resignation and a dash of hope.

Now alone, they stand face-to-face for a few beats of silence before Dr. Russo says, "Would you like to get a cup of coffee? In the cafeteria?"

"Yes," she says, feeling her pulse quicken in a way that both surprises and unsettles her. She feels nervous, but doesn't know why, and hopes that he can't sense her uneasiness.

"Great," he says, as they turn and walk toward the elevators. They do not speak along the way, other than an occasional hello to nurses. Valerie carefully studies their faces, their reactions to him, as she has for several weeks now. She has long since determined that Dr. Russo is admired, almost *revered,* in marked contrast to many of the other surgeons she's heard grumblings about, accusations of their being condescending or arrogant or downright rude. He is not overly friendly or chatty, but has a warm, respectful manner that, coupled with his rock-star reputation, makes him the most popular doctor at the hospital. *He is the best in the country,* she's heard again and again. *But still so nice. And quite the looker, too.*

All of this makes the invitation even more flattering to Valerie. She is certain he merely wants to discuss Charlie's upcoming skin graft or his overall progress, but has the sense that he rarely does so over coffee, particularly on a Friday evening.

A few seconds later, they arrive at the elevator, and when the doors open, Dr. Russo motions for her to go first. Once inside, they both stare ahead, silently, until he clears his throat and says, "He's a great kid."

"Thank you," Valerie says, believing him. It is the only time she is good at accepting compliments.

They exit the elevator and round the corner to the cafeteria. As Valerie's eyes adjust to the fluorescent lights, Dr. Russo asks, "When did he start getting so interested in classical music?"

"Over the past year or so," Valerie says. "Jason plays the piano and guitar and has taught him a lot about music."

Dr. Russo nods, as if digesting this information, and then asks whether Charlie plays any instruments.

"He takes piano lessons," she says, following the familiar route past the grill and fountain drinks to the coffee station.

Valerie can tell he's thinking about Charlie's hand as she continues, "He's pretty good. He can hear a song and just . . . figure out the notes, by ear." She tentatively continues, wondering if she is bragging too much. "Runs in the family. Jason apparently has perfect pitch. He once identified our doorbell as an A above middle C."

"Wow," Dr. Russo says, looking legitimately impressed. "That's rare, isn't it?"

Valerie nods as she takes a cup from the upside-down stack and scans the coffee options. "I guess it's one in ten thousand or something."

Dr. Russo whistles and then says, "Can Charlie do that?"

"No — no," Valerie says. "He's just a bit precocious. That's all."

Dr. Russo nods as he pumps a paper cup full of the regular blend. Meanwhile, Valerie chooses the hazelnut and stirs in a packet of raw sugar.

"You hungry?" he asks, as they pass a row of pastries and other snacks.

She shakes her head, having long since forgotten the feeling of hunger. In two weeks, she has lost at least five pounds, going from thin to very thin, her hip bones two sharp angles.

They make their way to the cash register, but when Valerie pulls out her wallet, Dr. Russo says, "I got this one."

She does not protest, not wanting to make a big deal of an eighty-cent cup of coffee. Instead she nonchalantly thanks him as he takes his change and leads her to a small booth in the back corner of the cafeteria, a place where she has sat many times before, but always alone.

"So," he says, sliding into his seat and taking a sip of his coffee. "How are you holding up?"

She positions herself directly across from him as she tells him she's fine, for the moment believing it.

"I know it's not easy," he says. "But I have

to tell you . . . I really think Charlie is doing so well. And in large part, I think it's because of you."

She feels herself blush as she thanks him and says, "The hospital has been wonderful. *Everyone* here is wonderful."

It is the closest she has come to thanking him, something she can't quite bring herself to do directly, for fear that she will break down. He nods, now his turn to look modest. "You're welcome," he says emphatically, in a much different tone than the one he used to return Rosemary's words of thanks.

Valerie smiles at her son's doctor; he smiles back at her. Then they sip their coffee in unison, all the while maintaining eye contact. Valerie decides that, by any measure, they have just shared a moment, and the joint acknowledgment of this moment renders them both silent for an even longer stretch.

Valerie's mind races, as she wonders what to say next. She resists peppering him with medical queries, as she feels she asks too many questions already. And yet, she doesn't feel quite comfortable broaching outside-world topics, as everything seems either too trivial or too personal.

"Well," he finally says, breaking their silence. "I wanted to talk to you about

Monday. Charlie's graft."

"Okay," she says, straightening her posture and wishing she had her spiral notebook and pen with her, so she could take notes, release nervous energy.

"I wanted to make sure you understand the procedure — and answer any questions you may have," he says.

"I appreciate that," Valerie says as she conjures the specifics from prior conversations with him, as well as bits and pieces from Charlie's nurses, and all that she has read on the Internet.

He clears his throat and says, "Okay. First thing Monday morning, an anesthesiologist will come in and put Charlie to sleep."

She feels herself tense as he continues. "Then I'll shave his hair and remove the burned skin from his face."

She swallows and nods.

"Then I'll take a special surgical instrument called a power dermatome and shave a layer of skin off his scalp to produce a split-thickness graft."

"Split thickness?" she asks, worried.

He nods reassuringly. "A split-thickness graft contains the epidermis and a portion of the dermis."

"And that will grow back? On his scalp?"

"Yes. The remaining skin still contains hair

follicles and sebaceous glands which gradually proliferate out to form a new layer of epidermis. We'll dress the area with a moist antibiotic-covered gauze to guard against infection . . ."

"Okay," Valerie says, swallowing, nodding. "And then? How do you put the skin on?"

"So. We'll take the skin and just drape it right over his cheek, and use a scalpel to punch little holes to allow blood and fluid to drain. We then secure the graft with fine sutures and a little biological glue and cover it with a moist, nonadherent dressing."

"Does it always . . . take?" she says.

"Typically, yes. It should attach and revascularize . . . and his scalp will be a fine match for his cheek."

She nods, feeling queasy but reassured, as he goes on to explain that after the surgery Charlie will wear a custom-fitted face mask in order to control facial scarring. "Basically, we want to keep the scars on the face flat, smooth, and pliable."

"A mask?" she says, trying to picture it, worrying, once again, about the social stigma her son will have to endure.

"Yes," he says. "An occupational therapist will be coming by later this afternoon to take a scan of Charlie's face. This data will be transmitted to a company that makes custom-fitted, transparent silicone masks. The mask will cover Charlie's entire face — except for holes for the eyes, nose, and mouth — and attach with straps."

"But it will be clear? See-through?"

"Yes," he says. "Clear so that we can observe blanching of the scar and see where pressure is being applied . . . Over time, the therapist will adjust the fit of the mask by making changes to the mold and reheating the plastic." He studies her face, as if searching for something. "Sound good?"

She nods, feeling slightly reassured.

"Any other questions?"

"No. Not right now," she says quietly.

Dr. Russo nods and says, "Well. Just call me if they come up. Anytime. You have my cell."

"Thank you, Dr. Russo," she says.

"Nick," he says. It is at least the fourth time he's corrected her.

"Nick," she repeats as their eyes lock again. Another stretch of silence ensues, much like the last one, but this time, Valerie feels more comfortable, nearly enjoying the quiet camaraderie.

Nick seems to feel the same, because he smiles and easily switches to a new topic. "So Charlie mentioned you're a lawyer?" he says.

Valerie nods, wondering when, and in what context, Charlie discussed her profession.

"What kind of lawyer?" he asks.

"I practice corporate litigation," she says, thinking of how far away and unimportant her firm and all its politics feel to her. Other than a few phone calls with the head of her department, in which he assured her that her cases and clients were covered and she should not worry about a thing, she had not given work a single thought since Charlie's accident and couldn't fathom why she ever let it stress her out.

"Did you go to law school around here?" he asks.

She nods and says, "Yeah. I went to Harvard," instead of the usual way she avoids that word, not out of a sense of feigned modesty the way so many of her classmates say, "I went to school in Cambridge," but because she still doesn't feel quite worthy of the name.

But with Nick, it is different, perhaps because she knows he went there, too — that he is as accomplished as they come. Sure enough, he nods, unfazed, and says, "Did you always know you wanted to practice law?"

She considers this — considers the truth

— that she had no real passion for the law, but simply wanted to achieve for the sake of achievement. Especially after Charlie was born, when she desperately wanted to earn a good living and be able to provide for her son. Do something that Charlie could be proud of so that she might somehow compensate for his not having a father.

But, of course, she does not divulge any of this, and instead says, "No, not really. I was a paralegal for a couple of years, and realized that I was as smart as the lawyers at my firm . . ." Then she smiles and goes out on a limb with a joke, her first in ages. "Probably what the nurses around here are saying about you."

"Probably so," Dr. Russo says, smiling modestly back at her.

"Oh, come on," she says. "You don't believe that. You even *told* me how good you are."

"I did?" he says, surprised. "When?"

"When we first met," she says, her smile fading as she remembers that night.

He stares at the air above his head, as if he, too, is reliving the night of Charlie's accident. "Yeah, I guess I did, didn't I?"

Valerie nods, then says, "And so far . . . I'd have to agree."

She gives him a look as he leans across

the table and says, "Just you wait. Give me a few months and a couple more surgeries . . ."

To this, Valerie says nothing, but she can feel her heart racing with gratitude and something else she can't quite name, as she silently grants him all the time in the world.

9
TESSA

It is Friday night, and I am sitting in the family room with my mother, brother, and sister-of-law, all in from Manhattan for a weekend visit. We are dressed for our eight o'clock dinner reservations, enjoying a bottle of wine in the family room while the four cousins, freshly bathed and fed, play upstairs under the supervision of a baby-sitter. The only thing missing from the picture is Nick, who is now twenty minutes late and counting, a fact that is not lost on my mother.

"Does Nick always work this late on the weekends?" she asks, crossing her legs as she glances purposefully at the Timex watch she now wears in lieu of the Cartier my father gave her for their last anniversary.

"Not usually," I say, feeling defensive. I know her question likely has more to do with her frenetic personality, and her inability to sit still for any length of time, but

I can't help taking it as a covert affront, a question along the lines of, *Are you still beating your wife?* Or, in this case, *Are you still letting your husband beat you?*

"He just needed to check on a patient — a little boy," I say, feeling the need to remind her of just how noble Nick's profession is. "He's having his first skin graft on Monday morning."

"Damn," my brother says, cringing and shaking his head. "I don't know how he does it."

"I know," my sister-in-law agrees with an admiring look.

My mother is not as impressed. She makes a skeptical face, then folds her cocktail napkin in quarters. "What time is our reservation?" she asks. "Maybe we should just meet him at the restaurant?"

"Not until eight. We still have thirty minutes. And the restaurant's very nearby," I say tersely. "We're fine, Mom. Just relax."

"Yeah. Chill out, Mom," my brother says teasingly.

My mother puts her hands up, palms out. "Sorry, sorry," she says, humming under her breath.

I take a long drink of wine, feeling as tense as my mother looks. Normally, I don't care when Nick is late, just as I'm a good sport when he gets paged. I've accepted these things as part of his job and our life together. But it is a different story when my family is in town. In fact, the last thing I said to Nick this afternoon when he told me he had "to run into the hospital for a few minutes" was, "*Please* don't be late."

He nodded, seemingly understanding all the nuances of the instruction — that for one, we don't want to give my mother ammunition to prove her point about his life taking precedence over mine. And for another, although I adore my older brother, Dex, and am very close to my sister-in-law, Rachel, I am sometimes a little jealous of, if not sickened by, what I perceive to be their perfect marriage and can't help using them as a yardstick of our relationship.

On paper, the four of us have much in common. Like Nick, Dex has a stressful job, working demanding hours as an investment banker at Goldman Sachs, while Rachel, too, gave up her legal career once she had children, first working part-time, then quitting altogether. They also have two children — Julia and Sarah (ages seven and four) — and like the dynamic in our house, Dex defers to Rachel when it comes to parenting and discipline (which, interestingly, does *not* rile my mother as it does when Nick takes a background role; to the contrary, she has occasionally accused Rachel of expecting *too* much of Dex).

But the most striking thing my brother and I share is our relationship history, as he, too, broke *his* engagement mere *days* before his wedding. It's crazy, really: two siblings born two years apart, both canceling weddings, also two years apart — a fact that any psychiatrist would have a field day analyzing and likely attributing to our parents' own split. Dex believes this is the reason for their incredible support both times around; they lost thousands of dollars in wedding deposits and must have been embarrassed in front of their more traditional friends, but they seemed to believe it was a small price to pay for making sure their children got it right on their first try. Still, the joint scandals scored us some rather ruthless ribbing from my mother, who felt the need to give us both the woolliest, thickest socks for Christmas — for our cold feet, naturally. In addition, we had to endure her endless advice that we *not* marry on the rebound. To which Dex, in his analytical way, argued that he could more readily identify "the one" on the heels of "the *wrong* one" — and that he was absolutely sure about Rachel. And which I simply rebutted with a straightforward: "Butt out, Mom."

As an aside, though, Dex's situation was far more scandalous as Rachel was actually *friends* with my brother's former fiancée — *childhood* friends, in fact. Moreover, I am fairly certain there was some cheating involved. This suspicion has never been confirmed, but occasionally Dex and Rachel will let a detail of their early days slip, and Nick and I will exchange a knowing glance. Not that these circumstances really matter at this point, years into their marriage, other than the fact that I think a shady genesis puts a greater burden on a relationship. In other words, if two people have an affair, they'd *better* stay together. If they do, they have this romantic "we were meant to be" story and a certain degree of exculpation for their sin; if they don't, they are just a couple of cheaters.

So far, Dex and Rachel fall squarely in the former camp, still sickeningly in love after all these years. Beyond this, they are truly *best* friends in a way that Nick and I simply are not. For one, they do absolutely *everything* together — go to the gym, read the paper, watch all the same television shows and movies, eat breakfast, dinner, and sometimes even lunch together, and, remarkably, go to bed at the same time every night. In fact, I once heard Dex say that he has trouble falling *asleep* without Rachel — and that they *never* go to bed angry at one another.

This is not to say that Nick and I don't love the time we spend together — because we really do. But we are not joined at the hip and never have been, even in the beginning. Our workout times (mine nonexistent as of late), bedtimes, and even mealtimes vary greatly. In the evenings, I am perfectly content reading a novel in bed alone, and have absolutely no trouble whatsoever falling asleep without Nick next to me.

I'm not sure that this means their marriage is superior to ours, but at times, it definitely gives me the unsettling feeling that we have room for improvement. Cate and April, with whom I've confided the issue, insist that *I* am the normal one, and that Rachel and Dex are atypical, if not completely freakish. April, especially, who has a marriage on the other end of the spectrum, maintains that Dex and Rachel are actually "unhealthy and codependent." And when I broach the topic with Nick, whether with a wistful or worried tone, he becomes understandably defensive.

"You're *my* best friend," he'll say, which is

probably true only because Nick doesn't really have close friends, typical of most surgeons we know. He once did — in high school and college and even a few in medical school — but hasn't made much effort to keep up with them over the years.

More important, even if I *am* Nick's best friend by default, and even if he is my best friend in theory, I sometimes feel as if I share more of my life with Cate and April and even Rachel — at least when it comes to the everyday matters that comprise my life — from the slice of cheesecake I regret eating to the killer sunglasses I found on sale to the adorable thing Ruby said or Frank did. Eventually, I get around to telling Nick this stuff, too, if it's still relevant or pressing when we're finally together at the end of the day. But more often, I mentally pare down the important issues and spare him the trivial ones — or at least the ones I think *he* would deem trivial.

Then there is the matter of Dex and Rachel's sex life, something I know about by accident, really. The conversation began when Rachel recently confided that they've been trying for over a year to have a third baby. This, in and of itself, gave me a pang, as Nick has long since ruled out a third in no uncertain terms — and although I overall agree with him, I sometimes long for a less predictable, two-child, boy-girl family.

In any event, I asked Rachel if they'd been working hard at it or just casually trying, expecting her to delve into the typical unromantic strategies and methodologies of couples trying to conceive. Ovulation kits, thermometers, scheduled intercourse. Instead she replied, "Well, nothing out of the ordinary . . . But, you know, we have sex three or four times a week — and no luck . . . I know a year of trying isn't *that* long, but it happened right away with the girls . . ."

"Three or four times a week when you're ovulating?" I asked.

"Well, I'm not really sure exactly when I'm ovulating. So we just have sex four times a week, you know . . . *all* the time," she said, releasing a nervous laugh, indicating that she didn't feel entirely comfortable discussing her sex life.

"All the time?" I repeated, thinking of the old Japanese adage that if a newly married couple places a bean in a jar every time they make love during their first year, and then remove one every time they make love thereafter, they will never empty the jar.

"Yeah. Why? Should we do it . . . less?" she asked. "Maybe save it up for the best

139

few days of my cycle? Could that be the problem?"

I couldn't hide my surprise. "You have sex *four* times a week? As in, every *other* day?"

"Well . . . yeah," she said, suddenly reverting to her old self-conscious self, the girl I worked so hard to bring out of her shell when she married my brother, with the hope that we would someday feel like sisters, something neither of us had growing up. "Why?" she asked. "How . . . often do you and Nick?"

I felt myself hesitate, then nearly told her the truth — that we have sex three or four times a *month,* if that. But a basic sense of pride, and maybe a little competition, kicked in.

"Oh, I don't know. Maybe once or twice a week," I said, feeling wholly inadequate — like the kind of old married women I used to read about in magazines and couldn't imagine ever becoming.

Rachel nodded and went on to bemoan her declining fertility and whether I thought Dex would be disappointed never to have a son, almost as if she knew I was lying and wanted to make me feel better by pointing out her own worries. Later, I raised the issue with April, who quelled my fears, likely along with her own.

"Four times a *week?*" she nearly shouted, as if I had just told her they masturbate in church. Or swing with their upstairs neighbors. "She's lying."

"I don't think so," I said.

"She totally is. Everyone lies about married sex. I once read that it is the most skewed statistic because nobody tells the truth — even in a confidential survey . . ."

"I don't think she's lying," I say again, feeling relieved to know I wasn't alone, and even more so later when Cate, who loves sex more than most pubescent boys, weighed in on the subject.

"Rachel is such a pleaser. And a martyr," she said, giving examples of such behavior from our girls' trips before we had children — how she always took the smallest room for herself, and defers to everyone else when it comes to dinner decisions. "I can totally see her stepping up to the plate even if she's not in the mood. Then again . . . your brother *is* pretty hot."

"C'mon. Stop," I say, my automatic response when my friends start going on about how hot my brother is. I've heard it my whole life, or at least since high school when his groupies emerged. I even had to jettison a few friends in those days on the suspicion that they were blatantly using me

141

to get to him.

I went on to tell her my theory that looks actually have little to do with attraction to your spouse. That I think Nick is beautiful, but on most nights, it's not enough to get past my clichéd exhaustion. Couples might fall in love based on looks and attraction, but those things matter less in the long run.

In any event, I am mulling all of this over when Nick finally rounds the corner into the family room, greeting everyone and apologizing for being late.

"No problem," my mother is the first to say — as if it's *her* role to absolve *my* husband.

Nick gives her an indulgent smile, then leans in to peck her cheek. "Barbie, dear. We've missed you," he says with a trace of sarcasm only I can detect.

"We've missed you, too," my mother says, giving her watch an exaggerated, brow-raised glance.

Nick ignores her jab, leaning over to plant a real, full-on kiss on my lips. I kiss him back, lingering for a millisecond longer than I normally would as I wonder what I'm trying to prove — and to whom.

When we separate, my brother stands to give Nick a man hug as I think what I always think when my husband and brother are standing side by side — that they could pass for brothers, although Dex is leaner with a green-eyed preppy look and Nick is more muscular with dark-eyed, Italian flair.

"Good to see you, man," Nick says, smiling.

Dex grins back at him. "You, too. How're things going? How's work?"

"Work's good . . . fine," Nick says — which typically is about the extent of their professional conversations, as Dex's understanding of medicine is as cursory as Nick's grasp of financial markets.

"Tessa told me about your latest patient," Rachel says. "The little boy roasting marshmallows?"

"Yeah," Nick says, nodding, his smile receding.

"How's he doing?" she asks.

"All right," he says, nodding. "He's a tough little kid."

"Is he the one with the single mother?" Rachel asks.

Nick shoots me an irritated look which I take to mean either, *Why are you discussing my patients?* or *Why are you getting sucked into this petty gossip?* Or likely both.

"What?" I say to him, annoyed, thinking of the harmless conversation I had with Rachel right after the accident. Then I turn to

Rachel and say, "Yes. That's the one."

"What happened?" Dex says, always ferreting out a good story. I mentally add it to the satisfying things about my brother — and perhaps one of the reasons he and Rachel are so tight. Without being girly or even metrosexual, Dex will partake in gossip with the girls, even flip through an occasional *People* or *Us Weekly*.

I give my brother a rundown of the unfolding story, as Nick shakes his head and mumbles, "Jeez, my wife is turning into such a yenta."

"What's that?" my mother says, visibly getting her fur up on my behalf.

Nick repeats his statement, more clearly, almost defiantly.

"*Turning* into?" she asks. "Since when?"

It is a test but Nick doesn't realize it.

"Since she started spending time with all these desperate housewives," he says, playing right into her hands.

My mother gives me a knowing glance and polishes off her glass of wine with purpose.

"Wait. Did I miss something here?" Dex says.

Rachel smiles and reaches out to squeeze his hand. "Probably," she says jokingly. "You're always one step behind, honey."

"No, Dex," I say emphatically. "You

missed *nothing* here."

"That's for sure," Nick says under his breath, shooting me another reproachful look.

"Oh, get over yourself," I say.

He blows me a kiss, as if to say the whole thing was a joke.

I blow him a kiss back, pretending to be just as playful, while doing my best to ignore the first seeds of resentment that my mother, in all her self-proclaimed wisdom, predicted.

Our collective good spirits are restored at dinner, the mood both fun and festive as we discuss everything from politics to pop culture to parenting (and grandparenting). My mother is on her best behavior, not once taking a jab at anyone, including her ex-husband — which might be a first. Nick, too, seems to go out of his way to be outgoing, and is especially affectionate with me, perhaps feeling guilty for being late or calling me a yenta. The wine doesn't hurt matters, and as the evening progresses, I find myself becoming looser and happier, buzzing with feelings of familial bliss.

But early the next morning, I awaken with throbbing temples and a renewed sense of worry. When I go downstairs to make coffee, I find my mother at the kitchen table with a cup of Earl Grey and a worn copy of *Mrs. Dalloway,* which I know to be her favorite book.

"How many times have you read that?" I ask, filling the coffeemaker with water and freshly ground beans before joining her on the couch.

"Oh, I don't know. At least six," she says. "Maybe more. I find it comforting."

"That's funny. I only conjure angst when I think of Mrs. Dalloway," I say. "Which part do you find comforting? Her never-consummated lesbian longing? Or her yearning for meaning in a meaningless life of running errands, child-rearing, and party-planning?"

It is a line right out of my mother's book, which she acknowledges with a snort of laughter. "It's not so much about the book," she says, "as it is the time in my life when I first read it."

"When was that? College?" I ask — which was when I first fell in love with Virginia Woolf.

She shakes her head. "No. Dex was a baby — and I was pregnant with you."

I cock my head, waiting for more.

She kicks off her pink fuzzy slippers that seem incongruous on my mother and says,

"Your father and I still lived in Brooklyn. We had nothing then . . . but were so happy. I think it was the happiest time in my life."

I picture the romantic brownstone floor-through, decorated in kitschy seventies style, where I spent the first three years of my life but only know from photographs, home movies, and my mother's stories. That was before my father built his law practice and moved us to the traditional Westchester colonial we called home until my parents divorced. "When did you and Dad . . . stop being happy?" I ask her.

"Oh, I don't know. It was gradual . . . and even up until the very end, we had some good times." She smiles the sort of smile that can either be a precursor to tears or laughter. "That man. He could be so charming and witty —"

I nod, thinking that he is *still* charming and witty — that those are the two adjectives people always use to describe my dad.

"It's just too bad he had to be such a womanizer," she says matter-of-factly — as if she's simply saying, *It's too bad he had to wear polyester leisure suits.*

I clear my throat, then tentatively ask for confirmation of something I've always suspected. "Were there other affairs? Before her?" I say, referring to my dad's wife,

Diane, knowing my mother hates hearing her name. I truly believe that she is finally over my father and the pain of her divorce, but for some reason, she says she will never forgive the "other woman," fiercely believing that all women are in a sisterhood together, owing one another the integrity that men, in her mind, seem to innately lack.

She gives me a long, serious look, as if debating whether to divulge a secret. "Yes," she finally says. "At least two others that I know of."

I swallow and nod.

"He confessed to those, came completely clean. Broke down, tears and all, and swore he'd never do it again."

"And you forgave him?"

"The first time, yes. I did completely. The second time, I went through the motions, but never felt the same about him. I never really trusted him again. I always had a sick feeling in my stomach as I searched for lipstick on his collar or looked for phone numbers in his wallet. I felt cheapened because of it. Because of him . . . I think I always knew he would do it again . . ." Her voice trails off, a faraway look in her eye.

I feel the urge to reach out and hug her, but instead ask another hard question. "Do you think it's made you . . . distrust all men?"

"Maybe," she says, glancing nervously toward the stairs as if worried that Nick or Dex will catch her bad-mouthing their gender. She drops her voice to a whisper. "And maybe that's also why I was so upset with your brother . . . when he broke his first engagement."

It is another first, as I had no idea my mother suspected any infidelity — or that she was ever upset with Dex about *anything*.

"At least he wasn't married," I say.

"Right. That's what I told myself. And I couldn't stand that Darcy," she says, referring to Dex's old girlfriend. "So the result was good."

I start to say something else, but then stop myself.

"Go ahead," my mother says.

I hesitate again and then say, "Do you trust Nick?"

"Do *you* trust Nick?" she shoots back. "That is the more important question."

"I do, Mom," I say, putting my fist over my heart. "I know he's not perfect."

"Nobody is," she says, the way gospel preachers say *amen*.

"And I know our marriage isn't perfect," I say, thinking of our rocky start last night.

"No marriage is," she says, shaking her head.

Amen.

"But he would *never* cheat on me."

My mother gives me a look, one that I would ordinarily construe as overbearing, but in the gauzy, golden light of dawn, I take only as maternal concern.

She reaches out and covers my hand with hers. "Nick's a good man," she says. "He really is . . . But the one thing I've learned in life is that you can never say never."

I wait for her to say more as I hear Frank call my name from the top of the stairs, breaking our intimate spell.

"And in the end," she says, ignoring her grandson's escalating calls, sitting so peacefully that it is as if she doesn't hear him, "all you really have is yourself."

10
VALERIE

Just after dark on Saturday, Jason shows up at the hospital with microwave popcorn, two boxes of Jujubes, and several PG-rated movies.

"I *love* Jujubes!" Valerie says, a preemptive strike against what her brother has been threatening for days.

Jason shakes his head and says, "It's boys' night."

Valerie grips the arms of her rocker, reminded of the frantic way she used to feel playing musical chairs. "You always say I'm one of the boys," she says.

"Not tonight. Charlie and I are having a sleepover. No girls allowed. Right, Charlie?"

"Right," Charlie says, grinning at his uncle as they touch fists, a left-handed, knuckle-bump handshake.

Valerie, who was stir-crazy just moments before, wondering what she and Charlie would do all evening, now feels a rising panic at the prospect of their separating. She has left the hospital for a few hours here and there, to pick up takeout or run a quick errand. One afternoon, she even returned home to do a few loads of laundry and sort through her mail. But she has not yet left Charlie at night, and certainly not overnight. He might be ready; *she* is not.

"Go ahead. Eat your candy and watch your movies," she says as casually as she can so as not to give away her panic and further entrench Jason's position. She glances at her watch and mumbles that she'll be back in a couple of hours.

"Nope," Jason says. "You'll be back *tomorrow*. Now go."

Valerie gives her brother a blank stare, prompting him to literally push her off the chair. "Skedaddle. Scoot. Begone, woman."

"Okay, okay," Valerie finally says, slowly gathering her purse and BlackBerry, charging in the corner of the room. She knows her feelings are not rational — that she should be relieved to have a good night's sleep in her own bed and a little privacy. More important, she knows Charlie's in good hands with Jason. He is safe and stable, and for the most part, perfectly comfortable — at least until his surgery on Monday. But there it is anyway — a feeling of deep reluctance in her gut. She takes a breath and slowly exhales, wishing she had a Xanax left in her prescription, something to smooth out her ragged, worried edges.

"C'mon, now," Jason whispers to her as he helps her with her coat. "Call a friend. Go get a few drinks. Have a little fun."

She nods, pretending to ponder her brother's advice, full well knowing she will do nothing of the kind. Saturday-night *fun,* at least the kind Jason means, was a rarity before this — and is certainly out of the question now.

She goes to Charlie and gives him a hug, followed by a light kiss on his cheek, alongside his scar. "I love you, sweetie," she says.

"I love you, too, Mommy," he says, quickly returning his attention to the selection of DVDs Jason has fanned out on the foot of the bed.

"Okay then. I'm off . . ." Valerie says, stalling as she glances around the room, pretending to look for something. When this charade is exhausted, she kisses Charlie once more, walks out the door, and makes her way down to the cold, dark parking garage. For a few moments, as she hunts for her dusty teal Volkswagen with its political bumper sticker now two elections old, she becomes convinced that it was stolen, somehow chosen over the trio of BMWs parked on the same level — and she feels one part relief that she'll have no choice but to go back inside. But then she remembers squeezing into a narrow space designated for compact cars after a burrito run a few days before, and finds it just where she left it. She peers into the backseat before unlocking the door, something she has done for years, since a teenager from her hometown was kidnapped in a shopping-mall parking lot days before Christmas — the chilling moment captured on a surveillance camera.

Tonight, though, Valerie's backseat search is not hair-raising, but perfunctory and halfhearted. It is a silver lining, she thinks — when a greater fear is realized, lesser ones fall away. Hence, she is no longer petrified of parking-garage rapists. She shivers as she slides into her car and starts the engine. The radio, left on high from her last trip, blares R.E.M.'s "Nightswimming," a song that vaguely depresses her, even under the best of circumstances. She exhales into her hands to warm them, then turns the dial, hoping for something more uplifting. She stops at "Sara Smile," figuring that if Hall & Oates can't help her, nobody can. Then she drives slowly toward home, humming an occasional refrain and doing her best to forget the last time she left her son for a boys-only sleepover.

Only she doesn't go home. Not right away. She fully intends to, even planning to return a few phone calls — to her friends at work and a few girls from home, even Laurel, who had heard through the grapevine, aka Jason, of Charlie's accident. But at the last second, she bypasses her exit and heads straight for the address she looked up on the computer, then MapQuested and memorized last night, just after Charlie fell asleep. She wants to believe her detour is a lark, a flight of fancy, but nothing can truly be called a lark or flight of fancy given the current state of things. It can't be boredom, either, as she is never bored; she enjoys solitude too much for that. She convinces herself that it must be a simple matter of curiosity, like the time in the mid-nineties when she and Jason went to L.A. for a cousin's wedding and drove by South Bundy, the site of the double homicide in the O.J. Simpson trial. Only tonight her curiosity is of the idle, not morbid, variety.

As she makes her way toward the heart of Wellesley, a light rain begins to fall. She puts her windshield wipers on the slowest setting, the mist on her window giving her the veiled feeling of protection. She is under-cover, gathering clues — about what she is not quite sure. She makes a left turn, then two rights onto the street — which is elegantly called a "boulevard." It is broad and tree-lined with neat sidewalks and clas-sic, older homes. They are more modest than she expected, but the lots are deep and generous. She drives more slowly, watching the odd numbers on the right side of the road diminish until she finds the house she is looking for — a storybook Tudor. Her heart races as she takes in the details. The twin chimneys flanking the slate roof. The huge birch tree with low, climbable branches just off center in the front yard. The pink tricycle and old-school red rubber ball, both abandoned in the driveway. The warm yel-low light in one upstairs bedroom. She wonders if it is his — *theirs* — or one of the children's, and imagines them all tucked neatly inside. She hopes that they are happy as she does a three-point turn and drives home.

Sometime later, she is taking a bath, her favorite Saturday-night pastime. Normally, she reads a magazine or paperback book in the tub, but tonight she closes her eyes, keeping her mind as blank as possible. She stays submerged, the soapy water up to her chin, until she feels herself nod off and it occurs to her that she might be tired enough to fall asleep and actually drown. Charlie would be an orphan, forced to forever speculate whether her death was a suicide — and if it were somehow his fault. She shakes the morbid thought from her head as she stands and steps out of the tub, wrapping herself in her coziest, largest bath towel — a bath *sheet,* to be precise. She remembers the day she ordered the set of fine, Egyptian-cotton towels, the most luxurious ones she could find, even opting for a French-blue monogram with her initials for an extra five dollars per towel. It was the day she received her first bonus check at her law firm, a reward for billing two thousand hours — a small fortune she had planned to spend on everyday creature comforts. After the towels, she ordered Austrian goose-down pillows, sateen sheets, cashmere cable-knit throws, heavy cast-iron cookware, and fine china for twelve — quality domestic goods that most women acquire when they marry, *before* they buy a house or have a baby. She was doing it backward, maybe, but she was doing it all by herself. *Who needs a man?* she thought with every item she added to her cart.

It became her mantra. As she worked long hours at her firm, saving more money until she and Charlie could finally move out of their depressing basement apartment — with its stark white walls the landlord wouldn't let her paint and the perpetual smell of curry and marijuana from the neighbors across the hall — into the cozy Cape Cod they still live in now. As she shoveled the driveway in the winter, watered grass seed in the spring, pressure-washed their front porch in the summer, raked leaves in the fall. As she did all the things to make a home and a life for Charlie. She was self-sufficient, self-reliant, self-contained. She was every empowered lyric that she heard on the radio: *I am woman, hear me roar . . . I will survive . . . R-E-S-P-E-C-T.*

Yet tonight, after she eats a peanut butter and jelly sandwich over the kitchen sink and tucks herself neatly into bed, wearing her favorite white flannel nightgown with eyelet trim, she feels a sharp lonesome pang, an undeniable sense that something is missing. At first she believes the void is Charlie, who, for the first time ever, is not sleeping in the room next to hers. But then she thinks of that upstairs glow in the stone Tudor, and realizes that it is something different altogether.

She stares into the darkness and tries to imagine what it would be like to have someone in bed next to her, tries to remember the feel of being entangled in another, sweaty, breathless, satisfied.

That's when she closes her eyes and sees his face, and her heart starts to race again, just as it did in the hospital cafeteria over coffee and in front of his house.

She knows it's wrong, having these thoughts about a married man, but she lets herself drift there anyway, rolling onto her side and pressing her face into her pillow. *Who needs a man?* she tries to tell herself. But as she falls asleep, she is thinking, *I do.* And more important, *Charlie does, too.*

11
TESSA

"How's the school search coming along?" Rachel asks me on Sunday morning as she sits cross-legged on the floor of our guest room and packs for their return trip to New York. It is the first we've been alone all weekend, and are now only because my mother had an early morning flight home and Dex and Nick are taking the kids out for a walk — or as Rachel called it after she peeled her girls off the couch, "a forced march outdoors."

"Ugh," I say, making a face. "What a pain in the ass the whole thing is."

"So you've definitely ruled out the public elementary school?" she asks, pulling her shoulder-length hair into a ponytail with the ever-present elastic band she wears on her left wrist, seemingly in lieu of a watch.

"I think so. Nick's in favor of it — probably because he went to public schools . . . But obviously Dex and I didn't . . . I think

160

it's all what you're used to," I say, hoping that this is the actual reason for Nick's public leanings — and not that he simply wants to get out of school tours and applications and conversations on the topic.

"Yeah. I was squarely in Nick's camp — public school girl all the way — but didn't think we could go that route in the city," she says as she lays one of Sarah's little floral blouses facedown on the floor, then neatly smooths out the wrinkles, tucks in the arms, and folds the whole thing into a neat square with the skill of a department-store clerk. I memorize her technique, but know I will never recall it — just as I can never quite remember how to fold our dinner napkins into the origami-like shapes Nick mastered while working as a waiter at a country club during college.

"I vowed not to let it stress me out," I say, "but now that it's upon me, I'm right there in the frenzy with everyone else."

Rachel nods and says, "Yeah. I was more stressed out filling out those applications for Julia and Sarah than I was when I applied to *law* school. It's one thing to brag about your own qualifications and credentials, but bragging about your five-year-old — it just feels so crass . . . Dex had an easier time with it. For our Spence essay, he actually dubbed Julia a 'bubbly, brown-eyed wonder.' "

I laugh. "He wrote that?"

"Sure did."

"So cheesy," I say, shaking my head, consistently amazed that my banker brother, who appears to be so cool and dignified, can be such a colossal dork behind closed doors. At the same time, I think this is part of why his marriage works so well. At heart, he *is* cheesy, the polar opposite of slick, and having observed many relationships over the years, I have discovered that slick does not a good husband make — my own father leading that charge.

"Yeah. No wonder they rejected us, huh?" Rachel says with a sardonic smile. For a high achiever, she seems to wear this rejection as a peculiar badge of honor, as if it is their loss entirely, and it occurs to me that although she is unassuming, sometimes even downright shy, she is actually one of the more confident people I know — as opposed to April and so many other mothers who seem to strive for perfection as a way of dealing with their underlying insecurities.

She continues, "I knew I should have edited Dex's essays . . . But deep down, I knew Spence wasn't the right fit for us anyway. So I didn't bother . . ."

I ask her why, always intrigued to hear the details of their life in the city — so different from my own childless memories of Manhattan.

"Oh, I don't know," she says, pausing before moving on to a pink cashmere sweater with tiny pom-poms sewn along the neckline. All of Julia and Sarah's things are exquisite and girly, which is incongruous with Rachel's own wardrobe of denim; cozy earth-toned sweaters; and long, bohemian-chic scarves that she drapes twice around her neck even in the summer. "You just hear all the stereotypes of all the schools . . . Chapin is blond, precious, WASPy . . . Spence is full of wealthy, connected society girls. Or spoiled, materialistic sluts, according to the haters . . . and Dex when we got rejected." She laughs and then imitates his low voice — "How dare they turn down our brown-eyed wonder!"

I laugh at my brother's expense and then ask about Brearley's reputation — which is the Upper East Side all-girls' school that Sarah and Julia attend.

"Hmm . . . Let's see . . . I'd say bedraggled intellectuals," Rachel says.

"You are a far cry from bedraggled," I say, pointing to her perfect piles that she is now stowing in the girls' monogrammed canvas

L.L. Bean bags.

She laughs and says, "So is Longmere still your top choice for Ruby?" she asks.

I nod, impressed with her memory of Boston schools and even more so when she asks, "That's where April's daughter goes, right?"

"Yeah . . . Which at the moment isn't a selling point for Nick," I say, giving her the full story about Nick's patient. "He wants to avoid the entire drama . . . Or at least avoid the types he perceives to be meddlesome, do-nothing drama queens."

"Meddlesome, do-nothing drama queens are *everywhere,*" Rachel says. "Private schools, public schools. Manhattan, the Midwest. They're unavoidable."

"Yeah," I say. "But tell that to Nick. He seems to have a chip on his shoulder these days."

As soon as the words are out, I regret them, both because I feel disloyal uttering them to Rachel who never breathes a negative word about her husband — and because I feel as if I've solidified my brewing criticisms of my own husband.

She gives me a sympathetic look which only sharpens my guilt. "Chip on his shoulder about what?" she asks.

"Oh, I don't know," I say, trying to backtrack slightly. "I understand where he's coming from. I totally see that April and Romy and everyone in their clique should back up and give this woman and her kid some space. And I told April as much — which wasn't an easy thing to say to a friend."

"I can imagine," Rachel says, nodding.

"But Nick takes it to such an extreme. You know how he can be. Self-righteous isn't really the word . . ."

"Blunt? No-nonsense?" she guesses.

"Well, yes, there is that. He's always been on the serious side," I say, realizing how difficult it is to describe the people closest to you, perhaps because you are aware of all their complexities. "But it's more that he has zero tolerance for anything he deems frivolous, be it gossip, celebrity magazines, excessive drinking or consumption."

She nods hesitantly, walking the fine line between supporting me and denigrating Nick.

"I know I'm making him out to be so humorless . . ."

"No, no. You're not. Listen — I know Nick. I get him. He has a great sense of humor," she says.

"Right," I say. "He just seems more reclusive lately. He never wants to get together

165

with friends . . . And as far as parenting goes, he's either the laissez-faire dad or Mr. Devil's Advocate . . . Or maybe I'm just noticing it more lately . . ." I say pensively, thinking of the recent conversations with my mother and tentatively sharing some of the lowlights with Rachel.

"Well, Barbie's a cynic. You have to take her with a grain of salt," she says. "You know what she recently said to me? Right in front of the girls?"

"What?" I ask, shaking my head in anticipation.

"She said getting married is like going to a restaurant with friends. You order what you want, and when you see what the other person has, you wish you had ordered that instead."

I drop my head to my hands and laugh. "Brutal," I say.

"I know. She made me feel like a big pork chop that Dex might send back to the kitchen."

"How about this one?" I say. "After she saw Nick open the car door for me recently she offered this nugget: 'When a man opens the door of his car for his wife, you can be sure of one thing — either the car is new or the wife is.' "

Rachel laughs and then says, "Well? Was

the car new?"

"Unfortunately, yes," I say. "Brand spanking . . . So *anyway,* I would never admit this to her, but quitting my job hasn't really been the panacea I was hoping for. I feel just as frazzled and exhausted — and there still doesn't seem to be enough time for the kids . . . For *anything,* really."

"Yeah. It almost makes you feel more guilty, doesn't it? For not being an arts-and-crafts kind of mom?"

"But you are," I say, giving her an accusatory look.

"I am *not,*" she says. "I can't tell you the last time I got out the art supplies with the girls. You theoretically have so much more time at home, but you fill it with the minutiae that you somehow managed to avoid when you were working."

"Yes!" I exclaim again, feeling intense relief, as there's nothing so despair-provoking as thinking you're the only one who feels a certain way, especially when it comes to matters of motherhood — and correspondingly, nothing more comforting than knowing you're not alone. "That's exactly it. I feel like I need a wife . . . Someone to handle the class projects and —"

"Run all the errands," Rachel says.

"And buy the gifts."

"And wrap them," she says.

"And write the thank-you notes."

"And put the photo albums together," she says, rolling her eyes. "I'm two years behind — and only halfway finished with Julia's baby book."

"Hell, forget the albums. I'd settle for some help *taking* the photos," I say, thinking of how I recently told Nick that if something were to happen to me, the kids would have no photos of their mother. He told me not to be so morbid, grabbing the camera from me and snapping a dark-circles-under-my-eyes, Clearasil-coating-a-big-zit-on-my-chin shot that I later deleted, shuddering to think that I might be remembered in such a grisly light. Or worse, viewed that way by another woman, Nick's second wife, the only mother my children would ever know.

Then, just as I feel our playful gripes transforming into a no-holds-barred bitch-fest, Rachel smiles and says, "Ahh. Yes. But lucky for them they are so darn cute. Inept though they are."

I smile, puzzled at the idea of calling children "inept" and then realizing that she is not talking about the kids, but rather Dex and Nick.

"Right," I say, my smile stretching wider.

168

"Good thing."

That night, long after everyone has departed and the kids have gone to sleep, Nick and I are in our room, getting ready for bed.

"That was a great weekend," I say, rinsing my face. I pat it dry and apply a generous amount of moisturizer to my face and neck. "I love seeing the cousins together."

"Yeah, it was fun," Nick says as he rifles through his drawer and pulls out a pair of chambray pajama bottoms. "And your mother managed to behave herself reasonably well."

I smile, going to my own dresser and selecting a black nightgown. It is made of a cotton-spandex blend and is not sexy in an obvious way, but the cut is flattering and I'm hoping it might spark something between Nick and me. It's not so much that I'm in the mood for sex as I am for the intimate aftermath.

"Yeah," I say. "But she gave me an earful yesterday morning."

"About what?" he asks.

"Oh, I don't know," I say. "She continues to worry . . ."

"What's she worried about *now?*"

"The usual stuff. How hard marriage is with small children. How I shouldn't have quit my job," I say, suddenly realizing that her worries are crystallizing in my head, becoming my worries, too. Or maybe they were already brewing and were simply unearthed by a mother's intuition.

"Did you tell her that we're fine?" he says, but seems distracted as he checks his Black-Berry, then types a rapid response, his agile thumbs working in tandem. Whenever I see his hands moving like this, I am reminded that he is a surgeon with the finest motor skills, and feel a wave of reassuring attraction. Still, I don't like his use of the word *fine*. I want to be better than *fine*.

"Yeah," I say. "I told her."

I watch Nick continue to type, his brow furrowed, and can tell it is a work-related exchange. He finishes abruptly, then pulls on his pajama bottoms, cinching the drawstring at the waist. *Do you always sleep topless?* I once asked when we first started to date. At which point he laughed and corrected me: *Girls wear tops; men shirts. Hence, topless and shirtless.* I watch him toss his clothes in the vague vicinity of the hamper, but missing so egregiously he couldn't really have been trying. It is not like him to be so haphazard, and as I stare down at the pile on the floor, his maroon Harvard baseball cap upside down on the heap, I feel something in me become faintly unhinged. I silently count to ten, waiting for him to say something, *anything,* and when he doesn't, I say, "So I printed out the application for Longmere."

The statement is fully architected to push his buttons, or at the very least engage him in conversation. I feel a tinge of shame for being so manipulative, but feel somehow justified.

"Oh?" he asks, making his way to the bathroom sink. I sit on the edge of the tub and watch the muscles flex in his back as he brushes his teeth with what I've always believed to be excessive force. I used to remind him about his gums, how bad his technique is for them, but have given up over the years.

"I think we should get rolling on the process," I say.

"Yeah?" he says, his tone bored, as if to tell me that this is on the long list of things that aren't his concern, along with class snacks and Halloween costumes.

Shit, I think. *My mother is right.*

"Yes. I'll put it in your briefcase. Do you think you could take a first crack at the essays? Maybe this week? Rachel said Dex did theirs . . ."

Nick gives me a look in the mirror and

then says through a mouthful of toothpaste, "Seriously?"

I give him a blank stare as he spits into the sink, rinses his mouth, and says, "Okay. Fine. But I have a crazy week coming up. Charlie's graft is tomorrow."

"Right," I say, my annoyance ratcheting up a notch at the mention of his patient's first name.

A moment later, he is following me to bed.

"So that's what we're doing?" Nick asks with a sigh. "We've decided to apply to Longmere?"

"It's a great school," I say. "It's where *Charlie* goes."

As soon as the words are out, I know I've gone too far.

"What's that supposed to mean?" Nick says.

"Nothing," I say with wide-eyed innocence as I adjust the covers around me.

"Okay. What gives, Tess? Are you angry about something?"

"No," I say as unconvincingly as possible, wanting him to probe one step further, so I can tell him all the things I am feeling, the frustration that approaches anger. Anger that feels justified half the time, paranoid and selfish the rest.

Only he doesn't probe, doesn't give me

the chance, doesn't ask any questions at all. Instead, he simply says, "Good. Now, c'mon. Let's get some rest."

"Right. I know. You have surgery tomorrow," I say.

Nick glances over at me, nods, and barely smiles. Then he absentmindedly checks his BlackBerry one last time before turning off his bedside light, clearly as oblivious to my sarcasm as he is to my little black nightgown.

12
VALERIE

On Monday morning, while Dr. Russo and a team of five doctors and nurses operate on Charlie, Valerie sits in the waiting room, doing just that — waiting — and nothing more. She waits alone, having insisted to her mother and brother that they come later, after everything is over. Valerie has never been one to want conversation or distraction during times of stress, and can't understand the psychology of those who cast about for diversions, like her mother who knits when she's upset or worried. As such, she does not once turn to watch the flat-screen television that is blaring CNN in the corner, or so much as glance at one of the dozens of women's magazine scattered on tables throughout the room. She does not even listen to Charlie's iPod, which she promised to keep for him while he was in the OR. She does not want an escape of any kind. Instead, she wants to remain alert, simply enduring the agonizing minutes, waiting for someone to emerge in the doorway and take her to her son. She hopes that someone will be Nick, for no other reason than she is certain that when she sees his face she will be able to tell right away that everything went smoothly. She knows by now that he is a straight shooter, and she spends her mental energy visualizing the moment she sees his reassuring smile, almost willing it to unfold accordingly.

Only at one point, about two hours after the surgery begins, does Valerie lose focus and let her mind wander to her foolish Saturday-night stunt. She feels her face grow warm with shame, even though she knows she escaped unnoticed, that nobody will *ever* know what she did, and that it will never happen again. Still, she asks herself what she had hoped to gain or glean. And, God, what if Nick had seen her — or worse, he and his wife had *both* spotted her? What then? Would they have chalked the maneuver up to a mother so distraught that she lost her moorings, pitying her in more ways than one? Or would their explanation have been less benign, accusing her of stalking? Would Nick have been disturbed enough to recuse himself and turn Charlie over to another, lesser surgeon? The thought makes her literally shudder as she pulls her cardigan more tightly around her.

She asks herself *why* again — what made her go there? — and does her best to ignore the disturbing answer taking form in her mind. That there is something between them. An attraction. Or at least a connection. She shakes her head, dismissing her conclusion as wrong, delusional. She couldn't possibly have feelings for a man she barely knows. And he certainly does not have feelings for her, other than mere compassion. She is just vulnerable, that's all, and he is her salvation. She tells herself that it must be a common phenomenon — patients falling for their doctors, confusing gratitude with something more. In fact, she remembers reading something about it when she was pregnant — how some women develop crushes on their obstetricians. She thought it seemed inconceivable at the time, but looking back, perhaps she was just too preoccupied with Lion for a crush of any kind, however fleeting, to materialize.

So that is it, Valerie decides. She is a textbook case, nothing more. It suddenly makes perfect sense to her, especially given that Nick is so frightfully good to look at. Anyone could plainly see his beauty — his eyes, that hair, those shoulders — which is why so many of the single nurses swooned and giggled around him. Even those who were married, the kind who carried around brag books filled with photos of their husbands and children, seemed smitten.

Valerie crosses her legs and shifts her weight in her armchair, feeling relieved to find such a logical explanation for her erratic behavior. Nick is a brilliant, handsome surgeon — and she, not only single but, these days, utterly walled off from the rest of the world. She looks up, watching the second hand sweep across the face of the clock above her, convincing herself that the crush will soon pass, until a figure moving behind the frosted glass door of the waiting room breaks her concentration. She sits up straighter, hoping it is someone for her, someone with news or an update of some kind. Hoping that it is Nick.

Instead, Valerie looks up to see two women looming in the doorway. She recognizes one, but is slow to place her. She finally does, stiffening as she hears the woman say her name.

"Romy," Valerie replies. "What are you doing here?"

Romy raises a big wicker basket filled with a bouquet of white and yellow flowers, which appear to be handpicked but artfully arranged, and fruit so waxy and perfect in appearance that it looks fake.

"I brought you this," Romy says, carefully placing the basket at her feet. Valerie looks down, noticing a bottle of wine, angled opposite the flowers, raffia tied around its neck. She scans the French label, registers that the bottle is from a vineyard in Provence — and feels a wave of rage at the inappropriateness of wine at a time like this one. She glances around the room, feeling trapped, realizing she has nowhere to go, no possible escape route short of pushing past the women and running out the door. And of course, she can't leave. She told Nick that this is where she would be.

Valerie acknowledges the basket with a nod, but refuses to thank Romy for the offering, instead turning to gaze at the other woman.

"Hello, Valerie," she says, speaking slowly as if communicating with a foreigner. "My name is April. My daughter, Olivia, is in Charlie's class. We just wanted to tell you that the whole class is behind you. The whole *school*. We're all so terribly sorry for you and Charlie. How is he?"

"He's fine," Valerie says, instantly regretting this answer, especially as she studies April's expression. There is something about it that Valerie finds distasteful — condescending and aggressive at once. Besides, Charlie's not fine. He's not fine at *all*. So she tells them, "He's in surgery now."

The two women exchange a surprised, uneasy glance, solidifying Valerie's cynicism and suspicion that Romy is worried about a lawsuit, about parting with some of her money. She suddenly remembers Romy's earrings — the big diamond studs she wore at the open house at school — and notices that small silver hoops are in their place. Gone, too, is her hulking engagement ring. Everything about her appearance is understated, a portrait of a woman trying hard to show she does not have deep pockets.

"Surgery?" Romy says.

"Yes. A skin graft."

Romy's hand reaches up to touch her own cheek. "How . . . is . . . his face?"

Valerie's response is reflexive and terse. "I'd rather not discuss it."

Another look is exchanged between the two friends, this one more overtly worried, self-interested. Romy's lower lip quivers as she says, "We were just concerned."

"About who?" Valerie snaps.

"About Charlie," April says, stepping in to defend her friend.

Valerie bristles at the sound of her son's

name, spoken by this stranger who has no business being here in the first place.

"Look. I'm not going to sue, if that's what you're worried about. No matter how negligent you were."

Romy looks as if she might cry, while April says, "She *wasn't* negligent."

"Oh?" Valerie says. "So you think it was a good idea to roast marshmallows at a birthday party with a bunch of little boys?"

"Accidents happen. Even when you're careful," Romy insists, her eyes now filling with tears.

"Well, can you tell me what happened?" she presses, her volume rising. She notices a man in the corner who has been engrossed in a book glance their way, sensing controversy. "Because your husband said he wasn't sure. Do you know? Does *anyone* know?"

Romy stops her tears on demand, further proof that they are fake. "The boys were roughhousing."

"Six-year-old boys will do that," April adds.

"Right. So once *again*," Valerie says, in her cross-examination mode, "how is unsupervised marshmallow roasting a good idea for a bunch of six-year-olds who are prone to roughhousing?"

"I don't know. I'm . . . I'm *sorry*," Romy

says, her words empty, hollow.

"You should have started there," Valerie snaps.

"She tried to start there," April says. "You won't take her calls."

"I've been a little busy here. Forgive me."

"Look," Romy tries again. "We know your son is hurt and that you —"

"You don't know anything about me," Valerie says, standing, her voice louder. "You think you know me. But you have no clue. None."

April taps Romy's shoulder, then nods toward the door. "Let's go," she says.

"Great idea. *Please.* Go," Valerie says. "And take your wine and flowers with you. Maybe you can use them at your next party."

Minutes after the women leave, Nick arrives in the waiting room. He is not smiling, but he might as well be. Valerie has learned that this is his version of a happy face — relaxed but dauntless — and she knows in an instant that Charlie is okay. She stands expectantly, awaiting confirmation.

"He did great," Nick says, which of course means that *Nick* did great.

This nuance is not lost on Valerie, who feels overcome with emotion as she says,

"Thank you so much."

Nick nods and says, "I'm really pleased with the results."

Valerie thanks him again, as Nick cautions her that she won't be able to tell much right now, that the graft still needs time to heal, the new vessels time to grow. "In other words, it might not look pretty to you — but it does to me."

"Well, that's what matters," she says, recalling the before and after images on the computer that she pored over this weekend, all the worst-case scenarios she read about, all against Nick's admonition to stay off the Internet. "Can I . . . see him?"

"Of course. He's still asleep, but should be waking up soon," Nick says, glancing curiously at the basket that the women left behind. "Is that yours?"

"No," Valerie says, stepping purposefully over it, as she follows Nick's eyes to the large white envelope clearly addressed to "Valerie and Charlie."

She awkwardly plucks the card out of the basket, drops it into her bag, and stammers, "I mean, yes . . . it's mine. But I think I'll just leave it here. For other families . . . to enjoy. I'm not really in the mood for wine these days . . ."

Nick shoots her a look, as if suspecting

182

more to the story, but says nothing as he leads her out of the room to Charlie. Along the way, he is all business, talking more quickly and excitedly than usual, giving her details about the procedure, telling her how well everything went. When they arrive outside the recovery room, he motions for her to go in first. Valerie braces herself, but not enough for her first glimpse of Charlie in bed, looking smaller than ever. His body is covered with blankets, his scalp and face with dressings, only his nose, eyes, and lips showing. As Valerie watches an unfamiliar nurse take his vitals, she has the sudden urge to go to him, touch the pink of his neck, but she hangs back, frightened that she will somehow infect him.

"How's he doing?" Nick asks the woman, who responds in a raspy voice, giving him numbers that mean nothing to Valerie.

Nick nods his approval as she makes notations on his chart and slips out the door.

"Come here," Nick says, motioning her over to the bed.

As Charlie's lids flutter and open, she feels ashamed for her hesitancy, for not being stronger in this moment. He is the one who has just endured four hours of surgery. He is the one with a mask over his face, an IV dripping into his body. All she had to do was wait.

"Hi, honey," she says, forcing a smile, feigning courage.

"Mamma," he says, the first name he ever gave her, when he was just a baby, abandoning it as he learned to talk and walk.

She feels overcome with relief to hear his voice, see the blue of his eyes.

"You did great," she says, tears welling as she sits on the bed next to him. She rubs his legs through several layers of blankets, watching him struggle to keep his eyes open. After several seconds, his lids grow heavy and close again.

"Here. Let me show you," Nick whispers, turning to put on a pair of latex gloves. He then goes to Charlie and, with the steadiest hand, removes the mask and peels back one corner of the dressing to reveal his work.

An uncontrollable gasp escapes Valerie's lips as she looks down at her son's face. Sheets of pale, translucent skin cover his cheek, all dotted with tiny holes draining blood and fluid. A ghostlike mask beneath his mask. A scene from a horror movie — the kind Valerie never lets herself glimpse, always hiding her face in her hands. She feels herself start to shake, but keeps the tears at bay.

"You okay?" Nick says.

She nods, gulping air, willing herself to exhale, get it together.

"Remember. It needs time to heal," Nick says as he replaces the dressing and mask.

She knows she should say something, but can't get any words out.

"It will look nothing like this in a few days. You'll be amazed."

She nods again, feeling dizzy, weak. She tells herself she cannot faint. That she will never forgive herself for fainting upon seeing her son's face.

"It will turn back to a normal flesh color as it regains vascularity. And it will move like normal, too, after the skin heals and adheres to the underlying facial tissue and muscle."

Say something, she tells herself as she sits on the edge of Charlie's bed.

"That's why we'll need that face mask, which should be here today or tomorrow. To keep constant pressure — to keep things in place as he starts to eat solid foods, talk, that sort of thing. It will also help control his pain —"

Valerie looks up at him, alarmed into finally speaking. "He's going to be in pain? I thought you said there were plenty of pain meds?"

Nick points to the IV and says, "There

185

are. But there will still be some discomfort — and the pressure helps with that."

"Okay," she says, the dizziness and terror clearing as she gathers facts she will need to help her son. "So he can drink now?"

Nick nods. "Yes. He can sip liquids, and we'll go to soft foods in the next day or so. And other than that, he just needs rest. Lots of rest."

"Right, big guy?" Nick says as Charlie opens his eyes again.

He blinks, still too drowsy to speak.

"Right," Valerie says for him.

"Okay then," Nick says as he removes his gloves and shoots them, basketball style, into a wastebasket in the corner. He makes the shot, looking satisfied. "I'll be back."

She feels a sharp pain, wishing he weren't going yet. "When?" she asks, instantly regretting the question.

"Soon," Nick says. Then he reaches for her hand, squeezing it once, as if to tell her again that everything is going exactly as he hoped, exactly as it should.

13
TESSA

"I hate to say 'I told you so,' " April calls to tell me on Monday morning while I maneuver my way down the crowded cereal aisle at Whole Foods.

"Nice try," I say, laughing. "You *love* to say 'I told you so.' "

"I do not," April says.

"Oh, yeah? How 'bout the time you told me that if I let Frank play in a public sandbox, he'd get pinworms?"

April laughs. "Okay. I loved that one — but not because he got pinworms! But because you and Nick mocked me for being paranoid."

"You *are* paranoid," I say. I often tease April about her incessant hand sanitizing and remind her that she does, in fact, have a few white blood cells. "But you were right . . . So what else were you right about?"

April pauses for a few seconds and then

says, "Valerie Anderson. I was right about Valerie Anderson. *What a bitch.*"

"What happened?" I say, bracing myself for the story to come, wondering if April somehow knew that Charlie was having surgery this morning.

"You won't believe it," April says, gearing up for her tale. Always colorful with anecdotes, even those involving minutiae of her life, April carefully sets the scene, describing the third-try care package that she and Romy so lovingly put together, how they had carefully selected the most exquisite bottle of wine from Romy's wine cellar and the perfect bouquet from Winston Flowers.

Careful not to sound vitriolic, I say, "I thought you were going to lay off with that stuff? Give her some time and space?"

"We did. We waited a week or so, just like you suggested . . . And then Romy thought she'd give it one last college try."

I toss a box of raisin bran into my cart, thinking that the expression *college try* really should be reserved for hitting on girls in bars, or negotiating a good deal on a used car, or running a six-minute mile. Not contacting the mother of a hospitalized child when she clearly doesn't want to be contacted. I am also thinking that giving advice to April is like giving advice to Ruby

— in one ear, out the other. The only difference is, April pretends to listen first.

"You know, extend the olive branch," April says.

"Hmm," I say, thinking this, too, is a very telling expression — and something of a contradiction to Romy's spin that her efforts to reach out to Valerie are about sympathy and support for a fellow mother, rather than a blatant and unabashed quest to absolve herself.

"So Valerie didn't take kindly to the gesture?" I ask.

"That's the understatement of the decade," April says, going on to give me a verbatim account of their exchange. How Valerie had refused the basket, telling Romy to use it for her next party. "She was so snide," April says. "A complete bitch."

"That's unfortunate," I say, choosing my words carefully and realizing that this might be the hallmark of a genuine friendship: how freely you speak.

"Yeah. And the more I think about it, the more I think it's really pretty sad. I feel sorry for her."

"You mean what happened to her little boy?" I ask purposefully, thinking that *this* is the understatement of the decade.

"Well, yes, there's that. And the fact that

she clearly has no friends."

"Why do you say that?" I ask.

"Well, for one, how could she have friends with such a bad attitude? And for another, why else would she be sitting in the waiting room alone? I mean — can you imagine if it were one of our children in this situation? We'd be surrounded by loved ones."

I start to remind April of my initial premise — that perhaps Valerie *wants* to be alone — but she cuts me off and says, "She just strikes me as one of those bitter single women who hates the world. I mean, wouldn't you think she'd be grateful? At least for Charlie's sake? Our children are in the same class!"

"I guess so," I say.

"So that's that," April says. "We officially give up. She's on her own."

"She might still come around," I say.

"Well, she'll have to 'come around' on her own. We're done."

"Understandable," I say.

"Yeah . . . Oh — and we ran into your sweet husband on our way out."

I stop in my tracks, praying that he wasn't abrupt or chilly with them. "Oh?" I say. "Did he know why . . . you were there?"

"Probably," she says. "But we didn't discuss it . . . I didn't want to put him in an awkward situation . . . So we just chitchatted. Talked about Longmere. And Romy made him the most generous offer to write Ruby a letter of recommendation. Told Nick she would be honored to do it. With a letter from a board member, you're a virtual shoo-in."

"Wow. That's really nice," I say.

"And I swear I didn't raise the subject with her — it was all her idea. Isn't she the *best?*"

"Yes," I say, feeling sickened by my two-facedness. "The *best.*"

Four errands in the rain later, I return home to a disheartening domestic scene. Dirty dishes and peanut butter and jelly remnants are strewn all over the kitchen, and our family room is an explosion of dolls, puzzle pieces, and miscellaneous plastic parts. Ruby and Frank sit comatose, inches in front of the television, watching cartoons, and not the wholesome variety, but the kind rampant with laser-shooting and sexism — men saving the day and helpless women with hourglass figures. There is a smear of grape jelly across Frank's cheek, dangerously close to the arm of a taupe chair I knew I should have ordered in a darker shade, and Ruby is sporting a terry-cloth beach cover-up, despite the forty-degree, rainy day.

Meanwhile, our usual babysitter, Carolyn, a twenty-four-year-old Jessica Simpson look-alike, double Ds and all, is reclined on the couch, filing her nails and laughing into her iPhone. As I listen to her brainstorm nightclub venues for a friend's birthday party, I marvel at her seeming inability to actually *work* during her measly ten hours a week in our home (as opposed to socialize, groom, snack, and obsessively e-mail and tweet) and feel a familiar brand of fury rising in my chest — an emotion I experience all too often since becoming a mother. It occurs to me to take my usual path of least resistance, nonchalantly head upstairs, pretending nothing is wrong, before speed-dialing Cate or Rachel with my standard Carolyn complaints.

But after my conversation with Nick last night, and the one with April earlier, I am in no mood to disguise my true feelings. Instead, I walk briskly past Carolyn and begin chucking toys into a wicker basket in the corner of the room. Clearly startled by my arrival, Carolyn hurries off her call, stows her nail file in the back pocket of her tight, skinny jeans, and straightens her posture. She does not, however, apologize for the mess or pitch in with my pointed cleanup effort, let alone sit up straight.

"Hi, Tessa," she says cheerfully. "How's it going?"

"Fine," I say, wishing I had enforced a little formality when she started working for us four months ago — maybe if I were "Mrs. Russo" she'd take her job a little more seriously. I grab the remote control from the coffee table and snap off the television to a chorus of protests.

"I don't want to hear it," I tell the kids with my sternest voice — which of course, only makes me feel worse. It's not their fault that their babysitter is such a slouch.

Wide-eyed and still staring at the now-black television screen, Frank thrusts his thumb into his mouth, and Ruby sniffs and says, "It was almost over."

"I don't care. You're not supposed to be watching television," I say, more for Carolyn's benefit.

"Carolyn said we could," Ruby retorts, an answer I couldn't have scripted better.

I turn and give Carolyn a raised-brow look as she flashes me an innocent, aw-shucks smile.

"They were being so *good*. And they ate every last green bean on their plates. I just thought I'd give them a special treat," she says, playing good cop in a way that enrages me further.

"Right, right . . . But next time, let's stick with Disney or Nickelodeon," I say, smiling brightly, knowing that I am enforcing a double standard. That when I'm on the phone, I'll let them watch most anything if it means a little peace. Then again, I am not financing Carolyn's club-hopping and extravagant shopping sprees at French Lessons so that she can be *me.*

"All right. Sure," Carolyn says, as I think back to the day we interviewed her — or more accurately, *I* interviewed her while Nick sat distracted in the corner, pretending to be engaged in the process.

Afterward, he gave her two thumbs up, calling her "sweet and smart enough," and accused me of being overly picky when I pointed out the red flags — namely her Rolex, Jimmy Choo sandals, and oversized Vuitton tote, along with her proclamation that housework wasn't really her "thing."

But I had to admit, she did have a good rapport with the kids, especially Ruby, who seemed to instantly adore her — or at least adored her long hair and magenta toenail polish. And she is better than the last three sitters we interviewed. One spoke little English; the next was a vegan who refused to even touch meat; the third an ideal Mary Poppins with clearly fictional references. And at this point, Carolyn is my only path to freedom — or at least freedom for ten hours a week. So I say her name as calmly as I can.

"Uh-huh?" she says, cracking her gum, as I plan my "I told you so" speech to Nick.

"I need to go upstairs and do a few things before you go. Would you please read them a book?"

"Sure," Carolyn says perkily.

"And put some warmer clothes on Ruby?"

"Sure," she says again. "No problem."

"Thank you *very* much," I say with exaggerated patience. Then I give both kids a perfunctory kiss, which only Frank reciprocates, and head up to my office, which is really more of a small alcove off our bedroom. It is one of the many things I wish I could change about our house, a Tudor built in 1912 that is long on charm but short on functional space.

For thirty minutes, I answer a few e-mails, order several long-overdue baby gifts, and download several hundred photos. Then, something compels me to open an old document, a syllabus for a class I taught called "Games and Sport in the Victorian Novel." It was only two years ago, but it seems much longer, and I feel a sudden wistfulness for the discussions I led, the lectures covering chess and sexual politics in *The Tenant of Wildfell Hall,* social game-playing in *Vanity Fair,* and outdoor sports and the genteel dance in *The Mayor of Casterbridge.*

Then, as I hear a loud shriek from Ruby that I determine is one of glee not pain, I am overcome with a feeling of regret, an intense pang of missing my old life. The oasis of calm in my on-campus office, the afternoons I had to meet with my students, the intellectual stimulation and, frankly, the escape from my mundane world. A sense of loss washes over me, and I tell myself to get a grip. I'm just having a bad day. I'm just upset about the fight with Nick last night, the unsettling conversation with April, the chaos downstairs. Which is how life goes — when there is discord in one sphere, it spills over to all others.

I pick up the phone to call Cate, to get a much-needed pep talk. But all Cate wants is what I have — at least that's what she thinks she wants — and I don't really want someone telling me how great I have it. I'm not even in the mood to talk to Rachel, who always knows the right thing to say, perhaps because, as much as she complains, I think at core she loves being a stay-at-home mother. I even consider calling Nick, just to clear the air and vent about April, but I know he won't be available to talk. And besides, I can just hear his neat solution to the problem, something like *Get your job back* or *Find new friends* or *Fire Carolyn.*

As if it's that simple or straightforward, I think. As if *anything* in life is ever that simple or straightforward.

14
VALERIE

Nick returns to check on Charlie every hour on the hour, until his last visit of the day when he shows up wearing Levi's and a gray turtleneck sweater, a black bag and wool coat slung over his shoulder, clearly on his way home.

"How's everyone doing?" he asks in a soft voice, glancing from a sleeping Charlie, to Jason, then finally to Valerie.

"We're fine," she whispers as Jason interrupts and says, "Hey, Doc. I was just telling Val she needs to get out. Go get some fresh air. Don't you agree?"

Nick shrugs, feigning helplessness, then says, "Yes. But she never listens to me."

"Yes I do," Valerie says in a tone that sounds more girly than she intended. She looks away, feeling transparent, exposed, as she pictures Nick's house and that golden light in the upstairs bedroom window.

"Oh, yeah?" Nick asks with a coy smile.

"So you get plenty of sleep? And you eat three meals a day? And you avoid reading worst-case scenarios on the Internet?"

She blushes, mumbling, "Fine. I'll go. I'll go." Then she stands, puts on her coat, and grabs her purse from her rocking chair.

"Where're you going?" Jason asks.

"Not sure," she replies self-consciously, aware that Nick is listening and watching her. "I'll probably just pick up some takeout. Do you want something? Mexican?" she asks her brother.

Jason makes a face. "Nah. Never thought I'd say this — but I'm sick of burritos."

"Have you tried Antonio's?" Nick asks them both.

Valerie shakes her head and says, "No. Is it nearby?"

"Yeah. Right across the street. On Cambridge. It's a little hole-in-the-wall — but the food is amazing. Better than anything on the North End. Best chicken and broccoli I've ever had — including my mom's," Nick says, patting the front pocket of his jeans as if checking for his keys.

"Sounds good," Jason says, pointing decisively at Nick. He turns to Valerie and says, "Could you pick me up a piece of lasagna?"

"Sure," she says.

"But take your time," he says. "Eat there.

199

I'm not that hungry."

"That's a first," Valerie banters, realizing that on the contrary, she, for once, is famished. She kisses Charlie, now snoring, on his good cheek, then walks out the door, feeling Nick trail several steps behind her.

"I'm on my way out, too," he says once they are alone in the hall. "I'll walk you over there?"

It is a tentative offer, and Valerie opens her mouth to refuse, not wanting to be any trouble. But at the last second, she changes her mind and says, "I'd like that."

Moments later, they are leaving the hospital together, entering a night so sharp and cold that it becomes an instant subject of conversation.

"Ugh," Valerie says, pulling her scarf around her face as they fall into a quicker stride. "It's freezing out here."

"Yeah. We didn't get much of a fall this year," he says.

"I know. I don't remember the leaves changing at all," Valerie says, thinking she wouldn't have been able to enjoy it anyway.

They look both ways, waiting a few seconds for traffic to clear before crossing Cambridge Street at a brisk clip, headed toward the black and white awning Valerie has seen many times in passing but not really noticed. As Nick opens the door for her, a stout man with a mustache — the exact type one would expect to greet you at a restaurant called Antonio's — bellows, "Dr. Russo, where you been, good man?"

Nick laughs. "Where've I been? I was just here last week."

"Oh, right. Guess you were," he says, giving Valerie a circumspect look.

She feels a wave of guilt-tinged nervousness, which dissipates as Nick says, "This is Valerie. My friend. Valerie, this is Tony."

She likes the plain introduction, the honest way it sounds — and tells herself that it *is* honest. They *are* friends. Almost so anyway.

Nick continues, "Just wanted to give Valerie a proper introduction to the city's best Italian."

"The city?"

"The world," Nick says.

"All right then. Dinner for two!" Tony says, rubbing his beefy hands together.

Nick shakes his head. "No. I can't stay. Not tonight."

Tony says what Valerie is thinking, "Oh, come on. One glass of wine? A little bruschetta?"

Nick hesitates, pushing the sleeve of his jacket up to check the time on his watch —

the bulky digital kind with lots of buttons on the side. Valerie has noticed it in the hospital and has imagined him setting it before the early morning runs she is sure he goes on, even in the dead of winter.

"Twist my arm," Nick says, peering into the dimly lit dining area. "And look. My table's free."

"Why of course! We saved for you!" Tony bellows. He winks at Valerie, as if she is an insider now, too, and leads them over to a two-top in the corner. He pulls out a chair for Valerie, hands her a large, laminated menu, and offers to take her coat.

"Thanks, but I think I'll keep it," she says, still chilled.

She watches Tony's lips move as he rattles off the specials, but has trouble concentrating on anything other than Nick, who is now discreetly checking his BlackBerry. She imagines the words on the screen — *Where are you?* Or maybe, *When will you be home?* She tells herself that that is none of her business, a convenient conclusion, as she orders a glass of Chianti at Tony's recommendation.

"And you, sir?" Tony says, waiting for Nick's order.

"The same."

Tony turns to go, and Valerie rests her

forearms on the glass-top table, as she recalls the pompous warning from the only attorney with whom she ever went out — that you should never order wine at a restaurant with checked tablecloths, paper napkins, or laminated menus. They were twenty minutes into their date when she determined that there wouldn't be a second.

"See. You were in the mood for a drink after all," Nick says.

Valerie looks at him, confused.

"You said you weren't in the mood for wine?" He smiles knowingly. "When you left the basket?"

"Oh, right," she says, trying to relax — or at least look relaxed. "Well, I guess I am now."

He seems to consider this, turning a little in his seat to look at her from a different angle. Then he clears his throat and says, "Why didn't you?"

"Why didn't I what?"

"Take the basket?" he says.

She swallows, choosing her words carefully. "I don't . . . exactly trust . . . the women who brought it."

He nods, as if this makes total sense, and then surprises her further when he says, "I don't trust them, either."

She gives him a puzzled look as he clarifies, "They were on the way out of the waiting room as I was on my way in. I had a brief chat with them."

"So you know them?" she asks.

He drums his fingers on the table and confirms, "Yeah. I know them."

She starts to ask how but stops herself, surmising that the connection involves his wife. She does not want to go down that road, fearing that he will respond awkwardly, breaking the rhythm of their tentative friendship, indicating that there might be something less than pure about it. She wants to believe that a true friendship is possible, one extending beyond Charlie's stay in the hospital. It has been a long time since she has forged a genuine bond with another — so long that she had just about given up on the notion. Jason consistently blames her for not trying harder, but she believes that it isn't really a question of effort. It is more a matter of being a single, working mother caught in no-man's-land — or more aptly, no-*woman*'s-land. She would never fit in with the stay-at-home mothers populating Wellesley, nor does she have time to bond with the childless attorneys at her firm. And for the most part, this has all been fine with her, just as she has learned to accept the rift with Laurel and her old high school friends. Everyday life kept her distracted from dwelling on these matters, on what was missing from her life. Yet glimpsing it now — the feeling of true companionship, the exhilarating tension between the familiar and the unknown — fills her with such intense longing that she has to catch her breath.

Fortunately, Nick appears oblivious to all of this and instead smirks at her, as if they've just shared an inside joke. Then he continues his rant, saying, "And even if I didn't *know* them, I know their type."

"And what type is that?" she asks, leaning forward in her chair, yearning for confirmation that he gets it, that they are like-minded in their observations of others and the circumspect way they view the world.

"Oh, let's see," he says, rubbing his jaw. "Superficial. Artificial. Sheep. They're more worried about how they come across to others than who they really are. They exhaust themselves in their pursuit of things that don't matter."

"Exactly," she says, smiling at how perfectly he has captured her sense about Romy and April. Then she blurts out exactly what's on her mind. "I think they're worried I'm going to sue," she says. "Especially if they know I'm a lawyer."

"Oh, I'm quite sure they've done a thorough background check on you."

"Yeah?" she says.

"What else do they have to do with their time?" he says, looking into her eyes.

"So you know the whole story?" she asks, staring back at him. "You know how . . . it happened?"

"Yes," he says, nodding. "I do."

She knows he is not talking about the basic information he gathered as a surgeon, the facts he needed the night Charlie was admitted. He is talking about the negligent backdrop, the rumors that she is sure are swirling out there in her elite community.

Sure enough, he says, "Boston can be a small town, you know?"

She nods, feeling a swell of pure affection for his honesty. His utter lack of bullshit.

"So are you?" he asks.

"Am I what?"

"Going to sue?"

She shakes her head as Tony returns with their wine and bruschetta, quickly leaving them again, seeming to sense that their conversation is a serious, private one. They clink glasses and make eye contact as they take their first sip, but offer no glib words.

Instead Nick lowers his glass and says, "You know, I might if I were you. They deserve it. What kind of a moron lets little kids play around a fire like that?"

"Believe me. I know. And I've considered it," she says, clenching her teeth and doing her best to suppress that toxic wave of anger that she allowed to surface this morning. "But . . . that wouldn't help Charlie. It wouldn't change anything."

"I know," he says, and they both take another long sip of wine.

"And besides." She pauses. "That's not my style."

"I know that, too," he says, as if they've been friends for a very long time. Then he gives her a full-wattage grin that, combined with the wine on her empty stomach, makes her dizzy.

His eyes still on her, he points toward the plate of bruschetta and says, "Go for it."

She smiles back at him, then transfers two slices of toasted bread to her plate, grateful for the distraction, hoping that he can't tell the effect he has on her.

"I think," she says, passing the plate back to Nick and continuing her earlier train of thought, "that the whole single-motherhood thing isn't helping my case with them."

"What do you mean?" he asks.

She shrugs, searching for words to describe her sense that being single — being different at *all* — is an obstacle to friendships, at least female friendships. Since elementary school, she has been keenly aware that girls look to befriend girls exactly like them, or at least who they aspire to be. "I don't know," she says, admiring the artful array of tomato, basil, garlic, and onion, broiled to the perfect golden hue. "I think people make assumptions . . . you know . . . that single mothers need the money . . . or that they might be . . . more opportunistic."

She looks up and sees Nick make a face, indicating that he does not agree with her theory, or at least does not share this belief. Then he says, "Were you married . . . at one time?"

She shakes her head as she swallows her first bite of bruschetta, commenting on the perfect flavor, the fresh ingredients.

He gives her a regretful look. "I'm sorry . . . I shouldn't have asked that . . . It's none of my business," he says.

Then he drops his eyes to his plate as if to reassure her that there will be no further questions. She knows she has her out and for a second she follows her usual instinct to remain close-lipped on her personal life. But then she takes a long sip of wine and chooses her words carefully. "No. I've never been married. Charlie's father was never in the picture . . . His name was Lion — which should tell you something." She smiles, giving him permission to do the same.

"He was an artist. A *talented* artist," she continues. "I thought I was in love. He told me he was — and I believed him. And then . . . well, it didn't work out." She laughs nervously. "More accurately, he disappeared right after I got pregnant. So he never saw his son. As far as I know, he doesn't know he *has* a son. Although, sometimes I find that very hard to believe. That none of his friends has ever seen me with a child. A child that has his curly hair. His diamond-shaped face."

It is more than she has ever said on the subject, and she feels drained by revealing so much of her life — but also relieved. She can feel Nick's eyes on her, and somehow finds the courage to look up and meet his gaze.

"Do you know where he is now?" he asks.

She sips her wine again and says, "I heard he moved out west . . . But I've never tried to find him . . . I'm sure I could, though . . . I'm sure he has exhibits . . . But I just . . . don't see the point. I've always believed that it was better for Charlie this way."

"That must have been hard," he says softly. There is warmth and understanding in his eyes, but no pity whatsoever.

"It was," she admits.

"Is it still?" he asks.

"Sometimes," she says, holding his gaze, thinking of the night of the accident, how terrified and alone she felt, even with Jason. "But not at this moment."

He smiles another glorious, broad smile that makes her heart race, and says, "I'm really glad to hear that." Then he glances at his watch and suggests that they order dinner.

"Don't you have to go?" she protests mildly.

"Not yet," he says, motioning for Tony and telling her how much she's going to love the spinach ravioli.

15
TESSA

I am hanging Frank's navy peacoat and Ruby's fluffy pink shawl on the coatrack in the mudroom when Nick comes flying through the side door as if eager to shave a few seconds off his two-hour delay. We have not spoken all day, other than an exchange of three messages. The first from me, asking him what time he would be home. The second, a voice mail from him, telling me he'd be home in time to put the kids to bed. And the third, a text informing me he'd be later than expected. Fortunately, I did not make any promises to Ruby and Frank, having long since learned that that is a risky proposition.

"I'm *really* sorry I'm late," Nick says earnestly, kissing me hello, his lips landing to the left of my mouth. He tries again, our closed mouths meeting this time, and in this instant, I have the uneasy feeling that he wasn't working when he sent me that final text message.

Some would call it women's intuition, like Cate, who rampantly uses the term when what she really means to say is that she's not completely blind and dumb and oblivious to a certain set of obvious facts, which tonight include the pungent aroma of garlic on Nick's skin and clothes. The fervent tone of his apology. And most of all, the guilty look in his eyes.

To be clear, it is *not* the guilt of a man who has cheated or has even contemplated cheating. That has never been my worry. Nor is it the guilt of a man who feels contrite for being a garden-variety bad husband — for missing his kid's soccer game or not noticing his wife's new haircut or getting paged in the middle of an anniversary dinner. The guilt on Nick's face right now is more subtle than that, yet still unmistakable. I try to place it, peering at him while trying to seem nonchalant, and decide that it is the guilt of someone who wishes he were somewhere else.

"It's okay," I say, looking into his eyes, hoping that I'm wrong, that I misread the clues, drew the wrong conclusion. That Nick actually rushed through the door because he missed me or was desperate to fix whatever happened between us last night. Even if that fix means pretending that *nothing* happened, which is our usual way.

So I say, as offhandedly as I can, all accusations stripped from my voice and face, "What was the holdup?"

"Oh, you know, the usual stuff," he says, avoiding my eyes as he walks into the family room with his coat still on.

"Like what?" I say, following him, thinking of so many scenes in movies where the husband stops off for a drink before coming home, taking his usual spot at the bar, spilling his troubles to the bartender or anyone who will listen. Or worse, stewing alone, keeping them all bottled in. I suddenly wonder whether Nick has troubles he's not sharing with me — beyond the typical worries of a pediatric surgeon. I recall one night last week when I looked out our bedroom window to see him pulling up the driveway after work. He parked the car, but then sat there, staring straight ahead. I watched him for a moment, wondering if he was listening to a song or simply lost in thought. Whatever the case, he was clearly in no hurry to come inside. And when he finally did walk in, a full five minutes later, and I asked what he was doing out there, he appeared bewildered, as if he didn't know the answer himself. He gives me the same quizzical look now.

So I ask the question more concisely, going out on a limb this time. "How was Antonio's?" I say, inhaling garlic again.

His silence is telling, and I look away before he can answer, glancing up at a cobweb in our chandelier, feeling somehow embarrassed for him — for both of us. It is the way I felt when I once walked in on him in the middle of the night, reclined on the couch, his jeans unbuttoned, one hand down his boxers, quietly moaning. I tried to creep out of the family room unnoticed, but tripped on one of Ruby's toys, both of us caught. He opened his eyes, looked at me, and froze, saying nothing. The next morning when he came down for breakfast, I expected him to make a joke about it, but he didn't. The idea of my husband masturbating didn't bother me, but his silence on the subject made me feel separate, the opposite of intimate — the same way I feel now.

"It was fine."

"So you already had dinner?" I clarify.

He quickly replies, "Just a little bite to eat. Was craving Antonio's."

"Did you bring me anything?" I ask, hoping that he simply forgot to remove the white to-go bag from his backseat. I am ready to dismiss my whole theory if he can just produce that bag.

He snaps his fingers with regret. "I should've. I'm sorry. I figured you ate with the kids?"

"I did," I say. "But I'd never turn down Antonio's. I could eat that ravioli for dessert."

"No doubt," he says, smiling. And then, clearly in a hurry to change the subject, he asks how my day was.

"Fine," I say as I try to remember how I filled the last twelve hours. My mind goes blank — which can be a good sign or a bad sign, depending on your perspective, your life at the moment. Tonight, it feels like a bad sign, along with everything else.

"And the kids? They're down for the count?" he asks, a throw-away question.

"No. They're out on the town." I smile to soften my sarcasm.

Nick smiles, nearly laughs.

"How was *your* day?" I ask, thinking that my mother is right. He is the one with something interesting to talk about. He is the one who had better things to do than come home on time tonight.

"The graft went well," he says, our conversation falling into autopilot.

Four words for a four-hour surgery.

"Yeah?" I ask, craving more details, not so much because I want the medical report, but because I want him to *want* to share with me.

"Yeah. Textbook graft," he says, slicing his hand through the air.

I wait several seconds until it's clear he has nothing more to offer. "So," I say. "April said she saw you at the hospital."

His expression becomes animated, nearly fierce, as he says, "Yeah. What the *hell* was up with that?"

"They didn't know the surgery was today," I say, wondering why I'm offering April and Romy an excuse — when I basically agree with Nick.

He snorts. "Even so."

I nod, my way of taking his side, hoping that the alignment will fix whatever is brewing between us. "I heard they brought wine," I say, rolling my eyes.

"Who brings *wine* to a waiting room?"

"In the morning, no less."

He unbuttons his coat, shaking his arms free. "You should cut her out of your life," he says adamantly.

"Cut April out?" I ask.

"Yeah. You have better things to do with your time."

Like, being with my husband, I want to say,

but restrain myself. "She has her good points," I say. "I really think she was trying to help."

"Help who? Her negligent friend?"

I shrug lamely as he continues, now on a roll. "They deserve to get their asses sued."

"Do you think that's a possibility?" I ask.

"No way," he says.

"Did the kid's mother discuss it with you?" I ask, intrigued more by the interpersonal side of his work than the medicine.

"No," he says curtly.

"Would we?" I ask. "Would you?"

"I might," he says, showing his vindictive side. A part of him that I don't particularly like, but still admire, right along with his bad temper, blind stubbornness, and unabashed competitiveness. All the hallmarks of an acclaimed surgeon — the very traits that make him who he is. "I might sue for no other reason than that offensive bottle of wine . . . And that look on her face . . . What's her name? Remy?"

"Romy," I say, marveling that the man managed to learn the name of every muscle and bone in the body, endless Latin medical terms, and yet he can't commit a few names to memory.

He continues, as if talking to himself. "That fake smile she has . . . I've just

217

finished a grueling surgical procedure and there she is grinning, wanting to chat me up about private schools."

"Yeah. April said she's going to write us a letter," I say.

"The hell she is," he says. "No way. I don't want a letter from her. I don't even want Ruby around those kind of people."

"I think that's a bit of a generalization," I say, my own frustration and anger starting to displace the forlorn feeling in my chest.

"Maybe," he says. "Maybe not. We'll see."

"*We'll* see?" I say. "So that means *you'll* look into it? Consider it?"

"Sure. Whatever," he says. "I told you I would."

"Did you look at the application today?" I ask, knowing that I am not really talking about an application — I'm talking about his connection to our family.

He looks at me and then says my name the way he says Ruby's name when he's asked her to brush her teeth for the tenth time. Or more often, when he's heard *me* ask her to brush her teeth for the tenth time.

"What?" I say.

"Do you know what my day was like?"

He doesn't wait for me to answer.

"I glued a kid's face back together," he says. "I didn't have time for kindergarten applications."

"But you had time for dinner at Antonio's?" I say, skipping the intermediate stages of anger and feeling rage rise in my chest.

He stands abruptly and says, "I'm going to take a shower."

"Of course you are," I say to his back.

He turns and gives me a cold, hard look. "Why do you do this, Tess? Why do you manufacture problems?"

"Why don't you want to come home?" I blurt out, expecting him to soften. Tell me that I'm being ridiculous.

Instead, he shrugs and says, "Gee. I don't know. 'Cause you make it so pleasant around here."

"Are you for real? All I *do* is try to make things pleasant for you. For *us*. I'm trying *so* hard here," I shout, my voice shaking, as my day comes into sharp focus. My grocery shopping, photo downloading, cooking, parenting. All the things I do for our family.

"Well, maybe you should stop trying so hard. 'Cause whatever you're doing, Tess, it doesn't really seem to be working," he says, his voice angry but as controlled and steady as his hands were during surgery. With a final disdainful glance, he turns again and disappears upstairs. A moment later I hear him start the shower — where he stays for a very long time.

16
VALERIE

"Are you a doctor, too?" A loud voice interrupts Valerie's thoughts, reminding her that she is still at Antonio's, waiting for Jason's lasagna, which she would've forgotten to order without Nick's reminder right before they finished their own dinner and he left for home.

She looks up and smiles at Tony, hovering nearby.

"A doctor? . . . No," she says as if the notion is ridiculous. In fact, it *is* ridiculous, considering the fact that the only failing grade in her life came in high school biology class when she flat refused to dissect her fetal pig that her football-playing lab partner insisted on calling Wilbur. She can still remember the dizzying smell of formaldehyde and the sight of the feathery taste buds on its pale pink tongue.

Tony tries again. "A nurse?"

It occurs to her to throw him off his line

of questioning by simply saying, "A lawyer," but she knows he's curious about her connection to Nick and the wine has softened her usual guardedness. Besides, there is something about Tony's open, affable manner that makes her think he can handle the truth.

So she nods in the direction of the hospital and says, "My son's a patient at Shriners."

"Oh," Tony says softly. He shakes his head regretfully as Valerie wonders whether part of that regret is not over her answer, but his question, the fact that his light small talk has somehow derailed into somber terrain. "How's he doing?"

Valerie smiles, doing her best to put him at ease, practicing for a conversation she knows she will have again and again in the months to come. "He's hanging in there. He's had two surgeries so far . . ." She pauses awkwardly, forcing another smile, unsure of what else to say.

Tony shifts his weight from one foot to the other and then leans over to rearrange a salt and pepper shaker on the table next to hers. "Dr. Russo's his surgeon?"

"Yes," she says, feeling somehow proud of this fact, as if their affiliation reflects on her parenting. *Only the best for Charlie,* she thinks.

Tony looks at her expectantly so she continues, offering more detail. "One surgery on his hand. And one on his cheek. This morning." She reaches up to touch her face, feeling the first jolt of anxiety since she left Charlie nearly two hours ago. She glances down at her cell phone, faceup on the table, the ringer on high, wondering if she could have somehow missed a call from Jason. But the screen remains reassuringly blank, a scene of a two-lane highway winding under blue sky and fluffy white clouds, disappearing into the distance.

"Well, then you know by now — Dr. Russo is the *best*. You and your son have the *best*," Tony says so passionately that Valerie wonders if he has firsthand experience with patients or their parents. He continues with reverence. "And he's so modest . . . But the nurses who come here — they've all told me about his awards . . . the kids he's saved . . . Did you hear about the little girl — the one in that plane crash up in Maine? Her dad was a hotshot TV executive? It was on the news — about two years ago?"

Valerie shakes her head, realizing that she will never again have the luxury of ignoring such a story.

"Yeah. It was one of those little single-engine numbers. They were flying to a wedding . . . the whole family . . . and the plane went down about a quarter of a mile off the runway, right after takeoff. Crashed into an embankment and everyone but that one little girl died right away from smoke inhalation and burns. The pilot, the parents, the little girl's three older brothers. Tragic," he says, looking mournful.

"And the little girl?" Valerie asks.

"Orphaned and alone. But she lived. She made it. 'Miracle girl' the nurses call her."

"How bad were her burns?" Valerie asks, her leg jiggling nervously.

"Bad," Tony says. "Real bad. Eighty percent of her body, something like that."

She swallows as she contemplates *eighty* percent, how much worse it could have been for Charlie. "How long was she in the hospital?" she asks, her throat suddenly dry.

"Oh, jeez," Tony says, shrugging. "A long, long time. Months and months. Maybe even a year."

Valerie nods, feeling a wave of pure heartbreak at the thought of the accident, the unfathomable horror on that embankment. As she begins to imagine the flames engulfing the plane and all those people inside, she shuts her eyes to stop the images from coming.

"Are you okay?" Tony asks.

She looks up and sees him standing closer to her now, hands clasped, head bowed, looking strangely graceful for such a squat, burly man. "I shouldn't have . . . It was insensitive."

"It's okay. We were very lucky in comparison," Valerie says. She takes her last sip of wine, suddenly desperate to get back to the hospital, just as a cook from the back emerges with a to-go bag. "Lasagna and house salad?"

"Thanks," Valerie says, reaching for her purse.

Tony holds up his hands and says, "No, no. Please. This one's on the house. Just come back and see us, okay?"

Valerie starts to protest, but then nods her thanks and tells him she will.

"How is he?" she asks Jason as she walks through the door and finds Charlie in the same position she left him.

"Still sleeping. He even slept through his dressing change," Jason says.

"Good," she says — because he needs his rest and because every minute of sleep is a minute not in pain, although she sometimes thinks his nightmares are worse than anything else. She kicks off her shoes and puts on her slippers, part of her nightly ritual.

"So?" Jason says. "How was it?"

"It was good," she says quietly, thinking of how fast the time flew by sitting there with Nick, how pleasant and easy it felt. "We had a good conversation."

"I meant the *food,*" Jason says, raising his brows. "Not the company."

"The food was great. Here." She tosses him the takeout bag as he mumbles something under his breath.

"What?" she says.

He repeats himself more slowly, loudly. "I *said* — I think someone has a crush on Dr. Beautimus."

"Dr. *Beautimus?*" she says, standing to close the blinds. "Is that some slang term I don't know about?"

"Yeah. Dr. Beautimus. Dr. Dime-piece."

She laughs nervously and says, "Dime-piece?"

"A perfect ten," Jason says, winking.

Valerie rolls her eyes and says, "I think *you're* the one with the crush."

Jason shrugs and says, "Yeah. He's hot. But I'm not trying so hard to deny it."

"I don't go for married men," she says emphatically.

"I didn't say you were *going* for him," Jason says. "I just said you have a *crush* on him."

"I do *not,*" she says, envisioning Nick's dark eyes, the way he squints with a slight grimace whenever he's making a point or being emphatic. It occurs to her that she might sound unduly defensive, that she shouldn't protest quite so hard — especially given the fact that she and Jason often banter about hot guys, such as the bachelor who lives across the street and occasionally mows his lawn shirtless, and that some of them happen to be married.

Jason opens the bag, inhales, and nods approvingly. "So what did you talk about all that time?"

"A lot of things," she says, realizing that she has not yet told Jason about the basket from Romy. She considers doing so now, but feels suddenly drained, deciding it can wait until morning. "Work. His kids. Charlie's school. A lot of stuff."

"Did you mention that you think he's smokin'?"

"Don't start," she says.

"Don't *you* start," he says. "It's a dangerous path, falling for a Baldwin like him."

"Whatever," she says, laughing at the term *Baldwin* and thinking that she *did* once have a crush on Billy — or whichever brother was in the movie *Flatliners* — and that Nick does bear something of a resemblance to him. Unfortunately for her, she thinks, as she watches Jason dive into his lasagna, Nick has even nicer eyes.

17
TESSA

"Tess?" Nick says that night when he finally comes to bed just after one in the morning. His voice is tender, almost a whisper, and I feel a rush of relief to hear him say my name like this.

"Yes," I whisper back, realizing that we've just made a rhyme.

He takes several deep breaths, as if collecting himself or deciding what to say, and it occurs to me to fill the silence with a question about what is going on in his head. But I force myself to wait, sensing that his next words will be telling ones.

"I'm sorry," he finally says, pulling me close to him, wrapping his arms around me. Even without the hug, I can tell he means it this time. Unlike his apology for being late, there is nothing obligatory or automatic in his voice now.

"Sorry for what?" I breathe, my eyes still closed. It is ordinarily a passive-aggressive question, but tonight it comes from a sincere place. I really want to know.

"I'm sorry for what I said. It's not true." He takes several more deep breaths, exhaling through his nose, and then says, "You're a great mother. A *great* wife."

He kisses my neck, just under my ear, and hugs me harder, all of his body now against mine. It has always been his way of making up — action over words — and although I've criticized and resisted this approach in the past, tonight I don't mind. Instead, I push back against him, doing my best to believe him, dismiss the brewing doubts about our relationship. I tell myself that Nick has always been a bit of a dirty fighter, quick with cutting words that he later regrets and doesn't really mean. Then again, I wonder if there isn't always a grain of truth in them, somewhere.

"Then why did you say it?" I whisper, between his kisses and some of my own. "Why did you say things aren't working?"

It occurs to me that the two things aren't mutually exclusive. I can be a great wife and mother — and things could still be broken. Or slowly breaking.

"I don't know . . . I just get frustrated sometimes," he says as he tugs down my sweatpants with rapidly building urgency.

I try to resist him, if only to finish our conversation, but feel myself caving to the overwhelming physical pull to him. The need for him. It is the way I felt in the beginning, when we'd rush home from school to be together, making love two or three times in a night. A way I haven't felt in a long time.

"I want you to be happy," Nick says.

"I *am* happy."

"Then don't look for problems."

"I don't."

"Sometimes you do."

I consider this, consider all the ways I could've greeted him differently tonight. Maybe it's my fault. Maybe I *do* manufacture trouble, like the housewives I once criticized for drumming up drama in order to alleviate the monotony of their days. Maybe there is a void in my life, one that I'm relying on him to fill. Maybe he really *did* simply have a craving for Italian food tonight.

"C'mon, Tess. Make up with me," he says, sliding off his pajama bottoms, pulling up my T-shirt, but not bothering to take it off. He kisses me hard on the mouth as he moves inside me, offering penance. I kiss him back just as urgently, my heart beating fast, my legs wrapping tight around him. All the while, I tell myself that I'm doing it because I love him. Not because I want to prove anything to him.

Yet, moments later, after I let go, and feel him doing the same, I hear myself whispering, *See, Nick? See that? It's working. It's working.*

18
VALERIE

Valerie watches Charlie intently coloring inside the lines of a jack-o'-lantern, alternating between an orange crayon for the pumpkin and a green for the stem, using careful, steady strokes. It is a boring project for a child his age, requiring no creativity whatsoever, but Charlie seems to understand that it is good for his hand and takes the assignment from his occupational therapist seriously.

She says his name as he draws a black cat in the background, exaggerating each whisker with long strokes. He ignores her, now staring at his drawing from several different angles, moving the paper rather than his head.

She says his name again, wanting only to ask what he wants for lunch. He finally looks up, but says nothing, making her wonder what kind of mood he's in. It has been a few days since his surgery, and although she is more accustomed to the mask covering his face, she is not yet used to the way it obscures his expressions, making it harder to tell what he's thinking.

"I'm not Charlie," he finally says, his voice low, scratchy, theatrical.

"Who are you then?" she says, playing along.

"An Imperial stormtrooper," he replies ominously, sounding as much like a grown man as a six-year-old can.

Valerie smiles. She silently puts it on the list of benchmarks — first solid food, first walk around the halls, first joke at his own expense.

"I don't even need a Halloween costume," he says as Nick walks in.

Valerie feels her own face light up and is sure Charlie's does, too. Never mind that they both know why he is here — to assess the graft and remove any accumulating fluid with a needle. The procedure is less painful than it looks, both because of the morphine Charlie's still receiving intravenously and because nerves have not yet attached to the graft — but it is still not a pleasant one. Yet Nick manages to distract them both, as if the procedure is an ancillary part of his visit.

"Why's that, buddy?" Nick asks. "Why don't you need a costume?"

" 'Cause I'm already wearing a mask," Charlie says, his voice a high soprano again.

Nick chuckles and says, "You got a point there."

"I can be a stormtrooper or a mummy."

"I'd go stormtrooper if I were you," Nick says. "And I'll be Darth Vader."

You cannot hide forever, Luke, Valerie thinks. And then, *I am your father.* The only two *Star Wars* quotes she knows by heart, other than *May the force be with you.*

"You have a Darth Vader costume?" Charlie asks him, reaching under his mask to scratch along his hairline.

"No. But I'm sure I could find one . . . Or, we could just pretend," Nick says, raising an imaginary weapon.

"Yeah. We could pretend."

Valerie feels a warm glow watching Nick and Charlie grin at one another, until Charlie's voice grows earnest and he asks, "Are you coming to the party?" He is referring to the Halloween party in the rec center downstairs; all the patients and their families are invited to attend. Of course, she and Charlie plan to go, along with Jason and Rosemary.

"Oh, honey. Nick has two kids — I'm sure he's taking them trick-or-treating," Valerie says quickly, as she unpackages the Spider-

235

Man costume that Jason picked up at Target yesterday, the only one he could find that fit her two criteria — no horror connotation and a mask that would cover Charlie's own mask.

"I'll be there," Nick says. "What time does it start?"

"Four o'clock," she says reluctantly, giving him a look that she hopes conveys gratitude but also makes clear that this is above and beyond his duties as their surgeon.

She turns to him, her voice becoming soft. "Really, Nick," she says. "You don't have to . . ."

"I'll be there," Nick says again, running his hand over the blond stubble beginning to sprout from Charlie's shaved, pink head.

She pictures Nick's wife and children at home, waiting for him, and knows she should protest one more time. But instead she basks in the warm feeling in her chest, slowly spreading everywhere.

"That's really nice of you," she finally says, and nothing more.

Later that afternoon, while Charlie naps, Valerie begins to have second thoughts about accepting Nick's spur-of-the-moment Halloween promise and feels the sudden need to let him off the hook. From years of logistical difficulties, she is well aware that Halloween is a two-parent operation, requiring one to stay home and pass out candy, the other to take the kids door-to-door — and recognizes the high likelihood of Nick's wife balking at his decision to attend the hospital party. She wants to spare him that domestic squabble and avoid the awkward exchange that will ensue in the event he loses the debate. More important, the thought of a broken promise or anything smacking of a disappointment in Charlie's life is too great for her to bear. So she decides to make a preemptive strike — a strategy she has come to know well.

She considers waiting for Nick's next round to have the conversation, but feels a sense of urgency to settle matters before she can change her mind again. Rapidly removing her BlackBerry from her purse and Nick's card from her wallet, she fights a wave of inexplicable nervousness and dials his number, hoping he'll answer.

After the third ring, he answers abruptly, impatiently, as if he's just been interrupted doing something very important — which is probably the case.

Valerie hesitates, suddenly regretting the call, feeling that she's just made things even worse, that she has no right to call his personal cell even though he gave it to her.

"Hi, Nick," she says. "It's Valerie."

"Oh! Hi, Valerie," he says, his tone transforming into a familiar, friendly one. "Everything okay?"

"Oh, yeah. Everything's great," she says, hearing background noise that does not sound like the hospital. "Is this a good time?" she asks, worrying that he might be with his family.

"Yeah," he says. "What's up?"

"Well, I just . . . wanted to talk to you about the Halloween party tomorrow," she stammers.

"What about it?" he asks.

"Listen. It was so nice of you to say you'd come . . . But . . ."

"But what?" he says.

"But it's Halloween."

"Yeah?"

"I'm sure you need to be somewhere else," she says. "With your family. Your kids . . . and I just don't feel comfortable . . ."

"Would it make you feel better to know that I was scheduled to work anyway?" he asks. "So unless you want to call the chief of staff and tell him that you think I should have the day off . . ."

"Are you really scheduled to work?" she

replies, now pacing in the hall outside Charlie's room, feeling simultaneously relieved and foolish for making such a big deal out of the party, and wondering why it never occurred to her that he could have been scheduled to work anyway. That his decision to attend might have *nothing* to do with them.

"Val —" he says, the first time he has used the abbreviated form of her name, a fact that is not lost on her, a fact that she can't help liking. "I want to be there. Okay?"

The warm glow returns to her chest. "Okay," she says.

"Now if you'll excuse me," he says. "I'm in the middle of buying a Darth Vader costume."

"Okay," she says. She feels a silly, uncontrollable grin spread over her face as she hangs up, doing her best not to admit to herself the real reason she just made the call.

19
TESSA

Over the next few days, the marital gods shine upon our house and things start to feel good again. Nick is a model husband — calling from work just to say hello, coming home in time to put the kids to bed, even making me dinner one night. And yet, his effort doesn't feel valiant or forced. Instead, he simply seems engaged, as if he's part of our family's biorhythms, absorbing the small moments that I sometimes feel I'm navigating alone. He's so attentive, in fact, that I start to blame myself for our fight — which is always something of a relief, if only because it puts you back in control of your own life. Rachel and Cate, both of whom I confide in, agree that I was at least *partially* to blame for our rough patch, pointing to hormones, boredom, and general paranoia — the hallmarks of motherhood, Rachel jokes.

Our only setback comes on Halloween,

mid-afternoon, when Nick calls from the hospital to tell me he likely won't be able to make it back for trick-or-treating — and will definitely miss the neighborhood gathering at April's beforehand. I refrain from reminding him that to children, Halloween is the second most sacred night of the year (perhaps the most sacred to Ruby, who has an epic sweet tooth), and that although I try not to subscribe to gender-role parenting, I believe trick-or-treating falls squarely in a father's domain. Instead, I focus on the fact that he took Ruby to school this morning, staying to videotape her costume parade through the preschool hallways, then coming home to spend time with Frank before he left for work.

"Are you all right?" I ask calmly, supportively.

"Yeah, yeah. Just a lot going on here," he says, sounding stressed and distracted but also disappointed, which has a way of mitigating my own disappointment. Then he asks if we'll be okay without him, as far as handing-out-candy logistics go.

"Yeah," I say. "I'll just leave a bowl on the porch. We won't be out very long. No big deal."

And it really isn't a big deal, I tell myself as

Ruby, Frank, and I walk up the hill to April's house just before dark and arrive to find her tying a cluster of orange and black balloons to her mailbox. I can tell at one glance that she's already had several glasses of wine, and I suddenly feel in the mood for one myself. She blows me a kiss and then raves about how adorable Sharpay and Elmo are, her voice and gestures boisterous.

"Thanks," I say, thinking that although they do look cute, her compliments are often over the top and that there's nothing *that* cute about two store-bought costumes — one utterly predictable, the other slightly tacky.

"Where's Nick?" she says, peering around, as if expecting him to jump out of the bushes and surprise her.

"He had to work," I report with my usual mix of pride and regret that comes with being married to a surgeon.

"Bummer," she says sympathetically.

"Yeah. What can you do?" I shrug, then glance up at her house, admiring her extensive decorations — the scarecrows lining the driveway, the little ghosts strung from trees, and the elaborately carved jack-o'-lanterns clustered on her front porch. I tell her everything looks beautiful, hoping to change the subject, if only for Ruby and

Frank's sake, seeing no point in drawing attention to their father's absence.

"Thanks!" she says. "There's a face painter in the backyard . . . And I'm on the fence about bobbing for apples. Do you think it's too cold? Too much trouble?"

"Yeah. Keep it simple," I say, recognizing that this advice is rather like telling Madonna to keep a low profile or Britney Spears to make good relationship decisions.

I tell her this and she laughs, linking her arm through mine and announcing that she's missed me — when what I think she means is that she's missed talking about something other than the Romy drama.

"I've missed you, too," I say, feeling content as we walk up the driveway. We watch Ruby and Frank greet Olivia with exuberant hugs, feeling a rush of satisfaction that comes from successfully engineering your children's friendships.

My good mood continues over the next hour, as I mingle with friends and catch up with neighbors, discussing the usual topics — how quickly the year is flying by, how much the kids are liking school, how we really should get together for a playdate soon. All the while, I do my best not to think of Nick's conspicuous absence from the group of fathers huddled with their red wagons filled with trick-or-treat bags for their kids and bottled beer for themselves, even when I'm asked, no fewer than a dozen times, where he is tonight. I can tell many are thinking of Romy, but only Carly Brewster has the nerve to directly raise the subject. Ironically, Carly is one of the most talked-about and least liked women in the neighborhood. A former consultant with an M.B.A. from Wharton, she seems utterly bored in her role as stay-at-home mother of four boys, compensating by inserting her nose in everyone's business and starting unnecessary battles in PTA and neighborhood association meetings. Last spring, she actually suggested that a leash law be enacted for *cats.*

In any event, she begins her inquiry nonchalantly while expertly bouncing her youngest in a Björn carrier. "How's that little boy doing?" she asks as if the story is vague in her mind. "The one who was burned at the Crofts'?"

"He's fine," I say, my eyes resting on the line of demarcation between her ash-blond hair and dark roots.

"Is your husband with him tonight?"

"I'm not sure. I didn't ask," I say pointedly, knowing she won't take the hint.

Sure enough, she inhales dramatically,

looks around, and drops her voice to a hushed whisper. "My husband works with his mother. Valerie Anderson. They're at the same law firm." Her eyes light up as she continues, "And he says she hasn't been to work in *weeks* . . ."

"Hmm," I say noncommittally, and then do my best to divert her attention to her own children, the only topic she's guaranteed to enjoy more than speculation about another. "How are the boys?" I say.

"Crrazy," she says, rolling her eyes, as she watches her second oldest, dressed as Winnie-the-Pooh, systematically pluck chrysanthemums from April's flower bed. Clearly, she is cut from the "my child can do no wrong" mold, as she lets him continue to pick away, saying, "Yeah. They are *all* boy."

As opposed to Frank, I think, who routinely clamors for my lip gloss, plays with Ruby's dolls, and recently announced that he wants to be a hairdresser when he grows up. I offer these details to Carly, who gives me a sympathetic head tilt and a lilting, "I wouldn't worry too much."

Her implication is clear — I should be *gravely* worried.

I watch Winnie-the-Pooh stomp on the crushed petals, smearing streaks of purple and pink along the driveway, feeling sure he kills bugs with the same diligence and thinking that I'd rather my son be gay than the testosterone-driven frat boy her son seems destined to become.

"And this is Piglet, I presume?" I say, smiling at the infant in her arms, wearing a hot-pink striped onesie and a little snout on his nose, and glancing around for Tigger and Eeyore.

She nods and I murmur, "Adorable."

"He's not so adorable at three in the morning," she says wearily, wearing her fatigue as a badge of honor. "I have a baby nurse — but I still get up to nurse every couple hours. So it really does no good."

"That's rough," I say, thinking that she just masterfully made two points: she's privileged enough to have outside help, yet committed enough to get up and nurse her child anyway.

"Yeah. It is. But *so* worth it . . . Did you nurse?"

None of your business, I think, as it occurs to me to lie as I have many times in the past. Instead I blurt out the truth, feeling liberated that I no longer guard the fact as a guilty secret. "For a few weeks. It didn't work out so well for me. I quit. We were all better off."

"Poor milk production?" she whispers.

"No. I just went back to work — and pumping was too hard," I say, spotting Ruby, who is doing her best to push a squawking Frank out the back window of a lavender Cozy Coupe.

"Hey! Ruby! Knock it off!" I shout across the lawn.

"It's my turn," Ruby yells back at me, a hysterical edge to her voice. "He won't share."

"He's two," I say. "You're four."

"Two is old enough to share!" she shouts, which, unfortunately, is a decent point.

"I better go handle this one," I say, grateful to excuse myself.

"This is when you wish their father was around, huh?" Carly says, giving me her very best "my life is better than your life" smile.

Later that night, after the kids are asleep, our porch lights are turned off, and I'm trying to resist candy, my mind returns to Carly's smug smile. I wonder whether it was in my head — whether I'm being oversensitive or defensive about Nick's work, projecting my own dissatisfaction. It occurs to me that she is not unique — that *all* women compare lives. We are aware of whose husband works more, who helps more around the house, who makes more money, who is having more sex. We compare our children, taking note of who is sleeping through the night, eating their vegetables, minding their manners, getting into the right schools. We know who keeps the best house, throws the best parties, cooks the best meals, has the best tennis game. We know who among us is the smartest, has the fewest lines around her eyes, has the best figure — whether naturally or artificially. We are aware of who works full-time, who stays at home with the kids, who manages to do it all and make it look easy, who shops and lunches while the nanny does it all. We digest it all and then discuss with our friends. Comparing and then confiding; it is what women do.

The difference, I think, lies in *why* we do it. Are we doing it to gauge our own life and reassure ourselves that we fall within the realm of normal? Or are we being competitive, relishing others' shortcomings so that we can win, if only by default?

The phone rings, saving me from my runaway thoughts and an unwrapped Twix bar. I see that it's Nick and answer hurriedly.

"Hey!" I say, feeling as if we haven't talked in days.

"Hey, honey," he says. "How'd it go tonight?"

"It was fun," I say, sharing the highlights of the evening — how Frank kept saying, "Treat or treat." How Ruby would remind him to say thank you. How proud she was whenever the big girls complimented her costume. "But of course it wasn't the same without you. We missed you."

"I missed you, too," he says. "All three of you."

I take one small bite of chocolate, knowing that I'm screwed with this fatal, first bite. "Are you coming home now?"

"Soon."

"How soon?"

"Pretty soon," Nick says. "But don't wait up . . ."

I swallow, feeling a wave of disappointment and defeat, followed by guilty relief that I have no witnesses to observe the look on my face now, as I hang up the phone, finish my candy bar, and go to bed alone.

20
Valerie

Valerie knows she's in trouble on Halloween. Not because of her deep-down knowledge that she called Nick, in part, just to hear his voice, and in part, so that he'd have her number. And not because he insisted on coming to the party, arriving in full Darth Vader garb. And not *even* because he stayed in their room long after Charlie fell asleep, leaning on the windowsill, talking in a hushed voice as they both lost track of time. Of course, all of those things were signs of trouble, especially the following morning when she played the reel back.

But the moment of certainty came when he called her on the way home to tell her "one more thing." It was something about Charlie — that much she would remember later — but all professional pretenses were erased by the hour of the call, and the fact that they didn't hang up when that *one thing* was communicated. Instead, they talked until he pulled into his driveway, some thirty minutes later.

"Happy Halloween," he whispered into the phone.

"Happy Halloween," she whispered back. Then she forced herself to hang up, feeling a mix of melancholy and guilt as she pictured his house and the three people inside. Yet she still went to sleep that night hoping that he'd call her in the morning.

Which he did. And then every day after that, except for the days when she called him first. They always began their conversation with a discussion of Charlie's graft or his pain meds or his mood — but they always ended with *one more thing,* and often *one more thing* after that.

And here it is, six days later, the phone ringing again.

"Where are you?" he begins, no longer announcing himself.

"Here," she says, watching Charlie sleep. "In the room."

"How is he?" Nick asks.

"He's good . . . asleep . . . Where are you?"

"Five minutes away," he says, talking to her until she can hear his voice in the hall.

"Hey," he says, rounding the corner, sliding his BlackBerry into his pocket, a broad smile on his face as if they've just shared an inside joke.

"Hi!" she says, feeling herself grin back, overcome with gladness.

But ten minutes of light conversation later, Nick's expression becomes grave. At first Valerie worries that something has gone wrong with Charlie's graft, but then realizes that the opposite is true, that it is simply time for Charlie to go home. She remembers Nick telling her it would be about a week for the new skin to adhere, remembers how he kept his eyes fixed on hers as if offering a guarantee. Yet she still feels shocked and overwhelmed, as if she never saw this moment coming.

"Today?" she asks, her heart racing with dread and the dawning, shameful realization that she does not want to go home. She tells herself it is only the place — the security of a hospital — but deep down, she knows that there is more to it than that.

"Tomorrow," Nick says, a fleeting look crossing his face that tells Valerie he feels the same way. But he quickly falls into his medical mode, talking about Charlie's progress and therapy, his long-term surgical plan, as well as his short-term outpatient plan, rattling off instructions and assurances.

"He can go back to school in another week or so. Ideally, he still needs to wear his mask about eighteen hours a day. But it can come off occasionally — unless, of course, he's playing sports, that sort of thing . . . And he needs to sleep with it, too. Same goes for the splint on his hand."

She swallows and nods, forcing a smile. "That's great. Great news," she says, feeling like a decidedly bad mother to receive the report with anything short of unbridled joy.

"I know it's scary," Nick says. "But he's ready."

"I know," she says, biting her lip so hard that it hurts.

"And so are you," he tells her, so convincingly that she nearly believes him.

The following afternoon, as Valerie works her way through all the paperwork and packing, she finds herself remembering the first time she left the hospital with Charlie, when he was just three days old. She has the same feeling of impending failure now, the fear that she will be revealed as a fraud once home alone with her child. The only thing that tempers her trepidation is Charlie's palpable excitement as he skips through the halls, handing out illustrated cards he made for everyone last night. Everyone but

Nick, that is, who is nowhere to be found.

Valerie keeps expecting him to show up, or at least call, and feels herself stalling, signing the discharge papers and loading the cart with their belongings as slowly as possible. At one point, Valerie even asks Leta, a matronly, soft-spoken nurse who has been with them since the beginning, if they should wait to see Dr. Russo before leaving.

"He's off today, sugar," Leta says, even more gently than usual, as if she's worried the news will upset Valerie. "He signed the order last night." She flips through Charlie's chart as if looking for some consolation, smiling brightly when she finds it. "But he wants to see you back in a few days," she says. "Call this number here," she says, circling Nick's office number on a form and handing it to her.

Embarrassed, Valerie takes the paper and looks away, wondering just how transparent she is, if all the nurses can tell how she feels, how close she and Nick have become. Or perhaps he is this way with all his patients and families — perhaps she has mistaken their friendship for a well-honed and finely tuned bedside manner. The thought that he is doing his job, that she and Charlie aren't unique, fills her with relief *and* disappointment.

Valerie zips the last duffel bag as Leta bustles out of the room, returning a moment later with a wheelchair for Charlie's final ride through these halls — and a lanky hospital page named Horace to do the pushing.

"I don't need that anymore!" Charlie says with a happy shout.

"It's hospital protocol, baby," Leta says.

Charlie stares at her, confused.

"Everyone gets wheeled out, sweetie pie," she tells him. "So hop aboard. Horace might pop a wheelie for you."

Charlie makes a gurgling, happy boy noise and climbs into the chair as Valerie glances around the bare room, and gives her last, silent thank-you to a place she will never forget.

Charlie doesn't ask about Nick until later that night when he is in his own bed, his artwork and cards from the hospital transferred to his honey-colored walls, his army of stuffed animals surrounding him, his iPod in the docking station, playing soft Beethoven.

"I never got to give Dr. Nick my card!" he says, suddenly sitting up. "I didn't get to say good-bye."

"We'll see him again in a few days," she

says, easing him back onto his pillow and turning his night-light on.

"Can we call him?" Charlie says, his voice quivering.

"Not now, honey. It's too late," she says.

"Please," he whimpers, reaching up to pull off his mask. "I want to say good night."

Valerie knows what the answer should be, knows that there are a dozen things she could tell her son to distract him from the subject of Dr. Nick.

But instead she puts her hand in her pocket and pulls out her phone that she has kept near her all day and types a rapid text: *We're home. Everything good. Call if you can. Charlie wants to say good night.*

She hits send, tells herself she is doing it for her child. She *is* doing it for her child.

Seconds later, the phone rings.

Valerie jumps. "It's him!" she says, pressing the talk button and holding the phone up to Charlie's ear.

"Hi, Dr. Nick," Charlie says. "I didn't get to say good-bye to you."

Valerie strains to hear his response. "No need for good-byes, buddy. I'll see you soon."

"When?" Charlie asks.

"How about tomorrow? Ask your mom if you're free?"

"Are we free tomorrow, Mommy?" Charlie asks.

"Yes," Valerie answers quickly.

Nick says something else that she can't make out and Charlie hands her the phone. "He wants to talk to you, Mommy," he says, replacing his mask before yawning and closing his eyes.

She takes the phone and says, "Hi, there . . . I'm sorry to bother you . . . on your day off . . . at night . . ."

"Stop it," Nick says. "You know I love when you call . . . I really wanted to come by today . . . I miss you. I miss you both."

Valerie walks out of the room, leaving Charlie's door open a crack, and whispers in the hall, "We miss you, too."

Silence crackles over the phone as Valerie makes her way to her own bed. "Is it too late now?" he finally says.

"Now?" she asks, confused.

"Can I stop by for a minute? Take a peek at him?"

Valerie closes her eyes and catches her breath long enough to tell him yes. Long enough to tell herself, for the hundredth time, that they are friends. *Just* friends.

21
TESSA

In the weeks leading up to Thanksgiving, I feel myself slipping into a holidays-suck-and-so-do-I malaise. It starts one morning when I am running late to pick up Ruby from school. My hair still wet and Frankie covered in crumbs, I strap him into his car seat, throw my minivan in reverse, and promptly slam it into the garage door — the *closed* garage door — resulting in a cool three thousand dollars' worth of damage.

Later that afternoon, in an apparent attempt to make me feel better, Larry, the tattooed, mustached garage-door repairman straight out of central casting, informs me that it happens way more than I'd think.

"And would ya believe it?" he continues in a thick Boston accent. "Most often the *men* ah to blame."

"Really?" I say, mildly intrigued by this bit of trivia.

Larry nods earnestly and says, "I guess

'cause men ah busiah, ya know?"

I give him an incredulous look, anger bubbling inside me as I resist the urge to share with Larry just how many things I was mentally juggling when I left the house that day — *way* more than my husband could have had in his head when he sailed out the door with a thermos of coffee and his new Beck CD. *Whistling.*

Beyond my own feelings of idiocy and Larry's sexist commentary, what disturbed me the most about the whole incident was my gut reaction as I stood there in the garage, assessing the crash scene. Namely, *Nick's going to kill me.* It is a sentiment I've heard time and again — almost always uttered by my stay-at-home-mother friends — and one that has always grated on my nerves, right up there with women who try to hide purchases from their husbands, for fear of getting in trouble. Which always makes me want to say, "Is he your father or your husband?"

To be clear, I wasn't *afraid* of Nick, but I *was* worried that he'd be disgusted with me. That he'd secretly wish his wife were a little more together. And I can't remember ever feeling that way before.

The fact that Nick turned out to be understanding, even mildly amused, when I confessed my mental lapse, wasn't much of a comfort because it didn't really change the underlying truth — that the power was shifting between us and I was becoming a needy, approval-seeking wife, someone I didn't recognize, someone my mother warned me about.

Several days later, the feeling returns after Ryan, my ex-fiancé, finds me on Facebook, requesting my "friendship" — and I find myself hoping that it might make Nick jealous, and thinking that I *want* him to be jealous.

Staring at the tiny photo of Ryan wearing Ray-Bans, a shimmering lake in the background, I call Cate and give her the news.

"I knew he would contact you eventually," she says, referring to our debate some time ago in which I insisted that we would never speak again. For one, I had a scorched-earth letter promising that to be the case. For another, nobody in our circle of friends had heard a peep from him since our five-year reunion.

"Should I accept the add?" I ask.

"Hell, yeah," Cate says. "Don't you want to see what he's doing? If he's married?"

"I guess so," I say.

"Besides, you can't *ignore* a friend request — it's rude," Cate continues. "Especially when you were the dumper . . ."

"So if he had broken up with me, I could deny his request?"

"Absolutely. It would still be a little rude, but you'd be well within your rights," Cate says definitively, the master of social networking nuances and scorned-lover tactics.

"Okay. Here goes," I say, my stomach churning with curiosity and anticipation as I click the confirm button, go directly to his page, and read his update, posted last night: *Ryan is taking the ferryboat home, all set to reread* Middlesex.

I pause, thinking how odd it is to have such a vivid glimpse into someone's life after having no clue what they've been doing for the last decade.

"What? What do you see?" Cate says.

"Hold on a sec," I say as I scan his page, quickly discovering that he lives on Bainbridge Island but works in Seattle — hence the ferry. He still teaches high school English. He's married to a woman named Anna Cordeiro, has one dog — a husky named Bernie. No children. His interests include politics, hiking, biking, photography, and Shakespeare. His favorite music: Radiohead, Sigur Rós, Modest Mouse, Neutral Milk Hotel, and Clap Your Hands Say Yeah. Books: too many to name. His favorite quote is from Margaret Mead: "Never doubt that a small group of thoughtful, committed citizens can change the world." No real surprises. I summarize for Cate, who says, "What's he look like?"

"The same. Except he got contacts," I say, remembering how blind he was without his thick glasses. "Or laser surgery."

"Does he still have his hair?"

"Yeah," I say.

"And his wife? Is she cute or not so much?" Cate clamors, as if it is *her* ex we're cyberstalking.

"I don't know. Cute enough. Short. Good teeth."

"Blond?" Cate guesses.

"No. She looks Latino — or very tan . . . Here. I'll copy and paste."

I send three photos to Cate — one of Ryan and Anna arm in arm on a pier, wearing red Patagonia fleeces, the dog standing alert at their feet. Another of Anna, grinning triumphantly on an ice-capped mountain. The third, a close-up of her with dramatic red lips, her hair in a smooth, low chignon.

A nanosecond later, Cate opens my e-mail and exclaims, "Shit. She's *young.* Rob the cradle, *Ryan.*"

"I guess she does look young," I say, realizing that I never seem to notice age, at least not when someone is younger than I am. It's as if I'm mentally frozen at about thirty-one.

"Does it bother you?" she asks. "Are you jealous? Do you feel anything?"

I smile at her frenetic questioning and tell her she needs to consider switching to decaf.

"I have," she says.

"Maybe you should get a fish?" I suggest teasingly. "Supposed to calm you down."

She laughs and asks again if I'm at all jealous.

"No. I'm not jealous," I answer truthfully, as I continue to click through eighty-seven photos of Ryan, Anna, and their dog, most in idyllic, outdoor settings. In fact, I tell her, it's almost as if I'm looking at photos of strangers, rather than the man I almost married. "He looks really happy. I'm glad for him," I say.

"Are you going to write him?" she asks.

"Should I?"

"Technically he should first since he added you . . . But go ahead and be the bigger person."

"What should I write?"

"Something generic."

"Like?"

"Like . . . um . . . 'Good to see you're doing well, still teaching, enjoying the outdoors. Take care, Tess.' "

I type the sentences verbatim and hit post before I can agonize over the wording. Instantly, my own posed photo appears on his wall. In comparison to his artsy shots, the stiff picture of me with the kids next to our Christmas tree looks utterly staged, lacking any of the sparkle or spontaneity captured in so many of Ryan's photos.

"Okay. Done," I say, thinking I really need to change my profile picture. Unfortunately, I don't have any majestic, mountaintop options. "It's posted."

"You posted it? On his *wall?*" Cate asks, horrified.

"You told me to!" I say, panicked and wondering what I just missed.

"No! No! I did not!" she says. "You should've just sent an e-mail. Privately. Not on his wall! He might not want his wife to see it! She might despise you. She might be totally bitter."

"I doubt that. She looks perfectly happy."

"You don't know what her issues are."

"Well, should I delete it?" I ask.

"Yes! Immediately . . . Oh, shit. I gotta go into hair and makeup . . . but keep me posted . . . No pun intended."

264

I laugh and hang up, now transfixed by the last shot — a black-and-white photo of Anna, wrapped in a big blanket by the fire, staring adoringly at the camera. I tell myself once again that I'm not jealous, but can't deny the tiniest, unidentified pang in my chest that returns several times over the course of the day, prompting me to sign back on to Facebook and check Ryan's page, again and again. By five o'clock, he has yet to respond to my post but has changed his update to: *Ryan thanks his wife for her foresight.*

Wondering what Anna's foresight involved, I return to the photo of her by the fire, finally pinpointing my earlier pang. It isn't jealousy, at least not any associated with Ryan or his marriage, but rather wistfulness over Nick, my *own* marriage, memories of how we met, how things used to be. If there is any jealousy at all, it is envy over the look of utter contentment on Anna's face. The fact that Ryan likely inspired her smile, then snapped the photo, then converted it to an evocative black-and-white image, then posted it on Facebook — all things that would never happen in my house. Not these days.

Later that night, after Ryan has finally e-mailed me back (*Good to see you, too.*

Beautiful kids. Are you still teaching?), I tell Nick about the exchange, hoping for a satisfying, territorial reaction. Or perhaps a little nostalgia over our relationship lore; after all, it was Ryan who brought us together.

Instead, he shakes his head and says, "Figures that guy has a Facebook page." Then he picks up the remote control and flips on CNN. Anderson Cooper is doing a retrospective on the tsunami, horrifying images of destruction flashing on the screen.

"What's wrong with Facebook?" I ask defensively — more for my sake than Ryan's.

"Well, for starters, it's a complete waste of time," he says, turning the volume up slightly for a British tourist's account of the tragedy.

I bristle at his implication that *I* have time to waste — whereas he is the busy surgeon with better things to do.

"No it's not," I say. "It's a great way to reconnect with old friends."

"Uh-huh. Tell yourself that . . . Better yet, tell what's-his-name that." Then he gives me a playful wink, before returning his gaze to the television, secure as he was in the very beginning, back when I broke off my engagement with another man for the mere chance to be with him. It was once the thing I liked most about him — his unwavering confidence — but now, it feels like a brand of indifference. And as I pretend to be as engrossed in the documentary as he is, my mind is racing, remembering how things used to be, remembering how they began.

Hi, Nick. It's Tessa Thaler. From the subway.
I remember writing the words down, working up the courage to call him, practicing for Cate, changing my tone from somber to sultry to sprightly.

"Do it again," Cate demanded from her favorite perch on my futon — and really the only place to sit since Ryan had moved out with our couch six weeks before. "And no up-talk this time."

"What?" I asked her, my palms sweaty.

"You're ending your sentences with the inflection of a question. Sounds like you're not sure who you are . . . It's Tessa Thaler? From the subway?"

"I don't think I can do this," I told her, pacing along the Asian-inspired screen separating my bed from the living area.

"You want him to start dating someone else? Or worse, forget you altogether?" she asked, the master of scare tactics. "C'mon. Timing is everything." She removed an emery board, a bottle of nail polish remover, and several cotton balls from her mammoth purse and began giving herself a manicure.

"I'm not ready for a relationship," I said.

"Who said anything about a relationship? Maybe you'll just have hot sex for once in your life. Would that be so bad?"

"For once in my life?" I said. "How do you know Ryan and I weren't having hot sex?"

She shuddered as if I were talking about her brother — which wasn't far from the truth given the fact that we had operated as a chummy threesome during much of college. "Well? Were you?"

I shrugged and said, "It was decent."

She shook her head, filing her nails into a shape she called "squoval." "Well, we're aiming for something north of decent. So pick up the damn phone and call him. Now."

And so I did, dialing the number on his business card, and taking a deep breath as the phone rang. Then, upon hearing his unmistakable hello, I read from my script, somehow managing to end all my sentences with a period.

"Who?" Nick said.

"Um . . . We met on the subway?" I said again, completely flummoxed and deflated.

"I'm kidding," he said. "Of course I remember you. How are you?"

"I'm good," I said, wishing I had practiced beyond the first three sentences. I looked to Cate for reassurance as she gave me a thumbs-up and a hand gesture to keep the conversation rolling. "How are you?"

"Can't complain . . . So how was the honeymoon?" he asked, no hint of light-heartedness in his question, although weeks later he confessed that it was an attempt at a humorous icebreaker — but that he felt insensitive as soon as the words were out.

I let out a nervous laugh and told him there was no honeymoon, no wedding.

"Oh," he said. And then — "I'm sorry? Congratulations?"

"Thanks," I said, which seemed to cover both sentiments.

"So? Are you just calling to share your news?" he said smoothly. "Or to ask me out?"

"To share my news," I said, his banter making me bold. "The asking out is up to you."

Cate raised her brows and grinned, clearly proud of my response.

"Well, then," he answered. "How 'bout tonight? You free?"

"Yes," I said, my heart thumping wildly —

a reaction I never had with Ryan, not even seconds before our first time.

"Are you a vegetarian?" he asked.

"Why?" I asked. "Is that a deal breaker?"

He laughed. "No . . . I was just in the mood for a burger and a beer."

"Sounds good to me," I said, thinking that sprouts and tofu would have sounded just as appealing. Anything with Nick Russo.

"Okay. I'll meet you at the Burger Joint at the Parker Meridien . . . Do you know it?"

"No," I said, wondering if it was something I *should* know — if it gave me away as the homebody I was with Ryan, something I had vowed to change.

"The hotel's on Fifty-sixth — between Sixth and Seventh, closer to Sixth . . . Go into the lobby — and right between the check-in desk and concierge stand, there's a little curtain and a sign that says BURGER JOINT. I'll be there, saving our table."

I furiously scribbled the instructions on the back of my script, my hands now sweaty *and* shaking. I asked him what time, and he told me eight.

"Okay," I said. "See you soon."

I heard the smile in his voice as he replied, "See you soon, Tessa from the subway."

I hung up the phone, closed my eyes, and screamed a giddy, girly scream.

"Holy shit. *Go,* Tess," Cate said. "I mean, technically you should have told him you had plans already. Next time, at least mute the phone and *pretend* to consult your calendar. And *never* agree to day-of plans . . ."

"Cate!" I said, racing to my closet. "We don't have time for a dating tutorial. I have to find something to wear."

Cate grinned. "Padded bra, black thong, stilettos."

"Fine on the padded bra and thong . . . But we're going to a place called 'Burger Joint.' Not so sure the stilettos will work."

Cate looked crestfallen as she followed me to my closet. "Burger Joint? God, I hope he's not cheap. Sort of defeats the purpose of dating a doctor."

"He's still in school," I said. "And I love burgers."

"Well, if he's as fine as you say he is . . . he can pull it off."

"He is," I said. "He's *that* fine."

"Well, then," Cate said, rifling through my clothes. "Let's get down to business."

Hours later, I was standing in the chilled lobby of the Parker Meridien wearing jeans, a black tank, and jeweled flip-flops, a casual look that would typically not meet with Cate's approval, but one she okayed that night on account of the grungy venue and the last-minute invite.

Still hot from my muggy cab ride, I fanned myself with my hand, inhaling my new perfume, bought earlier that day with Nick in mind, determined not to commingle old scents with fresh starts. Then I found the entrance to the restaurant, took a deep breath, and dramatically parted the floor-to-ceiling drapes sequestering the Burger Joint from the lobby. And there he was, standing before me, even finer than I remembered, his beauty a high contrast to the yellow lighting, vinyl booths, and random newspaper clippings taped to the faux-wood paneled walls.

He stepped toward me, smiling, then looked down at my left hand and said, "No ring."

"No ring," I said, nothing more, remembering Cate's admonition not to talk about Ryan.

"I like you even better this way," he said, smiling.

I smiled back at him, rubbing my thumb over my naked ring finger, feeling an affirming rush that I had done the right thing. Then he asked me what I like on my burger and when I told him just ketchup, he nodded and pointed to the only free booth in the corner. "You might want to grab that for us. This place fills up fast."

I followed his direction, taking a few steps over to the table, sliding into my seat while I kept my eyes on his back and tried to decide what I admired more about him — his take-charge attitude or the perfect fit of his faded jeans.

Minutes later, he joined me with two burgers wrapped in foil and a pitcher of beer. He poured two glasses, then raised his and said, "Here's to the best burger you'll ever have."

I smiled and thought, *Here's to the best first date I'll ever have.*

Then his face grew serious as he said, "I'm glad you called . . . I didn't think I was going to hear from you . . . I thought you'd go through with it."

"Why's that?" I asked, fleetingly disappointed that he hadn't had more faith in me.

"Because most people do."

I nodded, thinking of my brother, but deciding not to air my family laundry right out of the gate. It was one of Cate's many rules — no "my parents got a divorce" or "my dad cheated on my mom" or other hints of dysfunctional-family talk. I ticked through the other rules — no asking about

273

his exes, no excessive talk about grad school or work, show interest in him without interviewing him.

"I usually hate to be wrong," Nick said — which he would later tease was my official warning of his biggest character flaw. "But in this case, I'm glad I was."

Three hours of conversation, two pitchers of beer, and a shared brownie later, he led me to the Columbus Circle subway station, down the steps, and over to the turnstile where he inserted two tokens and motioned for me to go first.

"Where are we going?" I shouted over an approaching train, feeling tipsy from a good beer buzz.

"Nowhere," he said, smiling. "We're just going to ride the subway."

And so we did, making our way onto an empty train, but still opting to stand, holding on to a metal pole together.

"Think it's the same one?" he asked at one point.

"Same what?"

"Same car? Same pole?" he said, right before he leaned in for our first kiss.

"I think so," I said, closing my eyes and feeling his lips against mine, soft and sure and amazing.

Later, I called Cate and gave her the

report. She calculated the cost of the night, dubbing it a ridiculously cheap date, but still deeming it a success — a romantic home run.

"I think it's a sign," she whispered into the phone.

"Of what?" I asked, hoping that I had just kissed the man I would someday marry.

"Of hot sex to come," Cate said, laughing.

I laughed with her, hoping we were both right.

And within a month, I was sure we were. Cate considered it a miracle — that I had found the one guy in the city who was both thoughtful and reliable, yet also sexy and great in bed. He really was the best of everything. An unaffected, down-to-earth boy from Boston who loved burgers and beer and baseball. Yet he was also a Harvard-educated surgeon-in-training, a natural in Manhattan's swankiest restaurants. He was handsome without being vain. Scrupulous but not judgmental. Confident but not arrogant. He did exactly what he said he was going to do — no exceptions — yet retained an air of mystery that kept me on edge, kept me wondering. He cared little what others thought of him, yet seemed to earn everyone's respect. He was coolly aloof yet somehow still passionate. And I fell hard and fast in love with him, overwhelmed by the certainty that our feelings were as equal as they were real.

Then, six months later, in the dead of the winter, Nick took me back to our burger joint. And after we ate and drank and reminisced, he pulled his keys out of his pocket and carved our initials into the graffiti-covered corner table. Skillful, neat, deep grooves declaring his love. I couldn't imagine a sweeter gesture, until an hour later, in an empty subway car, he pulled a ring from his pocket and asked me to marry him, promising he'd love me forever.

22
VALERIE

As the days turn colder and shorter, they both continue to pretend. They pretend that the visits and phone conversations and texts are the normal course of doctor-patient follow-up. They pretend that their friendship is appropriate and unremarkable. They pretend that there is nothing to hide — that they are not *literally* hiding in Valerie's house. Most of all, they pretend that they can stay in this tenuous middle place, between their existence in the hospital and her official return to reality.

It almost reminds Valerie of the days she stayed home sick from school when she really wasn't. She always had the sense that Rosemary knew the truth, but went along with her feigned symptoms so that she could stay home from work and spend time alone with her daughter. They were some of her best childhood memories — being curled up on the couch in her Wonder

Woman sleeping bag, immersed in soap operas and game shows with her mother, who would bring her chicken soup and root beer floats on an orange lacquered tray, thoughts of school and homework and cafeteria happenings a million miles away. This was the escapism she felt when Nick came over with videos and music for Charlie, wine and takeout from Antonio's for them. It was as if she was shutting her mind down and living in the moment, forgetting everything else in the world, and especially his family, just a few miles away.

But the day before Thanksgiving, their charade becomes more difficult, when Nick stops by unexpectedly on his way home from work — minutes after Jason dropped by to pick up a card table for the feast he's hosting tomorrow. The second the doorbell rings, Valerie knows she's in trouble, especially because Jason is in the family room, nearer to the door. She freezes over the sweet potato casserole she's making, knowing there will be no explanation other than the truth. The *real* truth — not the one she and Nick have fabricated together.

"Nick," she hears Jason say, surprise commingling with disapproval and concern.

She arrives in the foyer in time to see Nick

reach out to shake her brother's hand and say, "I was just stopping by to check on Charlie." His forehead is lined with worry, and he is visibly flustered in a way that Valerie has never seen him before, studying his watch a beat too long, as if stalling to gather his thoughts. "Is he still up? Or did I miss him?"

"He's in bed," Jason says purposely.

"But he's doing very well today," Valerie finishes, carrying on the ridiculous house-call charade. "Would you . . . like to come in . . . anyway?"

He opens his mouth, poised to refuse the invitation, but she nods, eyes wide, a smile frozen on her face, as if to tell him leaving now would make things worse, *more* obvious — and that he has no choice but to stay.

"Okay. Sure. For a minute," he says.

Valerie takes Nick's coat, hangs it in the hall closet, and leads him into the living room where he sits in a chair he has never chosen before — an armchair from her grandmother's house and her grandmother's house before that. It is not a good antique — just an old chair covered in an unappealing mauve paisley, but Valerie can't bear to reupholster it for sentimental reasons. She keeps her eyes fixed on the design now, as she takes a seat on the couch opposite Nick. Meanwhile, Jason selects another chair, completing their triangle. His expression is inscrutable, but Valerie senses judgment in his silence, and wonders if it is about Nick's being here — or her keeping a secret from him. Secrets have never been something that existed between the two — other than the one she kept for the three days that followed her positive pregnancy test.

"So how are you doing?" Nick asks, glancing from twin to twin.

They both tell him they are fine and Valerie launches into a nervous, detailed account of Charlie's day — what they did, what he ate, how many times she changed his dressings. She finishes by saying, "He's going back to school on Monday." As if the instruction didn't come from Nick himself.

Nick nods and tosses out another question. "What are you doing tomorrow? For Thanksgiving?"

"We're all going to Jason's house," Valerie says — which, of course, Nick already knows. "Jason's boyfriend, Hank, is quite the cook."

"Is he a chef?" Nick asks.

"No. A tennis pro," Jason says. "But he knows his way around the kitchen."

"Ah. Okay," Nick murmurs. "Nice perk for you."

Valerie can tell her brother is resisting a smart-ass remark, probably something about the perk of dating a doctor — when he stands, rubs his hands together, and says, "Well. As much as I'd love to stay and chat, Hank and I have a turkey to baste."

Nick looks relieved as he stands and shakes Jason's hand again. "Good to see you, man," he says a bit too robustly.

"You, too, Doc," Jason says, flipping up the collar on his leather jacket. "It was a . . . nice surprise." On his way to the door, he shoots his sister a bemused look and mouths, "Call me."

Valerie nods, locking the door behind him, and steeling herself for the awkward exchange to come.

"Shit," Nick says, still sitting rigidly in her grandmother's chair, one hand gripping each armrest. "I'm really sorry."

"For what?" she asks, returning to her spot on the couch.

"For coming tonight . . . For not calling first."

"It's okay," she says.

"What are you going to tell him?" he asks her.

"The truth," she says. "That we're

friends."

He gives her a long look and says, "Friends. Right."

"We *are* friends," she says, desperately clinging to this version of their story.

"I know we're friends, Val," he says. "But . . ."

"But what?"

He shakes his head and says, "You know what."

Her heart stops and she considers a last-ditch effort to change the subject, get up, hurry out to the kitchen to finish her casserole. Instead she whispers, "I know."

He exhales slowly and says, "This is wrong."

She feels her hands clench into two fists in her lap as he continues, a note of panic in his voice. "It's wrong on several levels. At least two."

She knows exactly what those two levels are but lets him spell it out.

"For one, I'm your son's doctor — there are ethics involved. Ethics and rules designed to protect patients . . . It would be unfair of me to . . . take advantage . . . of your emotions."

"You're Charlie's doctor, yes . . . But that's not what this is about," she says adamantly. She has thought about it often,

282

and although she feels endlessly grateful to him, she is certain that she's not confusing gratitude with anything else. "Besides, *I'm* not your patient."

"You're his *mother*. It's actually, probably worse," Nick says. "I shouldn't be here. Jason knows it. You know it. I know it."

She nods, staring down at her hands, aware that he is referring to his second point, the one she has yet to address. The small issue of his marriage.

"So does that mean you're leaving?" she finally asks.

He moves to the couch, next to her, and says, "No. I'm not leaving. I'm going to sit here next to you and continue to torture myself." His eyes are intense, almost angry — but also resolved — as if he hates to be tested and refuses to lose.

Valerie looks at him, alarmed. Then, ignoring everything she believes, all that she knows to be right, she responds by pulling him to her in the embrace she has imagined so many times. After several seconds, he takes control, slowly lowering her to the couch, covering her with the weight of his body as their legs entangle, their cheeks touch.

After a long time like this, Valerie closes her eyes and lets herself drift off, lulled by his steady breathing, the feel of his arms encircling her, and their chests rising and falling, together. Until suddenly, she is awakened by Eminem's "Slim Shady," the ring tone that Jason programmed into her phone just for his calls. Nick jolts in such a way that she can tell he fell asleep, too — the idea of which thrills her.

"Is that your phone?" he whispers, his breath warm in her ear.

"Yes. It's Jason," she tells him.

"Do you need to call him back?" Nick asks, repositioning her slightly, just enough to look in her eyes. He reaches out and touches her hairline, so tenderly and naturally that it feels as if they've been together like this a thousand times and done everything else, too.

"No," she replies, hoping he won't move away from her. Hoping he won't move at all. "Not now."

Another moment passes before he speaks again. "What time do you think it is?" he says.

She guesses nine, even though she believes it to be later. "Maybe ten," she adds reluctantly, wanting to be truthful.

He sighs, then swings himself into an upright position, pulling her legs onto his lap before checking his watch. "Damn," he mutters, shaking his sleeve back over his watch.

"What?" she says, looking up at him, admiring his profile, yearning to touch his lower lip.

"Ten after ten. I better get going," he says, but does not move.

"Yes," she says, processing what has just transpired, wondering what will follow. She can tell he is doing the same, asking himself all the same questions. Would they retreat or move forward? Could they do this thing they were on the verge of doing? Did they have it in them to make a wrong decision just because it felt right?

Nick stares ahead, then turns to look down at her, his eyes jet black in the dimly lit room. He holds her gaze, then her hand, as if to tell her that the answer, *his* answer anyway, is *yes*.

Then he stands and collects his coat from the closet. She watches him, still unable to move, until he comes to her, taking her hands in his, pulling her to her feet. Wordlessly, he leads her to the front door, which she unlocks and opens for him.

"I'll call you tomorrow," he says, which has become a given. Then he hugs her hard, an upright version of their last embrace, his fingers cupping the back of her head, then running through her hair. They do not kiss, but they might as well, because in that silent moment, they both stop pretending.

23
TESSA

It is Thanksgiving morning, and I am in my kitchen, preparing dinner with my father's wife, Diane, and Nick's mother, Connie. In past years, the collaborative effort would have annoyed me, as much for Diane's gourmet airs as my mother-in-law's tendency to usurp my kitchen. But this year, oddly enough, my first Thanksgiving as a stay-at-home mother, I feel no sense of ownership of the meal, and am actually grateful to be stationed at the sink, peeling potatoes, the least important task on the Thanksgiving totem pole. It occurs to me, as I stare out the window into our fenced backyard, that I might be depressed — not depression-commercial miserable where the women can't get out of bed and look as if they've been beaten with a bag of rocks, but the kind of depressed that renders me unnerved, exhausted, and largely indifferent. Indifferent to whether we use rosemary or thyme to flavor the turkey. Indifferent that the children are running around in sweats instead of the matching chocolate-brown corduroy pants and jumper my mother sent. Indifferent to the fact that Nick worked late last night — again. And that we argued this morning — over nothing, really, which is the best kind of argument to have when a marriage is working, the worst when it's not.

"Tessa, dear, please tell me you have white pepper," Diane says, jolting me out of my thoughts with her usual sense of urgency and affected Jackie O accent. Earlier this week, she gave me a long list of ingredients for her various side dishes — but white pepper was not among them.

"I think we do," I say, pointing toward the pantry. "Should be on the second shelf."

"Thank *God*," Diane says. "Black pepper simply won't do."

I force a smile of understanding, thinking that Diane is a snob in the classic sense of the word, feeling superior on just about every front. She grew up with money and privilege (then married and divorced someone even more well-to-do), and although she does her best to hide it, I can tell she looks down on the middle-American masses — and even more so on the nouveaux riches — or as she calls them in a whisper, "parvenus." She is not classically beautiful, but is striking in the first-glance kind of way that tall, high-browed blondes often are, and looks a full decade younger than her fifty-eight years due to diligent grooming, obsessive tennis playing, and a few nip and tucks she openly, proudly, discusses. She also has a natural grace about her — the kind that comes from boarding school, years of ballet, and a mother who made her walk around balancing encyclopedias on her head.

In short, she is everything a first wife fears — refined and sophisticated with no trace of bimbo to be found — and as such, I do my best to disdain her on my mother's behalf. Diane makes the task difficult, though, for she's never been anything other than gracious and thoughtful to me, perhaps because she never had children of her own. She also makes a great effort with Ruby and Frank, lavishly gifting them and playing with them in a heartfelt, on-the-floor way that their two grandmothers never do. Dex, who is spending Thanksgiving with my mother in the city, is suspicious of Diane's efforts, certain that her kindness is more about showing off to my father and showing *up* my mother, but Rachel and I agree that her motivation doesn't much matter — it's the result we appreciate.

Above all, Diane keeps my father in line and happy. Even when she's complaining — which she often does — he seems content to remedy whatever's ailing her, almost inspired by the challenge. I remember April once asking if I ever felt in competition with her — if she had somehow eroded my "daddy's girl" status. Until she posed the question, I hadn't quite realized that my dad and I never had that kind of relationship. He was a good father, prioritizing our education, taking us on great European vacations, teaching us how to fly a kite, tie sailing knots, and drive a stick shift. But he was never particularly affectionate or doting, the way Nick is with Ruby — and I have the feeling it might have something to do with my mother and how closely I aligned myself to her, even as a child. It was as if he sensed my disapproval, my affiliation with a woman he was betraying, even before I knew what he was up to. So, in short, Diane's flamboyant arrival on the familial front didn't really change much between my dad and me.

I watch her now, reaching into one of her many personalized Goyard bags, retrieving a pair of cherry-red, jeweled, cat's-eye reading glasses that only a woman like Diane could pull off. She slips them on and peers down at her cookbook, also pulled from her bag, humming an indeterminable tune with an aren't-I-adorable expression — a look that she kicks into high gear as my father pops into the kitchen and winks at her.

"David, sweetheart, come here," she says.

He does, wrapping his arms around her from behind, as she turns and kisses his cheek before returning her full attention to her butternut squash soup.

Meanwhile, Connie is manning the turkey, basting it with peasantlike efficiency. In high contrast to Diane's ultrafeminine skirt suit and sleek crocodile pumps, Connie is wearing elastic-waist pants, a fall-foliage sweater adorned with a pilgrim pin, and tie shoes that are either orthopedic or her attempt to win an ugly-footwear contest. I can tell she disapproves of Diane's cookbook, as she is firmly in the no-frills-or-recipe camp, especially on Thanksgiving. In this sense — in *every* sense — she is utterly traditional, a subservient wife who thinks Nick, her only child, walks on water. She actually refers to him as a miracle child — as he came after her doctor's prognosis that she could not have children. Considering this, and the fact that Nick has met and surpassed all parental hopes for greatness, it is another miracle that Connie and I get along at all. But for the most part, she pretends to approve of me, even though I know it kills her that I'm not raising the kids in the Catholic church, or *any* church for that matter. That my father's Jewish (which, in her mind, makes me half Jewish, her grandchildren a quarter so). That I use spaghetti sauce from a jar. That although I love Nick, on most days I don't think he lassoed the moon. In fact, the only time she has ever seemed genuinely pleased with me was when I told her I was going to quit my job — an ironic juxtaposition to my own mother's views on the subject.

My hand sore from peeling, I set about filling a large pot with water while listening to two parallel conversations — one about Connie's neighbor's battle with ovarian cancer, another involving Diane's recent girls' spa trip, with only the most attenuated thematic connection between the two threads. It is one of the only things that Diane and Connie have in common — they are both big talkers, incessantly chattering about people I've never met, referring to them by name as if I know them well. It is an annoying trait, but it makes them easy to be around, requiring almost no effort other than an occasional follow-up question.

The next two hours continue in this vein, the noise level ramping up as the kids infiltrate the kitchen with their most nerve-trying toys, until I succumb to a string of Bloody Marys — which, incidentally, is the only other thing Diane and Connie have in common. They are both big drinkers. So by four o'clock, when we all come to the table, at least three of us are tipsy, possibly four if you include Nick's dad, Bruce, who has drained several Captain and Cokes but never talks enough to reveal any signs of consumption. Instead, he sits gruffly, and after a nudge from Connie, makes the sign of the cross and speeds through his standard prayer: *Bless us, O Lord, and these thy gifts which we are about to receive from thy bounty through Christ our Lord. Amen.*

We all mumble *Amen,* while Nick's parents cross themselves again and Ruby imitates them, with a few too many touches — in what occurs to me, with amusement, looks more like a Star of David than a cross.

"So!" my dad says, as uncomfortable with religion as he is with Nick's parents. "Looks delicious!" He directs his praise at Diane, who beams and helps herself to a comically small portion of mashed potatoes, then conspicuously refuses the gravy, passing it along to Nick's dad.

The conversation comes to a standstill after that, other than murmurings of how great everything looks and smells, and Frank and Ruby's discussion of what they do not want on their plates.

Then, about two minutes into dinner, Diane looks at me with alarm and says, "Oh, Tess! Do you know what we forgot?"

I glance around the table, finding nothing amiss, pleased that I remembered to get the rolls out of the warming drawer — which is my usual omission.

"Candles!" Diane says. "We *must* have candles."

Nick shoots me an irritated look that makes me feel fleetingly connected to him. Like we're on the same team, in on the same joke.

"I'll get them," he offers.

"No. I'll get them," I say, feeling sure that he has no idea where we keep such accoutrements. Besides, I know how Connie feels about her men getting up from the table during the meal, for *any* reason.

I return to the kitchen, standing on a stepstool to reach into a high cabinet for a pair of pewter candlesticks, two barely burned candles from last Valentine's Day still stuck inside. Then I open the drawer next to the stove where we normally house matches.

None to be found — which is par for the course these days in our disorganized house. I close my eyes, trying to visualize where I last saw a book of matches, one of those things, like safety pins or paper clips, that you find strewn everywhere unless you need them, and remember that I lit a candle in our bedroom one night last week. I run upstairs, open the drawer of my nightstand, and find a matchbox right where I left it. Out of breath from the biggest burst of exercise I've had in days, I sit on the edge of the bed and run my hand over the matchbox cover, reading the pink, distinctive-font inscription: *Amanda & Steve: Love Rules.*

Steve was one of Nick's better friends in medical school, now a dermatologist in L.A., and Amanda the model he met in his office when she came in for laser hair removal. *Love Rules* was the theme of their Hawaiian wedding, the three-day extravaganza Nick and I attended when I was a few months pregnant with Frank. The tagline was written everywhere — on their save-the-date cards, invitations, and Web site, as well as the canvas boat bags, water bottles, and beach towels given to all guests upon our arrival at the resort. The hip declaration was even scrawled across a banner, pulled by an airplane flying overhead on the beach just after the couple exchanged vows. I remember Nick, looking skyward, shading his eyes with amused cynicism, whispering, "Yo. Love rules, dude."

I had smiled back at him, feeling slightly foolish for being momentarily impressed by the spectacle he was clearly mocking, and simultaneously proud that our wedding had been the opposite of a production. Nick had deferred to me in our plans, but had lodged a strong request for a low-key affair, one that I obliged, in part, because of my embarrassment over my canceled wedding and all the costs our guests accrued; in part because I had seen the light, come to believe that a wedding should be about a feeling between two people, not a show for the masses. As a result, we had a small ceremony at the New York Public Library, followed by an elegant dinner at an Italian restaurant in Gramercy with only our family and closest friends. It was a magical, romantic evening, and although I occasionally wish I had worn a slightly fancier dress, and that Nick and I had danced on our wedding night, I have no real regrets about the way we chose to do things.

Love Rules, I think now, as I slowly stand, gathering strength for my return trip downstairs, reminding myself of all that I have to be grateful for. Then, just as I'm leaving our room, I spot Nick's BlackBerry on the top of his dresser and feel seized by the temptation to do something I have always said I would never do.

I tell myself that I'm being ridiculous, that I do not want to be a snooping, paranoid wife, that I have no reason to be suspicious. Then I hear the little voice in my head say, *No reason other than his withdrawn behavior, his long hours, our lack of intimacy.* I shake my head, dispelling the doubts. Nick isn't perfect, but he is not a liar. He is *not* a cheater.

And yet, I continue to walk toward his phone, strangely compelled to reach out and touch it. I take it in my hand, scroll through to the mail icon, and see that there is a new text message from a 617 area code, a Boston cell phone number. It is undoubtedly a colleague, I tell myself. A *male* colleague. A work situation that can't wait until tomorrow — at least not in the estimation of a fellow obsessed surgeon.

I click on it with equal parts guilt and fear and read:

Thinking of you, too. Sorry I missed your call. Will be home around 7 if you want to try again. Until then, have a happy Thanksgiving . . . PS Of course he doesn't hate you. How could anyone hate you?

I stare at the words, trying to determine who they could be from, *who* doesn't hate Nick, reassuring myself that there is a logical, benign explanation behind them, even for the "thinking of you, too" portion of the message. And yet, my head spins and heart pounds with worrisome possibilities, worst-case scenarios. I read the text twice more, hearing a woman's voice, seeing the vague outline of her face, a young version of Diane. I close my eyes, swallow back the panic rising in my throat, and tell myself to stop the madness. Then I mark the message as unread, slip his phone back on the dresser, and return to the table, candlesticks and matches in hand.

"Here we are!" I say, smiling brightly as I flank the autumnal centerpiece with the candles, lighting them one at a time, doing my best to steady my hands. Then I sit and eat in virtual silence, other than to remind the kids of their manners and occasionally fuel Diane and Connie's babble.

All the while, I replay the text in my head, stealing glances at Nick, and wondering if I could ever hate him.

24
VALERIE

She and Charlie spend Thanksgiving at Jason's, along with his boyfriend, Hank, and Rosemary. Although the day is quiet and low-key, it still feels like something of a test and a benchmark, as Hank marks the first official contact Charlie has had with anyone other than family or hospital personnel. Hank handles the interaction perfectly, earning Valerie's affection every time he looks Charlie directly in the eye, and without treating him with kid gloves, asks him questions about his mask, his surgeries and physical therapy, and how he feels about his upcoming return to school.

Meanwhile, Valerie neatly avoids being alone with her brother, ignoring his long stares and pointed remarks, until late in the day when he finally manages to corner her in the kitchen while the others are eating their second helping of pumpkin pie.

"Start talking," he says, casting furtive

glances at the door, safeguarding her privacy, even from their mother. *Especially* from their mother.

"It's not what you think," she says, still buzzing from the text message she read in the powder room right before dinner. It was from Nick — his third of the day — asking if Jason hates him, telling her he is thinking of her. She wrote him back, saying she was thinking of him, too — although *obsessing* was more the word for it. She dreamed about him all last night, and he has not left her mind once all day.

"So you're not getting busy with the doc?" he probes, under his breath.

"No," she says, as a vision of him weakens her knees.

"So he always makes house calls? Late at night? Unannounced? Wearing cologne?" Jason rattles off the questions.

"He wasn't wearing cologne," she replies a little too quickly, then attempts to cover up her intimate knowledge with a sidebar about how she has never trusted guys who wear cologne. "Lion wore cologne," she finishes.

"Aha!" he says, as if this is all the evidence he needs. Why else would she compare a man to Lion — the love of her life so far? Which isn't saying much. But still.

"Don't *aha* me," she says as Rosemary walks into the kitchen.

"What are you two all whispery about now?" she asks, opening the refrigerator.

"Nothing," they say in unison, clearly hiding something.

Rosemary shakes her head, as if she doesn't believe them but doesn't much care, returning to the family room with a container of Cool Whip and a large serving spoon.

"Carry on," she says over her shoulder.

Which Jason does, switching tactics, slipping into his straight-shooting mode. "Val. Just tell me. Is something going on?"

She hesitates, making a split-second decision that she does not want to layer a lie on top of everything else.

"Yes," she finally says. "But it's not . . . physical."

She thinks of their embrace last night, as intimate as any moment in her life, but decides that she is still telling the truth. Technically.

"Are you falling in *love* with him?" he asks.

She gives him a bashful smile that is more telling than anything she could say.

Jason whistles. "Wow. Okay . . . He *is* married, correct?"

She nods.

"Separated?"

"No," she says, answering questions the way she instructs her clients — as simply as possible, offering no extra information. "Not to my knowledge," she adds, entertaining the hopeful thought that this *could* be the case.

"And . . . ?" he says.

"And nothing," she says.

She has thought about his wife a thousand times, of course, wondering about her, their marriage. What does she look like? What is *she* like? Why did Nick fall in love with her? And more important, why has he fallen out? Or maybe he hasn't. Maybe this is only about the two of them, the feelings they share, the uncontrollable force bringing them together — and nothing else.

Valerie doesn't know which scenario she prefers, whether she wants to be a reaction to something that has already soured or to be something that has taken him by storm, out of the blue, overriding his contented existence with an offer of something more. Something better. All she knows for sure is that he isn't the kind of man who has done this before. She would swear anything on it.

Valerie sticks to the facts now. "He's married with two kids . . . And he's Charlie's doctor. It's an all-around big problem," she says succinctly.

"Okay," Jason says. "Now we're getting somewhere. I thought maybe it was just me."

"No. It's not just you. I am perfectly aware that there is nothing about this situation that is right," she whispers resignedly. "And for the record, he knows it's wrong, too. But . . ."

"But you're not going to stop seeing him?" Jason says in the voice of a brother, a best friend, a therapist, all rolled into one. "Are you?"

"No," she says. "I can't."

25
TESSA

That night, shortly after Nick's parents leave for home and my dad and Diane depart for Fifteen Beacon, their favorite hotel in Boston and where they always stay when they come to town, Nick pokes his head into the kids' bathroom where I am stripping off their clothes and corralling them into the tub.

"I'm going to run out. Be back in a few," he says.

"For what?" I ask, my heart sinking as I glance at my watch and note that it is nearly seven o'clock.

"Cherry Coke," he says.

Nick has always insisted that cherry Coke is more effective than Tylenol in curing headaches, which he claims to have tonight. And maybe he does. I desperately hope that he does, hope that he is on the brink of the worst migraine ever. "You want anything?"

"No, thanks," I say, frowning as I adjust

the temperature of the bathwater. I add more liquid soap, and a hill of bubbles appear as Ruby climbs in and I heave a squirming, giggling Frank over the edge. I sit on a stepstool, watching my children play, admiring their perfect pink bodies — their potbellies, their round, little bottoms, their stick-figure limbs. As Nick turns to leave the bathroom, I keep my eyes fixed on my children, telling myself that he would never do anything to hurt them or jeopardize our family.

Yet, the second I hear the garage door open, I race to our bedroom and, with a heavy heart, confirm what I already knew: Nick's phone is gone from the dresser. I tell myself that it's natural to take your phone, even on a short errand, yet I can't shake the image of my husband, in his car, speed-dialing another woman's number.

"I think Nick might be having an affair," I tell Cate the next day, when I finally get a hold of her after four tries. I am sitting on the floor amid three piles of dirty laundry — although it should be more like five if I weren't prepared to overstuff the washing machine. "Or at least contemplating one."

The second the words are out, I feel

intense relief, almost as if confronting my fears and saying them aloud makes them less likely to be true.

"No way," Cate says, as I knew she would. Which is, subconsciously, why I probably called her in the first place, choosing her over the other candidates: Rachel, my brother, April, or my mother, somehow knowing that Rachel and Dex would be too worried, April too likely to break my confidence, my mother too cynical. "Why do you think that?"

I share with her all my evidence — the late nights at the office, the text message, and the cherry Coke excursion that lasted close to thirty-eight minutes.

"Come on, Tess. That's a crazy conclusion to draw," she says. "He might have wanted to get out of the house for a few minutes. Shirk his bedtime duties with a little alone time. But that doesn't add up to an affair."

"What about the text?" I ask. "The 'thinking of you' . . . ?"

"So what? So he's thinking of someone . . . That doesn't mean he's thinking of *undressing* someone."

"Well, who could it be from?" I say, realizing that the very thing that gives me greatest pause — that Nick has so few friends, so seldom makes new connections

— is the thing that simultaneously reassures me.

"It could be from anyone. It could be a coworker who is getting a divorce and alone for Thanksgiving. It could be from an old friend . . . a cousin. It could be from a patient's mother or father. A former patient . . . Bottom line, Nick is not the affair type."

"My mother says all men are the affair type."

"I don't believe that. *You* don't believe that."

"I'm not sure what to believe these days," I say.

"Tess. You're just going through a little depression. A downturn. I'll tell you what. How 'bout you come here next weekend? I'll cheer you up, send you home happy. This is nothing that a little girl time won't cure . . ."

"Time to let Nick have an affair?" I say, now joking. *Mostly* joking.

"Time to let him miss you. Time to remind yourself that you have the best husband. The best marriage. The best *life*."

"Okay," I say, unconvinced but hopeful. "I'll come Friday — late afternoon."

"Good," she says. "We'll go out. You can watch me hit on some guys in bars . . . I'll show you exactly what you're *not* missing. I'll show you how good you have it there with your *loyal* husband."

"Until then, what's my strategy?"

"Your strategy?" she says excitedly; strategies are her specialty. "Well, for starters, no more snooping. I've been down that road . . . Nothing good comes from it."

"Okay," I say, cradling the phone under my ear, and stuffing a load of darks into the washer. A pair of Nick's red plaid boxers fall onto the laundry room floor, and as I pick them up, I tell myself that nobody has seen his underwear but me. "What else?"

"Exercise. Meditate. Eat healthy foods. Get lots of sleep. Brighten up your highlights. Buy some new shoes," she says, as if reading from a list of commandments about how to be happy. "And above all else, don't give Nick a hard time. No nagging. No guilt trips. Just . . . be *nice* to him."

"To give him an incentive not to cheat?" I say.

"No. Because you believe he's *not* cheating."

I smile my first real smile in days, glad that I confided in Cate, glad that I'm going to see her soon, glad that I married someone who has earned my best friend's benefit of the doubt.

26
VALERIE

On the night before Charlie's first day back to school, Nick stops over to wish him good luck, but ends up staying to make dinner, declaring himself a burger connoisseur as he prepares the patties, then hovers over the George Foreman grill. Although Valerie has exchanged dozens of calls and text messages with him, it is the first she has seen him since Thanksgiving and she feels giddy to be standing next to him, the only thing that could assuage her nervousness over Charlie's return to school.

She watches her son now, playing with his *Star Wars* action figures at the kitchen table, as he asks Nick about his mask — which is resting on the table beside him. "Do I have to wear it?" he says. "To school?"

"Yeah, buddy," he says. "Especially for gym and recess . . . You can take it off now and then if it's bothering you or making you sweaty or itchy, but it's a good idea to keep it on."

Charlie furrows his brow, as if considering this, and then says, "Do you think I look better with it or without it?"

Valerie and Nick exchange a worried glance.

"You look great both ways," Valerie says.

"Yeah," Nick agrees. "Your skin is healing great . . . but the mask is way cool."

Charlie smiles as Nick transfers their burgers onto three open buns, the sight of which gives Valerie a jolt of joy. "Yeah. You can tell your friends that you're a stormtrooper."

Nick nods. "And that *you* know Darth Vader."

"Can I?" Charlie says, looking expectantly at Valerie.

"Yes," she replies emphatically, thinking she'd say *yes* to just about anything tonight, that they have earned the right to do what-ever they want. She knows in her heart that it doesn't work like this. That misfortune doesn't give you the right to disregard oth-ers, ignore the rules, tell lies and half-truths.

Still considering this, she carries two of the three plates to the table, Nick with the third, Charlie trailing behind. The three of them sit together at the small, round kitchen table, covered with deep grooves and scratches and permanent marker from Charlie's art projects, a contrast to the fine, blue and yellow linen napkins and place mats that Jason brought back to her from his trip to Provence last summer, the one he had taken with his boyfriend before Hank.

"We're glad you're here," Valerie murmurs to Nick, her version of grace. She looks down at the napkin on her lap while Charlie offers a more formal blessing, giving himself the sign of the cross before and after, just as his grandmother taught him.

Nick joins in the ritual, saying, "I feel like I'm at my mother's house."

"Is that a good thing?" Valerie asks.

"Yeah," he says. "Only you look nothing like my mother . . ."

They grin at one another, launching into lighthearted topics while they eat their burgers, fries, and string beans. They talk about the big snowfall expected midweek. Christmas right around the corner. Charlie's desire for a puppy, to which Valerie can feel herself succumbing. All the while, she does her very best to ignore the thought of two other children, having supper at home with their mother.

After they finish eating, they clear the table together, rinsing, loading the dishwasher, laughing, until Nick abruptly tells them he has to go. As Valerie watches him kneel down to give Charlie a gift, a gold coin for good luck, she thinks that this is almost better than continuing what they had started three nights before. She loves spending time alone with him, but loves watching him with Charlie more.

"This was mine — when I was little," Nick says. "I want you to have it."

Charlie nods reverently, then takes the gift in his hands, his face lighting up, looking as whole and beautiful as she has ever seen him. She almost instructs him to say thank you, her instinctive response whenever Charlie is given a gift, but this time, she says nothing, not wanting to interrupt their moment, sure that Charlie's smile says it all.

"Reach in your pocket and touch this if you start to worry about anything," Nick says. Then he slips a piece of paper into her son's other hand. "And memorize this number. If you need to call me, for any reason, at any time, you call me."

Charlie nods earnestly, looking down at the paper, whispering the numbers aloud as she walks Nick to the door.

"Thank you," she says when they get there, her hand on the doorknob. She is thanking him for the burgers, the coin, the number in her son's hand. But most of all, for getting them to this night.

He shakes his head, as if to tell her that this, *all* of this, is something he *wanted* to do, something that requires no gratitude on her part. He glances in Charlie's direction, and upon realizing they are not being watched, he takes her face in his hands and kisses her once, softly, on the lips. It is not the first kiss she has imagined so many times, more sweet than passionate, but a chill still runs along her spine and her knees go weak.

"Good luck tomorrow," he whispers.

She smiles, feeling luckier than she has in a long time.

The next morning, she is up before dawn. She showers, then heads for the kitchen where she sets about making French toast for Charlie's first day back to school, her first official day back to work. She arranges all the ingredients on the counter — four slices of challah bread, eggs, milk, cinnamon, powdered sugar, and syrup. Even freshly cut strawberries. She takes out a small bowl, a whisk, and a can of nonstick spray. She is nervous and calm at once, the way she feels before a big case when she knows she's done everything she can to prepare but still feels worried about things out of her control. She tightens the belt of her fleecy white robe and shuffles over to the thermostat, turning it up to seventy-four, wanting Charlie to be warm when he comes down for breakfast, wanting everything to go right for him on this critical morning. Then she returns to the stove, where she whisks together the ingredients and sprays the bottom of her skillet as worrisome images flash in her head: Charlie falling off the monkey bars, tearing his new skin. Getting teased about his mask — or worse, teased if he chooses to take it off.

She shuts her eyes, tells herself what Nick has been telling her for days — that nothing is going to go wrong. That she has done everything she can to prepare for this day, including phoning the headmaster and school nurse and guidance counselor and Charlie's lead teacher to let them all know that Charlie will be back, that she will walk him in rather than dropping him off in the usual car-pool line, that she wants to be contacted at the first hint of a problem — whether emotional or physical.

"French toast!" she hears Charlie say behind her. Surprised that he woke up on his own when she usually has to drag him out of bed, she turns around to see him in his pajamas, barefoot, holding his mask in one hand, the gold coin in the other. He is smiling. She smiles back at him, praying that he stays in this mood all day.

And he does, at least that whole morning, showing no signs of worry or fear as they go through their morning ritual — eating, dressing, brushing teeth and hair — then driving to school, listening to the disc of soothing music Nick burned for him last week.

When they arrive in the parking lot, Charlie puts on his mask, quickly and quietly, as Valerie debates whether to say something to him. Something momentous or at least comforting. Instead, she follows his lead, pretending that nothing is out of the ordinary on this day, coming around to the backseat, opening the door for him, resisting the urge to help him unbuckle his seat belt or take his hand.

As they walk in the main entrance, a cluster of older kids — Valerie guesses fourth or fifth graders — look up and stare at Charlie. A pretty girl with long, blond pigtails clears her throat and says, "Hi, Charlie," as if she not only knows who he is, but knows every detail of his story.

Charlie whispers a barely audible hello,

nestling closer to Valerie, taking her hand. Valerie feels herself tense, but when she looks down at him, she can see her son smiling. He is okay. He is happy to be back. He is braver than she is.

A few moments and hellos later, they arrive in his classroom, his two teachers and a dozen classmates gathering affectionately, enthusiastically, around him. Everyone but Grayson, that is, who is in the corner by the hamster cage with an expression she can't quite place, the expression of a child who has overheard one too many adult conversations.

She lingers for as long as she can, casting occasional glances Grayson's way, until Charlie's lead teacher, Martha, a kindly grandmother type, flicks off the light, the signal for the children to go to the rug. At this point, Valerie hesitates, then leans down to kiss Charlie good-bye, whispering in his ear, "Be nice to Grayson today."

"Why?" he says. His eyes flicker with confusion.

"Because he's your friend," she says simply.

"Are you still mad at his mommy?"

She looks at him, feeling shock and shame wash over her, wondering how he has interpreted such a thing, what conversation *he* overheard, what else Charlie has picked up over the past few weeks, unbeknownst to her.

"No. I'm not mad at his mommy," she lies. "And I *really* like Grayson."

Charlie reaches up to slightly adjust his mask, processing this, nodding.

"Okay, sweetie," she says, feeling her throat constrict as it did on his first day of kindergarten, but for very different reasons now. "Be care —"

"I'll be careful, Mommy," he says, interrupting her. "Don't worry . . . I'll be okay."

Then he turns to walk away from her, going to the edge of the rug where he sits cross-legged, his back straight, his hands folded in his lap, the good one tucked over the bad.

27
TESSA

I'm not sure why I wait until Tuesday night to tell Nick about my trip to New York — or why I feel as anxious as I do, unable to look him in the eye, focusing instead on slicing open our American Express bill that just came in the mail. It's a sad day when you'd rather look at a credit card statement than your husband's face, I think, as I say as nonchalantly as possible, "I decided to go to New York this weekend."

"This weekend?" he asks, perplexed.

"Yes," I say, skimming the charges, surprised for the umpteenth time at how quickly things add up even when you're trying *not* to spend.

"As in this Friday?"

"As in this Friday," I say, giving him a sideways glance, feeling somehow emboldened by his look of bewilderment. Satisfied that, for once, *I* am the one catching *him* off guard; I am the one telling *him* what *my* schedule is going to be.

"Gee. Thanks for the notice," he says with good-natured sarcasm.

I bristle, focusing on the sarcasm, rather than his smile, thinking of the number of times he has failed to give *me* notice, or suddenly changed our plans, or canceled them, or left in the middle of dinner or the weekend. But following Cate's advice, I am careful not to start an argument, feigning a considerate, wifely tone. "I know it's sudden . . . But I really need some time away. You're not on call, are you?"

He shakes his head no as our eyes meet, a mutual look of skepticism passing between us. I suddenly realize that this will be the first time he's ever been alone with the kids overnight. *Ever.*

"So it's okay?" I say.

"Sure," he says reluctantly.

"Great," I return brightly. "Thanks for understanding."

He nods, then asks, "Are you staying with Cate? . . . Or Dex and Rachel?"

"Cate," I say, pleased that he asked the question so that I can say, "I'm sure I'll see my brother and Rachel. But I'm really in more of a go-out-and-get-drunk mode. Blow off some steam as only Cate knows how to do."

Translation: *Revert to my premarried self, the woman you couldn't keep your hands off, the girl you rushed home from the hospital every night to see.*

Nick nods and then picks up the AmEx statement, his eyes widening as they always do when he goes through our bills. "Damn," he says, shaking his head. "Just don't go shopping . . ."

"Too late," I say, pointing at my Saks bag in the hallway, further goading him. "Needed some new shoes to go out in . . ."

He rolls his eyes and says, "Oh, I see. I guess none of the thirty pairs you already own will suffice for a girls' night out?"

I roll my eyes back at him, feeling my smile stretch and tighten, thinking of Cate's closet. And April's. And even Rachel's — restrained by Manhattan banker wives' standards but still more indulgent than mine. The contrast between their rows and rows of jeweled and satin and edgy black leather, impossibly high-heeled designer footwear — and my understated, mostly sensible collection.

"You have no idea what a *lot* of shoes looks like," I say, a hint of defiance in my voice. "Seriously. I have a paltry wardrobe."

"Paltry? Really?" he says, raising one judgmental eyebrow.

"Well, not compared to a Somali villager . . . But in this context," I say, pointing 180 degrees around me, indicating our big-spending neighbors. "I am *not* a shopper . . . You know, Nick, you really should be glad you married me. You couldn't handle these other women."

I hold my breath, waiting for him to soften, smile a real smile, touch me, *anywhere,* and say something to the effect of: *Of course I'm glad I married you.*

Instead he appears thoughtful, moving on from the bill to a Barneys catalogue from which, incidentally, I have *never* ordered, as he says, "Do you think it's too late to get a sitter? For this weekend? I might want to go grab a few beers myself . . ."

"With whom?" I ask, instantly regretting it, trying to retract my suspicious question with a guileless smile.

It seems to work, although he still hesitates in a way that stabs my heart. I look at him, knowing I will replay this second of silence and the blank look on his face, just as I will replay the way he stumbles on his next words, "Oh, I don't . . . I don't know . . . Maybe alone . . ."

His voice trails off as I nervously fill the awkward gap. "I'll call Carolyn and see if she's free," I say, the word *enabler* springing to mind.

Then I turn and take my new shoes upstairs, thinking that if my husband is on the verge of cheating on me, at least he's not very good at it.

On Thursday morning, April convinces me to fill in for her usual doubles partner, who is home with a stomach bug, in a practice match against Romy and her longtime partner, Mary Catherine — known in tennis circles as MC because she occasionally bursts out with "Hammer Time!" when acing her opponents. In short, all three women take their tennis very seriously, and I am sure that my high school tennis team prowess won't live up to their religious ten hours a week of dedication to the game. And I'm even *more* sure when I see Romy and MC strut onto the indoor tennis court at Dedham Golf & Polo with their all-business, full-makeup game faces, and perfectly coordinated outfits, down to their matching wrist bands and sneakers — Romy in powder blue, MC in lavender.

"Hello, ladies," MC says in her husky voice. She removes her warm-up jacket and shakes out her arms, her biceps rippling like an Olympic swimmer's.

"Sorry we're late," Romy says, slipping

her short blond hair into a nubby ponytail and then stretching her hamstrings. "Nightmare of a morning. Grayson had *another* meltdown on the way to school. My decorator showed up thirty minutes late with positively *loathsome* fabric samples. And I spilled a bottle of nail polish remover all over our brand-new bathroom throw rug. I knew I shouldn't try to give myself a manicure!"

"Oh, honey! That sounds dreadful," April says, her tone changing as it always does when she gets around Romy. It's as if she wants to impress her or win her approval — which I find odd given that April seems smarter and more interesting than her friend.

"So. Tessa. April says you're a great player," MC says, cutting to the chase. She is the matriarch and captain of their tennis team, and apparently looking to fill one spot in their spring lineup. In other words, I am clearly auditioning today. "You played in college?"

"No!" I say, appalled with the misrepresentation.

"Yes you did," April says, running her hand across her newly restrung racket and then opening a can of balls.

"No, I *didn't*. I played in *high school*. And

I didn't touch a racket for years until I quit my job last year," I say, setting the record straight and lowering everyone's expectations, including my own. Still, I feel a surprising current of competitiveness, something I haven't experienced in a long time. I want to be good today. I *need* to be good today. Or at least competent.

For the next few minutes, the four of us make small talk and warm up, hitting ground strokes as I replay my tennis instructor's advice from a recent lesson — keep my feet moving, my grip tight, approach the net on second serve returns. But as soon as we begin the match, all my competency melts away, and thanks to my inability to hold serve or win a point on my return side, April and I quickly find ourselves down a set and three–love.

"Sorry," I mumble after one particularly embarrassing return, an easy shot that I hit directly into the net. I am speaking mostly to April, but to Romy and MC, too, as I know I'm doing nothing to help hone their skills or elevate their level of play.

"No worries!" Romy shouts, barely winded, her makeup still perfect. "You're doing fine!" Her tone is patronizing, but encouraging.

Meanwhile, I gasp for air and wipe my

face with a towel, then chug from my water bottle, returning to the court with fresh determination. Fortunately, my play seems to improve slightly from there, and I even hit a few winning points, but within thirty more minutes, we are still facing match point, which MC announces as if speaking into a microphone on Centre Court at Wimbledon.

I feel a sudden surge of intense nervousness, as if the next point could prove life-changing. Gripping my racket in the ready position, I watch MC line her toes up behind the baseline, bounce her ball three times, and stare me down, in what is either her pre-serve visualization or an obvious attempt at intimidation.

"Serve already," I hear April mutter, as she finally tosses her ball in the air, simultaneously coiling her racket behind her head, crushing a slice serve with a Monica Seles–esque grunt.

The ball whizzes over the net, spins sideways, and slides off the singles line in the wide corner of my deuce service box, pushing me off the court. I spot the spin and the angle, stretching into the tennis version of a warrior-three yoga pose as I fully extend my arm and flip my wrist. The frame of my racket barely makes contact with the ball yet I still manage a high, deep forehand return. Feeling satisfied, I watch the ball lob its way down the line toward Romy, who yells "Mine! Mine!" a crucial instruction when playing with MC.

Romy hits an overhead up the middle.

"You!" April shouts as I, once again, stretch to make contact, this time with an awkward backhand that somehow manages to place the ball on the other side of the net.

MC hits a high forehand volley back to April, who returns with a topspin forehand of her own. My heart races as Romy's half volley sends the ball back to me, and I return it with a lucky lob deep in MC's court.

And so on and so on until the point culminates in a dramatic, close-to-the-net, reflex-volley exhibition, finally ending when MC gets her racket over the ball, smashing it directly into me.

Hammer Time.

"Game, set, match!" she yells jubilantly.

I force a smile as we all walk to the sidelines, where we gulp from our water bottles and rehash the last point — or at least MC rehashes it. Then she turns to me and mentions that they are looking for a new team member.

"Would you be interested?" she asks while April beams, proud of her latest project — to remake me into one of the glamour girls of Wellesley.

"Yeah," I say, thinking that I could get used to this life, a thought I have again after we shower, reconvene, and indulge in an après-tennis lunch at the juice bar, sipping protein shakes and commencing rigorous girl talk. We cover shoes and jewelry, Botox and plastic surgery, our diet and exercise regimes (or lack thereof), and our nannies, babysitters, and housekeepers. The conversation is mostly shallow and mindless, but I enjoy every minute of it, loving the utter escapism, akin to opening a tabloid magazine. I sheepishly admit to myself that I also like the feeling of belonging, of being included in their elite clique. It occurs to me that I haven't had a true group of friends since Cate and I joined a sorority in college, perhaps because I typically prefer one-on-one friendships, but more likely because I have a family now. It also occurs to me that Nick would scoff if he could hear the Cliff's Notes of our conversation — which, in turn, makes me feel defensive and all the more resentful.

Perhaps for this reason, I am unfazed when Romy finally gets down to the subject of Charlie. "Charlie Anderson is back at school this week," she says, sipping her mango shake, gingerly broaching the subject.

"That's great news!" April says, her voice an unnaturally high octave.

I echo the sentiment, murmuring something noncommittal but supportive, my way of giving Romy permission to say more.

"Yeah, I know," Romy says, letting out a huge sigh.

"Tell them about Grayson," MC prompts.

Romy pretends to balk, shaking her head, looking down at the table. "I don't want to make Tessa uncomfortable," she says.

"It's okay," I say, meaning it. "And whatever you say, I'll keep it to myself."

She flashes me a small, grateful smile, and says, "Grayson's having a rough time at school," she says. "He's still going through post-traumatic stress syndrome and I think seeing Charlie again has brought back a lot of bad memories."

"That must be hard," I say, feeling genuinely sympathetic.

"And on top of that," Romy says. "Charlie's not being very nice to Grayson."

"Really?" I say, surprised to hear this — and still a bit skeptical of the source.

"Well, it's not that he's being *mean,* per

se. He's just . . . ignoring him. They aren't nearly as close as they once were . . ."

I nod, thinking of Ruby's class, how the mean-girl syndrome has already begun, the popularity dynamic shifting on a weekly basis as the girls recast their silent votes for four-year-old queen bee status and realign accordingly. So far Ruby has managed to dwell somewhere in the middle — not a victim, not the predator. It is where I always managed to linger, and where I hope she stays, too. "Maybe he's just shy?" I say. "Or self-conscious."

"Maybe," Romy says. "He is wearing a mask — as I'm sure you know."

I shake my head and say, "No. Nick and I really haven't talked about the case."

Romy says, "Well, in any event, I think Charlie being back just makes Grayson feel worse . . . Maybe even a little guilty since it happened at his party."

"He shouldn't feel guilty," I say, which is clearly the truth.

"And neither should *you,*" April says to Romy.

I nod, although I'm not sure I'm willing to go this far in the analysis.

"Have you run into her again? Valerie Anderson?" MC asks. "Since that day at the hospital?"

"No. Fortunately," Romy says, biting her lower lip, appearing lost in thought. She shakes her head. "I just don't understand that woman."

"I don't, either," April says.

Romy's face brightens as she turns to me. "Did April tell you we saw your cute husband at the hospital? What a doll."

I nod and smile, relieved that I don't have to weigh in on the issue of Romy's accountability and corresponding guilt.

"I love a man in scrubs," she says.

"Yeah. I used to feel that way," I say, cynicism creeping into my voice.

"What happened?" Romy asks, smiling.

"I married him," I say, laughing, but only half kidding.

"Yeah, *right,*" April says, then turns to Romy. "Tessa has the perfect marriage. They *never* fight. And he's watching the kids all weekend so she can go to New York and play."

"He can handle the kids alone?" Romy asks, amazed.

I start to tell her that I have Carolyn lined up to bridge the gap between my departure tomorrow afternoon and his return from work, as well as giving him a break over the weekend, but April answers for me, gushing, "He's great with the kids. The *best* father. I'm telling you — they have the *perfect* marriage."

I give her a look, wondering why she's trying to pitch me so hard — my children, my tennis game, now my marriage. I appreciate it, but have the sense she's overcompensating for something, perhaps for the fact that I don't pull off that instant, cool first impression. Although it's good to know that Nick does. In his scrubs.

Romy and MC give me a wistful look that makes me feel like a June Cleaver imposter as I consider what the past few weeks have looked like in my house.

"Nobody has the perfect marriage," I say.

MC vigorously shakes her head. "Nobody," she says, as if speaking from a wealth of experience.

We all fall silent as if contemplating our relationships until Romy says, "Speaking of . . . did you hear about Tina and Todd?"

"Don't *even* tell me," April says, covering her ears.

Romy pauses dramatically, then whispers, "With a *call girl.*"

"Omigod. You're kidding me," April says. "He seems like such a nice guy. He's an usher at our church, for God's sake!"

"Yeah. Well. Maybe he's stealing from the collection plate, too."

MC asks if it was a one-time thing and Romy turns to her and snaps, "Does that make a difference?"

"I guess not," MC says, finishing her shake with a final, long slurp.

"But for the record, no. It was *not* a one-time thing. Turns out he's been doing it for years. Just like — what was his name — that governor of New York?"

"Eliot Spitzer," I say, remembering how obsessed I was with that hooker scandal, and more specifically, with his wife, Silda. How I had marveled when she stood behind him at the podium, her eyes puffy and red, looking utterly defeated and disgraced as he confessed and resigned on national television. Literally standing by her man. I wondered how long she had deliberated on what to wear that morning. Whether she had Googled the hooker in question, poring over her pictures online or in the tabloids. What she said to her friends. To her three daughters. To her mother. To *him*.

"At least Tina doesn't have to face the nation," I say. "Can you imagine?"

"No," Romy says. "I can't believe these women go on television like that."

"Yeah," April says. "I'd be gone in a heartbeat."

MC and Romy murmur their agreement,

and then they all look at me, waiting for me to weigh in on the subject, giving me no choice but to tell them I am in perfect agreement. Which I am. I think.

"Would you find it harder to forgive a prostitute or a love affair?" April asks, reading my mind.

MC chortles. "Burned to death or drowned?" Then she turns to Romy and says, "Sorry, hon. Unfortunate choice of words. Damn. I always put my foot in my mouth . . ."

Romy shakes her head somberly and reaches out to pat MC's hand. "It's okay, hon. I know what you meant." Then she fiddles with her diamond ring, spinning it twice around, and says, "I could never forgive Daniel if he slept with a hooker. It's just so gross. I couldn't forgive anything that *sleazy*. I'd rather he fall in love with someone."

"Really?" MC says. "I think I could get over something physical — maybe not a hooker, but a purely physical, one-night-stand kind of thing . . . But if Rick actually loved someone . . . that's a different story."

April looks contemplative and then says to me, "What would bother you more, Tess? Hot sex or love?"

I consider this for a second, then say,

"Depends."

"On what?" Romy says.

"On whether he's having hot sex with the girl he loves."

They all laugh as I think of Nick's text, feeling sick to my stomach, hoping that I never have to find out exactly what I'd do in any of the above scenarios.

28
VALERIE

Charlie Anderson has a purple alien face.

They are words Valerie knows will be seared into his consciousness forever, part of his indelible life story, along with Summer Turner, the little girl who convinced him to remove his mask and show her his scars, right before issuing the cruel proclamation that made three children laugh, Grayson among them.

It happened on the Friday of Charlie's first week back to school, just as Valerie was finally feeling optimistic. Not home free by any means, but out of the danger zone. She had just successfully argued a motion for summary judgment in front of a notoriously misogynistic judge, leaving the courthouse with a renewed sense of confidence that comes with success, with the feeling of being good at something. Life was returning to normal, she thought, as she reached into her purse for her keys and checked her cell phone, seeing four missed calls, two from Nick, two from the school. She had only turned her phone off for an hour, a rule at the courthouse, and although it occurred to her that something *could* happen in that short a window, she didn't think that it actually would. Envisioning another accident, and knowing that she could get a report from Nick faster than a web of secretaries at the school, she frantically got into the car and dialed his number, bracing herself for his medical report.

"Hi there," Nick answered in such a way that confirmed to Valerie that the calls *were* about Charlie, and that something bad *had* happened, but that it wasn't as dire as she feared. She felt her panic recede slightly as she asked, "Is Charlie okay?"

"Yes. He's fine."

"He wasn't hurt?"

"No . . . Not physically . . . But there was an incident," Nick said calmly. "The school tried to call you first —"

"I know. I was in court," she said, feeling overwhelming guilt for being unavailable, and even more so for allowing herself to care about work, however fleetingly.

"Did you win?" Nick asked.

"Yeah," she said.

"Congratulations," he said.

"Nick. What kind of an incident?"

"A . . . playground incident."

Valerie's heart sank as he continued, "A little girl called him a name. A few kids laughed. Charlie got mad and pushed her off the monkey bars. She's a little scraped up. They're both here in the headmaster's office."

"Where are you?"

"With Charlie. I just stepped out of the office for a second to take your call . . . When your secretary told the headmaster you were in court, Charlie gave them my number. He was pretty upset — about the name-calling, about getting in trouble."

"Is he crying?" she asked, her heart breaking.

"Not anymore . . . He's calmed down . . . He'll be all right."

"I'm sorry . . ." Valerie said, feeling somewhat surprised that Charlie didn't call Jason or her mother before Nick. "I know how busy you are . . ."

"Please don't be sorry. I'm glad he called me . . . I'm glad I could come."

"I am, too," she said, stepping on the gas pedal, feeling a vague sense of déjà vu. "I'll be there as soon as I can."

"Take your time. Be careful. I'll be here."

"Thank you," Valerie said. She nearly

hung up, but instead mustered the courage to ask what the little girl had said to Charlie.

"What?" Nick said, clearly stalling, doing his best to evade her question.

"The little girl. What did she call Charlie?"

"Oh . . . That . . . It was ridiculous . . . It doesn't matter."

"Tell me," she said, steeling herself.

He hesitated and then replied, his voice so quiet and muffled that she wasn't sure she heard him right. But she had. She shook her head, seething, almost scaring herself by the venom she could feel for a six-year-old child.

"Val?" Nick said, the tenderness in his voice making her eyes fill with tears.

"What?"

"It'll only make him stronger," he said.

Minutes later, a school receptionist ushers Valerie into the headmaster's office, a stately room decorated with oriental rugs, antique furniture, and a large bronze statue of a horse. She sees Summer first, perched on a leather wing chair, sniffling and cradling her arm. With long platinum-blond hair, bright green eyes, and a delicate, upturned nose, she reminds Valerie of a preteen Barbie doll.

She clearly is a fast girl in the making, dressed in an alarmingly short jean skirt, pink Uggs, and sparkly lip gloss. Valerie remembers thinking she was trouble on the first day of school as she watched a trio of mousy-brown-haired girls follow Summer around the classroom like ladies-in-waiting. Ironically, she also remembers feeling grateful she had a boy. They were so much less complicated, especially those not yet prone to crushes. For the time being at least, Charlie was immune to the likes of Summer.

But that was before.

Purple alien face.

She makes eye contact with Summer, doing her best to telepathically communicate hatred as she steps the whole way into the office, now spotting Charlie, Nick, and Mr. Peterson, the headmaster, a tall, slender man with a youthful face, premature gray hair, and owlish, wire-rimmed glasses.

"Thank you for coming," Mr. Peterson says, rising from behind his hulking walnut desk. He has a slight lisp and modest manner that offsets his position of authority.

"Of course," Valerie says, then apologizes for being unavailable when he first called.

"Not at all . . . We were all fine. It gave us a chance to chat . . . And it was so wonderful to meet Dr. Russo," he says, just as Nick stands, looking uncomfortable. He murmurs to Valerie, "I'll wait for you outside," then exchanges final pleasantries with Mr. Peterson before making a discreet exit.

Valerie takes Nick's chair, resting her hand on Charlie's knee. She looks at him, but he refuses to look back at her, staring down at his double-knotted sneaker laces. His mask is back on, where Valerie has a feeling it will stay for a long time to come.

"We're just waiting for Summer's mother," Mr. Peterson says, drumming his long fingers on the edge of his desk. "She's coming from work, too. Will be here shortly."

A moment of small talk later, an older, heavyset woman with a severe bob and an ill-fitting, shoulder-padded suit bursts into the room, breathless. She does not wait for Mr. Peterson to make her introduction, reaching out to shake Valerie's hand with an unusual blend of confidence and shyness.

"I'm Beverly Turner," she says. "You must be Charlie's mother. I heard what happened. I'm so sorry." Then she kneels down and apologizes to Charlie while Summer begins to sob — an obvious bid for sympathy which does not work. Instead, Beverly shoots her a fierce look, one that further disarms Valerie. She can even feel herself softening to the little girl — which she

340

thought impossible only seconds before.

"Did you apologize to Charlie?" Beverly Turner asks her daughter, her face stern.

"Yes," Summer says, her bottom lip quivering.

Beverly is unfazed as she turns to Charlie and asks for confirmation, "Did she?"

Charlie nods, still staring at his shoes.

"But he didn't say *he* was sorry," Summer says, whimpering. "For what he did to me."

"Charlie?" Valerie prompts.

He adjusts his mask, then shakes his head in refusal.

"Two wrongs don't make a right," Valerie continues, although she secretly believes they almost might. "Tell her you're sorry for pushing her."

"I'm sorry," Charlie says. "For pushing you."

"Well, then. Very good. Very good," Mr. Peterson says, looking pleased. His palms come together as Valerie focuses on his gold signet ring. She pretends to listen to his eloquent speech that follows — graceful words about getting along and being respectful members of the community, but she can't stop thinking of Nick, waiting for them outside, both loving and fearing how dependent she has become on him.

Mr. Peterson concludes his talk, standing

and dismissing them all for the day, offering both mothers a final handshake. Once outside his office, Valerie breathes a sigh of relief as Beverly lowers her voice and apologizes a final time. Her expression is pained and sincere — more sincere than Romy's ever was.

"I know how much you've been through . . . I'm so sorry Summer added to that burden." She turns away from her daughter and says in an even lower voice, "I recently remarried . . . I have two stepdaughters now — teenagers — and I think the adjustment has been really tough for Summer . . . Not that I'm making any excuses for what she did."

Valerie nods, feeling genuine compassion for her situation, thinking that she'd almost rather have a victim than a mean child. Almost.

"Thank you," she says as she catches a glimpse of Nick, waiting for them by the exit, the sight of him making her pulse quicken. Charlie runs toward him, taking his hand, leading him toward the parking lot.

She says good-bye to Beverly, with the odd feeling that they could actually be friends, and a moment later, she is standing next to her car, watching as Nick opens Charlie's door, helps him into his seat, and pulls his belt across his narrow chest. "It's going to be okay, buddy," he says.

Charlie nods, as if he believes him, but then says, "I hate the way I look."

"Hey. Wait. Wait just a second here . . . Are you telling me you hate my work?" Nick reaches up and gently removes his mask, pointing at Charlie's left cheek. "I made that skin. You don't like my work? My art project?"

Charlie smiles a small smile, and says, "I *do* like your art project."

"Well, good . . . I'm glad . . . Because I like your face. I like it a *lot*."

Charlie's smile widens as Nick closes Charlie's door, then leans in to whisper in Valerie's ear, "And I love your face."

Valerie closes her eyes and inhales his skin, feeling a rush of attraction and adrenaline that causes her to forget where she is for a few disorienting seconds. As the feeling of light-headedness passes, something catches her eye across the parking lot. A woman sitting in a black Range Rover, watching them. Valerie squints into the sun, looking straight at Romy, who is peering back at her with an expression of surprise and distinct satisfaction.

29
TESSA

Going out with Cate is better than therapy, I decide, as we saunter down Bank Street right past the paparazzi gathered on the sidewalk outside the Waverly Inn, where she guarantees we can get in without a reservation, jokingly referring to her D-list fame.

"Did they know you were coming?" I ask, motioning toward the cameramen, who are standing around and smoking in their puffy North Face jackets and black skullcaps.

She tells me not to be ridiculous, that there must be a *legitimate* celebrity inside as a pair of twenty-something girls with artfully tousled, long-layered hair nod their confirmation.

"Yup. Jude Law," the brunette says, raising her hand to flag a cab, while the blonde expertly touches up her lip gloss, without a mirror, and dreamily murmurs, "He's so freakin' hot . . . His friend wasn't too bad, either."

The brunette adds, "I wouldn't kick either of them outta bed, that's for sure," right before the two slip into their taxi, on to their next venue.

I smile, thinking that this is exactly what I need tonight — to be at a trendy West Village restaurant in the company of paparazzi-worthy stars and a beautiful crowd, an absolute contrast to my real life. On some nights since I became a mother, such a scene might intimidate me, make me feel matronly and clueless, but tonight I have the feeling that I have nothing to lose. At least nothing I could lose at the banquette beside Jude Law, where Cate and I wind up sitting.

Just after we order two glasses of syrah, I consult my watch, thinking of the kids and Carolyn's scheduled hours, all the details I orchestrated to make sure that the weekend runs smoothly without me. Nick should be returning home from work just about now, and I take secret satisfaction in the fact that I am out and he is at home with bedtime duties.

"So," I say, glancing around the shabby but somehow still debonair dining room. "This is the new Manhattan hot spot?"

"Not *new*. God, Tess. You *have* been gone for a long time . . . But it's still hot. I mean, we're here, aren't we?" she says over the cozy din, gesturing between us, tossing back her richly highlighted hair, lately drifting toward the reddish-blond hues and quickly becoming her signature look. Aware that she is the recipient of a few double takes, she plays it cool, casually glancing in Jude Law's direction. She flashes a smile, her dimples emerging, then leans across the table and says, "Don't look now but guess who just checked us out?"

"I don't know who just checked *you* out," I say. "But I guarantee you, they're not checking *me* out."

"Yes they are," she says. "And that girl outside was right . . . his friend *is* cute. Maybe even cuter than Jude. Think of a cross between Orlando Bloom and . . . Richard Gere."

I turn and glance over my shoulder, more because I can't conjure such a combination than because I want the eye candy, as Cate hisses, "I said, '*Don't* look now.' "

"Whatever, Cate," I say, shaking my head. "It doesn't matter . . ."

"It *could* matter."

"For you maybe."

"For you, too. Never hurts to flirt."

"I'm the mother of two," I say. "I have no game."

"So? Did you somehow miss the expression 'MILF'?" she says.

I give her a puzzled look as she tosses her hair over the other shoulder and says, "Mother I'd Like to Fuck?"

"Cate!" I say, shaking my head. "Don't be so crass."

"Since when did you turn into such a prude?"

"Since I gave birth. Twice," I say, conscious of the fact that I become more uptight when I'm around Cate — while she diverges in a shallow, party-girl direction, neither of which reflects the real truth. It's almost as if we hope our extremes will bring the other back to a place somewhere in the middle — where we both began, years ago. Then again, maybe we *have* become exaggerated versions of ourselves. Maybe it will only get worse over time, I think — a depressing thought, at least for me.

She shrugs and says, "So? You're a mother of two? Does that mean you can't have a little fun? That you have to sit around in the suburbs in pastel scrunchies and pleated mom jeans?"

"As opposed to plain-front mom jeans?" I deadpan — although, in truth, I have not fallen this far, not yet lapsing into mom-jean terrain. "You think that's why Nick is cheating on me?"

She ignores this, just as she's ignored my last five references to Nick and infidelity, and says, "Back to Jude. Please."

"Didn't he sleep with his nanny?"

"I'm pretty sure he didn't sleep with *his* nanny," she says. "I'm pretty sure it was his *kids'* nanny. And, shit, Tess. That was a zillion years ago. You sure do hold a grudge . . . I guess you're still miffed at Hugh Grant for the Divine Brown incident? And Rob Lowe for the sex tape?"

"I'm not miffed at any of them. I'm all about second chances. For anyone but Nick," I say emphatically, thinking back to my discussion with Romy, April, and MC, finally feeling decisive on the topic. Hookers, love affairs — anything in between. All indefensible, all unforgivable. That is my final position, I silently decide.

She gives me an incredulous stare, steadfastly refusing to believe that Nick is capable of being anything other than a decent guy.

"C'mon. Please tell me you've rid yourself of this crazy notion?" she says, lowering her voice as our wine arrives.

"I don't know," I say, thinking of Nick's elusiveness this afternoon. How he was unavailable virtually all day, even when I called him three times from the airport. I take my first swallow of wine, feeling an instant buzz — or at least a good feeling, enough to numb me as I utter my next statement. "He's either up to no good or really out of it. Big-time disengaged. Something is up."

Cate smirks, refusing to take the subject seriously. "Okay. If he *were* up to something — and I know he's not . . . Would you go there?" she says, nodding toward the corner booth once again.

"Go where?" I ask.

"Would you get even? Take a lover? A revenge screw?"

I take a longer drink of wine and humor her. "Absolutely. Hell — I might even have a three-way," I say, doing my best to shock her, which of course doesn't work.

"Jude *and* his friend?" she asks, appearing intrigued by the notion — or perhaps visualizing such a tryst from her colorful past. Her still colorful present.

"Sure," I say, playing along. "Or Jude and his nanny."

Cate laughs and then flips over her menu, informing me that she already knows what she wants.

"What's that?" I say, perusing my options.

"The frisée aux lardons salad, the chicken-liver mousse, and the steamed artichoke," she rattles off, clearly a regular.

"And a little Mr. Law for dessert?" I ask.

"You got that right," she says, grinning at me.

But moments after our entrees are cleared, just as we're joined by Rachel and Dex for an after-dinner drink at the bar, Jude and his friend are joined by two blondes, both of whom appear to be models, hovering near six feet, crazy pretty with nary a line on their faces. Despite the fact that I know Cate was mostly kidding about Jude, I can tell she is also disappointed that her chances with him went from very slim to nil, and even more deflated by the fact that the girls must be a full decade younger than we are.

"That figures," she says, as the canoodling commences.

"What's going on?" Rachel asks.

"Jude Law," I say. "In the corner."

She turns ever so slightly to catch a glimpse as Dex does a rapid 180.

"Jeez. You two are clearly related," Cate says with a fond smile. "Your sister got whiplash, too."

Dex turns back around and drapes his arm around my shoulder, too confident to be shamed by Cate.

"So how was the show?" I ask, referring to the off-Broadway play they just went to see, one of the many things Dex gladly does with Rachel — either at her request or because he actually wants to, both scenarios filling me with envy.

"It was interesting," Dex says. "But Rach fell asleep."

"I did not!" she says, frowning at a loose button on her long, sheer black cardigan. "I just rested my eyes for a second."

"While you snored and drooled," Dex says, working his way into a space near the bar and ordering a vodka martini for Rachel and an Amstel Light for himself. Then he makes a face and says, "So Jude Law. Didn't he sleep with the nanny?"

I laugh, proud of my brother's tabloid knowledge, even prouder of his disapproval of such reindeer games, which, combined with my now strong buzz, prompts me to say, "Do you think Nick would ever do something like that?"

"I don't know," Dex says. "How hot are your babysitters?"

I force a smile, one that my brother must see through because he looks at me, confused, then shifts his gaze to Cate and says, "What's going on here?"

"Nothing," Cate replies, reaching out to

tap my thigh. "She's just being a Paranoid Patty."

Dex looks at me again, awaiting an explanation. I can feel Rachel's eyes on me, too, as I hesitate and then say, "I just . . . have a bad feeling lately."

"What do you mean?" Dex asks. "What kind of a bad feeling?"

I swallow and shrug, unable to reply for fear that I will start crying.

"She thinks Nick might be having an affair," Cate says for me.

"Really?" he asks.

I nod, wishing that I had kept things lighthearted, thinking there is something so depressing about having this conversation, drunk, at a bar.

"Tell her it would *never* happen," Cate continues with her usual verve and rah-rah conviction.

"I can't see it," Dex says more somberly while Rachel is tellingly silent.

"Are you really worried?" my brother says. "Or is this just one of your weird 'what if' questions?"

"I'm . . . moderately worried," I say, hesitating, then deciding it's too late to turn back now. I finish my wine, then confess all my fears, spewing a verbatim account of the mystery text and asking for his candid guy's opinion. "Honestly. Doesn't that sound . . . fishy?"

"Well . . . I'm not wild about the 'thinking of you,' " Dex says, running his hand through his hair. "It definitely sounds like a girl . . . But it really isn't all that damning. Is that all you have on him?"

"That and the fact that he just seems so distant lately . . ."

Rachel nods, a little too quickly for my comfort, as if to say she noticed the same behavior during their recent visit.

"You see it, don't you?" I ask her.

"Well . . . I don't know . . ." she waffles. "Not really . . ."

"C'mon, Rach," I say, relinquishing my usual competitive feelings about our respective marriages. "Tell me. Did he seem odd when you were in town?"

"Not odd," she says, exchanging a telling glance with Dex. Clearly they've discussed us. "He's just . . . a little distracted, by nature . . . And I think he's just really passionate about his work. Which is admirable. But I can see how that could become frustrating for you . . . None of that means he's cheating, though . . . necessarily." Her voice trails off, leaving me with a pit in my stomach.

"Why don't you just ask him?" Dex says,

as the bartender serves up their drinks and I order another. "Wouldn't that be easier? Instead of speculating?"

"What?" I say. "Just bust out with, 'Are you cheating on me?' "

Dex shrugs and says, "Why not? Rachel's asked me that question before."

She hits his shoulder and says, "I have *not*."

"Oh, right. That was *you* I had the affair with," he says — which marks the very first time he's openly admitted to their early circumstances. He taps her nose as she gives him a scornful look and begins to blush.

Meanwhile, Cate pretends that this is a shocking revelation. "You two had an affair?" she says, hungry for more scoop.

Dex nods nonchalantly and says, "Pretty much."

"When you were engaged to that other girl?" Cate asks.

"Yep," Dex says while Rachel squirms on her stool and says her husband's name in quiet protest.

"Oh, come on, Rach. What's the big deal?" Dex says. "That was years ago. We're married with two kids . . . And we're all friends again."

Rachel stirs her drink as Cate's eyes

354

widen. "You're still friends with what's-her-name?"

"Darcy," Rachel says, nodding. "Yeah . . . we're friends again."

"*Good* friends?" Cate says, aghast, finally reaching her shocked threshold.

"I guess you could say that," Rachel says with a sheepish look. "Pretty good friends. Yeah."

"They talk every day," Dex says matter-of-factly.

"Are you serious?" Cate says.

"*Every* day," Dex says. "Multiple times a day. They're planning a vacation together — a cozy foursome . . . I get to go on a ski trip with my ex-fiancée."

"Okay. So what's my takeaway supposed to be here?" I ask wryly. "That if Nick is having an affair, perhaps I'll have a new best friend? A travel companion?"

Rachel uncrosses her arms and slides an olive off her toothpick, popping it into her mouth. She chews and swallows, then says, "Yeah, Dex. What, exactly, *is* your point?"

"I dunno," he says, shrugging. "I just thought we were making confessions here. Tess reads Nick's texts. And I . . . I cheated on my fiancée with you . . ."

Rachel clears her throat and says, "His point, I think, is that even good guys can

355

cheat . . . But it only happens if they're in the wrong relationship — and only for the right person. And because you and Nick have a great relationship, you really have nothing to worry about."

Dex nods and says, "It might sound like an excuse . . . a justification. But I think it happens to people. But not if they're happy. Not if their relationship is where it should be."

I nod, reaching into my purse for my phone, hoping to see Nick's name in my in-box, feeling relief when I see that he called me twice in the past hour, then slight guilt for talking about him, albeit with family and my best friend.

"Did he call?" Cate asks.

"Yeah. Twice," I say, almost smiling.

"See? He's getting a bad rap. He's home, babysitting the kids, calling you multiple times —" Cate says.

I interrupt her and say, "It's not *babysitting* when it's with your own children." Then, just as I'm about to put my phone away, I notice an e-mail from April, the subject line marked *urgent.* Although I feel certain that it's anything *but* urgent, and that it is simply one of her usual e-mails, covering one of our everyday topics — the kids, cooking, tennis, retail decisions, neighborhood gossip — I still click on it and read.

"Shit," I hear myself say aloud, shaking my head as I reread her sentences: *Call me ASAP. It's about Nick.*

"What?" Cate says.

Speechless, I hand her the phone, and she silently passes it along to Dex as Rachel reads it over his shoulder. They all fall silent, as I look away, my vision growing blurry and my head pounding, as if fast-forwarding directly to the hangover I'm sure to have tomorrow morning.

My husband is having an affair, I think, feeling sure of it now. Someone has seen Nick with a woman. Someone knows something. And the information has worked its way to April, who feels that she has no choice but to tell me. There is no other explanation. Yet a small part of me still clings to the slimmest, fragile hope as I watch Rachel flounder about, grasping at the same slight possibility.

"It could be anything," she says, her voice soft, worried.

"Like . . . what?" I say.

She gives me a blank stare as Cate tries another reassuring angle. "April is an alarmist. She loves drama. You've said so yourself . . . It might be circumstantial evidence.

Don't jump to conclusions."

"Just call her," Dex says, his eyes flashing, his jaw falling into an angry line as I fleetingly consider who would win in a fight — my husband or brother. "Or call Nick. Call someone, Tess."

"Now?" I say, my heart starting to race, the room spinning.

"Yeah," he says. "Right now."

"At the bar?" Rachel says anxiously. "It's too loud in here."

"Way too loud," Cate agrees, shooting Dex an uneasy look.

They commence a discussion of my strategy, who I should call first, and where I should go to have the conversation that could potentially change my life — the ladies' room, another bar, the street, Cate's apartment. I shake my head and slip my phone back into my bag.

"What're you doing?" Dex says.

"I don't want to know," I say, completely aware of how foolish I sound.

"What do you mean?" he asks, incredulous.

"I mean . . . I don't want to know . . . Not now. Not tonight," I say again, surprising myself, right along with the three people who know and love me the most. Other than Nick. Maybe, apparently, *including* Nick.

30
VALERIE

Valerie spends the rest of the afternoon with Charlie, doing her best to distract him with some of his favorite things. They make hot fudge sundaes, watch *Star Wars,* read aloud from *A Wrinkle in Time,* and play whimsical duets on the piano. Despite the events of the day, they are having fun — the most satisfying, gratifying brand of parent-child fun. But all the while, she misses Nick, craving his touch and counting down the minutes until she can see him later as they have planned.

Now they are finally alone again, Charlie fast asleep upstairs, having literally nodded off in his chicken nuggets. They've just finished their own dinner — linguine and clams from Antonio's that they ate by candlelight — and have retired to the family room where the curtains are drawn, the lights are dimmed, and Willie Nelson is crooning "Georgia on My Mind" from a random mix of mellow songs that she made with Nick in mind. They have not yet touched, but she has the sense that they soon will, that something momentous, irreversible, and potentially life-changing is in the works. She knows that what she is feeling is wrong, but she believes in it — believes in *him.* She tells herself that he would not lead her down this path if he didn't have a plan — if he didn't believe in her, too.

He reaches out to take her hand and says, "I'm glad he pushed that little brat off those monkey bars."

Valerie smiles. "I know . . . Her mother was very nice, though."

"Yeah?" Nick asks.

"Yeah. Surprisingly so."

"It's always nice when people surprise you for the better," he says, swirling the wine in his glass, then taking a long sip.

She watches him, wondering what he's thinking but unwilling to ask such a sappy question. Instead she says, "How long can you stay?"

He gives her a candid look, clears his throat, and tells her that he has a babysitter — a young girl who thinks nothing of staying up to the small hours of the morning. Then he looks back down at his wine, and says, "Tessa's in New York for the weekend . . . Visiting a friend and her brother."

It is the first time he's directly mentioned his wife in weeks, since their attraction exploded into sexual tension, and the first he's *ever* said her name.

Tessa, she thinks. *Her name is Tessa.*

The sweet soft-whisper of a name conjures a gentle, mirthful animal lover. The kind of woman who wears brightly colored bohemian scarves, designs jewelry, and breast-fed until her children reached a year, maybe longer. A woman who ice-skates on frozen ponds in the winter, plants forget-me-nots in the spring, goes fishing in the summer, and burns incense year-round. A woman with one dimple or a small gap between her front teeth or some other charming physical quirk.

Valerie realizes suddenly that she subconsciously hoped for a harder, sleeker name, like Brooke or Reese. Or a frivolous, spoiled name, like Annabel or Sabrina. Or a fusty, stodgy one — like Lois or Frances. Or one so commonplace in their generation that it lacked any connotation, like Stephanie or Kimberly. But no — Nick married a Tessa, a name that fills her with unexpected sadness more troubling than the guilt constantly playing at the edges of her mind. A guilt she refuses to examine too closely for fear that it will interfere with what she desperately wants.

Nick touches his bare big toe to hers, their legs outstretched on the coffee table. She squeezes his hand, as if to squelch the guilt and shock that she is capable of doing such a thing. That she is here, like this, with a married man. That she hopes they will soon be touching everywhere, and that maybe, someday, he will belong to her. It is an outlandish, selfish dream, but one that seems frighteningly attainable.

But first, she must tell him about the moment today in the parking lot, the look on Romy's face, an omission she fears might be significant enough to divert the course they are on. So she holds his hand tighter and says, "I have to tell you something."

"What's that?" he says, raising her hand to his mouth, kissing her thumb.

"Today," she says. "In the parking lot after school . . ."

"Hmm-mm?" he says, looking at her, a trace of worry appearing between his brows. He swirls the wine in his glass, then takes a sip.

She feels herself falter, but forges on. "When we were standing by my car . . . I saw Romy. She was watching us. She saw us together."

He nods, looking worried, but pretending not to be as he says, "Well. That figures, doesn't it?"

Valerie isn't sure what he means by this so she says, "Do you think it's a problem?"

Nick nods and says, "It could be."

This is not the answer she hoped for. "Really?" she asks.

He nods and says, "My wife knows her."

"They're *friends?*" she asks, horrified.

"Not exactly . . . They are more . . . acquaintances," he says. "They have a mutual good friend."

"Do you think it will get back to her?" Valerie asks, wondering how he can stay so calm, why he isn't rushing to the phone to do damage control.

"Maybe . . . Probably. Knowing this town. These women. Yeah, it'll probably get back to Tess eventually . . ."

Valerie turns over the nickname in her mind, no less troubling than the full form of her name. *Tess.* A woman who throws Frisbees to dogs, sings eighties songs into her shampoo bottle, does handstands in the fresh summer grass, wears her hair in French braids.

"Are you worried?" she asks, trying to gauge exactly what is going on in his head

— and more important, his marriage.

Nick turns to face her, resting one arm along the back of the couch. "Romy didn't see us like *this,*" he says, touching her shoulder and leaning in to kiss her forehead. "We were just standing there, weren't we?"

"Yeah . . . but how will you explain being there in the first place? At the school with us?" As soon as the question is out, she realizes that they have officially become co-conspirators.

Nick says, "I'll have to tell her that we're friends. That we've become close . . . That Charlie called me when he got hurt at school. And that I came over. As his doctor and your friend."

"Has anything like this ever . . . happened before? Have you ever become close to a patient? Or a patient's family member?" she asks.

"No," Nick says quickly. "Not like this. Nothing like this."

Valerie nods, knowing she should move on. Instead, she presses him. "What will she say? . . . If she finds out?"

"I don't know," he replies. "I can't even think about that right now . . ."

"But should you?" Valerie says. "Should we talk . . . about it?"

Nick bites his lower lip and says, "Okay.

Maybe we should."

She gives him a blank stare, indicating that it is his conversation to begin.

He clears his throat and says, "What do you want to know? I will tell you anything you want to know."

"Are you happy?" she asks — one of the questions she vowed not to ask. She did not want this night to be about his marriage. She wanted it to be about them, only. But such a thing is not really possible. She knows this.

"I am now. At this moment. With you."

She is flattered by this answer — she is *overjoyed* by it. But it is not what she's asking and she does not permit the evasion. "Before you met me," she says, her stomach in knots. "Were you happy *before* you met me?"

Nick sighs, indicating the complexity of the question. "I love my kids. I love my family." He gives her a sideways glance. "But am I happy? . . . No. Probably not. Things are . . . complicated right now."

She nods, recognizing that the conversation they are having is one she would have scorned before now. She has heard clichéd versions of it many times before — in movies and from acquaintances and so many places that no one example comes to mind.

She can hear it, though, she can picture the "other woman" asking hopeful questions, pretending to be concerned, all the while plotting her coup. The man playing the victim, actually *believing* that he is the victim, when he is the only one breaking promises. And always before, she has thought, with respect to the cheater: grow up, be a man, suck it up or get a divorce. But now. Now she is asking questions, looking for shades of gray, explanations, loopholes in her once ironclad conscience.

Nick continues earnestly. "And I just can't help the way I feel about you . . . . I just can't."

"And how is that?" she asks, before she can stop herself.

"I'm falling . . ." he starts. Then he swallows and takes a deep breath before continuing, his voice dropping an octave. "I'm falling for you."

She looks at him hopefully, thinking that it all sounds so innocent, so simple. And maybe it is. Maybe this is how life works, how the story goes for a lot of people — some of whom are *good* people. Her heart pounds and aches at once, as she stares into his eyes and leans toward him.

What happens next she knows she will always remember, as vividly as any good or bad thing that has ever happened in her life. As much as the day she gave birth to Charlie or the night of his accident or anything in between, whether chronologically or emotionally. Their faces touch, their lips meet in a kiss that begins slowly, tentatively, but quickly becomes urgent. It is a kiss that lasts for hours, continuing as they recline on the couch, then roll to the floor, then move to her bed. It is a kiss that doesn't end until he is inside her, whispering that it is real, this thing between them, and that he has officially, completely fallen.

31
TESSA

"I regret saying anything to Dex and Rachel last night," I tell Cate over bacon, eggs, and home fries at Café Luka, one of our old Upper East Side haunts. I am hoping that the grease will cure my hangover, or at least put a dent in my nausea, although I know it can't lift my spirits.

"Why?" Cate asks, taking a sip of grapefruit juice. She makes a face to indicate its sourness, but then drains the glass, moving on to her ice water. Since getting her television gig, she has become obsessed with staying hydrated — which is hard to do given the amount of caffeine and alcohol she consumes.

"Because they'll worry. Because Dex might leak this to my mom. Because they'll never like Nick again . . . And because . . . I just don't want Rachel feeling sorry for me," I say, catching a glimpse of my puffy, bloodshot eyes in the mirrored wall next to the booth. I look away, thinking, *I'd cheat on me, too.*

"She's worried about you," Cate says. "But I don't think she *pities* you."

"I don't know. I hated the way she looked at me last night. The way she hugged me when they got in the cab. Like she'd rather be homeless than facing what I'm potentially facing . . ."

Cate reaches out and squeezes my hand, as I realize that I never resent her sympathy, and that I'm always willing to candidly confess any vulnerability, shortcoming, or fear, without ever wishing that I could take it back or revise my story later. As such, my self-image squares neatly with her image of me, no disparity between the two — which makes being in her company sheer comfort and luxury, especially when things are falling apart.

"But aren't you glad you told your brother?" she asks.

"Yes," I say. "I guess I just wish I had waited until I knew exactly what was going on. I could have called him next week — and had a sober conversation with him . . . I'm sure he'd tell Rachel anyway but at least I wouldn't have had to see that look on her face."

Cate rips open a packet of Equal, then

changes her mind, pouring white sugar from the table canister directly into her coffee. She stirs, then looks up and says, "Rachel is really nice — but she's such a little Polly Perfect, isn't she?"

"Yes," I say, nodding emphatically. "Do you know, I've never heard her swear? Never heard her bad-mouth Dex in anything other than a generic 'you know how men can be' way . . . Never really heard her complain about her children . . . Not even when Julia had colic."

"You think it's fake?" Cate asks. "Or is she really that happy?"

"I don't know. I think she's guarded, for sure . . . I think she has a big filter," I say. "But I also think she and Dex just have one of those lofty marriages. Those perfect relationships."

Cate gives me a look that conveys hope. Hope that such a thing is out there for her. It occurs to me that she once felt this way about my marriage.

"Look. Don't get me wrong," I say. "I want my brother to be happy. I want Rachel to be happy . . . But I can't help being a little sickened by them. I mean, did you see how they were holding hands? On barstools? Who holds hands on barstools? It's awkward . . ." I imitate her by reaching my hand out and holding air with an adoring expression. Then I say, "I thought she was going to pass out when Dex confessed their affair."

"You mean the one we all knew about anyway?" Cate says, laughing. "You think she gave him shit later?"

"I doubt it. I think they probably went home and made out. Gave each other massages. Whatever. It can be so draining being around couples like that," I say, realizing that jealousy takes a lot out of you.

"Look, Tess," Cate suddenly says, her expression becoming somber. "I know you're scared. I know that's why you aren't calling April back. But Dex is right . . . You really need to confront this head-on. Worrying about it is so much worse than the truth . . . And look, maybe it's nothing. Maybe Nick is getting a bum rap here."

"Maybe," I say, wondering how I can be so sure of an affair one minute — and just as sure that he would *never* cheat on me the next. "And if he *is* innocent, then I am the bad guy. Snooping through his things and smearing him like I did last night."

"You didn't smear him," Cate says. "But yes . . . this really could be a case of paranoia . . . He's probably at home, missing you."

I glance at my watch, picturing Nick in the throes of breakfast with the kids, crossing my fingers that he is engaged in the moment. That even if he's unhappy with some of the details of our life, the discontent will pass and things will work out in the long run. This is my desperate, hungover wish.

"Could you call April now? Please?" Cate says urgently.

I hold her gaze and nod slowly, thinking of all the times that Cate has encouraged me to do something I'm too scared or weak to do on my own, including that first phone call to Nick so long ago, thinking how different my life would be right now if I hadn't followed her advice. Then I pull out my phone and dial one of the few numbers I know by heart. April answers on the first ring, saying my name with a telling note of anticipation.

"Hi, April," I say, holding my breath, steeling my heart.

"Are you having a good time?" she asks, either stalling or prioritizing phone etiquette over everything else.

"Yeah. It's always good to be back in the city," I say, my voice becoming fake, wishing it were Cate on the verge of giving me bad news. I look across the table as she rests her fork on her plate, her expression of sick dread and suspense mirroring the way I feel.

"So," April says. "You got my text last night?"

"Yes," I say. "I did."

She begins to stammer, offering a rehearsed preamble about her duty as my friend to tell me what she's about to tell me.

"Okay," I say, my stomach in knots. "Go ahead."

April exhales into the phone and then, speaking as quickly as she can, says, "Romy saw Nick over at Longmere School. Yesterday afternoon."

I feel the tension drain from my shoulders, feeling profound relief that this could, in fact, be about private school rumors, and nothing else. I have never confirmed our intention to apply to Longmere for Ruby, and I can tell it is a source of intrigue among my so-called friends, perhaps because they want their own choices validated by my eagerness to get Ruby in.

I clear my throat and say, "Well, I did tell him the ball was in his court on the school front . . ." I nearly consider telling her that I knew he was going over to the school but don't want to risk being caught in a lie, and fear that Nick might have said something to contradict this story. So instead I say,

"Good for him for being proactive. He must have set up a tour. Or a talk with the head of admissions. Or maybe he actually submitted our application. Wishful thinking . . ."

"Yes — but . . ."

"But what?" I say, feeling a stab of intense loyalty to Nick, and simultaneous disdain for April.

"But . . . he didn't seem to be on a tour."

My silence is loud as she waits, then continues. "He was with Valerie Anderson."

Despite being clear on her implication, my head is still foggy. "What do you mean, *with* her?"

"They were in the parking lot," she says. "Together. With her son, Charlie. He was putting Charlie in the backseat of her car."

"Okay," I say, trying to get my head around the image, trying to find a logical explanation for it.

"I'm sorry," she says.

"What do you mean, you're sorry? What are you trying to say?" I ask, feeling my annoyance escalate.

"I'm not trying to *say* anything," April says. "I just thought you should know . . . I thought you should know that Romy said it looked . . . well . . . *odd* . . . the way they were standing together."

"And how was that?" I snap. "How were

they *standing?*"

"Well . . . like a couple," she says reluctantly.

Doing my best to control my voice, keep it from shaking, I say, "I think you both are jumping to a pretty dire conclusion."

"I'm not jumping to any conclusions," she says. "I realize it could be perfectly innocent. He could have gone to see the school to, like you said, investigate it for Ruby, and while there, he could have just run into Valerie . . . in the parking lot."

"What other scenario *could* there be?" I ask, indignation washing over me.

When she doesn't answer, I continue, becoming strident. "That my husband had an inappropriate rendezvous in the Longmere parking lot? I mean, April, I'm no expert on affairs, but I can think of a lot of better places . . . Like a motel. Or a bar . . ."

"I'm not saying he's having an affair," April says with a note of panic, clearly aware that I am royally pissed. She clears her throat and furiously backtracks. "I'm sure Nick would never develop an inappropriate relationship with a patient's mother."

"No. He would not," I say boldly. "He would not do that with *anyone.*"

Cate perks up in her seat, giving me a

"you go, girl" smile, pumping one fist in the air.

More awkward silence passes as April says, "You're not mad at me, are you?"

"No. Not at all," I say curtly, stiffly, wanting her to know just how mad I am. Wanting her to know that I think it is vastly uncool that she would perpetuate a rumor about my husband. That she would ruin my weekend with her fear-mongering, rumor-spreading, meddlesome ways. I almost tell her that maybe she is the one who should take a hard look at her life, consider what might be missing, what void she is trying to fill.

"Okay. Well. Good," April says, continuing to babble. "Because I would never want to start trouble . . . I just . . . I just would want you to tell me if you saw Rob with anyone . . . Even if it was perfectly innocent . . . I just think that's what friends are for. We girls need to stick together . . . look out for one another."

"I appreciate it. And you can tell Romy I said thanks, too. But there really is no need for concern." Then I say a terse good-bye and hang up, looking across the table at Cate.

"What happened?" she asks, her eyes wide, her long lashes still layered with black mascara from last night.

I give her the scoop, waiting for her re-action.

"I think there is a good explanation here. I think that's a lot of circumstantial bullshit. And I think your friend April sounds like an ass."

I nod, pushing my plate away.

"What do *you* think?" she asks carefully.

"I think . . . I think I need to go home," I say, my head swimming.

"Today?" she says, looking disappointed, but supportive.

"Yes," I say. "I don't think this can wait . . . I need to talk to my husband."

32
VALERIE

She awakens the next morning in something of a blissful stupor, unable to make herself move from the spot on her bed where Nick left her several hours before, kissing her one final time, promising to lock the door on the way out and call her in the morning, even though it was already morning.

Her eyes still closed, she rewinds the reel to the beginning of the evening, replaying every exquisite detail, all of her senses buzzing, in overdrive. She can still smell his musky scent on her sheets. She can still hear him breathing her name. She can still see the strong lines of his body, moving in the shadows. And she can still feel him everywhere.

She rolls over to glance at her clock, just in time to see Charlie tiptoeing past her room, clearly trying to be stealthy.

"Where are you going?" she says, pulling the covers up over her shoulders. Her voice is hoarse, the way that it is after a concert or an evening spent in a loud bar, which is puzzling, because she is quite sure she made no noise last night.

"Downstairs," he says.

"Are you hungry?"

"Not yet," he says, his left hand gripping the wide mahogany banister, one of the features she loves most about this house, especially at Christmas when she decorates it with swaths of garland. "I just wanted to watch some TV?"

She nods, giving him carte blanche permission. He smiles, then disappears from her view, down the stairs. Only then, as she is left staring at her ceiling, does the weight of her actions sink in. She slept with a *married* man — a *father* of *two* young children. And further, she did so with her *own* child under the same roof, breaking a cardinal rule of single parenthood, one of her own rules that she has vigilantly followed for six years. She reassures herself that Charlie is a sound sleeper, even after days filled with much less duress than yesterday. Yet that is beside the point, really, because she knows that he *could* have awakened. He *could* have come to her bedroom, pushed open the door held shut only by a small leather ottoman and a heap of their commingled clothing. He could have seen them together, moving under the covers, over the covers, all over the room.

She must be crazy, she decides, to do such a thing. *Initiate* it, in fact, both the walk upstairs to her bedroom and the actual moment when it happened, the moment she looked into his eyes and whispered, *Yes, tonight, please, now.*

There is only one other possibility, apart from lunacy — and that is that she, too, is falling in love, although it occurs to her, with equal parts cynicism and hope, that there might not be much of a gulf between the two. She thinks of Lion, the last time she felt anything remotely like this, remembering the temporary insanity of that relationship, how she believed it was real with her whole heart and mind. She wonders if she could be wrong again. Deluded by an intense attraction, a need to fill a void in her life, a search for a father for Charlie.

But she cannot make herself believe that any of these explanations are true, just as she cannot fathom Nick making love to her for the wrong reasons — for lust or conquest or fun. This does not mean that she is oblivious to the immorality of their actions. Or to the risks — the clear and present danger of emotional ruin. She realizes, fully, that this might end badly for her, for Charlie. For Nick and his family. For *everyone.*

Yet she also believes to her core, that there is a chance, albeit slim, for a happy ending. That maybe Nick and his wife have a loveless marriage, and that if it ends, everyone will wind up in a better place. She tells herself that she doesn't believe in much, but that she does believe in the essentialness of love, the thing that has been missing from her life. She tells herself that Tessa might be just as miserable married to Nick, that she might be having an affair of her own. She tells herself that their children might be better off with their parents happy and apart, than together and lonely. Above all, she tells herself to trust fate in a way she has never trusted before.

Her cell phone rings from her nightstand. She knows, *feels,* that it is Nick, even before she sees his name light up her screen.

"Good morning," he murmurs into her ear.

"Good morning," she says, smiling.

"How are you?" he asks, sounding self-conscious in that universal, morning-after-first-time way.

She isn't sure how to answer the question, how to convey the complexity of what she is feeling, so she simply says, "I'm tired."

He lets out an uneasy laugh and says, "Well, other than being tired, how are you? Are you . . . okay?"

"Yes," she says, offering no further explanation, wondering when she will let her guard down completely, finally spill her heart. Wondering if such a thing is even possible for her. She has the feeling that it just might be, with him.

"Are *you* okay?" she asks him, thinking that he has more on the line, much more to lose, and frankly, much more reason to feel guilty.

"Yeah. I'm okay," he says softly.

She smiles in response, but feels it fade quickly, her buzz displaced by a dose of heavy remorse as she hears the sound of piping voices in the background. His children. A far different matter from his wife. After all, she — Tessa, *Tess* — could be to blame in all of this, or at least a joint culprit in her own collapsing marriage. But there is no way she can reconcile what she is doing to his two innocent children, and certainly not with the convoluted rationalization that creating a family cancels out the breaking up of another — or that it exculpates her from the unabashed violation of the Golden Rule, in her mind, the only rule that really matters.

"Daddy. More butter, please!" she hears his daughter say, trying to picture her, grateful that she can't. She thinks of the framed black-and-white photos in Nick's office, the ones she has thus far managed to avoid.

"Sure, honey," Nick replies to the little girl.

"Thank you, Daddy," she chirps, her voice becoming singsongy. "Very! Very much!"

Her sweet voice and good manners stab at Valerie's heart, adding to her burden of guilt.

"What are you all having for breakfast?" Valerie asks. It is a nervous question, one designed to acknowledge his children without directly asking about them.

"Waffles. I'm the waffle king. Right, Rubes?"

She hears the little girl giggle and say, "Yes, Daddy. And I'm the waffle princess."

"Yes, you are," he says. "You're the waffle princess, for sure."

She then hears the little boy, talking exactly as Nick joked — like a cross between the Terminator and a European gay man, a staccato trill. "Da-ddeeeee. I. Want. More. But-tah. Tooo."

"No! That one's mine!" she hears the little girl say, remembering Nick's joke that Ruby is so overbearing that his son's first words were *help me.*

Valerie closes her eyes again, as if to shut out the sounds of his children, and all that she knows about them. Yet she still can't help herself from whispering, "Do you feel . . . guilty?"

He hesitates — an answer in itself — then says, "Yeah. Of course I do . . . But I wouldn't take it back."

"You wouldn't?" she asks, wanting to be certain.

"Hell, no . . . I want to do it again," he says, more quietly.

A chill runs down Valerie's spine, just as she hears Ruby ask, "Do what again? Who are you talking to, Daddy?"

"A friend," he tells her.

"What friend?" the little girl presses, as Valerie wonders if it is mere curiosity — or some sort of freakish intuition.

"Uhh . . . you don't know this friend, honey," he tells his daughter, carefully keeping the gender neutral. And then, to Valerie, in a hushed voice, "I better go. But can I see you later?"

"Yes," she says as quickly as she can. Before she can change her mind — or her heart.

33
TESSA

A short time later, after I've avoided two follow-up calls from April and exchanged somewhat tearful good-byes with Cate, I am on my flight back to Boston, eating a standard-issue bag of miniature pretzels and unwittingly eavesdropping on two loud-talking men in the row behind me. From a quick glimpse over my seat, I glean that they fall into the beefy, guy-walks-into-a-bar category, both sporting goatees, gold chains, and baseball caps. As I stare at the map in the back of my in-flight magazine, examining the myriad of domestic flight possibilities, I do my best to tune out the discussion of the "sweet Porsche" one wants to buy, and the other's "douche of a boss," before the conversation really revs up with the question: "So you gonna call that chick from the club or what?"

"Which club? Which chick?"

(Hearty laughter accompanied by either a

knee slap or high five.)

"The double-jointed chick. What's her name? Lindsay? Lori?"

"Oh yeah, *Lind*-say. Hell, yeah, I'm gonna call her. She was sexy. Sexy as *shit*."

I cringe, comparing them to my intelligent, respectful husband who would never, under any circumstances, think of putting *sexy* and *shit* in the same sentence. Then I close my eyes, preparing for our descent, imagining the likely scene upon my return: my family breaking all the usual rules, perhaps still in their pajamas, eating junk food, the house an utter wreck around them. I take strange solace in the thought of such chaos, the idea of Nick's domestic incompetence, the belief that he would be lost without me — in more ways than one.

Yet when I burst through my front door less than an hour later, I am dismayed to find my family gone, the house clean and orderly. The kitchen is sparkling; the beds are made; there is even a load of laundry, freshly washed and folded, in a wicker basket on the stairs. I wander aimlessly around the house, finding myself in the living room, the most formal and least used space in the house, eyeing the high-backed, rolled-arm couch that I don't think I've sampled since the day my mother and I chose it from a decorator's showroom. I remember the afternoon well, the hours we spent considering various styles, discussing fabrics and wood finishes for its graceful feet, debating whether to pay extra for stain guard. A project that now seems trivial.

As I carefully sit on it now, doing my best to enjoy the rare moment of peace, I can't make myself feel anything other than lonesome, disturbed by the loud silence, grimly imagining what it would be like if Nick and I ever split up — all the blank space and empty moments to fill. I remember once joking to him, after a particularly trying day, that I would make a superb mother if I were only on duty on Mondays, Tuesdays, and every other weekend. He laughed, telling me not to be ridiculous, that being a single parent would be miserable, that *he* would be miserable without me. I hold on to this thought as I dial his cell.

"Hey there!" he shouts into the phone. I feel instant relief just hearing his voice, although I can't shake the feeling that I'm in detective mode as I try to discern his background noise. It sounds like a mall, but the chances of Nick voluntarily going shopping are more unlikely than an affair.

"Hi," I say. "Where are you?"

"The Children's Museum," he says.

"With the kids?"

"Yeah," he says with a laugh. "It generally wouldn't be a place I'd come without the kids."

I smile at my silly question, feeling myself relax.

"How's New York?" he says. "What are you up to?"

I take a deep breath and say, "I'm home, actually."

"You're home? Why?" he asks, sounding startled.

"Because I missed you," I say, which isn't entirely untrue.

He says nothing in response, which unnerves me enough that I begin to ramble. "I just need to see you," I say. "I want to talk to you . . . about some things."

"What things?" he asks, a dose of unease in his voice — which could be because he's done something wrong. Or it could be that he's done *nothing* wrong and therefore assumes that *I* am the one with an issue.

"Just things," I say, feeling sheepish for my vagueness, suddenly questioning my judgment in coming home, initiating a conversation in this way. After all, I might have a legitimate reason to be worried, but was it really enough to cut my trip short by a night, without so much as giving Nick a heads-up before my arrival? It occurs to me that he could think this is a *true* emergency — a health crisis, an affair of my own, a foray into a deep depression — rather than what is likely going on here: April stirring the pot and me snooping through his text messages. *Two paranoid housewives.*

"Tessa," he says, agitated. "What's going on? Are you okay?"

"Yes. Yes. I'm fine," I say, feeling ashamed and more confused than ever. "I just want to talk. Tonight. Is Carolyn still coming? I was hoping we could go out . . . and talk."

"Yeah. She's still coming. At eight."

"Oh. Great," I say. "What . . . were your plans?"

"I didn't have specific plans," he replies quickly. "I was thinking of seeing a movie."

"Oh," I say again. "So . . . did you go out last night?"

"Uh . . . yeah," he says. "I did. For a bit."

I start to ask what he did, but stop myself. Instead I tell him I can't wait to see him and silently vow that I will not beat around the bush when we finally sit down to talk. I must be direct, confront the hard topics: fidelity, sex, his career, my lack of one, the underlying dissatisfaction in our marriage. It won't be easy, but if we can't have a frank discussion, then we really *are* in trouble.

"Me too. . . . But I better go now. The kids are running in two separate directions. So we'll just finish up here and be back by five or so? . . . Does that work for you?" he asks.

His words are innocuous but his tone is detached, with the slightest hint of condescension. It is the way he often talked to me when I was pregnant and, in his words, behaving irrationally — which I must confess was often the case, such as the time I actually *cried* over our Christmas tree, insisting that it was ugly, disturbingly asymmetrical, even suggesting that Nick unstring the lights and *return* it for a new one. In fact, I almost *feel* pregnant now — not physically, but emotionally, in a verging-on-tears, hormonal, utterly needy way.

"Sure. That works," I tell him, clutching the arm of the couch, hoping that I sound less desperate than I feel. "I'll be here."

I spend the next hour rushing around, showering, dressing, and primping, as if I'm going on a first date, all the while vacillating between despair and calm, at one moment telling myself my intuition must be on track and then berating myself for being so insecure, having such little faith in Nick and the bedrock of our relationship.

But when my family returns home, there is no denying the chilliness in Nick's hug, his kiss on my cheek. "Welcome home, Tess," he says, an ironic suspicion in his voice.

"Thanks, honey," I say, trying to remember how I interacted with him before all of this began, trying to pinpoint *when* all of this began. "It's so good to see you guys."

I kneel down to hug the kids, both of whom have clean faces and combed hair, Ruby even wearing a pink bow, a small triumph.

Frankie bursts into a mirthful laugh, clamoring for another hug. "Pick. You. Up. Mama!" he shouts.

I don't bother to correct his pronoun, but instead scoop him up in my arms, kissing both cheeks and his sweaty little neck, warm from all the layers his daddy remembered to bundle him in.

He giggles as I put him down and unzip his coat. He is wearing a mismatched outfit — navy cords with a striped orange and red shirt, the lines and colors slightly clashing, the first sign that their father has been on duty. Once free of his coat, Frank begins to spin in circles, flapping his arms, dancing in his rhythmless, random way. I laugh, for one moment forgetting everything else, until I turn to Ruby, who is doing her best to look miffed, steadfastly maintaining her position that she should have been invited on the girls' trip, although I know she secretly relishes time with her daddy.

She coolly regards me now and says, "What did you bring me?"

I panic, realizing that I never made it to the American Girl or Disney store as I promised. "I didn't have a chance," I say lamely. "I was going to do it today."

"Oh, *man,*" Ruby says, her lip curling into a pout. "Daddy *always* gets us something when he goes away."

I consider the trinkets that Nick has brought back from conferences, often cheap airport souvenirs, and feel guilty that I didn't at least save her my pretzels from the plane.

"Rubes. Be kind to your mother," Nick says, a mechanical reprimand. He then removes his own layers — a jacket, a fleece pullover, and a scarf — hanging everything on a hook by the door.

"She came home early," he adds. "That's your surprise. *Our* surprise."

"And my surprise was a clean house," I say, giving him a grateful look.

Nick smiles and winks, taking full credit, although something tells me that Carolyn did the laundry.

"Coming home early isn't a surprise," Ruby says.

"Maybe we'll get you a treat tonight. Ice cream after dinner?" I offer. Ruby is not sold on this, her pout conveying both disappointment and disgust.

She crosses her arms and attempts to negotiate a better deal. "With hot fudge?"

I nod while Frankie chortles unintelligibly, oblivious to his malcontent sister and the unspoken tension between his parents. I watch him flap his arms and spin again, filled with affection, admiration, and envy for my simple, happy child. As he falls down, dizzy and giggling, I say a prayer that Nick and I can somehow return to that pure place, where we want to drop everything we're doing, just be in the moment, and dance.

34

VALERIE

Hi, Val. It's me. Hope you guys are having a good day. We're here at the Children's Museum, in the Bubble Room. Good times . . . Anyway, I'm so sorry, but I'm not going to be able to see you tonight, after all . . . Give me a call if you get this message soon. Otherwise . . . I . . . might not be able to talk . . . I'll call when I can and explain . . . Anyway, I'm sorry. Truly . . . I miss you . . . Last night was incredible. You're incredible . . . All right. Bye for now.

Her heart sinks as she listens to the message in the parking lot of Whole Foods, having just gone shopping for tonight's dinner. Charlie and three bags of groceries are in the backseat behind her.

"Mommy!" Charlie says impatiently.

"What, honey?" she says, glancing at her son in the rearview mirror, doing her best to look and sound upbeat, the opposite of how she feels.

"Why aren't you driving? Why are we just sitting here?"

"Sorry . . . I was listening to a message," she says, starting the car and slowly backing up.

"From Nick?" he asks.

Her heart skips a beat. "Yes. That was Nick," she says, the risk of what she is doing further crystallizing in her mind, along with the realization that, already, Nick has become Charlie's first guess, even before Jason or her mother, just as he was the first one Charlie called from school when he couldn't reach her.

"What did he say?" Charlie asks. "Is he coming tonight?"

"No, sweetie," she says, turning out of the lot.

"Why not?"

"I don't know," she says, silently ticking through the possibilities. Maybe he couldn't find a babysitter. Maybe his wife came home a day early. Maybe he changed his mind about her, about them. Whatever the explanation, she realizes with acute sadness that this is how it's going to be, that these sorts of disappointments and messages and cancellations come with the territory. She can pretend and dream all she wants — and she certainly did last night — but there is no way around what they are doing. They are having an affair, and she is on the sidelines, along with Charlie. It will be her job to shield him from disappointment while hiding her own.

"Mommy?" Charlie asks, as she makes a turn onto a backstreet, taking the longer but more scenic route home.

"Yes, honey?" she says.

"Do you love Nick?"

Her mind races as she grips the steering wheel, searching for the right answer, *any* answer. "He's a good friend. He's been a great friend to us," she says. "In addition to being a wonderful doctor."

"But do you love him?" Charlie asks again, as if he knows exactly what is going on. "Like when you want to marry someone?"

"No," Valerie lies, doing her best to protect him — since it is too late to protect herself. "Not like that, sweetie."

"Oh," he says, clearly disappointed by her answer.

With a measure of trepidation, she clears her throat and says, "How do you feel about Nick?"

He pauses, then says, "I like him. I wish . . . I wish he were my daddy." His voice is wistful but apologetic, almost as if he's making a confession.

Valerie takes a deep breath and nods, having no idea what to say in response.

"Wouldn't that be nice?" she finally says, wondering if her words now, and what she is doing generally, make her a good mother or a decidedly bad one. She feels sure it is one extreme or the other, and even more certain that only time will tell which camp she's in.

35
TESSA

Thirty minutes before Carolyn is due to arrive, and just after I've put the kids to bed, I find Nick in the family room, sound asleep in a pair of old scrubs. I have a flashback to his residency, how he routinely fell asleep everywhere but our bed — on the couch, at the table, once even standing in the kitchen. He was making a cup of tea and nodded off in mid-sentence, awakening as his chin hit the counter. Despite more blood than I'd ever seen in real life, he refused to go back to the hospital where he had just completed a thirty-six-hour rotation. Instead, I took him to bed, holding a bandage to his chin for most of the night.

I sit on the edge of the couch now, listening to him snore for a moment before gently shaking him awake. "They wear you out, don't they?" I ask as his eyes flutter open.

He yawns and says, "Yeah. Frankie got up before six this morning. And your daughter

—" He shakes his head fondly.

"*My* daughter?"

"Yes, *your* daughter," he says. "She's too much."

We both smile as he continues, "She is one particular little girl."

"That's a delicate way to put it," I say.

He runs his hands through his hair and says, "She just about had a meltdown at the museum when her apple slices grazed her ketchup. And my God . . . to get that girl to wear socks. You'd think I was suggesting a straitjacket."

"Tell me about it."

"What does she have against socks, anyway?" he asks. "I don't get it."

"She says socks are for boys," I say.

"So bizarre," he mumbles. Then, through an exaggerated yawn, he says, "Would you be upset if we stayed in tonight?"

"You don't want to go out?" I say, doing my best not to take his position as an affront, a difficult thing to do given that he went out last night, and had planned to go to a movie tonight, solo or otherwise.

"I *want* to . . . I'm just so damn tired," he says.

Although I am also exhausted, and still have a residual headache, I believe that Nick will take the conversation more seriously if we are in a nice setting — or, at the very least, stay awake, which is only a fifty-fifty proposition if we stay in. But I resist making this inflammatory point, instead blaming Carolyn, telling him I don't feel comfortable canceling on her last-minute.

"So give her fifty bucks for the opportunity cost," Nick says, folding his hands on his chest. "I'd pay fifty bucks not to go out right now."

I look at him, wondering how much he would pay to avoid our discussion altogether. He stares back up at me, unyielding.

"Okay. We'll stay in," I relent. "But can we eat in the dining room? Open a good bottle of wine? Maybe get dressed a bit?" I say, eyeing his scrubs again, once a turn-on, now a grim reminder of one of the possible suspects in our rough patch. If I'm lucky, that is.

He gives me a look that conveys both annoyance and amusement, and I can't decide which offends me more. "Sure thing," he says. "Would you like me to wear a suit and tie? Perhaps a sweater vest?"

"You don't own a sweater vest," I say.

"Okay. So I guess that's out," he says, slowly standing and stretching. I study the lines of his back, feeling the sudden urge to throw my arms around him, bury my face in his neck, and confess my every worry. But something keeps me at a distance. Wondering if it is fear, pride, or resentment, I remain in my most efficient mode, informing him that I'll handle calling Carolyn and ordering dinner — and that he should go upstairs and change. "Relax a bit," I add with a strategic, indulgent smile. "Get your second wind."

He gives me a circumspect look, then turns toward the stairs.

"Sushi okay with you?" I call after him.

"That's fine," he says with a shrug. "Whatever you want."

A short time later, our sushi has arrived and we have reconvened in the dining room. Nick, wearing gray flannel slacks and a black roll-neck sweater, appears to be in a good mood yet shows signs of nervousness, cracking his knuckles twice before opening a bottle of wine and pouring two glasses.

"So," he says as he sits and gazes down in his miso soup. "Tell me about last night. Did you have fun?"

"Yeah," I say. "Until I started to worry . . ."

With a trace of scorn, he says, "What are you worried about *now*?"

I take a deep breath and a sip of wine before saying, "Our relationship."

"What about it?" he says.

I can feel my breathing grow shallow as I struggle to keep things nonaccusatory, strip any melodrama from my reply. "Look, Nick. I know life is hard. Life with little kids just beats you down and makes you weary. I know that the stage of life we're in . . . can put strains on relationships . . . even the best marriages . . . but . . . I just don't feel as close as we once were. And it makes me sad . . ."

As there is nothing in my statement that he can refute, he nods a small, careful nod and says, "I'm sorry you're sad . . ."

"How do you feel?" I ask.

He gives me a puzzled look.

"Are you happy?"

"What do you mean?"

I know he knows *exactly* what I mean, but I still spell it out for him. "Are you happy with your life? With *our* life?"

"I'm happy enough," he says, his spoon frozen in midair, his smile rigid, reminding me of a game show contestant who knows the answer but is still second-guessing himself before the final buzzer.

"Happy *enough?*" I say, stung by his quali-fier.

"Tessa," he says, his spoon returning to his bowl, his mood noticeably darkening. "What's this about?"

I swallow and say, "Something is wrong. You seem distant . . . like something's bothering you. And I just don't know if it's work or life in general or the kids. Or me . . ."

He clears his throat and says, "I don't really know how to answer that . . ."

I feel a rise of frustration and the first stirrings of anger as I say, "This isn't a trap, Nick. I just want to talk. Will you talk to me? Please?"

I wait for his reply, staring at the space below his bottom lip and above his chin, wanting to kiss and slap him at once.

"I don't know what you want here . . ." he starts. "I don't know what you're looking for." He holds my gaze for several seconds, before looking down to prepare his sashimi. He carefully pours soy sauce into his saucer and adds a dab of wasabi before mixing the two with his chopsticks.

"I want you to tell me how you feel," I say, now pleading.

He looks me directly in the eye and says, "I don't know how I feel."

Something inside me snaps as I unleash the first dose of sarcasm, nearly always lethal in a conversation between husband and wife. "Well then," I say. "Let's try an easier angle. How about telling me where you were yesterday afternoon?"

He gives me a blank stare. "I was at the hospital. I came home around five, had dinner with the kids, then went out for a few hours."

"You were at the hospital all day?" I press, saying a last-ditch prayer that Romy misidentified the man in the parking lot, that she is in dire need of glasses.

"Pretty much," he says.

"So you didn't go over to Longmere yesterday?" I blurt.

He shrugs, avoiding my gaze, and says, "Oh. Yeah. Why?"

"Why?" I say incredulously. *"Why?"*

"Yes. Why?" he snaps. "As in — *why* are you asking? As in — *why* did you fly home a day early to ask me that question?"

I shake my head, refusing to be fooled by his transparent tactic. "Why were you there? Did you go to take a tour of the school? Drop off an application? Did it have *anything* to do with Ruby?"

I already know the answer as he sighs and says, "It's a long story."

"We have time," I say.

"I don't really want to get into it right

now," he says.

"Well, you don't have that choice," I tell him. "Not when you're married."

"See. There you go again," he says, as if he's having an epiphany, a lightning bolt of insight into my mysterious, difficult persona.

"What's that supposed to mean?" I ask.

"It means . . . that there don't seem to be many choices left in this marriage. Unless you're the one making them."

"What?" I shout, becoming the first to raise my voice, something I vowed not to do.

"You have everything all mapped out. Where we live. What club we need to join. Where the kids should go to school. Who our friends will be. What we do with every hour, minute, *second* of our free time."

"What are you talking about?" I demand.

He ignores me, continuing his rant. "Whether it's going on a forced march through Target or a neighborhood Halloween party or a school tour. Hell, you even govern what I'm supposed to wear in my own house over takeout sushi. For *God's* sake, Tessa."

I swallow, feeling defensive yet outraged. "So tell me," I say, grinding my teeth between words. "How long have you been feeling this way?"

"For a while."

"So this has nothing to do with Valerie Anderson?" I say, going out on a dangerous limb.

He does not flinch. He does not even blink. "Why don't you tell me, Tessa? Since you seem to have all the answers."

"I don't have *that* answer, Nick. In fact, your little friendship was news to me. A great, big newsflash. While I'm trying to have a good time in New York with my brother and best friend, I'm getting a text that you're with another woman, sharing a cozy moment in the parking lot."

"That's great," he says with hushed sarcasm. "That's fucking great. Now I'm being watched — *followed* — like some kind of a bad guy."

"Are you?" I shout. "Are you a bad guy?"

"I don't know. Why don't you ask your posse of friends? Why don't you take a poll of all the Wellesley housewives?"

I swallow, then raise my chin with a self-righteous flourish. "For the record, I told April that you'd never cheat on me," I say.

I study his face, bearing an expression I can only describe as guilty.

"Why are you discussing me with April?" Nick asks. "Why is our marriage *any* of her concern?"

"She's not part of this discussion, Nick," I say, determined not to be sidetracked. "Other than the fact that she's the one who told me you were at Longmere with Valerie Anderson. When it was *you* who should have filled me in."

"I didn't know you wanted a report of everything I did," Nick says, standing abruptly and heading for the kitchen. A long moment later, he returns with a bottle of Perrier, refilling his glass as I pick up where we left off.

I shake my head and say, "I didn't ask for a report. I didn't want a report."

"Then why do you surround yourself with people who would give you that report?"

It is a fair question, but one that I feel is completely ancillary to the bigger picture, the one he is blatantly avoiding. "I don't know, Nick," I say. "You might be right about April. But this isn't about April and you know it."

He remains infuriatingly silent as I sigh and say, "Okay. Let's try this again, another way. Would you mind, now that we're on the topic, telling me what you were doing at Longmere?"

"Okay. Yes. I'll tell you," he says calmly. "Charlie Anderson, my patient, called me."

"He called you?" I say.

He nods.

"Was it a medical emergency?"

"No," he says. "It was not."

"Then why did he call you?"

"He was upset. There was an incident at school. A little girl teased him and he got upset."

"Why didn't he call his mother?"

"He did. He couldn't reach her. She was in court. She had her phone turned off."

"And his father?" I ask, even though I know the answer — that there *is* no father, perhaps the most unsettling fact in all of this.

Sure enough, Nick looks more impassioned than he has in the entire conversation as he says, "He doesn't have a father. He's a scared little kid who has been through hell and called his doctor."

"He has no other family?" I say, unwilling to feel sympathy for anyone other than myself — and potentially my children. "Grandparents? Aunts or uncles?"

"Tessa. Look. I don't know why he called me. I didn't ask him. I just went. I thought it was the right thing to do."

You are so fucking noble, I think, but instead press on. "Are you friends with her?"

He hesitates, then nods. "Yes. I guess you could say we're friends. Yes."

"*Close* friends?" I ask.

"Tessa. C'mon. Stop."

I shake my head and repeat the question. "How close are you?"

"What are you getting at here?"

"What I am getting at," I say, pushing my plate away, wondering how I possibly thought I could be in the mood for raw fish, "is what is going on with us. Why we don't feel close anymore. Why you didn't tell me that Charlie Anderson called you. That you're friends with his mother . . ."

He nods, as if granting me a small point — which has a way of softening my next words. "And maybe, just *maybe,* this nagging worry I have about our relationship . . . maybe it's all in my head. Maybe I need to take some antidepressants or go back to work or something." I pick up my chopsticks, holding them skillfully in my hands, remembering how my father taught me to use them when I was a little girl, about Ruby's age.

He nods again and says, "Yes. Maybe *you're* the one who isn't happy. In fact . . . I can't remember the last time you seemed happy. First it was that you worked too much and were overwhelmed and resented the professors without kids who didn't understand your situation. So I tell you to quit, that we will be fine without two incomes. So you do. And now. Now you seem bored and frustrated and annoyed by mothers who care too much about tennis or post inane Facebook updates or expect you to make homemade snacks for school parties. Yet you still fret about all of those things. You still play their game."

I try to interrupt, try to defend myself, but he continues with more conviction. "You wanted another baby. Desperately. Enough that sex turns into a project. A nose-to-the-grindstone project. Then you have Frankie and you seem on the edge. Postpartum. Miserable."

"I wasn't postpartum," I say, still focusing on the sting of his description of our sex, awash with remorse and inadequacy and fear. "I just had the baby blues."

"Fine. Fine. And I understand that. I understand how hard it was. Which is why I took the early morning feeding. Why we hired Carolyn."

"I know," I say. "Nobody's ever accused you of being a bad father."

"Okay. But look. The point is — I don't feel like I've changed. I feel like I've stayed the same. I'm a surgeon. That's who I am."

"That's who you are, yes. But that's not *all* you are. You're also my husband. Ruby

410

and Frank's father."

"Right, I know. I know. But why does that mean I have to have a full social calendar? And that my kids have to go to a fancy private school? And that my wife has to be consumed with what other people think of us?"

"That's how you see me?" I ask, my tears at their final tipping point. "As some kind of a lemming?"

"Tess. No. I don't see you as a lemming. I see you as a smart, beautiful woman who . . ."

I begin to cry as he reaches over to touch my hand. "Who what?" I ask through tears.

"Who . . . I don't know . . . Tess . . . Maybe something has changed in our life. I'll grant you that. I just don't think that thing is me."

I look at him, feeling light-headed, the weight of his words making it difficult for me to breathe. It is the admission I have been driving for and now that I have it, I have no idea what to do with it.

"Maybe it is partly my fault," I somehow manage to say, too afraid to ask about the text or anything else about Valerie. "But I still love you."

Several seconds pass — seconds that feel like hours — before he replies, "I love you,

411

too, Tess."

I look at him, holding on to the edge of the table and his words, wondering what kind of love we're talking about and whether it will be enough.

36
VALERIE

She waits. And waits. And waits some more. She waits for ten excruciating days, the longest stretch of time she can remember, almost as agonizingly slow as the early days at the hospital. She stares at her BlackBerry, sleeping with it next to her pillow, the ringer on high. She parts the curtains, looking for his car whenever she hears a door slam outside. And when she can't bear the waiting and wondering another second, she even breaks down and sends him a text that simply says, *Hope you're okay?* She adds the question mark for the sole purpose of requesting a response, but she still hears nothing from him. Not a single word.

At first she gives him the benefit of the doubt she believes he's earned, coming up with all sorts of excuses on his behalf. There's been an emergency at work or at home. Someone's hurt. *He's* hurt. And the most implausible scenario of all — that he told his wife he is in love with another woman, that he is unwinding his marriage, filing for divorce, wishing for a clean break before they continue, together, on an honest, true path.

She feels foolish for even conceiving of such a notion (let alone dreaming about it, and once, in an especially desperate moment, even *praying* for it) when she knows what is far more likely. That he regretted what they did and what he told her. Or worse, that he didn't mean it in the first place.

The emotions send her reeling back in time, to what she has come to call her stupid years, before she learned to protect herself with a wall of distrust and cynicism and apathy. The wounds Lion inflicted, wounds that she thought had healed long ago, are suddenly fresh and raw. She begins to hate him all over again, because it is easier than hating Nick. But she hates herself most of all — for being the kind of woman who gets herself in these situations.

"What is wrong with me?" she says, when she breaks down one bleak Tuesday afternoon at work, calling her brother, confessing what she did with Nick, and that she hasn't seen him since, hasn't even heard from him since his obligatory morning-after call.

"Nothing is wrong with *you,*" her brother says, sounding half-asleep or stoned — maybe both.

"*Something* is wrong with me," she says, staring out her office window into another office across the block, where two men are *literally* standing next to a water cooler, laughing. "He had sex with me once, then ended things."

"He didn't exactly end things. He just hasn't . . . followed up . . ."

"It's the same difference. And you know it."

Jason's silence erases another sliver of hope.

"So what do you think it was? Am I not pretty enough?" she asks, knowing she sounds like an anguished, broken teenager. She desperately doesn't want to be in this category of women who gauge their self-esteem by a man, pin their hopes on another. Yet that is exactly what she did, what she continues to do by asking these questions.

"Are you kidding? You're fucking gorgeous," Jason says. "You got the face. The body. The whole package."

"So what, then? Do you think it's the sex? Maybe I suck in bed?" she says, just as she pictures Nick's face, twisted with pleasure as he came inside her. The way he stroked her hair afterward. Kissed her eyelids. Ran his hand over her stomach and thighs. Fell asleep holding her, clutching her to him.

Jason clucks his tongue and says, "It's usually not about sex, Val."

"Then what is it? Am I boring? Too negative? . . . Too much baggage?"

"None of those things. It's not you, Val. It's *him* . . . Most guys are assholes. The gay ones, the straight ones. Hank's a diamond in the rough," he says, his voice radiant, the way it always is when he speaks of his boyfriend. The way she might have sounded only a few days ago. "But Nick . . . Not so much."

"He was so *amazing* with Charlie," she says, snapshots filling her head. "They had a rapport. A bond. You could see it. You can't fake that."

"Just because he's a great surgeon and became attached to the best kid in the world doesn't make him right for you. Doesn't make him a good guy, either," Jason says. "But I can see why you'd confuse the two. Anyone would. That's what makes it even worse — what he did. It's like . . . he took advantage of his position."

She sighs in agreement, although she can't quite make herself believe that he is that manipulative, that awful. It would be easier if she could. Then she could agree with her brother, agree that this rejection would be about *his* flaws, not hers.

"Charlie has an appointment with him next week. And we have another surgery scheduled for February," she says, thinking of the number of times she has looked at her calendar, wondering what she will say to him when she walks in his office. "Should we find a new doctor?"

Jason says, "He's the best, right?"

"Yes," she says quickly, her heart breaking, but her loyalty, bizarrely, still intact. She remembers how she continued to praise Lion's talent for months after their breakup. "Nick is the best," she says.

"Well, then keep him as Charlie's doctor," Jason says.

"Okay," she says, wondering what she will tell her son, what explanation she will give him as to why Nick no longer comes around, why it isn't a good idea to call him from school or anywhere else. Why they only see him at the hospital or his office.

"How guilty should I feel?" she asks, thinking of Charlie, his words in the car about wishing Nick were his daddy.

"About what? Tessa?" Jason asks.

She freezes in her chair. "I was talking

about Charlie. Not Nick's wife . . . And would you care to tell me how you know her name?"

"Didn't you . . . tell me . . . her name?" he stammers.

"No," she says with absolute certainty. "I did not."

"You must have."

"Jason. I *know* I didn't. I've never said her name aloud. How do you know her name?" she demands.

"Okay. Okay . . . So get ready for this one . . . It turns out Hank's her tennis instructor."

"You're kidding me," she says, dropping her head to her free hand.

"Nope."

"So Hank knows? About Nick and me?"

"No. I swear I didn't tell him."

She isn't sure she believes him, given the fact that Jason is an open book even when he's *not* in love, but at this point, she practically doesn't care, and numbly listens to her brother's ensuing explanation.

"She's been taking lessons with him for a while . . . Hank knew her husband was some hotshot surgeon, but he didn't put it all together until last week when she mentioned one of her husband's patients — a kid who burned his face at a birthday party."

Valerie's heart races. "What did she say about Charlie?"

"Nothing. She just said that Nick works a lot . . . Hank asked what kind of surgeon he was — and she told him. Used Charlie as an example . . . Small freaking world, huh?"

"Yeah. But I wouldn't want to carpet it," she says, one of their father's favorite sayings.

"Exactly," Jason says, the smile back in his voice.

She sighs, processing this new profile of Tessa, picturing a country-club lady of leisure. A Botoxed, lithe-limbed blonde indulging in midday tennis matches, shopping sprees at Neiman Marcus, champagne lunches at white-linen-tablecloth restaurants. "So she plays tennis? How nice for her," Valerie says.

"You should pick up tennis," Jason says, clearly trying to change the subject. "Hank said he'd give you free lessons."

"No, thanks."

"Why not?"

"I have to work, remember? I'm not *married* to a plastic surgeon. I only sleep with one when his wife's out of town."

Jason clears his throat and says her name as a "buck up, sis" reprimand.

"What?" she replies.

"Don't let this thing sour you."

"Too late."

"Happiness is the best revenge, you know? Just be happy. It's a choice."

"Be happy, huh? Like Nick's wife?" Valerie snaps. "Did Hank tell you how *happy* she is?"

Jason hesitates and then says, "Actually, he said she's very pleasant. Down-to-earth."

"Great. Fantastic," she says, the guilt and remorse from Saturday morning replaced by a thick, strangling jealousy. "Is she gorgeous, too?"

She braces herself, realizing that there is no answer Jason can give her that would satisfy her. If Nick's wife is unattractive, she will feel used. If Tessa is gorgeous, she'll feel inferior.

"No. She's not *gorgeous*. He said she's attractive. But not gorgeous by any stretch."

Valerie groans, feeling queasy and lightheaded.

"Just remember, Val, she's married to a cheater. You should feel sorry for her. Not jealous of her," Jason says.

"Yeah," she says, trying to convince herself that her brother is right, that she is better off without him, without any man. That he is Tessa's problem, not hers. But in her heart, she knows that the only thing that has changed since Saturday morning is that he stopped calling her. She knew all along that he was married. She knew all along that he had a wife. She knew all along that she wanted something — *someone* — that didn't belong to her and probably never would. This is what she gets. This is *exactly* what she deserves.

Jason blows his nose and then asks her if she's going to be okay. She tells him yes, and hangs up, willing herself not to cry as she swivels her chair and stares up at a watermark on the ceiling.

Seconds later, the phone rings, the screen lighting up "private caller." She answers it, assuming it is Jason with some follow-up Nick bashing, some nugget of relationship wisdom.

"Yeah?" she says.

"Hi, Val. It's me," she hears. She catches her breath, realizing that it is still her favorite voice in the world.

Rage and relief battle inside her as she says, "Hello, Nick."

"How are you doing?" he asks.

"I'm fine," she says as quickly and convincingly as she can. Her voice is cold — too cold to indicate indifference.

"I'm sorry I haven't called . . ." he says.

"It's okay. I understand," she says, even

though it isn't and she doesn't.

"I've just been confused . . . trying to work through some things . . ."

"You don't have to explain. It's really not necessary," she says, hoping that he will anyway.

"Val," he says, anguish in his voice that gives her a small degree of comfort. "Can I see you? Can you meet me somewhere? I need to see you. Talk to you."

Her mind races. She knows she should say no. She knows she must protect her son's heart, even if she isn't willing to protect her own. Charlie is attached to Nick now — *fiercely* bonded — but if she continues to see him, it will only be worse when Nick disappoints her again. Her chest tightens as she prepares to tell him that it's not a good idea, that Friday night was a mistake, and that she can't afford to make another one. But she can't do it. She can't make herself shut the door completely. Instead, she opens her mouth and tells him she was just about to go for a walk in the Common, that he is welcome to join her.

"Where?" he says. "Where can I meet you?"

"By the Frog Pond," she says as nonchalantly as she can, pretending that it isn't a hopeful, sentimental choice. That it isn't because she wants to walk with him in a place she loves, breathing in the cold winter air together. That it isn't because she imagined the two of them taking Charlie there, ice-skating and drinking hot chocolate afterward. That it isn't to create a vivid backdrop to the memory she hopes he wants to make. The explanation, the affirmation, the promise of what's to come.

Minutes later, after touching up her makeup, running a brush through her hair, and telling her secretary she has to step out for an appointment, she is bundled up in her heavy black trench coat, making her way past the wharfs, emptied of their boats for the winter. She inhales the sharp, cold air, her eyes fixed on South Station looming ahead, set against a colorless sky. She crosses into the gritty downtown, passing electronics shops and Laundromats, dive bars and ethnic restaurants, falafel stands and roasted nut vendors. She keeps walking, amid throngs of holiday shoppers and aimless tourists, turning down Franklin Street, lined with its stately gray buildings, and finally reaching Tremont Street, with its view of the State House and the historic, cobblestone section of town. All the while, the wind whips in from the harbor, taking her breath away, slicing through her.

As she crosses the street and approaches the Common, she sees the infamous old homeless man, known by many as Rufus. He has been around for as long as she can remember, but hasn't appeared to age, his dark skin lined with no more wrinkles than it was a dozen years ago, the gray hair only at his temples. She makes eye contact with him and thinks what she always thinks when she sees him in the cold winter months, *Why not move to Florida, Rufus?*

He smiles at her, as if he remembers her from her last walk along this route, and says, "Hey, darlin' . . . Lookin' mighty fine today, darlin' . . . Got a dollar? Some change to spare?" His voice is low and raspy and strangely comforting. She stops and hands him a five, and as he takes it, he tells her she has beautiful eyes.

She thanks him, choosing to believe he means it.

"God bless," he says, putting his fist over his heart.

She nods, then turns and keeps walking. Her pointy-toed black boots are not made for walking, and her toes are now numb, the cold stripping her of any dwindling optimism. She takes longer strides, moving toward Nick and her destiny. She tells herself not to be overdramatic, that he is just another guy, another chapter in her lackluster love life. She tells herself she'd rather *know* than wonder — that the wondering is always the worst part.

And then she is in the Common, approaching the Frog Pond, teeming with ice-skaters, some accomplished, most teetering, all gleeful. The sun suddenly breaks through the clouds, reflecting off the ice. Having forgotten her sunglasses, she shields her eyes with her hand, looking for Nick along the circumference of the pond and even on the ice, as if he might actually stop and put on some skates for a quick spin. She finally spots him in his navy overcoat, a generous gray scarf looped several times around his neck. He is squinting toward her but she can tell he does not yet see her. She studies him for a full minute or more before their eyes meet. His face lights up without smiling and he begins to trek toward her, looking down at his feet, his hands thrust deep in his pockets.

She waits for him, rearranging her expression several times, then making it as blank as possible. She has no idea what to expect — yet she knows *exactly* what to expect.

"Hi, Val," he says when he is standing before her. His eyes are bright — as bright as brown eyes can be — but something in them tells her that he is here to break her heart. Still, when he reaches out to hug her, she does not resist. Her cheek rests against his broad shoulder as she says hello, her voice lost in a sudden gust of wind.

As they separate, he looks into her eyes and says, "It's great to see you."

"You, too," she says, her chest knotted with anticipation approaching fear.

He presses his lips together, then reaches into his pocket and pulls out a lone cigarette and a pack of matches. She has never known him to smoke — would have bet all odds against it — but does not ask him about it, whether it's a new habit or an old one returning. He inverts the pack's cover, striking a match with one gloveless hand, reminding her of just how skillful they are.

"You have one of those for me?" she asks as they begin to walk.

"Sorry. That was my last one," he says, his voice tight, uneven. He reaches out and offers it to her.

"That's okay," she says, shaking her head in refusal. "I was sort of kidding. I don't smoke . . . unless I'm drinking."

"Should we go drink?" he asks with a small, nervous laugh.

When she doesn't reply, he tries again

with another question. "How's Charlie?"

"He's fine," she says, bristling, refraining from telling him anything more.

He nods and raises his cigarette to his lips. Closing his eyes, he inhales, then turns his head to the side. He does not exhale, but simply opens his mouth, the smoke swirling above his head and quickly vanishing. Then he glances around, mumbling something about a bench. She shakes her head and says she'd rather walk, that it's too cold for sitting.

So they move forward, encircling the pond, their eyes on the mirthful skaters moving counterclockwise across the ice in a blur of bright colors.

"Can you skate?" he says, their elbows occasionally touching.

She readjusts her stride, moving away from him, and says, "Yes." Then she sighs, signaling that she is not here to chat. After a full lap around the ice, he speaks again.

"Val," he says. "Our night together . . . it was amazing."

She nods her agreement — there is no way to deny this, no way she could ever deny this.

"*You* are amazing."

She feels herself tense, her throat constrict. She does not want compliments, whether real or consolatory. She can tell where this is going, and only wants the bottom line.

"Thanks," she says again — and then as flatly as she can, "You are, too."

He stops walking suddenly and grabs her arm, "Can we go somewhere to talk? Somewhere inside?" he says.

She can no longer feel her feet, and her nose is beginning to run so she nods reluctantly and then follows him to 75 Chestnut, a restaurant on the street with the same name. They find a table in the back and when the waitress comes to take their order, she says, "Nothing for me," with a gesture toward Nick.

He shakes his head, overriding her decision, ordering two spiced ciders.

"Just tell me, Nick," she says when the waitress is gone. "Tell me what you're thinking."

"I'm thinking a lot of things," he says, scratching his jaw, covered with several days of growth.

"Like?"

"I'm thinking that I'm crazy about you."

Her heart jumps as he continues, now leaning across the narrow table, their faces inches apart.

"I'm thinking that I love the way you look and feel and taste. I love the sound of your voice and the way you look at me with those eyes . . . I'm thinking that I love the way you are with Charlie. The way you *are*."

"Maybe it's just physical?" she calmly offers, pretending not to be deeply moved by his words.

"No," he says, shaking his head adamantly. "It's not a physical thing. It's not a crush. It's nothing like that. I love you, Val. It's the truth. And I'm afraid it will *always* be true."

She now has her answer, the word *afraid* giving him away. He loves her but wishes he didn't. He wants her but can't have her. This is his decision. She feels herself collapse inside as the waitress returns with their cider. She wraps her hands around the warm mug, inhaling the musky apple scent as he continues, almost as if talking to himself. "I know the moment it happened. The night we went to Antonio's and you told me Charlie had no father."

"Is that why?" she asks, doing her best to stay calm, strip any bitterness from her voice. "Is this a savior thing? You saved Charlie — and you wanted to save me, too?"

"I've considered that," he says, and the fact that he doesn't automatically refute it gives his answer more credence.

"I've thought about that — just as I've wondered whether that is your attraction to me." He takes a long sip and then finishes, "But I know that's not it. Not entirely anyway."

"That's not it for me, either," she says, the closest she's come to admitting that she loves him, too. "I don't need to be saved."

"I know you don't *need* to be saved, Val. You don't *need* anybody — you are the strongest person I know."

She forces a smile as if to prove his theory right — even though she doesn't believe it herself.

"You don't think you're strong," he says, as if reading her mind. "And the fact that you think you're barely keeping it together . . . is so . . . is so . . . I don't know, Val. It's just another thing I love about you. You're strong and vulnerable, at once."

He leans toward her, tucking a piece of hair behind her ear.

She shivers and says, "But?" She knows there is a *but* — that there has *always* been a but.

"But . . . I can't . . ." His voice cracks. "I can't do this . . ."

"Okay," she says, taking this as his final word, seeing no reason for a belabored discussion on *why* he can't do it.

"Don't 'okay' me, Val," he says. "Don't let me off the hook this easily."

"There is no hook."

"I don't mean 'hook' like that . . . I just mean . . . I just mean that I made a mistake by going down this road with you. I thought that if I felt this way about you — that it would make what we were doing okay. That I could separate myself from the men who have affairs for all the wrong reasons . . . But then Tessa came home from New York . . . and . . . I can't carve out this exception for myself. For *us*. Not without impacting everyone around me. My kids . . . Charlie . . ."

"And your wife," she finishes for him.

He nods sadly and says, "And Tessa, yes . . . Things are not great with us right now. And I'm not sure what the future holds . . . But I respect her. And I still care deeply for her . . . And unless I'm ready to throw all of that away, all of those years, and the home and family we built . . . unless I'm ready to do that right *now*," he says, tapping the table, "today, at this very *second*, then I can't be with you. It's just not right, as much as I want it to be. It's just not."

She bites her lip and nods as tears sting at her eyes.

"Believe me, Val, I've looked at this from every angle. I've tried to find a way to do the one thing I want to do . . . which is to take you back to your bed right now . . . hold you, make love to you . . . just *be* with you."

She bites her lip harder, her breath quickening in a final attempt not to cry.

"I'm so sorry," he says. "I'm so sorry that I did this to you. It was selfish and wrong . . . And part of me wants to say . . . that maybe someday we can be together . . . maybe someday things will be different . . . but saying that would be just as selfish . . . a false promise . . . a way to hold you on the line while I try to fix what I've done at home."

"You *should* fix it," she says, wondering whether she means it and why she's saying it if she doesn't.

He nods, looking grave and grief-stricken. "I'm going to try."

"That's all you can do," she says, wondering what that entails. Wondering if he will make love to his wife tonight. Whether he already has since last Friday night.

"Is there another doctor? Another doctor we can see?" Her voice cracks, but she manages to keep it together. "I don't think it's a good idea for Charlie to keep seeing you . . ."

He nods in agreement, then reaches into

his pocket for a business card, sliding it across the table.

She glances down at it, her vision growing blurry, only half hearing his words of praise for another surgeon. "Dr. Wolfenden is wonderful," he says. "I learned much of what I know from her. You'll love her. Charlie will love her."

"Thank you," she says, blinking back tears.

Nick nods, blinking in unison.

She picks up the card and says, "I have to go."

He grabs her wrist and says her name. "Val. Wait. Please."

She shakes her head, telling him there is nothing left for him to say. The conversation is over. *They* are over.

"Good-bye, Nick," she says. Then she stands and walks away from him, back into the bitter cold.

37
TESSA

As the days pass, and the countdown to Christmas begins, I feel as if I'm stuck in a bad dream, watching myself from afar, watching someone else's marriage implode with all the clichéd benchmarks of depression. I drink too much. I have trouble falling asleep at night and even more difficulty getting out of bed in the morning. I can't satisfy my deep, ravenous hunger, no matter how many comforting white carbs I down. I am lonely, yet avoid my friends, even Cate, and especially April, who has left me multiple messages. I lie to my family, shooting them chatty updates, snapshots of the kids on Santa's lap, and uplifting YouTube clips with notes such as *This is cute!* or *You'll love!,* always with exclamation points, sometimes with emoticons. I overcompensate with my children, a fake smile plastered on my face as I hum Christmas carols and punch open days of our Advent calendar with wild enthusiasm. I lie to Nick, curling against him every night, wearing his favorite perfume, pretending that I had another productive, festive day. Most of all, I lie to myself, telling myself that if I keep pretending, I can change the course of my life.

But I cannot escape her. I cannot escape the obsession with a woman I've never laid eyes on. I am not sure of the details. I do not know if the text I saw was from her, or if Nick was with her the night I was in New York. I do not know what, exactly, Romy saw in the parking lot. Whether it was innocent or not. I do not know whether he made love to her or kissed her or held her hand or simply stared longingly into her eyes, thinking about any of the above. I don't know if he told her about our problems or has otherwise betrayed me.

I do know one thing, though. I know that my husband is in love with Valerie Anderson, the only woman he's ever befriended, other than me. The woman for whom he left work, in the middle of the day, in order to drive over to a school that I've wanted him to visit for months, whispering with her in a parking lot, for Romy and all the world to see, risking his career, his reputation, his family. The woman he met on our anniversary, the starry night it all began, the night he first saw her face and her child's face, the one he has since fixed and memorized and maybe even come to love. I know this by the way Nick opens the refrigerator and stares inside, as if he forgets what he was looking for in the first place. I know by the way he pretends to be asleep when I whisper his name in the dark. I know by the mournful way he tucks the kids in at night, as if contemplating what it would be like if he were separated from them. I know with a deep-to-the-bone certainty that comes with the impending loss of something you desperately don't want to lose. I know because I just know.

And then one cold, cloudless, blue-sky afternoon, ten days before Christmas, when I can't stand it another second, he walks in the door with a look that tells me that he can't stand it another second, either. His face is chafed, his nose red, his hair windblown. He shivers as I go to him and unwrap the scarf from his neck.

"Where have you been?" I ask, hoping he was out Christmas shopping for the kids. For me.

"In the Common," he says.

"What were you doing there?" I ask.

"Walking," he says.

"Alone?" I ask.

He shakes his head, looking mournful.

"Who were you with?" I say, my stomach dropping.

He looks at me and I hear her name in my head just as he says it aloud. "Valerie Anderson," he tells me. "Charlie's mother." His voice cracks and his eyes appear glassy, as if he might cry, which horrifies me, as I have never seen my husband cry.

"Oh," I manage to say — or something like that. Some monosyllable to indicate that I heard her name, that I understand what is happening here.

"Tessa," he says. "I have to tell you something."

I shake my head out of fear. I know it's not good, this thing he wants to tell me, this thing I already know deep inside, but don't want confirmed once and for all. Then he falls to one knee, just as he did the day he proposed.

"No," I say, as he takes my hands, pressing my knuckles to his cold cheeks. "Tell me you didn't."

He stares, motionless, then nods, his chin moving ever so slightly.

"No," I say again.

He pulls me down beside him, right onto the floor, and whispers, yes, he did.

"Was it just a kiss?" I say, looking into his eyes.

He whispers no, it wasn't just a kiss.

"Did you have sex with her?" I ask, my voice so calm that it scares me and makes me wonder if I love him. If I *ever* loved him. If I have a heart at all. Because nothing is breaking inside me. Nothing even hurts.

"Once," he says. "Just one time."

But he might as well have said ten or a hundred or a thousand. It might as well have been every night since the day we married. And now tears are welling in his eyes, and he *is* crying. Something he did not do the last time he was on one knee before me. Something he didn't do on our wedding day, or the day I stood before him with the plastic stick and pointed to the red lines and told him we were having a baby, or the moment he first held Ruby in his arms and officially became a father, or the moment when he learned we were having a boy, that he was going to have the son he always wanted.

But he is here now, crying. For *her.* For Valerie Anderson.

I reach out and wipe a tear from his cheek, wondering why I am doing it, whether it will be our final tender exchange.

"I'm sorry, Tessa. I'm *so* sorry," he says.

"Are you leaving me?" I ask, as if I'm consulting him before checking *beef* or *fish* on a reply card.

"No," he says. "I ended it. Just now."

"Just now?" I say. "On your walk?"

He nods. "Yes. Just now . . . Tessa . . . I wish I could take it back. I would take it back if I could."

"But you can't," I say, more to myself than to him.

"I know," he says. "I know."

I watch him, my head spinning, ticking through all the times I've seen this scenario unfold. To the greenest of teenaged girls who believe they will never love again and to silver-haired, wrinkled women without time to find another. To ordinary housewives and to some of the most beautiful, famous women in the world. I conjure a list with almost no effort, as if I've been subconsciously preparing for this moment: *Rita Hayworth, Jacqueline Kennedy, Mia Farrow, Jerry Hall, Princess Diana, Christie Brinkley, Uma Thurman, Jennifer Aniston.* Yet the list provides me no comfort, no reassurance that his act isn't about me, isn't a rejection of me, of everything I am.

I think of that theoretical conversation — the "what would you do?" conversation, all the times I had it, including very recently with Romy and April, when, for all I know, Nick could have already slept with her. *What if Nick did this unspeakable thing to me? What would I do?*

And now I'm about to find out; I am watching myself again.

I discover that I do not cry. I do not shout. I do not fall apart or crack at all. I keep my voice low, thinking of my children upstairs in the playroom, knowing that this will be a day that they will someday ask about, wondering what I will tell them. I think of my mother — then my father — then my mother again. I think of the fights I overheard and the ones I never knew about. Then I stand, straight and tall, and tell him to leave.

"Please," he says, a word that doesn't soften me, but rather, fills me with hate. Hate that gives me strength. *This is not the way it's supposed to be,* I think. Hate is not supposed to make you strong. But that is what it is doing.

"Go," I say just as it occurs to me that I would rather be the one to leave, that I want to be alone, out of this house. That if I stay, maybe my strength will expire. Maybe I'll collapse on the kitchen floor and won't be able to microwave the chicken nuggets or sit through the Charlie Brown Christmas special with the kids that I've promised they can watch. That the sight of Linus, encircling that scrawny tree with his blue blanket, will be too much for me to bear.

"Get out now," I say.

"Tessa," he says.

"Now," I say. "I can't stand to look at you."

Then I step away from him, backing up slowly, as if keeping a close eye on my enemy. The *only* enemy I've ever had. I watch him put his scarf back on, throwing it over his neck, as I flash back to the day we met on the subway, the day I knew that marrying Ryan — sweet, simple Ryan — was a mistake. And the irony of that, the irony of thinking I was *saved* by Nick, slashes through me, along with profound regret. Regret for every single thing about our life together. Our first date, our wedding day, our move to Boston, our home and everything in it, down to the dustiest can of lentil soup in the back of our cupboard.

Then, for a fleeting second, I even regret our children — a thought that fills me with intense guilt and grief and even more hatred for the person I once loved more than anyone. I silently take it back, frantically telling God that I didn't mean it, that Ruby and Frank are the only *right* decisions I've ever made. The only things I have left.

"I'm sorry," he says, looking bereaved, wilted, lost. "I will do *anything* to fix this."

"There is *nothing* you can do," I say. "This cannot be fixed."

"Tessa — it is over with her . . ."

"It is over with *us*, Nick," I say. "There *is* no us . . . Now get out."

38
VALERIE

She starts to hail a cab back to work, but decides to walk instead, hoping that the cold will numb her heart right along with the rest of her. But by the time her office building is in sight, she knows that the strategy hasn't worked, not even close. She considers going back inside, if only to turn off her computer and retrieve her briefcase full of documents she needs for an early morning meeting, but she can't bear the thought of seeing anyone, certain that they would be able to see right through her, somehow tell that her heart had just been broken. *Poor Valerie,* they will say to one another, the news making its rapid rounds among partners and associates alike. *She just can't seem to catch a break.*

So she heads for her car, parked on the fourth floor of the parking garage, listening to the echo of her boots on the cement floor. Her gloveless fingers are so stiff that she has difficulty unlocking her door, and wonders if she could actually have frostbite. It is the sort of question she would have posed to Nick only days ago — *how do you know if you're frostbitten?* — not just because it's a vaguely medical inquiry, but because she had begun to discuss nearly everything with him, down to the smallest minutiae of her day. And the thought that she will never be able to call him again — for reasons big or small — takes her breath away.

She shivers, then slides into her car and starts the engine, staring ahead at the dingy cinder-block wall, coming in and out of focus. After a while, she stops blinking back the tears, her vision growing more blurry, her shoulders shaking with small, stifled sobs. Some time later, when there is nothing left in her, she takes a deep breath, blows her nose, and wipes the mascara from her face. Then she backs out of her spot, weaves her way down to the exit, past the gold-toothed attendant named Willie, who gives her his usual salute good-bye.

That is that, she thinks to herself as she drives to Jason's house to pick Charlie up, early. *Time to move on.*

But the next morning she wakes up feeling worse — *much* worse — as if the disappointment needed a night to solidify. The realization that Nick is gone, that there is no possibility of a future, or even another night together, makes her ache everywhere, as if she has the flu. She gets out of bed, steps into the shower, then goes through all the other motions of her day, feeling a void deeper than she ever imagined possible for someone in her life in such a brief period of time. It is a void she knows she will never fill — never even *try* to fill. It's not worth the downside. She wonders what fool ever said that it's better to have loved and lost than to have never loved at all — she has never disagreed with something so much.

But as hard as she tries to push him from her mind, the more she misses him and everything about him. His name lighting up her phone, his voice, his hands, his smile. Most of all, she misses the feeling that something special was happening in her life, that *she* was special.

The only silver lining, she decides, is the timing. For although the approach of Christmas makes her grief more palpable, it gives her a quiet purpose and focus as she sets about her usual goal of single-handedly creating the sort of Norman Rockwell traditions that comprise the best childhood memories. She takes Charlie caroling with a group from her mother's church, she builds gingerbread houses with him, she helps him write letters to Santa. All the while, she holds her breath, hoping that Charlie doesn't ask about Nick, determined to create enough magic in her son's life so that he won't realize anything is missing.

Two days before Christmas, on the eve of Christmas Eve, as Charlie calls it, she is feeling particularly satisfied with her efforts. As she and Charlie sit by the tree, sipping eggnog, she tells herself that it is only she who feels Nick's absence — that Charlie is content. Sure enough, he looks up at her and announces that their Christmas tree is the best, better than the one in the lobby of his school, even better than the one at the mall next to Santa.

"Why's that?" she asks him, milking the compliment, feeling proud, even moved.

"We have more colorful ornaments, fuller branches . . . and more lights."

She smiles at him, thinking that stringing lights is one of those things she has always put in the category of fatherly tasks, like taking out the trash or mowing the lawn, only much more critical to a child. Because of this, she has always ensured that no man could do a finer job, taking hours to intertwine dozens of strands of blinking, colored lights through the branches, making them as dense as possible, perfecting their placement as if an army of elves were in on the action. She sips her own liberally spiked eggnog and says, "Well, I think I'd have to agree with you. We have a mighty fine tree."

One beat later, Charlie sprawls out on the floor, resting his chin in his hands, and says, "When is Nick coming over to see it?"

She freezes, his name spoken aloud making her heart flutter, then sink. She has only heard it once since he ended things — when Jason asked for an update. She responded simply, told him that it was over and that she didn't want to talk about it — an answer her brother wordlessly accepted.

But she cannot give her son the same line now. So instead, she waffles. "I don't know, sweetie," she says, feeling guilty for stringing him along but determined not to taint his Christmas, this moment, desperate for the conversation to wait until January.

"When are we going to see him?" Charlie asks, seeming to detect something wrong in his mother's voice or expression.

"I don't know," she says again, forcing a smile. She clears her throat and tries to change the subject back to the tree, remarking on a snowman ornament she made as a child.

"We have to see him before Christmas," Charlie says. "To exchange gifts."

Valerie tenses, but says nothing.

"Don't you have a present for him?" he presses.

She thinks of the vintage postcards of Fenway Park that she bought for Nick on eBay, now tucked into her sock drawer, and the tickets to the symphony she bought for Charlie to give him, imagining the two going alone together, but shakes her head. "No," she lies to her son. "I don't."

"Why not?" he asks, looking confused. In the dim, reddish glow of the tree, she can barely make out the burn on his cheek, and she thinks of how far they have come in two months, how she never imagined that they would be here, like this, that she could *ever* worry about anything other than Charlie's basic health. She feels fleeting comfort in this until she considers the emotional damage that this setback could cause. Perhaps more lasting than a scar on his face. "Why don't you have a present for Nick?"

Her insides seize as she carefully replies, "I don't know . . . Because he's not family."

"So? He's our friend," Charlie says.

"Yes . . . But I really only buy presents for family," she says lamely.

Charlie seems to consider this and then

says, "Do you think he got us one?"

"I don't know, honey. Probably not . . . But that doesn't mean he doesn't care about you . . ." she says, her voice trailing off.

"Oh," Charlie says, looking momentarily hurt. Then his face clears as he says, "Well, that's okay. I still have something for him."

"What do you have for him?" she asks nervously.

"It's a secret," he says, his voice mysterious in the way of a little boy trying to be mysterious.

"Oh," she says, nodding.

He looks at her as if he is concerned that he just hurt her feelings. "It's a *Star Wars* thing. You wouldn't understand, Mommy."

She nods again, adding this to the growing list of things she doesn't — and likely never will — understand.

"Mommy?" Charlie asks after a few beats of quiet.

"What's that, Charlie?" she says, hoping that the next words from her little boy will be about *Star Wars,* not Nick.

"Are you sad?" he asks her.

She blinks and smiles and shakes her head. "No. No . . . Not at all," she says as convincingly as she can. "It's Christmas. And I'm with you. How can I be sad?"

He seems to accept this, adjusting the

Nativity scene along the Christmas tree skirt, pushing Joseph's and Mary's heads together as if in a symbolic gesture before his next question. "Did you and Nick break up? Like Jason always does with his boyfriends?"

She looks at him, stunned, then flounders for the right words. "Honey, we weren't together like that," she says. "Nick is married."

It is the first she's discussed this basic truth with her son, a fact that fills her with even more guilt.

"We were just friends," she finishes.

"But you're not friends anymore?" he asks, his voice trembling.

She hesitates but dodges the question. "I will always care about him," she says. "And he will always care about you."

Charlie is not fooled, staring into her eyes and asking, "Did you get in a fight?"

Valerie knows she cannot evade his questions anymore, that she has no choice but to crush him. Two days before Christmas.

"Charlie. No. We didn't get in a fight . . . We just decided that we shouldn't be friends anymore," she says, flustered and feeling certain that she chose the wrong words. Again.

He looks at her as if she just told him that

there is no such thing as Santa Claus. Or that he's real, but just won't be coming around to their house this year.

"Why?" Charlie says.

"Because Nick is married and has two children of his own . . . and he's not in our family."

And he never will be, she thinks. Then forces herself to say the words aloud.

"Is he still my doctor?" Charlie asks, his voice strained, panicked.

She shakes her head and says, as cheerfully as she can, that he has a new doctor now — a doctor who taught Nick everything he knows.

Hearing this, Charlie begins to choke up, his eyes growing huge, red, wet.

"So I can't be friends with him, either?" Charlie asks.

Valerie shakes her head slowly, barely.

"Why not?" he says, now shouting and crying. "Why can't I?"

"Charlie . . ." she says, knowing that there is no explanation she can give him to make sense of this. Knowing that all of this could have been avoided if she hadn't been so selfish.

"I'm going to call him now!" Charlie says, pushing up to his knees and then feet. "He told me I could call him anytime!"

451

Her heart fills with guilt and sorrow as she reaches out for her son.

He angrily resists, swatting at her hand. "He gave me his number!" Charlie sobs, his scar now aglow in a new angle of light. "I have a present for him!"

She tries to hold him again, this time catching him, wrapping her arms around him as tightly as she can.

"Sweetie," she says, holding him to her. "It's going to be okay."

"I want a daddy," he says, sobbing as he goes limp in her arms.

"I know, sweetie," she says, her heart breaking even more — something she didn't think possible.

"Why don't I have a daddy?" he continues to cry, his sobs gradually losing their edge, turning into soft whimpers. "Where *is* my daddy?"

"I don't know, sweetie."

"He left us," Charlie says. "Everybody leaves us."

"No," she says, breathing into his hair, now crying herself. "He left me. Not you."

She isn't sure who she is talking about, but she says it again, more firmly. "Not you, Charlie. Never you."

"I wish I had a daddy," he whispers. "I wish you could find my daddy."

She opens her mouth to tell him what she always tells him — that families are all different and that he has so many people who love him. But she knows that it will not be good enough. Not now, maybe not ever. So she just says his name, again and again, holding on to him under their perfectly lit tree.

39
TESSA

I told him to go. I *wanted* him to go. But I still hate him for listening to me, for not staying and making me fight. I hate him for walking so calmly toward the door, and for the look on his face as he turned back toward me, his lips parted, as if he had one last thing to say. I waited for something profound, some indelible sentiment that I could replay in the hours, days, years to come. Something to help me make sense of what had just happened to me and our family. Yet he didn't speak — perhaps because he changed his mind and thought better of it. More likely because he had nothing to say in the first place. Then he disappeared around the corner. Seconds later, I heard the door open and then shut again with a definite, final thud — the sound of someone leaving. A sound that has always made me fleetingly sad even when I know they'll be coming right back, even when it's a houseguest I am *ready* to see go. So it shouldn't have surprised me that that moment and the eerie calm that followed were worse than the actual moment of Nick's confession.

And there I stood, alone, dizzy and breathless, before turning to sit on the couch, waiting for the rage to overcome me, for the uncontrollable urge to go destroy something. Slash his favorite shirts or smash his framed Red Sox memorabilia or burn our wedding photos. React the way women are supposed to react in this situation. React the way my mother did when she smashed my father's new car with a baseball bat. I could still hear the sound of glass exploding, see the carnage that remained in the driveway long after my father came to sweep and hose down the crime scene, how those stray shards glistened on sunny days as a reminder of our fractured family.

But I was way too exhausted for revenge, and more important, I wanted to believe that I was too good for it. Besides, I had children to feed, practical matters to attend to, and it took all my energy to head for the kitchen, set the table with the kids' favorite Dr. Seuss place mats, prepare two plates of chicken nuggets and peas and mandarin oranges, then pour two glasses of milk, adding a dash of chocolate milk. When everything was ready, I turned toward the stairs, noticing the chicken breasts I had begun to thaw just before Nick came home. I put them both back in the freezer, then called the names of my children, listening to the sound of rapid footsteps. It was a rare, immediate response, especially for Ruby, and I wondered whether they detected the urgency and need in my voice. As their faces appeared in the stairwell, I realized how much I *did* need them — and the intensity of that need scared me and filled me with guilt. I remembered how much my mother needed Dex and me in the aftermath of her divorce, the burdensome weight of that responsibility, and said a quick prayer that I would be stronger. I reassured myself that my children were too young to understand the unfolding tragedy in their lives — which felt like a small consolation, until I realized that this was a tragedy in itself.

"Hi, Mommy," Frankie said, blanket in tow, smiling at me in mid-flight down the stairs.

"Hi, Frankie," I replied, my heart aching for him.

I watched Ruby bound down the stairs, past her brother, peering into the kitchen and asking me in an ironically accusatory tone, "Where's Daddy?"

I swallowed hard and told her that Daddy had to go back to work, wondering, for the first time, where Nick had actually gone. Was he at work? Was he driving aimlessly around? Or had he gone back to her? Maybe this was the result he wanted all along. Maybe he wanted *me* to make the choice, to play my hand like this. Maybe he assumed I would be just like my mother.

"Was it an emergency?" Ruby pressed, furrowing her dark brow, exactly as her father does.

"Yes. It was," I told her, nodding, then shifting my gaze back to Frankie, who looks *nothing* like his father — a fact that I suddenly found comforting. "Okay, then! Let's wash hands," I called out merrily, forging ahead with our evening, on some sort of bizarre autopilot, pretending that it was any other ordinary day. Pretending that my life — and theirs — hadn't just been shattered and smashed like my father's Mercedes, so long ago.

Later that night, I am curled up in a fetal position on the couch, wondering how I have managed to keep it together for so many hours, not shedding a single tear, even mustering a lighthearted bedtime story for the kids. I want to believe that it speaks volumes of my character, the core of who I am as a person and mother. I want to believe that it shows I am capable of being brave in a crisis, dignified in the face of disaster. That I am still in control of myself, even though I am no longer in control of my life. And maybe, in part, that is all true.

But more likely, I am simply in shock — a feeling that doesn't begin to recede until now, as I pick up the phone to call Cate.

"Hey, girl," she says, the sounds of Manhattan in the background — cars honking, buses grinding to a halt, a man shouting something in Spanish. "What's going on?"

I hesitate, then listen to myself say the words aloud.

Nick cheated on me.

And it is in this instant that my new reality comes into sharp focus. The reality that Nick is, and forever will be, one of those men. And by virtue of *his* choice, I have become one of those women. Cheater and victim. That's who we are now.

"Tessa. Oh, my God . . . Are you sure?" she asks.

I try to answer but can't speak, the dam of tears finally breaking.

"Are you sure?" she says again.

"Yeah," I sob, hugging a box of Kleenex to my chest. "He told me he did it . . . Yes."

"Oh, Tessa . . . *Shit,*" she whispers. "I'm *so* sorry, honey. I'm so sorry."

She listens to me cry for the longest time, murmuring her support, cursing Nick's name, and finally asking me if I want to share any of the details. "It's fine if you don't . . . If you're not ready . . ."

"There's not much to tell," I say, struggling to get my words out. "He came home this evening. Said he had just gone for a walk in the Common with her."

"Her?" Cate presses gently.

"The one we suspected. The one Romy saw him with." I am unable to say her name, vowing *never* to say her name again — suddenly understanding exactly how my mother has felt for all of these years.

"And he just told you . . . that he was having an affair?"

"He didn't call it that. I don't know *what* you would call it . . . He said it only happened once. He had sex with her once," I say, the words a knife in my heart, my tears still coming in streams. "He said he ended things today. And that's his story. As if his word means *anything.*"

"Okay. Okay!" She interrupts me with optimism I find confusing.

"Okay what?" I ask.

"So he's not . . . leaving?"

"Oh, he left," I scoff, anger resurfacing, temporarily halting my tears. "He's gone. I told him to get out."

"But I mean — he's not leaving *you*. He doesn't want to . . . be with her?"

"Well, clearly he wanted to *be* with her," I say. "Pretty damn badly."

"Once," she says. "And now he's sorry. He regrets it. Right?"

"Cate," I say. "Are you trying to tell me that this is no big deal?"

"No. Not at all . . . I'm just feeling somewhat hopeful that he confessed. As opposed to getting caught . . ."

"What difference does that make? He did it. He *did* it! He *screwed* another woman," I say, becoming hysterical.

Cate must hear it, too, because she says, "I know. I know, Tess . . . I am not minimizing it — at all . . . But at least he told you. And at least he ended things with her."

"Or so he says. He could be doing it again right now. This very *second,*" I say, the sickening images beginning to materialize in my head. I picture a blonde, then a brunette, then a redhead. I picture large, full breasts, then small, high ones, then perfect in-between ones. I don't want to know what she looks like — and at the same time, I *desperately* want to know everything

460

about her. I want her to be like me; I want her to be nothing like me. I no longer know what I want, apparently any more than I know the man I married.

"He's not with her," Cate says. "No way."

"How do you know?" I ask, wanting her to reassure me despite how hard I am resisting her positive spin.

"Because he's sorry. Because he loves you, Tessa."

"Bullshit," I say, blowing my nose. "He loves himself. He loves that damn hospital. He loves his patients and apparently their mothers."

Cate sighs, her background noise suddenly disappearing as if she just stepped off the street or got in a cab. Then she says, "What are you going to do?"

For a few seconds, her question empowers me, in the same way that telling Nick to leave empowered me. But the feeling quickly vanishes, crystallizing in fear. "You mean am I leaving him?" I say.

It is the million-dollar, until-now-theoretical "what would you do if" question.

"Yeah," Cate says softly.

"I don't know," I say, recognizing that I probably *might* have a choice. I could take him back, and live a sham of a life. Or I could do the thing I always *said* I would do — I could leave him. I could sit the kids down and give them the news that would change the face of their childhood, and color every major, important event of their adulthood. Graduations, weddings, the births of their children. I imagine Nick and me standing apart, either by ourselves or with someone new; either way, the distance between us creating unspoken tension during a time that should only be about joy.

"I don't know," I say, realizing with anger and grief and panic and fear that I have no good option left. That there is no possibility of happily ever after.

Every hour over the next few days, and virtually every *minute* of every hour, is torture, marked by a range of emotions too varied to chart but all shades of bleak and bleaker. I am ashamed for what has happened to me, *humiliated* by Nick's infidelity even as I look in the mirror, alone. I am furious when he calls (six times), e-mails (three), and drops off letters in the mailbox (twice). But I am frantic and filled with deep despair when a stretch of time goes by that he doesn't. I scrutinize his silence, imagining them together, jealousy and insecurity pulsing inside me. I scrutinize his

words even more, his apologies, his procla-
mations of love for me and our family, his
pleas for a second chance.

But with Cate's help, I remain vigilant and
strong and do not contact him — not once.
Not even in my weakest late-night moments
when his messages are soft and sad, and my
heart aches with loneliness. I am punishing
him, of course — twisting the knife with
every unreturned message. But I am also
doing my best to prove to myself that I can
survive without him. I am gearing up to tell
him that I meant what I said. That we are
done, and that he no longer has a place in
my home or heart. Moving forward, he will
be the father of my children, nothing more.

To this point, my first communication
with him is two days before Christmas, an
e-mail of precise instructions regarding the
children and the visit I am granting him on
Christmas Eve. I hate that I have to give
him that much, that I have to contact him
at *all,* for any reason, but I know he has a
right to see the kids — and more important,
they have a right to see him. I tell him that
he may come to the house at three o'clock,
that Carolyn will be here to let him in. I am
paying her for four hours, but he is free to
let her go, so long as she is back by seven
when I return. I do not want to see him. I

tell him to have the kids fed, bathed, and dressed in their Christmas pajamas, and that I will put them to bed. He should retrieve any belongings he needs for the next few weeks, and that we will schedule a weekend in January for him to get the rest. I am all business. Ice-cold. I reread, fix a typo, hit send. Within seconds, his response appears:

Thank you, Tessa. Would you please tell me what you've told the kids, as I want to be consistent?

The e-mail stabs at my heart, not for what is there, but for what *isn't*. He didn't ask to see me. He didn't ask for the four of us to be together. He didn't ask to come over on Christmas morning and watch the kids open their presents. I am enraged that he seems to be throwing in the towel, but then tell myself that I would have refused him anyway, and that I didn't leave him even a slight opening to ask for more. And that is because there *is* no opening. There is nothing he can say or do to change my mind. My hands shaking, I type:

I told them that you've been working very hard at the hospital because a little boy was badly hurt and that he needs you to make him better. They seem satisfied with this explanation for now. We will have to handle after the holidays, but I do not want their Christmas ruined by this.

There is no mistaking the little boy I am referring to, no mistaking the subtext: *You put another child above your own. And because of that choice, our family is broken forever.*

Later that afternoon, the doorbell rings. Expecting it to be the UPS man with a final delivery of catalogue-purchased Christmas gifts for the kids, I answer the door. But instead, I find April with a bag of presents and a tentative smile.

"Merry Christmas," she says, her smile growing broader but no less uneasy.

"Merry Christmas," I say, feeling conflicted as I force a smile of my own. On the one hand, I am still angry at her for handling things the way she did, and have the irrational feeling that she and Romy somehow *made* this happen to me. On the other hand, she has arrived at a very lonely moment, and I can't help feeling relieved and a little bit happy to see my friend.

"Would you like to come in?" I ask,

somewhere between formal and friendly.

She hesitates, as drop-in visits, even among close friends, are firmly on her list of faux pas, but then says, "I'd love to."

I step aside and lead her through the foyer into my very messy kitchen, where she hands me a bag of beautifully wrapped presents.

"Thank you . . . You shouldn't have," I say, thinking that I *didn't* this year, for the very first time deciding that gifts to friends and neighbors simply weren't going to happen. And for once, I let it go, let myself off the hook with no feelings of guilt.

"It's just my usual pound cake. Nothing fancy," she says — although her pound cakes are a thing of beauty. "And a little something for the kids." She glances around and asks where they are.

"Watching television," I say, pointing toward the stairs. "In my room."

"Ah," she says.

"There's been a lot of television watching these days," I admit.

"Television is crucial this time of year," she agrees, a rare admission. "My kids are bouncing off the walls. And the threat of Santa Claus not showing up has really lost its teeth."

I laugh and say, "Yeah. That one doesn't

work so well with Ruby, either. *Nothing* works with Ruby."

Then, after one awkward beat, I ask if she'd like a cup of coffee.

"I'd *love* a cup," she says. "Thank you."

She takes a seat at the kitchen island as I turn and flip on the coffeemaker and reach into the cabinet for two matching mugs. Upon realizing that most are still dirty in the dishwasher, others piled in the sink, I mentally shrug, grab two random cups, and forgo saucers and place mats altogether.

The next few minutes are awkward, and I am grateful for the task of brewing coffee, while fielding questions from April about holiday shopping and where I am on my various lists. But by the time I hand her a cup of black coffee, I have worked up the nerve to address the real reason I know she stopped by.

"Well. You were right about Nick," I say, catching her off guard. "And you were right about that woman . . . I kicked him out last week."

She lowers her mug, her face crumbling with genuine sympathy. "Oh, God," she says. "I don't know what to say . . . I'm *really* sorry."

I nod and numbly thank her as her expression becomes anguished. "I promise I won't

467

tell anyone. Not a soul. Ever."

I give her an incredulous stare and say, "April. We're separated. He's not living here. People are going to find out sooner or later. And anyway . . . what people are saying about me is really the least of my concerns right now . . ."

April nods, gazing into her still untouched coffee. Then she takes a deep breath and says, "Tessa. I have something to tell you . . . Something I want to tell you . . ."

"April," I say drolly. "No more bad news, please."

She shakes her head and says, "This isn't about you and Nick . . . It's about . . . me. And Rob." We make fleeting eye contact as she blurts the rest out. "Tessa, I just want you to know . . . that I've been where you are right now. I know what you're going through."

I stare at her, processing her words, the very last thing I expected to hear from her. "Rob cheated on you?" I ask, shocked.

She nods the smallest of nods, looking the way I feel — ashamed. As if Rob's actions are her failure, her humiliation.

"When?" I say, recalling our recent doubles match and her bold insistence that she would leave if it ever happened to her. She had been so convincing.

"Last year," she says.

"With who?" I ask, then quickly add, "I'm sorry. That's none of my business. And it doesn't matter."

She bites her lips and says, "It's okay . . . It was with his ex-girlfriend."

"Mandy?" I ask, recalling April's Facebook obsession with Rob's high school girlfriend and how ridiculous I thought she was being at the time.

"Yes. Mandy," she says, her voice dropping an octave.

"But . . . doesn't she live in one of the Dakotas?" I say.

She nods. "They reconnected at their twenty-year reunion," she says, making quotes around *reconnected*. "The Fargo-sounding whorebag."

"How do you know? Are you sure?" I ask, envisioning a scene like the one following Nick's walk in the Common.

"I read about fifty back-and-forth e-mails. And let's just say . . . they left very little to the imagination. He might as well have taken pictures . . ."

"Oh, April," I say, letting go of any residual resentment toward her — for her call, for her condescending tone when she told me about Nick being spotted by Romy (a tone that was likely in my head), and most of all, for what I believed to be her perfect life. My mind races as I try to remember any time last year when April was less than her cool, collected self — but come up empty-handed. "I had no idea," I say.

"I didn't tell anyone," she says.

"No one?" I ask. "Not even your sister? Or mother?"

She shakes her head again. "Not even my therapist," she says, releasing a nervous laugh. "I just stopped going to her . . . I was too embarrassed to tell her."

"*Shit,*" I say, exhaling hard. "Do they *all* cheat?"

April looks out the window into the back-yard and shrugs despondently.

"How did you get through it?" I ask, hoping to at least glean an alternative route to the one my mother took.

"We haven't," she says.

"But you're together."

"Cheaply," she says. "We haven't had sex in nearly a year . . . We sleep in separate beds . . . We haven't even been out to dinner alone . . . And I . . . basically despise him."

"April," I say, reaching out for her hand. "That's no way to live . . . Did you . . . Is he sorry? Do you ever consider forgiving him?" I ask, as if it's a simple matter of choice.

She shakes her head. "He's sorry. Yes. But I can't forgive him. I just . . . *can't*."

"Well, then," I say, hesitating, thinking of my father, then Rob, then Nick. "Do you ever consider leaving him? Ending things?"

She bites her lip and says, "No. I'm not going to do that. My marriage is a joke, but I don't want to lose my whole *life* because of what he did. And I don't want to do that to my children, either."

"You could start over," I say, knowing that it's not nearly as easy as I'm making it sound. That dissolving a marriage is one of the hardest things a person can go through. I know this because I saw it firsthand with my parents — and because I've been imagining it every day, nearly every *hour,* since Nick dropped his little bomb on me.

"Is that what *you're* going to do?" she asks.

I shrug, feeling as forlorn and bitter as she looks. "I don't know," I say. "I honestly don't know *what* I'm going to do."

"Well, I can't start over," she says, shaking her head sadly. "I just can't . . . I guess I'm not that strong."

I look at my friend, overwhelmed with confusion. Unsure of what April should do. What *I* should do. What a strong woman

471

would do. In fact, the only thing that I am certain of is that there are no easy answers, and that anyone who says there are has never been in our shoes.

And now it is Christmas Eve and I am driving through the dark, mostly empty streets, watching snow flurries dance in my headlights. I have another hour before I can go home and have already exhausted my errands: buying a few final stocking stuffers for the kids, returning the sweaters I bought for Nick, stopping by the bakery to pick up the pies I ordered only minutes before Nick returned from his walk in the Common — including the coconut cream he dared to request the day before, knowing what he knew.

I try not to think about this, try not to think about anything as I weave my way through the public gardens, turning onto Beacon, then over the Mass Avenue Bridge. As I reach Memorial, my phone rings in the passenger seat. I jump, wondering whether or maybe even *hoping* that it's Nick — if only so that I can ignore him once again. But it is not Nick; it is my brother, who does not yet know what has happened. I tell myself not to answer because I don't have it in me to lie, and I don't want to burden him on Christmas. But I can't resist the thought of his voice — the thought of *any-one*'s voice. So I slip on my headset and say hello.

"Merry Christmas!" he booms into the phone over his usual background din.

I glance at the Hancock Tower, its spire aglow with red and green lights and wish him a Merry Christmas back. "Got your card today," I say. "What a gorgeous photo of the girls."

"Thanks," he says. "Rachel gets the credit on that one."

"Obviously," I say, smiling.

"So what are you guys up to?" he says, sounding the way you're supposed to sound on Christmas Eve — buoyant, blithe, blessed. I can hear Julia singing the kitschy version of "Rudolph the Red-nosed Reindeer," her voice high and off-key, and my mother's bell-like laughter, as I envision the sort of scene I used to take for granted.

"Um . . . not too much," I say as I drive across the Salt-and-Pepper Bridge, back into Beacon Hill. "Just . . . you know . . . Christmas Eve." My voice trails off as I realize I'm making no sense at all, not even putting a proper sentence together.

"You okay?" Dex asks.

"I'll be fine," I say, knowing how revealing

this statement is, and that there is no turning back now. But as guilty as I feel for tainting his night, I feel a sense of relief, too. I want my brother to know.

"What happened?" he says, as if he already knows the answer. His voice is more angry than worried, the one thing absent from Cate's reaction.

"Nick had an affair," I say, the first I've used the word, having decided only a few hours ago, in the bakery, that even "one time" constitutes an affair, at least when there is emotional involvement leading up to it.

Dex does not ask for details, but I give a few anyway, covering Nick's confession, that I kicked him out, that I have not seen him since, and that, although he has a few hours with the kids now, he will be spending Christmas alone.

Then I say, "I know you're going to want to tell Rachel. And that's fine. But please don't say anything to Mom. I want to tell her myself."

"You got it, Tess," Dex promises. Then he exhales loudly and says, "Dammit."

"I know."

"I can't fucking *believe* he did this."

His loyalty, so fierce and unwavering, makes my eyes water, my heart ache. I tell myself I can't cry. Not right before going home. Not on Christmas Eve.

"It's going to be okay," I say as I pass the Church of the Advent where families are mingling on the sidewalk, a service just over or one about to begin.

"Can I call him?" he says.

"I don't know, Dex . . ." I say, wondering what good could possibly come from it. "What would you say?"

"I just want to talk to him," he says, making me think of a mobster going to "talk" to someone with a pistol tucked into his waistband.

I drive along Charles, its storefronts closed and dark, and say, "There's no point really . . . I think I've made my decision."

"Which is?"

"I think I'm leaving him . . . I don't want to live a lie," I say, thinking of April, suddenly deciding that her way is not an option for me.

"Good," he says. "You should."

I am surprised by his definitive answer, especially because of how much he has always liked Nick.

"You think he'd do it again, don't you?" I ask, thinking of our father, certain that Dex is, too.

"I don't know. But I don't think you

should stick around and find out," Dex says.

I swallow hard, wondering how I could feel so conflicted by his sure advice. Although I am comforted by his black-and-white stance, I also feel the urge to soften it, force him to acknowledge that this is murky terrain.

"You would never do this to Rachel," I say. "Would you?"

"Never," he says with all the certainty in the world. "Absolutely never."

"But . . . you —"

"I know," he says, cutting me off. "I know I cheated before. But not on *Rachel*." He stops suddenly, likely realizing his painful implication. That he wouldn't cheat on his wife, the love of his life. That people don't cheat on their true love.

"Right," I say.

"Look," Dex says, trying to backtrack. "I'm not saying Nick doesn't love you. I'm sure he does . . . But *this* . . . This is just . . ."

"What?" I say, bracing myself.

"This is just *unforgivable*," Dex says.

I nod, my eyes filling with tears as I replay the word in all of its forms — *unforgivable, forgive, forgiven, forgiveness*. It is the word that echoes in my head as my brother and I exchange *I love you*s and *good-bye*s and I drive back to Wellesley, past April's house, its windows trimmed with scarlet-bowed wreaths, then into my own driveway where I see Carolyn's white Saab parked in Nick's usual spot. I can still hear it as the kids and I put sugar cookies and eggnog out for Santa and while I sit in the basement, wrapping presents, reading leaflets of small-print instructions, and assembling plastic parts. *Can I forgive Nick?* I think with every ribbon curled, every turn of the screwdriver. *Can I ever forgive him?*

There are other questions, too — more than I can possibly keep track of, some that seem to matter, others that don't at all but still can't be silenced. *What would my friends do? What will my mother say? Do I still love my husband? Does he love me, or another woman, or both of us? Does she love him? Is he truly sorry? Was it really only once? Would he ever do it again? Does he want to do it again? What does she have that I don't? Did he confess out of guilt or loyalty? Did he really end things — or did she? Does he truly want to come home or does he simply wish to keep his family together? What is best for the kids? What is best for me? How would my life change? Would I be okay? Will I ever be okay again?*

40
VALERIE

Valerie can never decide whether New Year's Eve is more about looking backward or ahead, but this year, both make her think of Nick, both make her equally miserable. She misses him terribly, and is certain she still loves him. But she is angry, too, especially tonight. She feels sure he never confessed a thing to his wife, and can't shake the romantic, cozy images of the two of them, ushering in the new year with champagne toasts and lingering kisses and grand plans for their future — perhaps a new baby so that Nick can really wipe last year's slate clean.

At one point, she becomes so convinced that he has forgotten her altogether, that she nearly breaks down and sends him a text, an innocuous one-line happy-new-year greeting, if only to spoil his evening and remind him of what he did.

But she decides against it, both because she is too proud and because she doesn't really mean it. She doesn't want his new year to be happy. She wants him to suffer as much as she does. She is ashamed of this, and ponders whether you can truly love someone you wish misery upon. She is not sure of the answer, but decides it doesn't much matter, because the answer won't change anything. There is *nothing* she can do to change anything, she thinks, as she sits down at the kitchen table with Charlie and suggests that they write down resolutions for the coming year.

"What's a resolution?" Charlie asks, as she slides a sheet of lined yellow notebook paper toward him.

"It's like a goal . . . A promise to yourself," she says.

"Like promising to practice the piano?" he asks, something he hasn't done much since the accident.

"Sure," she says. "Or resolving to keep your room clean. Or make new friends. Or work *really* hard in therapy."

He nods, gripping his pencil and asking her how to spell *therapy*. She helps him sound out the word, then writes on her own paper: *Eat fewer processed foods, more fruits and vegetables.*

For the next thirty minutes, they continue like this, concentrating, spelling, discussing, until they've each come up with five resolutions — all practical and predictable and utterly doable. Yet as she tapes their lists to the refrigerator, she knows that the exercise, while productive, was something of a sham — that there is only one resolution that matters to both of them right now: *get over Nick.*

To that end, she makes the night as fun and festive as possible, playing endless rounds of go fish, watching *Star Wars,* and letting Charlie stay up until midnight for the first time ever. As the ball drops in Times Square, they drink sparkling cider out of crystal flutes and toss handfuls of confetti that they made with a hole punch and construction paper. Yet all the while, she can feel the hollow, forced joy in her efforts, and worse, she senses it in Charlie, too, especially as she tucks him into bed that night. His expression is too earnest, his hug around her neck too tight, his words too formal as he tells her how much fun he had, actually *thanking* her.

"Oh, sweetie," she says, thinking that she must be the only mother in the world who wishes her son would *forget* to say thank you. "I love spending time with you. More than anything."

"Me too," he says.

She pulls the covers up to his chin and

kisses both of his cheeks and his forehead. Then she says good night and goes to her own bed, checking her phone one last time before she falls asleep and wakes up to the new year.

She has always hated January for all the usual reasons — the postholiday letdown, the short, dark days, and the miserable Boston weather that, despite having never lived elsewhere, she knows she will never get used to. She hates the nor'easter gales, the ankle-deep gray slush, the endless stretches of painful, single-digit cold — so bitter and biting that thirty-degree days actually feel like a reprieve, a tease for spring, until the rain comes and the temperature drops like a stone, freezing everything solid once again.

But this year, *this* January, is especially unbearable. And as the days pass, she starts to worry that she will never emerge from her funk. She feels profound disappointment over Nick, along with near-constant worry for Charlie, both coagulating in her heart, fading into plain old bitterness, a state of being she has always guarded against, even at her lowest.

One afternoon toward the end of the month, Summer's mother calls her while she is at work. She feels a spike of negativity, remembering her daughter's words on the playground, bracing herself to hear about another incident.

But Beverly's voice is warm and breezy, no hint of trouble anywhere. "Hi, Valerie! Did I catch you at a bad time?" she asks.

Valerie glances at the pile of documents on her desk, her stomach in knots as she replies, "No. Not at all . . . It's nice to have a break from the fascinating world of insurance recovery."

"Sounds only slightly better than the fascinating world of accounting," Beverly says, laughing robustly, reminding Valerie that, against all odds, she actually *likes* this woman. "So how've you been? Did you have a good holiday?" she continues.

"Yeah," Valerie lies. "It was good. How was yours?"

"Oh — it was okay, but absolute *chaos*. We had my husband's kids this year — all four of them — *and* his former in-laws . . . which is a long, totally bizarre story I won't bore you with . . . So to tell you the truth, I was really ready to go back to work. And I don't even *like* my job." She laughs again as Valerie decides, with relief, that if something went wrong at school today, it can't be all that dire.

"So did you hear the news?" Beverly asks, amusement in her voice.

"The news?" Valerie says, refraining from telling Beverly that she is not in the social loop at school — or anywhere, for that matter.

"About the latest love connection?"

"No," Valerie says, unwittingly picturing Nick, *always* picturing Nick.

"Summer and Charlie," Beverly says, "are an item."

"Summer and *Charlie?*" Valerie echoes, sure that Beverly has her facts wrong — or perhaps is making some sort of bad joke.

"Yeah. Apparently it's pretty serious . . . In fact, we should probably sit down and start hammering out the details for the wedding and rehearsal dinner. I think we should keep it low-key . . . don't you?"

Valerie smiles, slightly disarmed, as she says, "Low-key is always good with me . . . Although, I must confess, I don't have a lot of experience with wedding plans."

It is something she wouldn't ordinarily say, the sort of personal information she always keeps close to the vest, and feels uneasy until Beverly laughs and chimes in with, "No worries. I've done it three times. So together we're just about normal."

Valerie laughs a real laugh, her first of the

year, and says, "Normal would be nice."

"Normal would be *very* nice. I can't fathom it, though . . ." Beverly says with merry acceptance. "So anyway. Yes. Charlie and Summer . . . I'm really pleased . . . Wasn't wild about her last boyfriend. At least, I wasn't crazy about his mother — which is all that matters, right?"

Valerie asks who her last boyfriend was, feeling a rush of cheap delight when Beverly says Grayson's name. But she still refrains from making a derogatory comment about Romy, and instead says, "Did they have a . . . falling-out?"

"Not really sure of the details. I know they — *she* — called it quits right before Christmas. I think his gift wasn't up to snuff . . . or at least it couldn't compete with the beaded bracelet Charlie gave her."

Valerie's mouth falls open, as she remembers the bracelet Charlie made in therapy, the one she assumed was for her, but never showed up under the tree. "Really? He didn't tell me," she says, shocked — in a good way.

"Yeah. It was purple and yellow — Summer's favorite colors . . . You've clearly taught him well."

Valerie smiles, appreciating this spin on Charlie's gesture, appreciating any scrap of approval she can get, especially in the parenting department. "I try," she says.

"So anyway, I was just calling to see if the two of you wanted to join us this Saturday for a playdate? A chaperoned first date of sorts?" Beverly says.

Valerie turns toward the window, watching dusk and sleet fall upon the city. "That sounds great. We'd love to," she says, surprised to realize that she actually means it.

Later that night, over tacos at Jason's, she decides to tell Charlie about the playdate with Summer. She is excited for her son, although part of her still wonders if the crush has been manufactured by Beverly, spawned from maternal guilt.

"Oh, Charlie," she says nonchalantly, spooning diced tomatoes and onions onto her plate in the assembly line Hank has created along the kitchen counter. "Summer's mother called today."

Out of the corner of her eyes, she sees Charlie look at her, his small eyebrows arched with curiosity. "What did she say?" he asks.

"She invited you over to play on Saturday. She invited both of us over. I told her yes. Is that okay? Would you like to go?"

She looks at him, awaiting his reaction.

"Yes," he says, a small smile flashing across his face, confirming everything.

Valerie smiles back at him, feeling happy to see *him* happy, but also awash with a new brand of protectiveness — the kind that comes when things are going well. It occurs to her that she has always believed in keeping expectations low. You can't get hurt if you don't care. Nick has proven that theory.

"Now. Wait. Who is Summer?" Jason asks — even though Valerie is sure that he knows exactly who Summer is — while Hank looks on curiously.

"A girl in my class," Charlie says, his ears turning a telling shade of pink.

Hank and Jason exchange a knowing smirk and then Hank breaks the ice with a hearty, "Charlie! Do you have a *girl*friend?"

Charlie hides another, broader smile with his taco shell and shrugs.

Jason reaches over and punches him on the shoulder. "Go, Chuck! Is she pretty?"

"She's *beautiful,*" Charlie says, his voice and expression so pure and sincere and angelic that Valerie feels an inexplicable knot in her chest — a feeling that she can't quite place as good or bad.

Later that night, as she applies vitamin E ointment to Charlie's cheek, the feeling in her chest returns when he looks at her, wide-eyed, and says, "You know, Mommy. Summer is sorry for what she said."

She feels herself tense, remembering those words, that day.

"Oh?" she says carefully.

"About having an alien face," Charlie says matter-of-factly.

"Really?" she says, not knowing what else to say.

"Yes. She said she was sorry. And that she takes it back. She said she likes my face the way it is . . . And so . . . and so I . . . forgave her. And that's why she's my friend."

"I'm so glad," Valerie says, awash with raw emotion. She looks at Charlie and can't decide whether he is enlightening her or asking her permission for his feelings.

"Forgiveness is a good thing," she says — which seems to cover both possibilities. And in that moment, looking upon her son's scarred but contented face, she lets go of some of her bitterness, and feels her heart start to mend, just a little.

41
TESSA

In the days that follow, I discover that anger is easier to handle than grief. When I am angry, I can make everything about Nick — *his* failure, *his* mistake, *his* loss. I can focus all my energy on punishing him, refusing to see him, ultimately leaving him. In one very dark moment, I even consider turning him in to the Ethics Committee at the hospital. I am comforted by anger's sharp, precise lines, its definite road map. Anger makes me believe that my brother is right — there should be no forgiveness or second chances. Life will be different moving forward, but it will go on.

Grief is a more complicated matter. It is something I can't direct at Nick, as it is also about *my* loss, my *children's* loss, the loss of our *family* and everything I once cherished and believed in. It has a component of fear and one of regret — of wishing I could turn back the clock and do things differently, more vigilantly guard my marriage. Be a better wife. Pay him more attention. Have more sex. Be more attractive. When the grief hits, I find myself looking inward, blaming myself for somehow allowing this to happen, for not seeing it coming at all. Grief also has a disorienting effect, offering no game plan whatsoever, leaving me only one option: to suffer there in the moment, until it is usurped by rage once again.

On the morning of my thirty-sixth birthday, a dreary, blustery Monday in January, I find myself squarely in the anger camp, and am further riled when Nick calls in the morning, just after Carolyn has arrived to watch Frankie and I've dropped Ruby off at school. I nearly answer the phone, but keep my track record alive and let him roll to voice mail, even showering before I check his message. When I finally listen, I detect a note of desperation in his voice as he wishes me a happy birthday, followed by an urgent plea to see me, if only to have cake as a family. I delete it immediately, along with an e-mail letting me know that if I won't see him, he will leave my gift on the front porch as he did with my still-unopened Christmas present, a box that is too small to be anything but jewelry. I flash back to our tainted anniversary, feeling a rush of resentment toward him — for not giving me a gift that night, not even a card. For not switching his call in the first place. For *everything.* I hold on to this anger, determined not to dwell on Nick or my situation on my birthday.

Then, in an ironic twist, my divorced parents, neither of whom I've yet told my news, are both in town. My mother's visit was always a given, as she almost never misses seeing me or my brother on the "anniversary of our births," as she calls them, while my father is in Boston for a last-minute meeting. He calls to wish me a happy birthday, then informs me he has several hours before his flight back to New York. "Can I take my little girl to lunch?" he asks, sounding chipper.

I scribble on a notepad, *Dad's in town,* and hold it up for my mother, who forces a broad, fake smile. I see right through her, feeling stressed at the mere idea of being at a table with both of them, and say, "Shoot, Dad. I already have plans. I'm sorry . . ."

"With your mother?" he asks, knowing that she owns this day, that he relinquished all birthday rights, along with the furniture and photo albums and Waldo, our beloved (by everyone but my mother) basset hound. It was always clear to Dex and me that my mother kept Waldo out of spite, a reaction that once annoyed me, but I now understand.

"Yeah. With Mom," I say, overcome by two emotions, seemingly at odds. On the one hand, I feel intensely loyal to my mother, along with a fresh sense of empathy for all she went through; on the other, I am frustrated for her, *with* her, wishing she could get over the bitterness I know she still feels. Bitterness that does not bode well for my future — or Ruby's and Frank's, for that matter.

"Right. I figured as much," he says. "But I was hoping to see you, too." A note of exasperation creeps into his voice, as if to say, *It has been years since the divorce. Can't we all be grown-ups here and move on?*

"Are you . . . alone?" I ask gingerly, knowing that Diane's presence would be a deal breaker in the scenario I am actually contemplating.

"She's in New York . . . C'mon, hon, let's do it. Wouldn't it be nice if *both* of your parents took you to lunch, together, on your thirty-fifth birthday?"

"Thirty-sixth," I say.

"We can pretend," he says, a smirk in his voice. My father hates growing older more than I — or any woman I know — which my mother ascribes to what she calls his boundless vanity. "So what do you say, kiddo?"

"Hold on a sec, Dad," I say, then cover the phone and whisper to my mother, "He wants to join us. What do you think . . . ?"

She shrugs, smiles again, and says, "It's up to you, honey. It's *your* day."

"Can you handle it?" I say, not at all fooled by her cool-as-a-cucumber facade.

"Of *course* I can handle it," she says, looking vaguely insulted.

I hesitate, then return to my father, giving him instructions on where to meet us. Meanwhile, out of the corner of my eye, I watch my mother reach for her compact, carefully, nervously, touching up her lipstick.

"Fabuloso," my father says.

"Dy-no-mite," I deadpan, wondering if I will ever achieve the indifference that has so clearly eluded my mother. Or whether, years from now, I will hear my ex-husband's name and feel just as frantic to look my best. To show Nick what he's missing, what he destroyed and lost, so long ago.

Thirty minutes later, I am seated with both my parents at Blue Ginger, a sleek, bamboo-paneled Asian restaurant, sharing the lobster roll appetizer. My father is intermittently humming a tune I can't quite identify while my mother taps her nails on her wineglass and chatters about the bonsai trees ornamenting the bar. In short, they are both nervous, if not downright tense, and the fact that the three of us have not been in the same room together since the night I married Nick is not lost on any of us. Yet another layer of irony in our family infidelity files.

Then, after a glib discussion of Ruby and Frank and other neutral topics, I try to muster the courage to break my news. It occurs to me that it is unfair to do it this way, at least to my mother, but part of me thinks that it will help me maintain a degree of dignity and pride that I feel I've lost. Because no matter how many times I tell myself otherwise, how many times Cate and Dex reinforce the notion that Nick's affair is no reflection on me, it still feels like *my* humiliation. I am deeply ashamed of my husband, my marriage, *myself.*

"So. I have something to tell you," I say during the next lull. I feel stoic, if not strong.

I look at my mother, then my father, their expressions so worried, nearly fearful, that my eyes begin to water. Upon realizing what they might be thinking, I reassure them that the kids are fine and that nobody's sick.

It is a thought that puts all of this in perspective, although in some ways I'd rather be ill. Then I could have a diagnosis, a treatment plan, and faith — or at least hope — that things could somehow work out. I take a deep breath, searching for the right words, as my father puts down his fork, reaches for my hand, and says, "Honey. It's okay. We know. We *know*."

I stare at him, slowly processing what he's telling me.

"Dex told you?" I say, too relieved that I don't have to actually say the words aloud to be angry at my brother. Besides, in the context of broken promises, his is not so egregious.

My mother nods, reaching for my other hand, her grip as tight as my father's.

"Should we sing 'Kumbaya'?" I ask, laughing so I won't cry. And then, "Dex sure has a big mouth."

"Don't be upset with Dexter," my mom says. "He told us out of love and concern for you . . . He and Rachel are *so* worried about you."

"I know," I say, thinking of how many times they've both called me in the past few days, calls I've been too upset to return.

"How are the kids?" my mom asks. "Have

494

they figured it out?"

"Not yet," I say. "Which tells you something, right? That's how much he works . . . He's only seen them four or five times since Christmas and they don't seem to notice that *anything* is different."

"Have you . . . seen him yet?" my mother continues, now in her information-gathering mode.

I shake my head.

My father clears his throat, starts to speak, then stops and starts again. "I'm sorry . . . Contessa, honey, I'm *so* sorry."

"Contessa" has been his special nickname for me since I was a little girl, one that he only breaks out at emotional moments, and I know, even without looking at him, that he is apologizing in more ways than one.

I bite my lip, pull my hands free, resting them on my lap. "I'm going to be fine," I say, sounding far more convincing than I feel.

"Yes," my mother says, lifting her chin, looking more regal than she usually does. "You *will* be fine."

"No matter what you decide to do," my father says.

"Dex told us *his* advice," my mother says.

"And I'm sure you're on the same page," I say to her, no longer caring about any possible innuendo. The parallels are obvious and I feel too defeated and exhausted to pretend they're not.

My mother shakes her head and says, "Every marriage is different. Every situation is different."

It occurs to me that that's what I've been telling her for years, and yet here she is finally agreeing with me now that her theory has been proven correct. I quit my job, prioritized my husband and family, and ended up in her shoes, just as she predicted.

"Tessa, honey," my dad says after the waiter refills our wineglasses and scurries discreetly away, likely sensing that something is amiss at our table. "I'm not proud of what I did . . ."

"Well, that's comforting," my mother scoffs under her breath.

He exhales, appropriately shamed, and tries again. "Okay. That's an understatement . . . I'll *always* regret behaving the way I did . . . Behaving so . . . dishonorably . . ."

As far as I know, this is the first he's ever admitted any wrongdoing and, as such, it feels like a shocking admission. It must to my mother, as well, because now she looks like *she* might cry.

He continues, more gingerly, "I wish I had

handled things differently . . . I really do. Things weren't going well with your mother and me — I think she'd agree with that." He glances her way and then continues, "But I looked for solutions in all the wrong places. I was a *fool.*"

"Oh, David," my mother says under her breath, her eyes welling.

"It's true. I was stupid," he says. "And Nick is stupid, too."

My mother gives him a knowing look as it suddenly dawns on me that their intervention was not only planned, but possibly rehearsed. Then she says, "Although, obviously . . . we don't know what was in Nick's head . . . or why he did what he did."

"Right. Right," my dad says. "But what I'm trying to say . . . is that I think your mother and I —"

"We made a lot of mistakes," she interjects as he nods.

I feel a wave of nostalgia, remembering our dinner conversations growing up, how much the two used to interrupt each other, more when they were getting along and happy than when their relationship was stormy, marked by silent gridlocks and standoffs. "I was depressed and frustrated and hard to live with. And *he,*" she says, pointing at my father and nearly smiling, "was a cheating son of a bitch."

My dad raises his brows and says, "Gee. Thanks, Barb."

"Well, you *were,*" she says, releasing a high, nervous laugh.

"I know," he says. "And I'm sorry."

"Duly noted," she says — which is as close as she has *ever* come to forgiving him.

I look from one parent to the other, unsure if I feel better or worse, but thoroughly perplexed as to their overarching point. Are they implying that I somehow contributed to this mess? That Nick had an affair because he's not happy? That marriage is more about how you manage a catastrophe than commitment and trust? Or are they simply caught up in their own bizarre feel-good moment?

My father must sense my confusion because he says, "Look, Tess. Your mother and I are just trying to impart some of the wisdom we collected the hard way. We're just trying to tell you that sometimes it's not about the affair —"

"But you *married* Diane," I say, avoiding eye contact with my mother.

He waves this off as if his current wife is utterly beside the point. "Only because your mom left me . . ."

Clearly liking this version of their history,

she smiles — a warm, *real* smile, allowing him to continue.

"Sweetie, here's what we're trying to say," my father says. "Marriages are funny, complicated, mysterious things . . . and they go through cycles. Ups and downs, like anything else . . . And they shouldn't really be defined by *one* act, albeit a terrible one."

"Multiple acts, perhaps," my mother says, unable to resist the softball. "But not *one*, singular mistake."

My father raises his palms in the air as if to say he has no defense, and then continues her train of thought. "That said, you don't have to be okay with his transgression. You don't *have* to forgive Nick," my dad says. "Or trust him."

"They aren't the same thing," my mother says. "Forgiving and trusting."

Her message is clear — she might have forgiven my father the first time around, but she *never* trusted him again, not even for a second. Hence her undercover work and her grim, but unsurprising, Diane discovery.

"I know, Barbie," he says, nodding. "I'm just trying to say that Tess has a decision to make. And it is *her* decision. Not Nick's — or her brother's, or mine, or yours."

"Agreed," my mom says.

"And no matter what, we're on your side," my father adds. "Just as we've always been."

"Yes," my mother says. "Absolutely. One hundred percent."

"Thank you," I say, realizing that this might be what hurts more than anything else — the fact that I always thought *Nick* was that person who would always, no matter what, absolutely, one hundred percent, be on my side. And the fact that I was absolutely, one hundred percent wrong.

And just like that, my anger dissipates, supplanted once again by a thick, murky grief.

A short time later, the three of us return home from lunch, and are standing together in the driveway, saying our extended goodbyes before my father leaves for the airport. My parents both appear perfectly at ease, and to watch their casual body language, you'd think they were very old friends, not two people who were married for nearly twenty-five years before going through a bitter divorce.

"Thanks for coming to Boston, Dad," I say, ready to get out of the cold. "I really appreciate it."

My father gives me another hug — his third since we left the restaurant — yet makes no move toward his rental car, instead commenting that he could take a later flight.

I look at my mom, who shrugs and smiles her permission.

"Would you like to come in for a while?" I say. "The kids will be home soon. Carolyn's picking Ruby up from school now."

My father quickly agrees, and minutes later, we have moved inside, congregating in the kitchen, discussing my dad's recent trip to Vietnam and Thailand. It is the sort of exotic travel my mother craves but doesn't undertake — either because she's too busy or doesn't want to do so alone. Yet she doesn't appear to begrudge my dad the experience, asking friendly, open questions. My father answers them, avoiding any plural pronouns or mention of Diane, although I know that she was with him — and I'm sure my mom does, too.

"You really should go, Barb. You'd love it," my dad says, eyeing a corked bottle of red on the counter and suggesting that we have one more glass. Against my better judgment, I shrug and say sure, watching as he pours three generous glasses, handing one to me, the other to my mother. She takes it and matter-of-factly clinks her glass against his, then mine. She offers no toast, just a wink and smile, as if acknowledging how bizarre, yet somehow pleasant, the afternoon has been. I take a long sip just as Ruby and Frank burst through the front door, Carolyn trailing behind.

"Nana and Pappy!" they shout in unison, seemingly unfazed by seeing their grandparents together.

In a surreal, bittersweet moment, I watch the four of them embrace, as I turn to handle more quotidian matters — paying Carolyn, retrieving Nick's predictably small gift from the front porch, wiping down the table, still covered with crumbs from Frank's lunch. Then, while my father does magic tricks for the kids and my mother adds her color commentary, I quietly excuse myself, relieved when no one objects or even seems to notice.

Once alone in my room, I down my wine and curl up on my made bed. After a few minutes of staring into space, I close my eyes and listen to the faint sound of my parents and children laughing downstairs, mulling over the strangeness of the afternoon — how surprising and sad and soothing it has been all at once.

As I hover near sleep, I find myself thinking about Dex's words on Christmas Eve — how he'd never cheat on Rachel — and only cheated *with* her because he was in love. Then I think of my father's comments about Diane at lunch today, his implication that she was utterly beside the point, not the catalyst for my parents' split, but merely a symptom of their problems. Then, against my will, I think of *her.* Valerie. I wonder which category she falls in and whether she and Nick could possibly end up together if I opt out of the equation for good. I imagine my children with her, stepsiblings to her son. Then I drift off, imagining the new blended family, riding in a pedicab in Hanoi while I remain home, sweeping crumbs under the kitchen table, bitter and alone.

I awaken to find my mother sitting on the edge of my bed, watching me.

"What time is it?" I murmur as my eyes flutter open.

"A little after six. The kids have eaten — and your dad gave them a bath. They're in the playroom now."

Startled, I sit up, realizing that I've been asleep for over two hours. "Is he still here?"

"No. He left a while ago. He didn't want to wake you. He said to say good-bye — and tell you he loves you."

I rub my eyes, remembering my full dream about Nick and Valerie, more graphic and disturbing than my vision of them in a pedicab.

"Mom," I say, overwhelmed by the sudden, startling conviction of what I need in order to move on, one way or the other. "I have to know."

She nods, as if she understands exactly what I'm thinking, what I'm trying to say.

"I *need* to know," I say, unable to shut down the images from my sleep. Nick making her laugh in the kitchen while they cook Thanksgiving dinner. Nick reading bedtime stories to her son. Nick soaping her back and kissing her in a beautiful claw-foot tub.

My mom nods again and puts her arms around me as the haunting reel continues. I try to pause it, or at least rewind it, wondering how it all began. Was it love at first sight? Was it a friendship that slowly became physical? Was it an epiphany one night? Did it come from something wrong in our marriage or the truest, deepest feelings or mere empathy for a hurt child and his mother? I need to know exactly what happened in the middle, and how and why it ended. I need to know what she looks like, what *she's* like. I need to hear her voice, see the way she moves, look into her eyes. I need to know *everything*. I need to know the whole, painful truth.

So before I can change my mind, I pick up my phone and dial the number I memorized on Thanksgiving. I am gripped by fear, but undaunted, as I close my eyes, take my mother's hand, and wait for my discovery to begin.

42
VALERIE

She is browsing the shelves at Wellesley Booksmith, while Charlie is at his piano lesson, when she hears her phone vibrate in her bag. Her heart jumps with the dim, unrealistic hope that it could be him, as she balances three novels under her arm and reaches inside her bag to check the caller ID. An unfamiliar local number lights up her screen, and although it could be just about anyone, she has the cold gut feeling that it is her. *Tessa.*

Everything in her signals a flight instinct, warns her not to answer, and yet she does, whispering a hushed hello into her phone.

She hears a woman's low, nervous voice say hello back to her, and now she is certain. She takes a gulp of air, desperate for more oxygen, as one of her books tumbles to the floor, landing spine up, pages bent and splayed. A teenaged girl standing near her stoops to pick it up, handing it to Valerie with a smile.

The voice on the other line asks, "Is this Valerie Anderson?"

"Yes," Valerie replies, filled with fear and guilt. She glances around for a chair, and upon seeing none, sits cross-legged on the threadbare carpet, bracing herself for whatever is to come, knowing she deserves the worst.

"We've never met . . . My name is Tessa," the woman continues. "Tessa Russo. I'm Nick Russo's wife."

Valerie replays the word *wife,* over and over, squeezing her eyes shut, seeing a kaleidoscope of color as she concentrates on breathing.

"I . . . I was wondering . . . if we could meet?" she asks without menace or malice, only a trace of melancholy, which makes Valerie feel that much worse.

She swallows and with great reluctance replies, "Okay. Sure. When?"

"Could you do it now?" Tessa asks.

Valerie hesitates, feeling sure she should prepare for this meeting the way she prepares for trials, with intense, careful attention to detail. Yet she knows the anticipation would be excruciating — for both of them — so she simply says yes.

"Thank you," Tessa says. And then,

"Where?"

"I'm at Wellesley Booksmith . . . Would you like to come meet me here?" she says, wishing she had worn a nicer outfit, and bothered to run a brush through her hair, then realizing this is probably a good thing.

Valerie listens to a silence so thick that she wonders if Tessa hung up or muted the phone until she hears, "Okay. Yes. I'll be right over."

And now she waits. She waits in the front of the store, next to the shelves of greeting cards and wrapping paper, staring past a window display onto Central Street, a hundred, disjointed thoughts spinning in her head. She waits for fifteen, then twenty, then thirty minutes as a dozen or more women walk through the door. She remains convinced that none is Tessa until *this* second when *this* woman walks in. A woman who, very clearly, has not come to shop for books.

Valerie studies her hungrily, memorizing the way she unbuttons her long camel coat, exposing an elegant yet understated ensemble of slim black pants, an ivory crewneck sweater, and matte gold flats. She admires her thick, honey-colored hair that falls to her shoulders in soft waves, and features that are vivid and strong, unlike so

508

many of the generic beauties populating Wellesley. If she is wearing makeup at all, Valerie decides, it's the subtlest of applications, although her full lips are shiny with peach gloss.

The woman glances furtively around the store, somehow missing Valerie upon first scan despite how close they are standing. Then, suddenly, their eyes lock. Valerie's heart stops, and she considers running out the door. Instead, she takes a step forward, no longer protected by the buffer of greeting cards.

"Tessa?" Valerie says, a chill running up her spine.

The woman nods, then extends her arm, offering her hand. Valerie takes it, her heart aching as she feels her smooth, warm skin and catches a whiff of a citrus fragrance.

As their hands fall to their sides again, Tessa swallows and says, "Can we go find a place to sit down?"

Valerie nods, having already scoped out a table in the back children's section, saving it with her puffy parka and stash of books. She turns and walks toward it now, and seconds later, the two women are seated across from one another.

"So," Tessa says. "Hello."

"Hello," Valerie echoes, her throat dry and

palms wet.

Tessa starts to speak, then stops, then begins again. "How's Charlie?" she asks, with such genuine concern that for one hopeful second Valerie thinks that she has it all wrong — and that Tessa is only here to check on her husband's patient.

But as Valerie replies that Charlie is doing much better, thank you for asking, she sees Tessa's lower lip quiver tellingly. And Valerie knows that she knows.

"Good. Good," Tessa manages. "I'm glad to hear it."

Then, when Valerie can't take the suspense another second, Tessa draws a deep breath and says, "Well. Look. I think we both know why I'm here . . . Why I wanted to meet you."

Valerie nods, her throat becoming tighter and drier by the second, her cheeks blazing.

"I'm here because I know," Tessa says so matter-of-factly that for a second Valerie is confused.

"You know?" she says, instantly regretting the question. She has no right to be cagey. She has no right on her side at all.

"Yes. I know," Tessa replies, her eyes flashing. "I know *everything*."

43
TESSA

There is no denying that she is pretty, *very* pretty, her eyes a disturbingly deep blue. But there is nothing *sexy* about her. With a petite, narrow frame, and almost no hips or chest, she is more boyish than bombshell. Her face is pale against her stick-straight ebony hair, which is pulled into an uninspired low ponytail. In short, as I say her name and watch her nod back at me, I feel a strange sense of relief that this is the woman, that she is the one. I am relieved by her frail handshake, her thin voice, and the frightened way her eyes dart about while I stare directly at her.

"Can we go find a place to sit down?" I say, determined to be in charge of this encounter, keep the upper hand.

She nods, and as I follow her to the back of the bookshop, I am speaking to Nick. *This is who you picked? This woman? This woman I would pass on the street without a second glance? This woman I'd overlook at a dinner party?*

And yet. He *did* pick her. Or at least he let her pick him. He had sex with this person, now seated across from me at the table she apparently reserved for our conversation.

We exchange awkward hellos, and I force myself to ask about her son. Several long seconds pass and when it becomes clear she is waiting for me to speak, I clear my throat and say, "Well. Look. I think we both know why I'm here . . . Why I wanted to meet you."

I tell her this, even though I am not completely sure of my mission — whether it is one of discovery or about preserving my pride or finding closure of some kind or another. But no matter what, I am relieved to get this inevitable moment over with, ready for anything she might tell me, bracing myself for the worst.

She looks at me and waits.

"I'm here . . . because I *know*," I tell her, which seems to cover all the above. I lean across the table, holding her gaze so that there is absolutely no mistaking my message and no possible escape for her.

"You know?" she says. She gives me a puzzled look that infuriates me, and I resist the sudden, intense urge to reach across the table and strike her. Instead I continue calmly, determined to maintain my dignity and composure.

"Yes. I know . . . I know *everything*," I say — which of course is not entirely true. I know a few facts — but none of the details. But I continue the lie, hoping that it will prevent her from doing the same. "Nick told me *everything*," I say.

She starts to speak, then stops, her eyes filled with unmistakable hurt and surprise that brings me a measure of comfort. Until this moment, she likely believed, or at least hoped, that I was here only on a hunch, or as a result of some solid spy work. It is clear by the look on her face that she did not know that Nick confessed. As I stare at the sharp lines of her chin, memorizing the facets of her diamond-shaped face, I suddenly realize that I couldn't have called her, and certainly couldn't be here facing her, had I learned the truth any other way. It's almost as if the facts about my discovery level the playing field between us. She slept with *my* husband, but he told me *their* secret. So in the end, he betrayed her, too.

"It was just once," she finally says, her voice so soft that I can barely make out the words.

"Oh. Just once," I say. "All right then."

I watch her cheeks turn a deeper scarlet as my sarcasm registers, further shaming her. "I know. I know . . . It was one time too many . . . But —"

"But *what?*" I snap.

"But we were mostly just friends," she says, the way Ruby sounds when making up an excuse for her blatant disregard of a basic rule. *Yes, Mommy, I know I scribbled all over the walls, but isn't it a lovely picture?*

"Friends?"

"He was so . . . so kind to Charlie," she stammers, "and such an amazing surgeon . . . I was so . . . grateful."

"So grateful that you had sex with him?" I whisper.

Her eyes fill with tears as she shakes her head and says, "I fell in love with him. I didn't mean for it to happen. I don't know exactly how or why it happened. Maybe it's because he saved my son . . . Or maybe I just fell in love with him . . . *because.*"

Her voice trails off as if she's talking to herself. "I've never met a man like him. He is . . . exceptional."

I feel a fresh rise of fury that she would dare tell me about my husband. Someone she's known for a measly three months as opposed to our *seven years* together. But instead of pointing this out, I say, "Excep-

514

tional men don't cheat on their wives. They don't have affairs. They don't put a cheap thrill ahead of their children."

As I say the words, the paradox of the situation crystallizes in my head. If she was a cheap thrill, then Nick isn't worth fighting for. But if she is a person of quality for whom he had genuine feelings, then what? Where does that leave me?

"I don't think that's what he did," she says, but I can tell she is wondering, questioning what they had.

"Did he tell you he loved you?" I fire back at her, realizing that *this* is why I am here. This is the linchpin for me, everything turning on this one singular fact. He slept with her; he clearly had feelings for her; and I believe, from the bottom of my heart, that he was — maybe still is — in love with her. But if he told her he loved her, or if he told her he didn't love me, we are finished forever.

I hold my breath, waiting, exhaling as she shakes her head, slowly, emphatically.

"No," she says. "He didn't feel the same. He doesn't love me. He never did. He loves *you.*"

My head spins as I replay the words, searching for the truth in them. I want to believe her. I *desperately* want to believe her. And maybe, *maybe* I actually do.

"I'm sorry, Tessa," she continues, her voice cracking, anguish and shame all over her face. "I'm sorry for what I did. To you. To your children. Even to my own child. It was wrong — and I'm . . . I'm *so* sorry."

I take a deep breath, imagining her with Nick, her eyes closed, holding him, telling him she loves him. Yet as much as I want to blame her and hate her, I don't — and can't. Instead, I feel pity for her. Maybe it's because she is a single mother. Maybe it's because her son was hurt. Maybe it's because she's in love with someone she can't have. *My* husband.

Whatever the case, I look into her eyes and say the thing I never dreamed I'd say in this moment.

"Thank you," I tell her, and as I watch her accept my gratitude with the slightest of nods, then gather her belongings and stand to leave, I am shocked to realize that I actually mean it.

44
VALERIE

Time heals all wounds. She knows this better than most. Yet she still feels surprised by it now, marveling that the mere passage of days can feel like gradual magic. She is not yet over him, but she no longer misses him in an acute, painful way, and she has made peace with what happened between them, even if she doesn't fully understand it. She thinks about what she told Nick's wife — that he never loved her — and wonders if this is true, part of her still clinging to the belief that what they shared was real.

But as more time passes, this hope dwindles and she begins to see their relationship merely as an impossible fantasy, an illusion born from need and longing. And she decides that just because two people believe in something, however intensely, doesn't make it real.

And then there is the matter of Tessa, the woman she envies and pities, fears and respects all at once. She replays their conversation a hundred times, even repeating it to Jason, before she can fully grasp what transpired in the back of the bookstore on that bitterly cold January evening. Nick's wife had *thanked* her. She had listened to another woman confess to falling in love with her husband, *making love* to her husband, and yet she *actually* thanked her, seemingly accepting her apology, or at least not rejecting it. The whole scenario was so unlikely, so far-fetched, that it began to almost make sense, just as it began to seem perfectly logical that Charlie would come to love Summer, a girl who had once tormented him on the playground.

It was about grace, she decides, something that has been missing from her own life. Whether she was born with a shortfall of it or lost it along the way, Valerie can't be sure. But she wants it now. She wants to be the kind of person who can bestow unearned kindness on another, replace bitterness with empathy, forgive only for the sake of forgiving.

She wants this so desperately that she does the very thing she once vowed she'd never do. She makes a phone call — and she makes it from the waiting room at the hospital while Charlie is in his second hour of surgery with his new surgeon. She listens to the phone ring, her throat constricting as she hears the apprehensive hello on the other line.

"Is this Romy?" she asks, her heart pounding.

The woman replies yes, and Valerie feels herself hesitate, thinking of the night of the accident and what she is still sure was Romy's negligence; then Charlie's last surgery when Romy barged, uninvited, into this very room; then the afternoon in the school parking lot when Romy spotted her with Nick.

Despite these images, she stays on course, saying, "This is Valerie Anderson."

"Oh! Hello. How are you? How is Charlie?" Romy asks, a gentleness in her voice that was either missing in prior exchanges or that Valerie had simply overlooked.

"He's doing well. He's in surgery now," she says.

"Is he okay?" Romy asks.

"No. No . . . I didn't mean . . . I mean, yes, he is fine. It's a routine surgery to refine an earlier graft. He's good. He really is," Valerie says, realizing that she is no longer nervous about Charlie's face or hand or heart. Not in the way she once was.

"Thank *goodness*," Romy says. "I'm so

happy to hear it. So happy. You just don't know."

Valerie feels herself choke up as she continues, "Well. I just wanted to call and tell you that. That Charlie is doing well . . . And that . . . Romy?"

"Yes?"

"I don't blame you for what happened."

It's not exactly the truth, Valerie recognizes, but is close enough.

She doesn't remember the rest of the conversation, or exactly how she and Romy leave things, but as she hangs up, she feels a heavy burden being lifted from her heart.

And it is in that moment that she decides she has another phone call to make, one that is six years overdue. She does not yet know what she will say, whether she will even be able to find him, or whether forgiveness will flow in either direction. But she knows that she owes it to him, and to Charlie, and even to herself, to try.

45
TESSA

When I return home from the bookstore, I find my mother sitting on the couch, reading a magazine and eating Godiva chocolates.

I sit beside her, and carefully select a dark, heart-shaped piece. "Well, look at me," I say. "The angry housewife eating bonbons."

My mother lets out a snort of laughter, then quickly sobers and asks me how it went.

I shrug, indicating that I do not want to discuss all the gory details, then say, "She wasn't what I expected."

"They never are," she says with a long sigh.

We eat in silence for another moment before my mother continues her train of thought. "But it's really not about them, is it?"

"No," I say, realizing that I might finally stop obsessing over the "other woman," now that I've met her. "It really isn't."

My mom's face brightens as if thrilled for my potential breakthrough. Then she gives me a sideways glance and tells me that she is taking the kids to the city for the weekend, that she's already discussed it with my brother. "You need time to yourself," she says.

"No, Mom. That's too much for you," I say, picturing her on the train, frantically corralling Ruby and Frank.

She shakes her head and insists that she has it under control — and that Dex is meeting her at Penn Station so she won't have to maneuver through the city alone.

I start to protest again, but she cuts me off, saying, "Dex already told Julia and Sarah that their cousins are coming for the weekend. And I already told Frank and Ruby. We can't disappoint the kids, now can we?"

I bite my lip, and acquiesce. "Thanks, Mom," I say, feeling closer to her than I have in a long time.

"Don't thank me, sweetie. I just want you to do this. I just want you to face this head-on and figure out what is right for you."

I nod, still afraid and still *very* angry, but finally, *almost* ready.

■ ■ ■ ■

The next morning, after my mother and children have departed for New York, I am in my kitchen, drinking coffee, with the frantic, dawning realization that there is nothing left to be done. There is no family left to tell or opinions to garner. There are no discoveries to be had or facts to uncover. It is time to talk to Nick. So I pick up the phone and call my husband of seven years, more nervous than when I phoned a perfect stranger the night before.

He answers on the first ring, breathlessly, as if he had been expecting this call, at this very moment. For a second, I wonder if my mother — or Valerie — prepared him.

But when he asks me if everything is okay, I hear sleep in his voice and realize that I must have just awakened him; that is all.

"I'm fine," I say, taking a deep breath, making myself continue as I unwittingly picture him, shirtless, in whatever bed he's been sleeping in for all these weeks. "I just want to talk . . . I'm ready to talk. Could you come home?"

"Yes," he says. "I'll be right there."

Fifteen minutes later, he is standing on the

porch, knocking on his own front door. I open it, and find him unshaven and bleary-eyed in an old pair of scrubs and a faded baseball cap.

I let him in, avoiding eye contact and mumbling, "You look dreadful."

"You look beautiful," he says, sounding as sincere as he ever has, despite the fact that I'm wearing jeans and a T-shirt, my hair still damp from my shower.

"Thanks," I say, leading him to the kitchen, taking my usual seat at the table and pointing to his spot, across from me.

He sits, takes off his cap, and tosses it onto Ruby's chair. Then he runs his hand through his hair, longer than I've ever seen it.

"I know. I know," he says. "I need a cut. You didn't give me much of a warning here . . ."

I shake my head, indicating that his grooming is the least of my concerns, then burst out with it. "I met her last night. I called her," I say. "I needed to see her."

He furrows his brow and scratches his jaw. "I understand," he says, and then stops short of asking any questions, which seems to require a certain measure of restraint.

"She was nice," I say. "I didn't hate her."

"Tessa," he says, his eyes begging me to stop.

"No. She *was* . . . She was honest, too. She didn't try to deny anything, like I thought she would . . . In fact, she actually admitted that she's in love with you," I say, unsure of whether I'm baiting him, punishing him, or simply telling the truth. "Did you know that? I'm sure she told you, too . . ."

He shakes his head, rubs his eyes with the palms of his hands, and says, "She's not in love with me."

"She was."

"No. She never was."

"She *told* me she was, Nick," I say, my anger ebbing and flowing by the second, with his every word, every fleeting expression.

"She *thought* she was," he says. "But . . . she wasn't. Love doesn't work like that."

"Oh?" I say. "How *does* it work, Nick?"

He stands and rotates to Frankie's seat, now next to me, where he reaches for my hand. I shake my head in refusal but when he tries again, I reluctantly give it to him, my eyes welling with his touch.

"Love is sharing a life together," he says, squeezing my hand. "Love is what *we* have."

"And what did you have with her?"

"That was . . . something else."

I stare at him, struggling to make sense of

his words. "So you didn't love her?"

He sighs, glances at the ceiling, and then looks at me again. I say a prayer that he doesn't lie to me, that he doesn't issue a flat-out denial when I know he loved her. Or at least thought he did.

"I don't know, Tess," he begins. "I really don't . . . I wouldn't have done what I did if I didn't have strong feelings for her. If it wasn't something at least approaching love, something that looked and felt like love . . . But those feelings — they don't compare to my love for you. And the moment I came home and looked into your eyes and told you what I had done, I knew that . . . Tessa, I messed up so bad. I risked everything — our marriage, my job, this home. I still don't know why I let it happen. I *hate* myself for letting it happen."

"You didn't *let* it happen, Nick," I say, pulling my hand away from him. "You *made* it happen. It took two. It took both of you."

As I say the words, though, I am struck by how much they apply to us, as well. That it took two to get us here. That it *always* takes two. For relationships to work, for them to break apart, for them to be fixed.

"I know," he says. "You're right. I'm not trying to shift the blame to anyone else . . . I'm just trying to tell you how much I love *you.*"

"Then *how* could you do it?" I say, my voice soft now. It is a question — not an accusation.

He looks at me, struggling for words. "I think . . . I think . . . I was looking for something I thought I needed."

"And what was that? What was it that you weren't getting here? From me?" I ask as I begin to answer the question for myself. I refuse to accept any blame for his infidelity, and yet I can't deny that things have changed between us. That I've changed. And that, in many ways, I'm not the person he married. I think of Nick's recent accusations, as well as my mother's observations. That I am never happy; that I have lost some of my passion; that I focus on things that don't matter, rather than our relationship, the bedrock of everything else. "What did she give you?"

He shakes his head. "It wasn't like that . . . It was more . . ." He glances up at the ceiling, searching for words, then looks at me and says, "the way I felt when I was around her reminded me of the way I felt for you in the beginning."

My heart breaks hearing the two of us compared, yet there is comfort in his honesty, in the pain on his face, how much he also wishes it weren't true.

He continues, "And there were other things, too . . . I felt . . . I felt this *need* to fix things for that little boy — a need that got convoluted and somehow extended to his mother . . . Part of it was probably my ego . . . wanting that feeling — that feeling of being young . . . of being needed and wanted." His voice trails off, as I remember how vulnerable I was on the subway the day we met.

"*I* needed you. *I* wanted you," I say, using the past tense, even though a big part of me *still* needs him, still wants him. "But maybe you're no longer . . . attracted to me?"

I look at him, knowing that he will deny this accusation, but hoping he can do so convincingly.

"No," he says, letting one clenched fist fall to the table. "That's not it. It's not about sex. Except for maybe the feeling of being connected that sex can give you . . . It's just . . . It's not that simple, Tess . . . It's no one thing you can point to."

I nod, thinking of how difficult marriage can be, how much effort is required to sustain a feeling between two people — a feeling that you can't imagine will ever fade in the beginning when everything comes so easily. I think of how each person in a marriage owes it to the other to find individual happiness, even in a shared life. That this is the only real way to grow together, instead of apart.

He continues, as if reading my mind. "Life can be tough. And monotonous . . . and exhausting. And it's not the romantic ride you think it's going to be when you start out, in the beginning . . . But that doesn't mean . . . that doesn't give anyone the right . . . It didn't give me the right to do what I did . . . Look, Tess. Whatever the reason, it wasn't a good one. And lately, I think there was no reason at all. Which might be worse. But it's the truth. And it's all I have to give you."

I swallow and nod. Then, despite my determination not to make this conversation about her, I ask whether he's spoken to her since the day he came home from his walk in the Common.

"No," he says.

"So you're not his doctor anymore?" I ask, avoiding Charlie's name, right along with his mother's.

"No."

"And you're not going to be in his life?"

"No."

"Not at all?"

"No."

"Does that make you sad?"

He sighs, then grimaces. "I'd be lying if I told you I wasn't sad . . . that I don't miss that little boy and feel tremendous guilt for being part of his life and then abruptly leaving. I feel guilty for any pain I could have caused a child. For breaking the first rule of medicine."

Do no harm, I think, and then consider *all* the harm he did.

He continues, "But I feel more guilty about you. I can't really think beyond you . . . *us. My* kids. *Our* family. Most of the time, I can't think at all. I'm just feeling and remembering and wishing."

"And what's that?" I ask, something inside me softening. "What are you feeling and remembering and wishing?"

"I'm feeling . . . the way I felt when I met you on the subway. You were standing there with that ring on your finger, looking so sad. So beautiful . . . And I'm remembering our early days when we were broke and in school and splitting Stouffer's lasagna for dinner and . . . and when you were pregnant with Ruby and eating two of those lasagnas by yourself." He stares into space with a faint smile.

"I was eating for two," I say, the line I used despite the fact that I was actually eating as if pregnant with triplets.

He continues, a faraway look in his eyes. "And I'm wishing . . . I'm wishing that I could somehow get you back. I want you back, Tessa."

I shake my head, feeling profound sadness for myself and the kids — but also, for the first time, for Nick.

"It won't be the same," I say.

"I know," he replies.

"It will *never* be the same," I say.

"I know," he says. "But maybe . . ."

"Maybe *what?*" I ask hopefully.

"Maybe it can be better," he says — which is exactly what I wanted him to say. "Can we try and find out? Can we try for Ruby and Frank? Can we try for *us?*"

I feel myself start to crumble as he stands and pulls me to my feet, taking both of my hands in his. "Please," he says.

"I don't know if I can," I say, tears spilling down my face. "I don't know if I can *ever* trust you. Even if I wanted to."

He starts to hold me, then stops, as if realizing he hasn't yet earned that right. Then he whispers my name and says, "Let me help you."

My tears continue to flow, but I do not tell him no. Which, of course, we both know is very nearly a yes.

"I can't make any promises," I say.

"But I *can*," he says.

"You did that once," I say, my voice cracking.

"I know. And I'll do it again. I'll do it *every* day. I'll do whatever it takes. Just give me one more chance."

One more chance.

Words that my mother heard, more than once. Words that women debate. Whether you *can* forgive and whether you *should* trust. I think of all the judgment from society, friends, and family, the overwhelming consensus seeming to be that you should not grant someone who betrayed you a second chance. That you should do everything you can to keep the knife out of your back, and to protect your heart and pride. Cowards give second chances. Fools give second chances. And I am no coward, no fool.

"I'm so sorry," Nick says.

I envision him on our wedding day as we exchanged our vows, hearing his words: *Forsaking all others as long as we both shall live.*

That was the way it was supposed to be.

That didn't happen.

Yet here we are, two children and a broken promise later, standing before each other, just the way we stood that day at the altar, with equal parts love and hope. And once again, I close my eyes, ready to take a leap of faith, ready for the long, hard road ahead. I have no idea how it's going to turn out, but then again, I never really did.

"Can I make you breakfast?" he says. "Eggs, sunny side up?"

I look into his eyes, nod, and nearly smile. Not because I'm happy — or hungry. But because my husband is home. Because he knows that sunny-side-up eggs are my favorite. And because I believe that, buried beneath disappointment and fear, anger and pride, I just might find it in my heart to forgive.

ABOUT THE AUTHOR

Emily Giffin is the *New York Times* best-selling author of *Something Borrowed, Something Blue, Baby Proof,* and *Love the One You're With.* She lives in Atlanta with her husband and three young children. Vist her website at www.emilygiffin.com.